Making a Beeline Home

Making a Beeline Home

Pam Estes

Library of Congress Control Number: 2011913582
ISBN: Hardcover   978-1-4653-4569-1
               Softcover   978-1-4653-4568-4
               Ebook   978-1-4653-4570-7

To order additional copies of this book, contact:
Xlibris Corporation
1-888-795-4274
www.Xlibris.com
Orders@Xlibris.com
101393

Dedicated to our much loved Allie and Bobbie and to all the special people in this book who were a part of Allie and Bobbie's lives, shaping them into such wonderful individuals. May their legacy of love of family and community continue on through the lives of their children, grandchildren, and great-grandchildren for many years to come.

Acknowledgements

I would like to thank many individuals for their encouragement and help in writing, Making a Beeline Home. First, I would like to thank my mother, Allene (Allie), whose remarkable memory made it possible to include so many wonderful details in this story. Next, I express heartfelt appreciation to family members who shared their precious memories and allowed me to include them in this book. Evelyn, Frank, and Joe, you offered suggestions and encouragement when I needed it the most. Finally, I thank Jim for everything.

Chapter 1

Memories! What a wonderful thing the memory is. It is a gift of God. There is a special place somewhere in one's mind that is reserved for remembering, the place my beloved teacher of long ago called the gray matter. When we had trouble remembering certain things, he would always say for us to dig back into our gray matter. If we ever knew it, he insisted, it was still back there somewhere. I shall never forget Mr. Schauffler with his kind blue eyes and wide grin that showed a pale-gold tooth when he smiled. I believe he was my fifth-grade teacher.

—Allie (2010)

Bobbie

January 1941

Bobbie's eyes flew open. He quickly rose up on his elbow and looked out the window. Although it was still dark outside, he had the sinking feeling that he had overslept. He listened to Jake's soft breathing beside him on their cot and then rolled to his side and crawled out from under the layers of quilts. The air was frigid, and he shivered as his feet touched the cold wooden floor. The boards creaked underneath his weight as he stood. Opening the door of the cookstove for a little light, he checked the time on the clock beside the radio. It was 4:45. He was fifteen minutes behind schedule!

During the winter, Bobbie and Jake slept on a cot that Momma pulled into the kitchen every night. They shared a bedroom the rest of the year, but in the winter, Momma worried about them getting too cold in the back of the house. The fire in the cast-iron cookstove made the kitchen the warmest room in the house, and Bobbie knew it must be close to zero outside for the kitchen to be so cold this morning. He pulled his heavy twill pants over his long underwear. Quietly he made his way to the side of the stove where he had left his boots to dry. He leaned against the wall and balanced as he pulled on one boot first and then the other. After slipping his suspenders over his shoulders, he adjusted the damper on the stovepipe, opening it to allow a pull. He opened the door and gently placed a big stick of wood into the fire. Sparks jumped nervously around before settling once more. There was still a good bed of coals, an orange nest that accepted the log he placed inside. Momma would be getting up before too long to start breakfast. She would appreciate a warm kitchen. Bobbie made as little noise as possible, not wanting to wake his little sister Audie or his little brother Rex. They slept in the front room. He looked in on them, two round mounds under the covers. Audie's blond curls spread across the pillow, Rex crossways in the bed with one chubby leg stretched out from beneath the stack of quilts. Bobbie took a minute to tuck it back under the warmth of the covers. Returning to the kitchen, he lifted his patched coat from the back of the wooden chair and slipped out the side door.

The cold wind nearly took his breath as he rounded the corner of the house, making his dark hair stand up on end. His eyes stung from the cold and began to water. Bobbie wiped at his eyes and yanked his worn gray woolen hat out of his pocket. Pulling it down over his ears, he gave a low whistle. Fancy and Buck, Dad's old foxhounds, came out from under the front porch where they slept on a mound of hay. They walked in a stiff manner, arching their backs and stretching their stiff legs, opening their mouths in wide yawns. Bobbie smiled as he gave Buck a quick scratch behind the ears. Even though those dogs must be bone tired after foxhunting with Daddy last night, they faithfully fell into step behind him as they did every morning as he made his way down the path and out the front gate.

The night was clear. The stars were endless, and the moon made a silvery glow on the worn path ahead of him. Bobbie was thankful for the light. It would make his trip faster, and if he ran, he could probably make up for lost time. His brown boots pounding the frozen ground beat out a rhythm that matched his short breaths. That and the sound of the dried leaves dancing in the sharp wind were the only sounds in the early morning. The smell of chimney smoke permeated the air as early risers coaxed flames from sleeping coals. Bobbie glanced to his right and saw a light on in Aunt Francie's house as he passed. Her house was a small one with only one room. He could see her shape moving behind the thin curtains as she crossed in front of the window, probably getting breakfast ready. He knew from passing her house every morning that she began her day at an early hour.

Bobbie was on his way to the old two-room schoolhouse up ahead. He had turned ten in August and was in the fourth grade at the school. He made the trip to school at least twice a day, but the first trip each day was always the hardest. Bobbie's breath came in deeper puffs as he quickened his pace down the path. It was his job to build a fire every morning in the two rooms at the old school. He had to get the fires started by five o'clock to give them enough time to heat the rooms before Mr. Schauffler and Mr. Blue arrived around seven. He hoped he wouldn't have trouble getting the fires going this morning since he was running a little behind.

Thankfully, it wasn't far from his home to the school, only about half a mile. Maybe that was why Mr. Schauffler had given him the job in the first place. When Mr. Schauffler had mentioned needing someone to help him with the fires, Bobbie had been the first one in line for the job. Money was scarce at his house, as in most every other house in this part of the country, and it would be good to have his own spending money. He felt proud that Mr. Schauffler had trusted him with the job. This was the second year he'd helped out with the fires, and he had satisfaction in knowing he was good at it. Bobbie beamed as he remembered Mr. Schauffler's words: "Bobbie, you're as good at building fires as you are at ciphering." It was true what his teacher said about his way with numbers. Bobbie could put down all the kids in the little room when Mr. Schauffler led them in a ciphering match each Friday. For some reason, adding numbers just came easy for him. Maybe it was counting his hard-earned money over and over that had made him so good at his sums.

Mr. Schauffler gave him a dollar every week for his job building fires, and Bobbie had almost worn those dollar bills out; he had counted them so many times. His white teeth shone in the darkness as he smiled just thinking about what he was going to buy with all that money. He had spent a little of the money on a pair of boots to start this school year, but most of the money was stuffed down into one of Daddy's old Prince Albert tobacco cans. He kept his treasure hidden under the loose board in the floor of the smokehouse. Each time he collected ten of those dollar bills, he took them up to Jim Andy's store and traded them for a whopping ten-dollar bill. Bobbie had saved twenty-seven dollars, and when he held all that money in his hands, he felt rich.

In no time at all, Bobbie was trotting up the slope to the school.

2 Room schoolhouse in Elizabeth, Arkansas

In the moon's light, the building stood tall and patient like it was waiting for him. The paint on the old white building was peeling and looked about as tattered as his old coat. Just like his momma had patched his coat over and over, the school had gotten its share of mending too. This past summer, Mr. Stephens had to fix that hole in the roof to stop the rain from coming in and to nail down some of the floorboards that were lifting up. Bobbie had noticed lately that the rain had started coming in around the stovepipe where it went up through the roof. That was going to have to get fixed too. He pulled open the heavy door and walked in with Fancy and Buck following behind. Taking the lantern from the rusty hook by the door, Bobbie lit the kerosene-soaked wick, adjusted the flame, and placed it back in its place. His eyes scanned the room. The school had two rooms, a little room as it was called and a big room. The wall separating the two rooms was really a partition that could be raised and lowered. The wall could slide up and down between two rows of slats that were built into the wall, making a kind of casing. This wall was loose inside the slats and heavy. It took at least four strong men to slide it up. When the wall was at its highest point, someone else had to be there to put a pole under each end to keep it in place. Even though it was a little scary to watch, Bobbie loved to see the wall go up. He always worried that some man was going to lose his grip and drop it, but no one ever had. Through the week, the partition was always down dividing the single room into the two smaller classrooms, but on special occasions, like for a play or the graduation from the little room to the big room, it was raised. Also, on the weekends, the school was used as a meeting place for the church. When they had a large attendance, the wall was raised for the needed space then as well. The little room at the front of the school was for the younger kids in the first grade up through grade four. This was where Mr. Schauffler did his teaching and where Bobbie learned. The other room, which was slightly larger, was called the big room. The room was not named for its size. The name *big room* just meant it was the room for the older kids. Bobbie couldn't wait until next year when he would be in there with the older students. He would miss having Mr. Schauffler for his teacher, he had to admit. In Bobbie's mind, he was the best teacher there ever was.

Bobbie grabbed a pine knot and some small pieces of wood beside the potbellied stove and got to work on the fire. He put them carefully in the stove. Next, he reached into his coat pocket and pulled out some sagebrush he'd gathered a couple of days ago for just this purpose. He poked it in among the sticks. When he had everything laid out to his liking, he opened the damper and carefully struck the match on the rough grate of the stove. Biting the corner of his lip in concentration, he placed the flame under the dried sagebrush. The glowing tendrils began almost immediately to burn. Smoke circled upward, trailing along like the strings of a kite. Bobbie blew gently on the flame, and soon, the pine knot ignited and began to burn brightly.

Satisfied, he closed the door and stood up. The dogs settled in around the stove waiting for the heat as Bobbie lifted the lantern from the hook and started through the door beside the partition that led to the big room. As Bobbie went through the doorway at the end of the partition, he glanced up to the big bell. He was always a little bit tempted to give the long rope that hung down from the bell a quick yank. That would wake everybody up, he thought. He could just imagine the panic everyone would have thinking they were late for school. Sometimes Mr. Schauffler did let some of the kids ring the bell. It would lift the smallest kids right off the floor as they hung on. Mr. Schauffler always laughed when this happened, but Bobbie knew he sure wouldn't be laughing if he heard the bell ring at five o'clock in the morning. Bobbie decided he'd better leave it alone.

Going through the same steps in the big room as he had in the little room, the fire began to burn steadily. The big room was somewhat different from the little room. For one thing, in the little room, there was a recitation seat. It was a long bench up by the blackboard, worn smooth by the many years of use. Mr. Schauffler would call the different grades up, one grade at a time, to recite their lessons. Bobbie wasn't that good at reciting. He always felt a little self-conscious up there with everyone watching him. He didn't like being the center of attention. He was afraid he'd mess up, and he often did. When this happened, his face would grow hot and red. The redness would start at his neck and crawl up his face and even out to the tips of his ears. He would slump down and feel downright humiliated.

Bobbie couldn't help remembering a time when he was younger that he had embarrassed himself. It was in this very room back when he was Audie's age and in second grade. He'd never forget what happened. It was picture day. Once a year, a traveling cameraman would make his way around country schools to take pictures of all the students. Then a few weeks later, he would return with the black-and-white photographs to sell to the parents. On this particular day, Bobbie waited patiently in line for his turn. When at last his turn came, Mr. Schauffler helped him climb up on the tall stool. Just when the photographer had him positioned and was fixing to squeeze the bulb, Bobbie had lost his balance on that wobbly old stool and had fallen flat to the floor. He wasn't hurt, but he would never forget how everybody laughed at him, even the picture man. It was no wonder that he looked like a little orphan boy in the picture with his hair sticking up on one side of his head and the shame still on his face. A moment captured eternally in that snap of the camera.

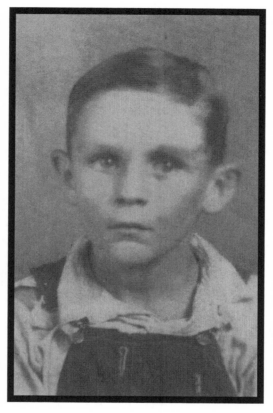

Bobbie, right after he fell off the stool when getting his
picture taken in second grade at the Elizabeth school

He never thought about his momma buying his picture
from the picture man; there was never enough money
for that. But when she had taken a look at his odd pitiful
expression in that year's photo, she had somehow managed
to scrape together enough money to buy it. That picture
now sat on Momma's side table in her bedroom, an immortal
reminder of that hideous day.

Nope, he didn't like that recitation seat in the little room and its threat of embarrassment looming over him. He'd had his share of that. But those girls, now, they seemed to love getting to go to the front of the class to recite. They would stand prim and proper and recite whatever Mr. Schauffler asked. Montene was one of the best. Just yesterday, she had rattled off a piece of that story from their reader: "Little goat, if you are able, please bring me my little table." Her dark curls bobbed up and down as she nodded her head to the rhythm of the story. What did that mean anyway? Why in the world would a little goat be taking someone a little table? Bobbie didn't take much to those silly stories. He wished they could work with numbers all day and leave off those storybooks. Thank goodness he'd be done with the recitation bench when he got to move up to fifth grade.

Both rooms had a blackboard, and Bobbie always took a minute each morning to look at what Mr. Blue had written on his board. This morning there was something about lines and angles scrawled in white on the blackboard. He hoped he would be able to understand that kind of math when he got to move in here. Mr. Blue was somewhat of a strict teacher and he was also a preacher. Bobbie guessed being stern just came naturally to a preacher man. He could make people squirm in their seats through the week and then again on Sunday morning. He must feel like he lived in this building, teaching here all week and then preaching here on Sundays. Mr. Blue was a scrawny little man who took the smallest steps. He walked somewhat stooped over and always tipped a little bit forward as he walked like he was in a hurry to get things done, and that's how he went about his teaching and preaching too.

All the desks in both rooms had double seats, and there was a space underneath to put your books. Some of the older kids had scraped their names into the old wooden desktops. Others had been so bold as to put their sweethearts' names along with theirs inside a heart. This had been done over and over through the years so that now it was sometimes hard to tell which names went together. Bobbie often walked around the room when he was waiting for the fires to get going to read some of the names on the desks. He wondered if his name would be there one day inside a heart.

He checked the fires once more. If the fire in the stove was too hot when school took up, the kids who sat in the desks at the front of the room near the stove would have bright red faces from the heat while the ones in the back were shivering and complaining about cold feet. Bobbie liked to make a hot fire and have the whole room warm when the second bell rang. Then the dampers could be closed off, and the fire didn't have to burn so hot. It would be hard this morning though with this cold.

Bobbie swept up the wood chips from around both stoves and adjusted the dampers on the stovepipes. Fancy and Buck got to their feet and fell into step behind him as he got ready to go. After taking one quick glance around, he blew out the wick in the lantern and hung it back on its hook. He walked out the door and down the steps of the school. It was time to head back home. Momma would have breakfast started by now.

Momma wasn't one to stay in bed in the morning. She claimed she got up with the chickens, but truth be told, she beat them out of bed by a good bit. She always had her day planned the night before, and she was anxious for morning to arrive to get it started. It seemed she was never still even for a minute. It amazed Bobbie at everything she could get done during the day. In the summer, Momma would make a garden, and it was always the best one for miles around. The family feasted in the summer on new potatoes, green beans, summer squash, juicy tomatoes, and corn on the cob. Momma wasn't satisfied with just one round of gardening either. Along about the end of July, she'd plow up what was finished bearing and plant another round. Yes, they certainly fared well in the summer. Momma never wasted a thing either. What they didn't eat, she canned. She would can just about anything: vegetables, berries, eggs, even fish. Bobbie and Willie helped her out as best they could by picking berries by the bucketfuls and bringing home stringers full of trout. By the end of fall, the board shelves that held the jars of food sagged beneath the load. Bobbie didn't know how the family would have gotten through the winter months without Momma's careful planning and preparation during the other seasons. No, there wasn't a lazy bone in Momma's body, of that he was sure. Bobbie didn't waste any time getting home to see what was on the breakfast table.

Bobbie's Momma, Eva Crotts James

As Bobbie walked into the warm kitchen, the good breakfast smells greeted him. Momma was standing beside the stove stirring a big skillet of bubbly gravy. She had just taken a pan of golden biscuits from the oven, and there was sausage in the warming tray on top of the stove. She grinned when he came through the door. Bobbie's mouth watered as he gave Momma a morning kiss on the cheek. Momma smiled and said, "Law, Bobbie, you brought the cold in with you this morning." She moved over to make room for him by the stove. "Scooch over here a little bit closer and warm up!"

Bobbie sidled up closer to Momma. He loved to watch her when she cooked. Her hands reminded him of hummingbirds darting this way and that, never staying very long in one place. They hovered first in one place then flew to another, never stopping to roost. Momma had her shoulder-length brown hair pulled back in a loose ponytail at the base of her neck. She was wearing a brown print dress with a red gingham apron tied around her waist and at the neck. Her face shone in the hot glare of the stove. The most amazing thing about her to Bobbie, though, was her smile. Momma kept her smile handy, and there was usually a bubble of laughter that came along with it. You weren't around Momma long before you had a smile on your own face.

"Reckon it must be down around zero out there this morning," Bobbie complained as he grabbed a piece of sausage from the platter and stuffed the whole thing in his mouth. The warm juicy flavor spread throughout his mouth leaving him wanting more. "My breath near about froze to my nose with every breath this morning." Momma reached over and pulled him in close to her.

Daddy was sitting at the table, a steaming cup of coffee in his hand. Daddy liked his coffee strong and hot. Bobbie had often watched his daddy pour himself a cup of boiling coffee from the pot right off the stove and then turn it up for a noisy slurp. How it kept from scalding the hide right off his tongue and throat, Bobbie didn't know. Momma liked to pour a little of her coffee into her saucer and blow on it a bit before sipping it. Daddy would just throw back his head and laugh when he saw her do that and say, "Why heat it up in the first place?" The day started early for Daddy too. He had on his work clothes: denim jeans, heavy woolen shirt with a red long-handle shirt underneath. His boots were brown and patched. There were sewn strips of leather over the toes where he had cut some leather from an old pair of boots and patched the hole in these. His pant legs were tucked down into his boots with the shoestrings still untied. He worked at one of the sawmills in town.

Sawmill work, left to right: Claud Blair, Raymond Stephens, Delford James (Bobbie's Dad)

There were actually two mills in town. One was owned by Daddy's brother Jim and a man named Claude Case.

Mr. Stephens owned the other one. A good many of the men in the area worked at one of the mills. It was hard work, dangerous too, but the men who worked there were just thankful for the job. Times had been hard these past several years with the Depression, but Mr. Roosevelt had the country headed in the right direction now. The sawmill had gotten increased orders in the past several months due to the new construction going up through the WPA. There was even talk of not one, but two dams that might be built over the rivers in the next county and that would call for even more lumber supplies. This news had the men excited and talking.

Momma called for the others to wash up and come to the table. Audie was seven and a spindly little thing. She had golden hair that hung in loose ringlets to her shoulders. This morning she had on one of Momma's brown knitted shawls over her faded blue nightgown. Jake followed his big sister into the kitchen. Momma always put Jake in the front room with the other two kids when she started breakfast. He had just crawled out of bed, and, even though his hair was sticking out in every direction, he looked about as cute as one of Fancy's little pups. He crawled up into Daddy's lap. Jake's hair was long and he could sure do with a haircut, but Momma just couldn't make herself cut off those long blond curls yet. Audie had been four when Jake was born, but, even though little Rex had come along last year, Momma still treated Jake like he was her baby too. He got a bit too much babying as far as Bobbie was concerned, with his Momma and Audie both catering to him. He was cute though, Bobbie had to admit. Rex was still snoozing under the covers. He would be one year old next month, and Momma liked for him to stay asleep until she had the rest of the family fed. Once Rex woke up, he would be hungry. Then Momma would have to stop what she was doing and take care of him.

After breakfast, Momma gathered up the remains of what was left and packed Daddy a lunch. She wrapped the biscuits and sausages in a rag and Daddy put it down in his coat pocket. Daddy just ate at the mill every day, not wanting to take time to come home for lunch. The men didn't take a long break, just enough time to eat a little lunch and have a cigarette break. Daddy, like most of the men, smoked cigarettes from Prince Albert tobacco. Bobbie liked to watch him roll his cigarettes. He'd take out a paper from the little OBC package and hold it in between the pointer finger and middle finger of his left hand. Then he'd open the top of the Prince Albert tobacco can and tilt the can, pouring the loose tobacco along the paper. Next he'd shut the can and take the paper to this mouth and seal it by licking the edges together. Finally, he'd light it, inhaling deeply and blowing out a stream of smoke. Daddy lit his first cigarette now as Momma handed him another cup of coffee. He leaned back in his chair and stretched out his legs. This was his final bit of relaxation before beginning his labors at the mill.

Unlike Daddy, the kids usually came home from school to have lunch with Momma. Momma said growing sprouts needed a hot meal to keep them healthy, and she always had something warm waiting for them when they got their lunch break from school. More times than not, it was what was left from breakfast, but she'd also open up a jar of peaches or berries she'd canned to cater to their sweet tooth. Every now and then, she'd save some of the biscuit dough from breakfast and make fried pies with the fruit. Now that sure made the walk home worthwhile. Momma was known around these parts for her mouthwatering fried peach pies. Bobbie never complained about gathering peaches in the summer because he knew Momma would put them to good use. It made his mouth water just thinking about them. He didn't know how Momma could get them so golden and crispy on the outside without burning them. She always sprinkled a little sugar over the tops that made them sparkle in the sunlight. When he sank his teeth into one, the oozy peach filling filled his mouth with such sweetness. There was a tinge of tartness mixed in with the sweetness that made every one of his taste buds smile. He'd have to ask Momma if she would make some fried peach pies real soon.

Bobbie began his morning chores. First, he gathered in some wood. The wood was stacked in neat rows out behind the house. It was amazing how much wood it took for a family each day. In the winter, a fire was always kept in the Franklin stove in the living room, not to mention the wood needed for the cookstove. Then when Momma washed, she had to have wood to put under the black kettles out back. He loaded up his arms with as many sticks as he could carry. He put some wood in the kitchen's wood box and stacked the rest on the end of the porch. Next, it was time to get the water. Some families were fortunate enough to have a well of their own, but his family didn't. There was a spring down in the holler just behind the house about halfway to Grandma's. In fact, the spring was one reason Daddy had decided to buy this place. Springs meant fresh water that could be counted on. In the summer, the family got their water from there. Daddy always said there was nothing sweeter than water straight from a spring. It was also a good place to store the milk and butter in the summer to keep them cold. They would place the items in a wooden box that they kept tied to a rock. Momma liked to tell of the time after a big rain that she found her precious food washed away. Bobbie guessed that was the reason she always asked if the box was tied down good and tight when they returned from storing food in the spring.

In the winter, the family drew water from the community well in the center of town. He didn't know who had built the well in town or even how long it had been there. It had been there as long as he could remember; he knew that much. When his family moved to this house three years ago, Bobbie had been given the job of taking care of the water, and he'd had the job ever since.

Grabbing two buckets from the counter, he emptied the remains of what was still in them into the water reservoir in the cookstove. Momma needed warm water for washing up the breakfast dishes. Then he headed off to the well. On wash days, Bobbie had to draw enough water to fill both washtubs and the kettle. Every time he had to do this, he thought his arms were going to fall right off, not to mention how tired his legs got from the walks back and forth to the well. He was thankful wash day came only one day a week and that was usually on Thursdays. He always had to complain just a little to Momma when he had to fill her tubs, but he couldn't act mad for long the way she'd go on and on about how he was building up his muscles when he drew water. She would have to let out the seams in his shirtsleeves before long because his muscles were just fixing to burst right through his sleeves. Momma's laugh was infectious, and it wouldn't be long before he was pumping his arms showing off his muscles and laughing right along with her.

When he had the water buckets filled and placed back on the counter, he ran back outside and across the yard and threw open the door to the chicken coop. He latched the door open by twisting the piece of wire around the nail behind the door. Momma had nine hens and one ole white rooster and Audie had named them all. She insisted on calling the rooster Henny Penny even though Bobbie and Willie had tried to explain to her that Henny Penny was a girl's name and a rooster shouldn't have a hen's name. Audie was stubborn though, and once she had something in her mind, there was no convincing her otherwise. Bobbie stopped at the smokehouse and dipped out a can of corn from the barrel and sprinkled it over the ground for the chickens. He replaced the lid and headed toward the house. It was about time to light out for school. Audie was just finishing with her own chores when he stepped inside.

It was Audie's job each morning to help Momma with the breakfast dishes and to help Jake get dressed while Momma fed Rex. Momma didn't want Audie outside on cold mornings, so Bobbie fed the chickens for her during the winter months. After school, Audie would gather the eggs, wash them, and place them in the wire basket on the counter. Bobbie opened the door and went inside. He moved to the stove and ladled out a dipper full of warm water into the wash pan. He washed his face and ran a comb through his tangled hair. Momma was fretting over Audie, making sure she had on two pairs of stockings and an extra layer of clothes. "I went ahead and fixed you a lunch this morning," Momma was saying to her, "so you won't have to get back out in the cold at dinnertime. What about you, Bobbie? I can throw something together for you too if you'd like me to."

Bobbie shook his head and dried his hands. "Nope, I'll just come on home. It won't be so cold by noon." He gave Momma a quick kiss and gave little Jake's head a playful rub. "Come on, sis," he hurried Audie. "We're going to be late if we don't get going." Momma tucked Audie's scarf tightly around her neck and gave her a hug.

"Bobbie, you watch out for Audie and help her this morning in the cold, you hear? And make sure Willie makes it to school!" He nodded at Momma and opened the door.

Willie was Bobbie's younger brother. He had just turned six in December. Willie lived with Grandma James most of the time. She lived just up the road from them. Grandma had lost Grandpa a couple of years ago. Willie hadn't even been five then, but Grandma thought she couldn't stay by herself with Grandpa gone. Willie had started spending the night with her every now and then, and now he practically spent every night there. It wasn't like he was never home with them; he just slept at Grandma's and had most of his meals with her. Grandma was doing better and maybe Willie would be able to be back home with them before too long. Bobbie always thought it a little odd. How could such a young boy make Grandma feel safer? He guessed Willie just provided company for her and kept the house from seeming so empty. Bobbie missed Willie though and hoped it wouldn't be long before he was back at home where he belonged.

This second walk to school each day was a lot slower for Bobbie than his first. For one thing, Audie's little legs were no match for Bobbie's long strides. He pulled her along, her gloved hand in his. This was her second year of school, and Bobbie had taken the responsibility of helping her with the trip back and forth to school very seriously, not that he had to help her that much. She was small for her age that was sure. She was tough though and quick to let everyone know she could do things for herself. Bobbie tugged at Audie's hand to hurry her along. Audie didn't object to holding Bobbie's hand as long as they were out of sight of the others, but when they came in sight of the other kids, Bobbie knew her hand would quickly pull away.

They were just coming into town, not far from Cap's blacksmith shop, when the first bell sounded. They quickened their pace. There were always two bells to announce school. The first bell rang at 7:50. That bell meant that school would be taking up in a few minutes. The second bell rang at 8:00; that meant that every boy and girl should be at school and making their way down the aisle to their seats. The teachers were strict about this and didn't take tardiness lightly. As they entered the school, Bobbie and Audie hung their coats on the hooks that hung on the wall. They noticed Willie's coat already hanging on his peg, so they knew he had beaten them there. Lunches that children brought from home were lined up in a neat row underneath the coats like students standing at attention. Some children brought their lunches in baskets or wrapped in cloth. Most, though, brought a bucket of some kind that had a lid and handle, such as a lard bucket. Most schoolchildren carried their lunches to school because it was too far for them to go home during the lunch hour.

The students made their way into the little room. Bobbie smiled to himself as he felt the warmth of the room wrap its arms around him. Even with the cold outside, it was plenty warm inside the school. There would be no cold feet this morning after all. He caught Mr. Schauffler's eye and nodded at him. Mr. Schauffler gave him a friendly wink, letting Bobbie know the room's temperature was to his liking. Bobbie headed to the back of the room to the seat he shared with Cody. Cody was ten like most of the other kids in fourth grade and one of Bobbie's best buddies. Bobbie headed for his spot beside him on the double seat closest to the wall, but Cody was in that spot today. Bobbie shrugged and slid in the aisle side of the seat. Cody didn't even look at him. *Let him be that way*, Bobbie thought, not caring if annoyance showed on his face. He thought back to their marble game yesterday. It wasn't like Cody to hold a grudge, but what else could Cody be mad about? It had to be the marble game. Cody had gotten so upset at Bobbie for winning his yellow cat's-eye marble from him. Bobbie had won it fair and square. They had been playing for keeps, and Bobbie had knocked one of Cody's special marbles outside of the circle. Cat's-eye marbles weren't that rare, but

Cody was the only one around with two yellow-eyed ones. Correction, one yellow-eyed one. Bobbie now held its twin in his own pocket. Cody claimed the marbles came from New Orleans, and he had managed to hang on to them ever since his uncle had given them to him last summer. That was until yesterday. Bobbie didn't care that much for marbles, and he had intended to give it back to him. After seeing the fit Cody threw though, going as far as calling him a cheat, Bobbie had decided to hang on to it for a while. He threw Cody a dirty glance, took out his writing tablet, and got ready for the school day.

Mr. Schauffler walked to the front of the room ready to lead the children in their morning song. He waited a few minutes until everyone had taken their seats, and then tapped his stick on his desk and began the morning song:

Good morning Mister Zip, Zip, Zip
With your hair cut just as short as mine

Mr. Schauffler had a booming voice that rattled the windows. When he sang, he held nothing back. He walked around the room as he sang, making eye contact with each of his students urging them to sing along. He always ended the song with a great big smile that exposed his shiny gold tooth toward the back of his mouth. He always said, "A smile is a curve that sets everything straight!" When the students had asked Mr. Schauffler about this song, he had explained that it began during the time of World War I or the Great War as it was called. He liked the snappy tune and believed it started everyone's day off in a good way. After finishing the song, he dropped his smile and got right down to the business of instruction.

Mr. Schauffler always began the day working with the first-grade students and then continued with the second, third, and finally the fourth. He would assign the older students some seat work to complete until it was their turn to come to the front. This morning, Bobbie, along with the other fourth-grade students, was working on his multiplication facts. They were supposed to write each multiplication fact five times each. Bobbie knew his facts by heart already, but some of the kids were still stumbling over some of them, especially the eights and nines. Bobbie pulled out his pencil and began his work. As he made his way down the page of facts, he heard a scratching sound beside him. He glanced over at Cody out of the corner of his eye and saw that he had his pocketknife out. At first, Bobbie thought Cody was just sharpening his pencil, but as he watched, he saw that Cody was carving on the desk. Bobbie couldn't believe it. Carving names on desks was not unusual in the big room, but Bobbie knew for a fact that there were no names carved on the desks in here. What would Mr. Schauffler think? What would he do? Bobbie squirmed in his desk and scratched at the back of his neck. He had an uneasy feeling about this. He finally got back to his work and tried to concentrate while Cody continued to carve. He couldn't stay focused though for the irritating sound of the knife on the wood. Glancing back over, he noticed that Cody had carved the name Allie on the desktop. *I can't believe this!* Bobbie thought to himself. Should he tell Mr. Schauffler? Should he ask Cody to stop? He punched Cody with his elbow and gave him a dirty look. Cody frowned at him but just kept carving. Finally, Bobbie got so worked up, he was about ready to explode. He couldn't just sit there; he had to do something or he was going to pop.

He slowly slid out of his seat and walked to the front of the room. Audie's little second-grade class had joined the first graders and was spelling some words from their simple story. "C-A-T," spelled Patty.

"Good, good," praised Mr. Schauffler smiling. He looked up as Bobbie approached. "Yes?" he asked sternly. Mr. Schauffler didn't like to be interrupted when he was teaching.

"Mr. Schauffler, sir, may I leave the room?" asked Bobbie. Mr. Schauffler looked surprised that Bobbie would need to go to the outhouse this soon after second bell. He nodded though, and Bobbie walked out the door. The cold air felt surprisingly good to his hot face. He closed the door softly, but then stomped down the front steps and headed toward the back of the school. He didn't really know why he was so upset with Cody. Was it because he felt that Cody was being disrespectful to Mr. Schauffler, or was it something else?

What was Cody doing writing Allie's name? Could it be that Bobbie was a little jealous thinking someone else liked Allie? He had to admit he thought Allie was pretty and had said as much to Cody just the other day. Bobbie had been watching Allie at recess when the girls were playing drop the handkerchief as he sat with Collin shooting marbles. She had such a pretty smile, and, most of the time, she wasn't loud and bossy like some of the other girls. Bobbie liked her quiet manner and the way she worked hard in class. You could tell Mr. Schauffler was proud of her by the way he always smiled and nodded when she read aloud or recited. She made Bobbie smile too. It actually made him a little sorry for her when he was up against her at ciphering and put her down, being faster with his work than she. Bobbie had leaned in close to Cody and said, "Now if I was to ever have a girlfriend, that's who it would be." He'd nodded in Allie's direction. Cody had looked first at Allie and then at Bobbie and smiled. He'd punched Bobbie with his elbow and grinned.

Cody knew Bobbie had a spark for her, so why was he carving her name on the desk? See if he told Cody anything ever again. He supposed Cody had the right to like any girl, but he couldn't help thinking he was just doing it to spite him. No use getting all worked up over it, he guessed. He decided he should just forget the whole thing and let Mr. Schauffler take care of the matter himself.

There were two outhouses behind the school. They were spaced far apart with the girls' on the right and the boys' on the left. He turned to the left and headed down the hill. Maybe just this short walk would be enough to calm him down. He could hear the townspeople going about their day. The logs from the sawmill made thumping sounds as they rolled and clattered together and hit the ground. He could hear some of the men at the mill calling out things to one another. He wondered if one of the voices he heard was Daddy's. In the distance, he could hear the pounding of Cap's hammer as he worked shaping the iron on a wheel or some tool at the blacksmith shop. He liked the sound of work. As much as he enjoyed school, he looked forward to the time when he would be a man and could work alongside his dad and the other men at the mill. He would work hard. He had already learned a lot about sawmill work by watching the men as they did the various jobs. He might even start his own sawmill one day. He felt better as he walked back up the worn path from the outhouse and into the building.

As Bobbie walked back into the room, he sensed a change. All heads turned toward him as he went inside. The children at the recitation seat were silent and curious. There was a noticeable interruption in routine and the normal activities. Mr. Schauffler cast a hard and stern look in his direction. His left eyebrow rose in a questioning manner. The whole room wore a feeling of uneasiness and dread. Bobbie was confused. Had he been gone too long? Did he make too much noise coming back in? He ducked his head slightly and slowly walked back to his seat. He noticed that Cody was no longer in his spot but was now in his usual spot closest to the aisle. Bobbie went around the back of the seat and took his usual place by the wall. He folded his hands on his desk and dropped his head to avoid the conspicuous stares. As he looked down, his eyes bulged and his mouth dropped open. He saw now that his name was carved underneath Allie's name on the desk and there was a big heart around both names. His face burned. Why had Cody done such a thing? Was Mr. Schauffler upset that he hadn't let him know what Cody was doing? Worse yet, did Mr. Schauffler think Bobbie had done it?

His teacher cleared his throat. The room itself seemed to hold its breath for what was to come next. Mr. Schauffler stood and slowly strode back to Bobbie's desk. With his hands clasped behind him, he rocked somewhat on his feet. Speaking clearly with no hesitation, he said, "Bobbie, would you like to explain to me why you have damaged school property by carving on the desktop?"

Bobbie was dumbfounded. He opened his mouth to speak, but no words found their way past his lips. He could feel his face burning and he had a sinking hollow feeling to his stomach. His hands felt sweaty, and he had the sudden urge to jump up and run out the door and down the steps of the school. He glanced around the room. Everyone was looking at him. He could see smiles tugging at the corners of some of the boys' mouths. They didn't dare let them out though. A log dropped inside the stove and made a crackling sound. Someone was tapping a pencil in the far corner of the room and another student coughed nervously. Bobbie bit down on his lip and thought of what to say. Shyly he glanced in Allie's direction. She had her back turned to him, sitting as rigid and stiff as the poker beside the stove. Did the others know what was written on the desk? Did she? Mr. Schauffler looked at Bobbie one last time and turned on his heels and walked to the front of the room. "Mr. James, we'll discuss this at a later time. Let's have the third graders up at the front, please. Everyone else should continue with morning work."

The morning crawled. Bobbie couldn't concentrate. As Mr. Schauffler worked with the third-grade students, Bobbie looked sideways at Cody. He had a good mind to give him a stout shove that would send him sprawling into the aisle. That would serve him right. He had considered Cody one of his best buddies. When he had shared with him his secret of liking Allie for his girlfriend, Cody had double swore not to tell anyone. Cody had better watch out at recess. Bobbie planned to jump him the first chance he got and teach him a thing or two for messing with him. He just wasn't going to get by with this. He'd tell Mr. Schauffler the truth. He'd tell him how Cody had been sitting in his seat this morning and how he had seen him carving on the desk. Mr. Schauffler would believe him. He'd apologize to Bobbie and make Cody apologize to him too. He'd tell the whole class he had made a mistake and that Cody was the one who broke the rule, not Bobbie. He stared at Cody who sat working diligently on his morning work as the clock slowly made its way to recess time, the time of reckoning.

Chapter 2

I'm not sure if one can pinpoint his first memory. I remember my first home with Mama and Dad. It was a four-room unpainted board house with a porch across the front. It had wooden shingles for the roof, which proved to be disastrous for us later on. I remember the flat rocks Dad had placed from the porch to the gate for a walkway. We had a picket fence that had jonquils bordering it at the front. The back gate that went out to the chicken houses had bordering it what we called snow-on-the-mountain. We had two chicken houses. One of them was later used as a place where my dad made brooms. I think the broom factory, as we called it, belonged to both my dad and Uncle George. In the backyard, there was a wide hole where Dad had started to dig a cellar but didn't ever finish it, so it just sort of filled up with dirt and weeds. Our vegetable garden was out back of the house.

I remember the catnip herbs that grew in the shade of the seedling peach trees. Mothers with new babies thought they couldn't raise a child if it wasn't given catnip tea. I remember Mama giving my baby sisters tea from a spoon because they had no baby bottles. I remember them getting strangled on it very often, but with Mama patting them on the back and raising their little arms up and down, they soon were ready for more catnip tea.

—Allie (2009)

Allie

January 1941

Allie, clad in her saddle oxford shoes, slowly dragged her feet along the rutted dirt road as she and her sister walked home from school that late January afternoon. Her socks had slipped down around her ankles, but she didn't bother to pull them up. Her brown woolen coat was buttoned to her neck and a brown-speckled scarf was wrapped around her head and up over the lower part of her face to protect it from the cold. Her hands were freezing. She had pulled them up into the sleeves of her coat to try and keep them warm, but they had long since gone numb. The lard bucket that held the remains of her hardly touched lunch hung over her arm making a clanking sound as it swung back

MAKING A BEELINE HOME

and forth with each step. Allie held her *McGuffey Reader* tightly against her chest like a shield. This had been one of the worst days of her life.

It was a little less than a mile walk from the school to their home. Allie usually didn't mind the walk to and from school, in good weather anyway. In fact, it was usually a lot of fun. She and her sister often sang songs and talked about what had happened at school during the day. Often they met up with some of the other kids walking to and from school. Today though, with the brutal weather and the humiliation of the day, the trip seemed endless. Today they walked home alone. The other children, sensing the seriousness of her mood, had hurried toward home without stopping to wait for their friends. Allie still couldn't believe the events of this day. She would never get over the embarrassment as long as she lived. She hated, hated, hated that James boy. How could he do such a thing? She always had been a little leery of him anyway, the way he acted older than the other kids in her class. Allie remembered how he liked to hang around her daddy's sawmill and even help out at times like he was one of them. He was the one who built the fires in the school every morning, a job you would expect a much older boy to do. It was like he was tired of being a child and was making the leap into manhood way before his time. Allie supposed she shouldn't be surprised at this joke of his. After all, it wasn't uncommon for the boys in the big room to carve on their desks, and she guessed he thought of himself as one of them. But still, still she was surprised. Bobbie had always seemed a little bit shy, too shy for a bold act like this. And for the life of her, she couldn't understand what had made him carve her name. He must have known how much it would embarrass her. He didn't like her, not like that. She wouldn't even consider that. He had barely said a word to her, probably never even knew her name. Allie searched her brain for some understanding or reason, but there was none. It was just a mean thing for him to do, and she would never speak to him again for the rest of her life.

Winna, Allie's older sister, walked a few paces ahead of her. She kept turning around every so often to try and get Allie to catch up. She hadn't seen what happened today since she was in the big room at school, but she had heard about it. Everyone had heard about it! It was all the kids were talking about, and they had all gathered around the door at recess trying to listen as Mr. Schauffler had talked to Bobbie. Bobbie had rejoined the others at recess in a little while before books had taken up again, but he didn't look all that upset or worried. He had just come down the steps and walked over to where some of the older boys were shooting marbles. They had huddled around him. Allie could see them asking him questions, but it didn't look like he was telling them much. Bobbie did look over at Allie, just for the briefest second as she stood with some of her friends, and he seemed to look regretful. It had been just that instant when their eyes had met, Allie, curious at his punishment, noticed when he glanced over at her that he looked sad somehow. She had quickly looked away. She had to give him that though; he did look as if he were sorry. A lot of good that did! Yes, the kids were all talking about it, and Allie would be surprised if Mama and Daddy hadn't heard about it by now too. She felt the whole world was laughing at her.

"Come on, sis," Winna coaxed. "You didn't do anything wrong. Boys do the dumbest things. They can't help it; that's just the way they are. You should see how some of them act in the big room. Everyone will have forgotten all about it by tomorrow anyway. Just you wait and see." Winna came back and looped her arm through the crook in her sister's arm. "It will be all right, I promise." Allie had held the tears in until now. Somehow, she had been so angry all day she had never once cried, not one tear. Suddenly, it was just all too much. She just shook her head and let the tears fall. They dripped off the end of her nose, soaking her scarf.

The sun's rays had begun to cast shadows of the girls as they walked up the final hill to their house. It was a weathered gray board house, never painted. It had a porch that went all the way across the front where the family gathered on warm summer evenings. An equally gray picket fence went around the house, and in the summer, jonquils grew in clusters around the front gate. The sisters turned in at the gate and walked up the flat rocks Dad had placed there long ago as stepping stones from the gate to the porch.

Mama, Daddy, Winna, Allie, and baby Betty

The warmth of the room embraced them as they opened the door and stepped inside. It was a four-room house with a front room, kitchen, and two bedrooms: Mama and Daddy in one bedroom, Allie and Winna sharing the other. A younger sister, Betty, sat playing with some dominoes on the floor. She was dropping them in one of Mama's kitchen pans, enjoying the clanging sound as they bounced on the bottom. She looked up with a dimpled grin as the sisters came in. Dropping their things to the floor, Winna and Allie hurried over to the fire to warm their frozen hands and feet.

Mama came around the corner from the kitchen with a smile and a plate of chocolate rolls warm from the oven. The chocolaty aroma wafted through the room. "How was school?" Mama asked. She set the rolls on the corner table as she helped them out of their coats and scarves.

Winna smiled up at Mama and said, "It was okay for me, but Allie is mad at what one of the boys did to her today."

"What happened?" Mama asked with concern, looking at Allie. She waited as the girls rubbed their hands together and sat down on the padded patchwork stool in front of the stove. Winna began untying her shoes, slipping them off. Allie slumped down onto the stool like a limp rag doll.

She didn't answer Mama's question. Her bottom lip was stuck out, and she was wearing her pouting face. Mama knew that face well. Allie was usually a happy, mild-mannered daughter, but when she was upset, there was no denying it. It was as plain as a wart on the end of her nose. Allie propped her elbows on her knees and rested her chin in her hands with a deep sigh. "What's wrong, honey?" Mama asked again. She waited while Winna placed her shoes beside the stove. Mama picked up the chocolate rolls and held out the plate to them. "Come on now, girls," she chided.

"Shocolate roll!" Betty cried as she clumsily got to her feet and reached for the plate.

"Hold on a minute, sugar," Mama replied. She sat down the plate once again and lifted Betty up onto Winna's lap and broke off a part of the chocolate roll and handed it to her. Betty started eating it greedily, crumbs tumbling onto Winna's blue skirt.

"Shocolate, good!" she smiled as she stuffed more into her mouth. Mama smiled.

"Now go on," Mama insisted, looking intently at Allie. "Tell me what happened."

Allie took a deep breath. She began the account at the awful moment when Cody had raised his hand during class and told Mr. Schauffler that Bobbie had carved something into his desktop. Cody had told Mr. Schauffler that he didn't want to be a tattle, but he thought Mr. Schauffler needed to know what Bobbie had done. He knew his teacher would be upset at anyone vandalizing the school property, and he felt it was his duty to report it. Allie then shared with Mama how all the kids had turned openmouthed to stare at her when Cody read what Bobbie had written. Tears filled her eyes at the thought of those accusing eyes like she herself had done something wrong.

Mama sighed and shook her head. "Oh, honey, it's all right," she soothed. "We can't always help what other people do. We just have to always try and do what's right ourselves."

"But why would someone do that?" sobbed Allie. "Why would he do that to me when I've never done anything to him?"

"I don't know, sweetheart, but I don't want you worrying anymore about it. Mr. Schauffler will take care of punishing him, and I'm sure it will never happen again." Allie sniffed, and tears rolled down her cheeks.

"Bite shocolate, sissy?" Betty asked as she raised her eyebrows. Her eyes were round as buttons as she offered her last bite of chocolate roll to Allie. Allie looked down at her little sister's chocolaty smile and bright eyes looking up at her. Chocolate was smeared from her chin up to the tip of her nose. That seemed to lighten the mood. The sob turned into a giggle as Allie looked down at the adorable face of her baby sister.

"Thank you, Betty Boo," Allie said with a tearful smile to her little sister, giving her a kiss on the nose, as she opened her mouth and accepted the bite Betty held out to her.

Betty had seemed almost like a miracle baby to her family, and she was loved and pampered by every one of them. Eight years separated Allie and Betty, and there were ten years between Winna and Betty. At times, it seemed there were three mothers watching out for her. Betty would turn three in May. It felt like the family had been holding its breath during the time she'd been with them. Every sniffle and sneeze was a source of worry. When she came down with a fever last winter, both Mama and Daddy had stayed up all night watching over her. Allie didn't think the family could have gone on if anything had happened to Betty. The devastation they had experienced at the loss of two other baby girls before Betty had taken its toll on the family. Even though Allie had been very young, she could still remember how quiet and empty the house had seemed after their deaths. It had been a gray time, a black time, and Betty had helped pull the family out of that pit. She had brought so much joy back into the family, joy they so desperately needed. Every new word, every silly face, just about everything she did was a source of pleasure for them all. And now, Mama was expecting again. In fact, the baby could come any day. It might even be born on Allie's own birthday, the fifteenth.

Allie glanced up from the book she was reading. After Mama had reassured her that everything would be okay, she had stretched out on the sofa with her head on the big print pillow. She was on page 189 in her *Basic Reader* book from school. The name of the story was "Rumpelstiltskin." What a funny story. Imagine trying to guess someone's name! She had Mama's crocheted afghan pulled up over her, and she felt as snug as a bug in a rug. Mama was saying something. "Girls, it's time to go after the night water." Allie let out a quiet moan. Each night before supper, Allie and Winna had to walk down to the spring and get the water. No matter how tired they were, how cold it was, how hot it was, how hard it was raining or snowing, the family had to have water. Heck, they could probably be in the middle of a tornado, and if it were time to get night water—off they'd have to go. It was something they could count on like clockwork—getting the night water. Allie pulled herself off the sofa and stretched. She slowly began pulling on her shoes. Winna came in from the bedroom where she had either been napping or reading. Allie dreaded getting out in the cold air again. She thought of her cousins who lived down the road from them. She couldn't help but be a little jealous of Erma Fay and Joanna. They had no idea how lucky they were. They lived in a big log house with five rooms instead of four like her own. Allie loved their house, especially the kitchen with its green walls. It had a big porch that went all the way across the front. It was a nice house, and Aunt Lottie had it decorated so pretty. However, the best, best, best thing about their house was that they had their very own well right on their screened-in back porch. What a luxury. Allie could hardly even imagine what it would be like to just walk out your kitchen door and draw up a bucket of fresh cold water, never again having to walk the steep hill down to the spring and stagger back up the hill with the heavy buckets of water. No sir, those girls had no idea how lucky they were.

Allie and Winna passed through the kitchen where Mama was fixing supper. She was just pouring the cornbread into the skillet and the pinto beans were bubbling slowly on the back side of the stove. Mama was frying some bacon and the potatoes were browning in the hot oil. It smelled so good,

Allie's mouth began to water. "Daddy will be home from the sawmill anytime, girls. You need to hurry," she said. Mama stopped in the food preparation and poured up the last of the water into the wash pan and handed the empty bucket to Winna. The other three buckets were sitting on the end of the cabinet. Winna grabbed the handle of one more bucket, and Allie picked up the other two. They went out the kitchen door and down the back steps swinging the buckets beside them. It was still cold outside, but the wind wasn't blowing now so that helped. The girls walked out across the yard and past the big hole.

Several years ago, Daddy had started digging the family a storm cellar. He had begun it one late evening around sundown and had worked at it into the night. It was something that never got finished though. For whatever reason, the cellar never got dug out completely, and the hole never got filled in. It just sat there for weeks. Finally, grass began growing both down in the hole and on the mound of earth on the sides of it. When they got a heavy rain, water collected there, and the girls pretended they had their own swimming hole, even though the water was never more than a few inches deep. The hole had been there so long now that it just seemed a natural part of their yard. Allie did remember that it was in April when Daddy began digging the cellar and it was soon after little Shirley had died. Allie remembered standing in the back door and watching him swing that shovel down hard over and over again in the darkening night. Even after she had gone to bed that night, she could hear the *whack, whack* sound of the shovel striking the hard earth. Daddy must have worked on that hole most of the night because in the morning there it was—a big gaping hole in the earth. As Allie looked at the hole, she couldn't help but think it was not unlike the gaping hole in their hearts. Uncle George, Daddy's brother, had come by the next day to see if he could give Daddy a hand, but Daddy had just waved him off saying he needed to do it himself. Daddy stopped digging the cellar that afternoon and, as far as Allie knew, had never worked on it again.

The girls walked along the edge of the hole and went out the back gate where the peach trees stood motionless, lifting their arms toward the rose-streaked sky. Catnip grew all along the edge of the fence around the gate, meandering back and forth among the rocks. Allie loved to play in the backyard in the spring and summer. Around May when the peach trees were in bloom and the larkspurs were heavy with flowers, the scent was intoxicating. Also Mama grew herbs: sage, rosemary, and mint. The aroma of the flowers and herbs mixed together in such a wonderful blend; Allie would spread a blanket and spend hours dreaming the day away. She pulled her scarf tighter around her head. Brrrrrr! Tonight, spring seemed so far away. The girls passed by the chicken house. It was a small gray weathered building with a front door and a tin roof. It was built off the ground and rested on glade rocks that were stacked at the corners of the house. They would shut the chickens up when they came back up the hill with the water in a few minutes. A few of the fowl were still scratching around in the dirt for a final nugget of food before retiring.

Leaving their own yard, they walked toward their grandparents' house that was only a few yards from their own. The pathway between the two houses was a well-worn and much-loved path.

Grandma and Grandpa Shoemate

Passing the window in the front of the house, they saw their grandpa sitting in the old rocker with the green padded seat cushion. He had his worn Bible in his hands.

Glancing up, he grinned widely and threw up his hand at the girls. Grandpa Shoemate was short, but he stood ten feet tall to Allie. He was somewhat round, making the front of his overalls stretch tight over his fat stomach. Grandpa's complexion was ruddy, and there were red spidery veins that ran over his nose and out over his cheeks. Allie knew his hair must have been dark-brown at one time, but now it was a light-brown with a mixture of gray. It was thin and combed back from his round face. His eyes were the color of the golden sorghum in the jelly jar that sat on Grandma's red-checked tablecloth.

Grandpa was a farmer. He always planted a big garden, and it amazed his granddaughters at the tricks he knew when it came to his garden plants. For instance, when he planted his sweet corn, he would also plant some pole beans in among them so the beans would grow and vine up around the corn stalks making the perfect poles. The cucumbers were planted by the fence where the vines seemed, to Allie, to have a lovely time seeing which of them could be the first to make it to the top of the fence. Later, cucumbers hung down from the vines making them easy to pick. Each spring, along about the first of May, Grandpa would hitch his mules to the old iron plow he kept stored in the barn during the winter months. He would throw their reins over his shoulder and give a click of his tongue. Those mules must have understood his language because they would prick their ears and take off across the field. Grandpa hung on to the handle of the plow, walking behind them in the furrowed earth. When he wanted the mules to go right, he would say, "Gee!" and when he wanted them to go left, he would say, "Haw!" Allie loved to watch her grandpa garden and listen to him talk to the mules. She would often fall into step behind him and follow along mimicking his every move and practicing mule talk. Over the years, she must have walked a hundred miles in his tracks, stretching her legs to place her bare feet into the large prints of her grandpa's boots. She loved following her grandpa and knew in her heart that his steps would never lead her in the wrong direction. Grandpa's footprints were unique. His feet turned outward as he walked leaving prints much like one of Grandma's ducks. No, Grandpa didn't have a graceful walk according to some people, but to Allie, everything about Grandpa was perfect.

Grandpa also worked at the sawmill. He'd work all day long behind his mule as he skidded logs. Grandpa wasn't afraid of work, and he gave it all he had. Allie had often seen him come home in the summer after working and sweating all day long, and his chambray shirt and blue denim overalls would be white with salt from his own sweat. It was said of Sam Shoemate that he would work just as hard when the boss wasn't around as when he was. He always gave a day's work for a day's pay, and a lot of those workdays only paid $1. In Allie's mind and heart, he was the best man she had ever known. He had the biggest and kindest heart one could ever have, and it made her wonder at her fortune at having him as her grandpa.

She loved Grandma too. Where Grandpa was short and round, Grandma was just the opposite. She reminded Allie of a dandelion: tall, thin, and fragile. Allie always feared a strong wind could whish her away just like the fragile fluff off the head of a dandelion. Her whitish-gray hair was usually pulled back in a bun at the nape of her neck. Her hair was actually very long. In fact, it had never been cut. Allie loved to watch Grandma comb it. She would bend from the waist and comb it up over her head and all the way down. It would almost touch the floor. After she had it all combed, she would begin to twist and twirl it around. She had hairpins, and she would put it up in a bun with it all combed back from her face. She would keep it in place with the hairpins and use ivory combs to secure it. Grandma got around a little slow, and she swayed from side to side when she walked like the pendulum of her old clock. Grandpa adored Grandma and treated her like a queen. Every Sunday, Grandpa would saddle up their old mule for Grandma to ride to church. It was quite a chore for her to get up on the mule, but Grandpa would push and pull and coax and soothe until he had her sitting tall and prim astride the mule like an honored queen. Allie and Winna would hurry outside or at least rush to the window when they saw Grandpa leading the ole mule from the barn so they could watch the ordeal. Once Grandpa got her settled, he would take the reins in his calloused hands and gently lead the mule down the hill and over the road that took them to church. Grandma and Grandpa were dedicated Christians, and they never missed attending services.

The girls went through their grandparents' front yard and out the side gate that led to the barn and chicken house. The barn was on the right and the chicken house was on the left. The chicken house was much like their own. It was made of gray boards, but the barn was made of logs. Grandpa had built the log barn himself. It had a loft and a corncrib. Allie loved to play inside. When the sun was shining, the rays coming through the spaces between the logs made patterns of light and dark on the dirt floor. She would play hopscotch along the patterned floor. Grandpa raised his own corn, and he stored it in the corncrib in the barn. He wouldn't pick his corn until it was dried, and then he'd load the dried corn, husks and all, into his wagon and haul it over to the barn. He'd toss it into the crib until he needed it. What fun to play among the crackling corn.

The girls loved feeding Grandma's chickens. They'd get several corncobs from the crib and shell off the kernels. The dried kernels fell off easily as they rubbed the cob between their hands. It left them with an empty cob just asking to be made into a corncob doll. Allie looked over at the barn and noticed Brendie, Grandpa's cow, munching some hay just inside the barn door. Her ears pricked forward as she glanced curiously over at the girls when the gate squeaked shut behind them.

"Race you to the bottom!" Winna suddenly squealed as she took off in a head start down the hill swinging her water buckets beside her.

"No fair," Allie grumbled as she lit out after her. The hillside was rocky. Allie's shoes rolled and her feet twisted on the loose stones as she stumbled along after her sister. More than once, she caught herself just before she went down. Limbs and briars reached out prickly fingers to slow her, and her buckets clanked and rattled as they brushed up against the bushes that hugged the path. The buckets clamored against her ankles. As Winna made her way down the hill, her brown hair flew out behind her like Mama's long brown stockings blowing on the clothesline. She made it to the bottom and gave a loud whoop. Winna was bent at the waist, her breaths coming in puffs and laughing, when Allie caught up with her. "Told you I'd beat you," she teased.

Allie set her buckets down and gave Winna a playful shove. "You always cheat! Come on, let's hurry. I'm so hungry, I can't wait till supper." The girls dipped their water buckets down into the spring being careful not to spill water onto their clothes. It was cold enough out here this evening without having wet clothes clinging to them. The water was crystal clear. Mint grew abundantly along the water's edge. Mint grows upward in long branches. When it gets too tall to support its weight, it bends over and then the part that touches the ground roots making the plant spread. Mint has such a fresh flavor to it. When Allie chewed on mint though, a funny thing happened. It seemed to open her nose up wide making the air she breathed in really cold and fresh. This was great in the summer when she was hot and sweaty, but in the winter, she didn't like the cold air. She decided to leave the mint alone today.

Allie looked down into the clear water. The trees made slender shadows on the surface of the water. Grandpa had to clean the spring every few weeks. Leaves and branches and other debris would hang up and collect in the ditch downstream of the spring making the water back up. That would keep the water from flowing smoothly. The spring had to always be flowing to keep it fresh. Rocks were placed around the sides to collect more water and make it deeper, and someone had placed some flat stones on the bottom. This kept the water from getting stirred up as they dipped their buckets down into it. Grandpa had built a little wooden fence around the spring to keep animals out of it. A spring was a wonderful thing to have, and Daddy and Grandpa did everything they could to take care of it.

A small coffee can was tied to a low-hanging branch of a sassafras tree that grew beside the spring. Several trees grew around the spring. This one was a tall thin tree with several limbs. The leaf of a sassafras has three lobes or parts to it. Of course, the tree was bare at this time of the year, but in the spring and summer, it made a nice shade.

Allie lifted the coffee can down from the branch. "Do you want to go first, sis?" she said with a smile. In the summer, Allie and Winna had a little game they would play. They would see if they could drink the number of cans of water as their ages. It began one hot summer day when Winna was especially thirsty and bragged that since she was eight, it would take eight cans of water to cool her off. Allie, not to be outdone, followed suit and drank six for her age. For whatever reason, the silly ritual had stuck and had been going on for several years now. It wasn't so bad back when they were younger, but she was going to be eleven in a few days and Winna was already thirteen. That's a lot of water. Allie smiled at Winna, "Hope you're thirsty!" This was one time when Allie was glad to be a couple of years younger than Winna. She didn't know how Winna's stomach held two more cans of water than hers. When Allie would finish her last can, her stomach looked as big as a watermelon that could win a ribbon at the fair. Winna's stomach must be bigger than her own. "Did a person's stomach keep growing year after year?" Allie wondered. She thought of Grandpa's fat stomach and thought surely it did.

Winna smiled and shook her head. "I think I'll pass today. I don't think I can carry two buckets in my stomach and two more in my arms up that hill today! I just don't have the energy." Allie laughed as she hung the can back on the branch.

When both girls had their buckets filled, they began the slow trip back. There would be no racing going up the hill. Allie led the way ever cautious of where she placed her feet. One stumble and she could drop her bucket and spill every bit of her water. Then it would be back down the hill to refill it. She didn't want that! She was thankful as she neared the top of the hill and saw the flat rock. This was the girls' stopping place. The flat surface made a level spot to set their buckets while they rested their hands for a minute and caught their breath. Not much farther now.

Grandma was gathering some of Grandpa's overalls off the clothesline in the back of the house as Winna and Allie passed through their yard once again. Grandma was moving more slowly than ever. Washing was hard work, and the girls knew she was probably worn out and her back aching after a day of carrying water, scrubbing on the washboard, and wringing out Grandpa's heavy overalls. "Grandma, do you want a drink of some good fresh water?" Winna called out. Grandma looked up from her basket as she was placing a pair of folded overalls into it. She put her hand to the small of her back as she slowly stood up.

"Oh, I've just been choking for a good drink," she called back. The girls set down their buckets and waited while Grandma walked over and got the dipper from the side porch and walked over to them. She dipped it down into the water and took a big gulp and wiped her mouth. "Ummm, that's just what I needed," she said with a smile. Allie and

Winna's dimpled smiles lit their faces as they giggled out loud. They knew Grandma probably wasn't a bit thirsty, especially on this cold afternoon. It was just a little game they played with her. If they happened to see her on their way back from the spring, they always offered her a drink, and Grandma was always just choking for a drink. They gave Grandma a quick hug and started for home. "Thanks for that drink," Grandma called out after them.

Grandma and Grandpa also got water from the spring. They did have their own cistern out back of their house, but the water in it was not fit for drinking. They used it for washing, bathing, and cleaning, just not for drinking or cooking. Their cistern also made a nice place in the summer to keep their milk and butter. Grandma would put the milk in a jar and secure the lid tightly. Then she'd wrap a thick towel around it and place it in the bucket. Next, she'd wrap a rag around the butter jar and place it alongside the milk. Finally, she would put them in the water bucket and lower it down into the cool hole, just above the water. She had to be really careful though and make sure the milk didn't spill. If that happened, the water in the well would smell like soured milk and wouldn't even be fit for washing or cleaning.

Grandpa had dug the cistern not long after he finished building his and Grandma's house. Aunt Ethel helped Grandpa build the house. Grandpa and Grandma had six children: Rufus, Gracie (Mama), Ethel and Ellen (who were twins), Ed, and Bernice. Aunt Ethel was living at home with Grandma and Grandpa at this time and helped Grandpa not only build the house, but the cistern too. First, Grandpa dug a big hole in the earth. When the hole got deep enough to get down into, Grandpa would crawl down inside the hole and send up buckets of earth. Aunt Ethel would empty the bucket and send it back down for more dirt. Allie knew it must have been such hard work making a cistern. Once the hole was deep enough to hold a lot of water, all the inside had to be plastered and smoothed with mortar. This kept the water from leaking out. Grandpa built the sides of the cistern up from the ground using rock and mortar. He built it up about four feet off the ground. For the top, Grandpa had found a large flat glade rock. A hole had been hewn in the center of the rock making a circle large enough for a bucket to fit through, and this was placed over the top of the cistern making the top. Finally, two poles were placed on either side of the cistern with a smooth post going across from pole to pole. A metal pulley was attached to the post, and the rope ran up and over the pulley. The water bucket was tied to the end of the rope and could be lowered and raised using the pulley system. A cistern was somewhat like a big water barrel. The difference though was that it was in the ground where the water could stay cold and dirt and leaves could be kept out. Unlike a well that collected underground water, the water in a cistern just collected rainwater. Grandpa attached a metal trough to the side of the roof of the house. When it rained, the water ran off the roof and into the metal trough. The trough was tilted so the water ran through the trough and into the cistern. During rainy weather, the cistern collected a lot of water. Sometimes when it got really full, the trough was moved so no more water could run into it. During the summer when the weather turned drier, the water level in the cistern got really low. Allie was glad that her grandparents had the cistern. It made wash day a little easier for Grandma.

Before the girls went through their own gate, Allie set her water buckets beside Winna's. "Wait for me while I shut up the chickens," she said. She ran over to the chicken house door. Mama was proud of her chickens and insisted they be locked up safely each evening before dark. Coyotes, foxes, or even dogs were known to catch and kill a whole flock of chickens if they got the chance. Allie loved taking care of the chickens. In the summer, it was her job to feed them and gather the eggs. Mama took care of that when school was in session though. Allie looked in the door and counted them. Yes, they were all there, even the ornery red rooster who liked to chase them around the yard. They all sat humped up looking like the frog hills Allie and Winna made in the sand. The hens were scattered apart on the roosting poles Daddy had made. He had made the roosts out of slim saplings he'd cut and tied together with bailing wire. The hens and rooster were perched on those poles ready for sleep.

Quietly, Allie stepped in the door and went over to the nests to check for any eggs the hens might have lain since Mama gathered them earlier. She loved checking for eggs. There were four nests built up against the wall. The boxes were placed on a shelf with sections in between the boxes. A board went across the front to keep any eggs from rolling out of the nests. Daddy always kept straw in the boxes, making a nice place for the hens to sit while they dropped their eggs, and it also kept the eggs from rolling around in the nests and possibly breaking. Allie took a breath taking in and enjoying the scent of the dried straw. She searched the nests for the oval gifts. To Allie's disappointment, the nests were empty except for the smooth round stone that was used as a nest egg.

"Hurry up, slowpoke!" Winna hollered from outside. The sound stirred the hens making them shift on their roosts.

Allie didn't answer. She quietly slipped over to one of the hens roosting on the bottom roost. Did hens dream when they were asleep? She stared at the hen and watched her eyelids. She's always heard that when a person was dreaming, his eyelids fluttered. The lids on the white hen were quivering just like Winna's did sometimes. She wondered what hens dreamed about. Was this one dreaming about a big juicy grubworm? She loved it when the hens were asleep and she could get right up close to them and study them. It made her feel sneaky, like a detective.

At one time, Mama had two chicken houses, but Daddy had turned one of them into his broom factory. Now they only had this one henhouse and twelve chickens. Most of the hens were white leghorns, but they had a few brown hens too. Allie could always tell which eggs had been laid by the brown hens and which were from the white ones. She had learned that brown hens produced brown eggs and white chickens produced white eggs. She also knew which egg was laid by Mama's oldest hen. It was always the biggest egg in the basket. The older the hen, the bigger and stronger her eggs, and the younger the hen, the smaller the egg. At one time, Mama even had a hen that laid eggs that had a blue tint to them. Allie was especially sad when something killed that chicken because she felt like she was finding an Easter egg when she gathered a blue egg out of the nest. Mama didn't sell her eggs like some people did, but the family always had plenty of eggs for egg custards, deviled eggs, and always eggs for breakfast. Some of the hens would make a nest and sit from time to time and hatch out little chicks. When there got to be too many hens, Daddy would have to kill some of them.

Allie didn't want to be anywhere around when Daddy killed a chicken. You might not think so, but a chicken can be fast. She knew from experience that a chicken can run extremely fast for a short distance. If you happened to be outside when Daddy got after a chicken, you were likely to be run over by one. You couldn't outrun one either; you might as well not even try. She had learned that the hard way. Once when Daddy was chasing a big red hen, Allie had happened to be playing in her playhouse. When she saw the commotion, she went screaming across the yard trying to get out of the way. The hen took out after her. Its claws caught in her own long hair as it sailed up and over her. She shrieked and fell to the ground flapping and squawking as loudly as the chicken. It took Mama and Daddy both to wrestle that chicken and untangle it from her hair. That was when Allie decided the best place to be when Daddy went out to kill a chicken was in the house under her bed.

Chickens had their own way of talking to one another too. Once when a blacksnake got inside the henhouse, the hens set up a squawking the likes of which you've never heard. One hen squawked out a warning and three or four more answered her. Before long, the whole henhouse was as noisy as one of Grandma's quilting bees. Allie was surprised the snake didn't run out of that henhouse holding his ears before his eardrums popped. Did snakes have eardrums? Did they even have ears? Allie shrugged her shoulders in answer to her own question. She didn't know for sure, but she did know it about popped her own eardrums with their squawking. But she had also heard the chickens make a completely different sound when Daddy got hungry for chicken and dumplings and started for the henhouse with his ax. When the first chicken saw him coming, she commenced warning all the others. Before long, there wasn't a chicken within earshot that wasn't giving Daddy the evil eye and telling the world what a mean man he was. It was a different type of squawk that they made when a snake or other animal came around threatening them. Allie wished she could understand their language. She'd like to know what they were saying.

Some people killed their chickens by wringing their necks. Allie had seen Aunt Ollie do this. First, she'd catch a chicken by grabbing it by its legs and holding it upside down. It's easier to catch a chicken when it's still in the chicken coop. When they are outside, they take off running and flapping their wings so that a person can't get anywhere close to them. Aunt Ollie usually tried to catch them first thing in the morning before they were let out for the day. Aunt Ollie didn't mind killing a hen; in fact, she seemed to enjoy it. After she caught it, she would grasp the chicken by the neck and sling its head up and then down very quickly. *Flip-flop*! You could actually hear the snap as the bones in the neck broke. Then she'd let it down, and it would actually run around the yard until it died. Yuck! Now Daddy didn't wring a chicken's neck like Aunt Ollie; he chopped off its head on the chopping block. Once again, it took the chicken a while to realize what had happened. The body, without the head, would put on a runaway as it ran in circles around the yard for a full minute or two before it fell over. Allie was sure being chased around the yard by a headless chicken would even be worse than being chased by a live one. It made the term *running around like a chicken with its head cut off* take on a whole different meaning. It gave Allie the creeps. She would always stay inside until Mama started plucking off the feathers. Allie didn't mind this part. In fact, she would help once the large feathers were removed.

Mama would hang the chicken upside down from the low branch of one of the poplar trees in the front yard. First, she'd take off the wing feathers and then the large feathers. The feathers had to be taken off one at a time. If you tried to remove too many at one time, it would pull off chunks of the chicken. Next, it was time to remove the fluffy down feathers. Winna and Allie helped with this part. It was harder to do than it might seem. Allie would pick a few down feathers off and then spend the next ten minutes trying to shake them off her own fingers. They stuck like pine rosin. These feathers were saved for pillows or mattresses. Allie preferred to hold the sack while Winna pulled off the downy feathers and placed them in the sack. Usually, Winna went along with this plan. Next, Daddy or Mama would hold the naked chicken over a flame to singe the rest of the feathers from the bird. Finally, the insides had to be removed and the chicken was ready to be washed and cooked. Allie forgot all the awful details of killing a chicken when she took her first bite of Mama's chicken and dumplings.

Allie took one last look at the sleeping chickens and eased her way out of the chicken house and latched the door. She looked around for Winna and caught a glimpse of her already going in the back door of their house. "Winna," she screamed, "I told you to wait!" Allie stomped over to her buckets and jerked them up making the water ripple and splash in the bucket. The bottom of her skirt was sopping wet by the time she made it to the door. She turned the doorknob and stomped inside. Plopping the buckets down, she slammed the door.

"Woaaaa!" laughed Daddy as Allie faced them all with a scowl. "And a howdy doodie to you too!"

"Winna never waits on me, and she makes me do all the work, and it's been the worst day of my life," Allie complained to Daddy as she stalked over to let him give her a hug.

Daddy laughed as he caught her up in a bear hug. "What's wrong with my Peeny?" Allie melted into his hug. She always felt better when Daddy held her like that. She slowly relaxed and told him about her bad day.

Allie and her Family: Mama holding
Betty, Winna, Daddy, and Allie

Chapter 3

One time we were going to have company. I think it was Aunt Susie and Uncle Charlie from South Carolina. Mom was going to kill four young chickens to cook. It was my and Erma Lou's job to pour hot water on the chickens and pluck the feathers off. Mom had wrung the heads off three chickens and had one more to go. Rex came along and wanted to wring the head off the last chicken. Mom said, "Go ahead." Rex picked up the chicken, turned his own head away from the chicken, shut his eyes, and wrung and wrung. He turned the chicken loose, and the chicken ran off with its head lying to the side. Rex ran after it, caught it, and tried again. The second time Rex turned it loose, the same thing happened. Mom finally had to finish the chicken off with one pop. I don't think Rex ever tried wringing a chicken's neck again.

—Betty (Bobbie's younger sister) (2010)

Bobbie

January 1941

Bobbie leaned against the side of the huge white oak, its bark rough against his back. He looked up at the massive limbs stretched naked against the bright blue sky above him. How many other children had sat beneath these branches over the years? This tree must be five hundred years old at least. It was recess, and the squeals and laughter of the children escaped the confines of the schoolyard and skipped and danced throughout the town. The weather had warmed, and the children celebrated the unexpected break in the weather by playing all those games they had longed to play the past several weeks. Some of the girls were playing drop the handkerchief in a flat area in front of the building. Bobbie watched Audie chase Racine around the circle, arms outstretched. Audie's spindly legs a blur as she gave all her energy to the race. Racine, breathless, dodged into the open space in the circle just avoiding Audie's tag. Giving a loud moan, Audie began her second rotation around the circle of laughing girls. She swung the white handkerchief determinedly at her side, eyeing the girls as she considered who would be her next target. Bobbie smiled as he watched his little sister. She amazed him. Her self-confidence, bordering on stubbornness, allowed her to do anything she set her mind to. Even now, circling the group of older, faster kids, she wore that determined look that left no doubt she would tag the next runner.

Most of the older boys were playing coach whip. The teachers frowned on this game saying it was too dangerous. Naturally, this only made the game even more enticing to the students. Bobbie usually loved coach whip, but today he didn't feel like playing. The group was at the side of the building, hoping they were out of sight of Mr. Schauffler and Mr. Blue. Bobbie supposed it was a little dangerous the way the older boys played it. Maybe that was why none of the girls or the smaller boys joined them today. To play the game, everyone joined hands in a line. Then everyone began running. The line went faster and faster. Then all of a sudden, the person on the end swung the line back the other way. This gave everyone a jerk causing the person on the end of the line, maybe even two or three people, to go sailing off from the others like a coach whip. That person almost always ended with a thump, sometimes a pretty rough thump, end over end. The rougher the landing though, the louder came the hoots of the ones still in the line.

As Bobbie watched the others playing, his concentration was on the marble game over by where the dirt road wound past the schoolhouse. The marbles rolled easily there on the smooth packed earth. Some of the boys had drawn a big circle in the dirt, and Cody was down on one knee as he eyed the position of the marbles. He positioned his knuckle almost to the ground and prepared to take his shot. SNAP! He flicked the shooter. It scooted across the ground in a straight line and struck another marble. That marble rolled to the outside of the circle. Cody smiled, picked it up, and stood. He dusted off the knees of his pants and pocketed the marble. "That's one for me!" he bragged. Shine pulled at the bill of his cap, a stern look on his face. He dropped down on one knee, eye close to the ground, as he determined the angle he should shoot to claim one of Cody's marbles.

Bobbie saw Cody glance over at him. He quickly looked away. He reached down into his trousers and took out his pocketknife. He opened the knife and ran his finger over its smooth sharp edge. Picking up a twig from the ground, he began whittling. The strips of wood fell in fat chunks as he pushed the knife away from him along the slender stick. He had been practicing his whittling strokes, trying to learn to shave the wood instead of whacking it off in chunks. The chips had grown a little smaller, but he wasn't satisfied with his whittling yet.

He loved to watch the men who sat on Jim Andy's store porch. They could shave the wood as fine as tissue paper with their knives. Bobbie gathered their shavings in his hands and crumbled them with his fingers, amazed at the fineness. He wanted to be able to whittle like those men. Brigham, one of the regulars at the porch, just smiled when he saw Bobbie trying to mimic his stokes. He'd pause and spit a stream of tobacco juice off the store porch making a dark stain in the sand. Then he'd look at Bobbie and wink. "Give it time, son, give it time," he'd say.

Bobbie's pocketknife was white with a single blade. He had gotten it as a Christmas present three weeks ago, and he had polished its blade every day since. He was never going to let a speck of rust or dirt gather on its shiny blade. Daddy had picked it out for him in Batesville when he'd gone with Claude Case to delivered a load of lumber from the sawmill to the Barnett family who lived there. Bobbie couldn't believe his luck when he'd opened his only gift under the tree on Christmas morning. He'd let out a whoop that shook the house. Daddy's bellowed laughter was almost as loud as his own shout. This was Bobbie's first knife. He had used Daddy's knife a few times but had never owned one of his very own.

He had felt so proud showing his knife to the other boys. They had gathered around him and admired the gleaming pearl-like handle and the sharp blade. Maybe this was what had given Cody the idea of using the knife to get him into trouble. Mr. Schauffler knew of Bobbie's knife and his joy at using it. Bobbie was still madder than a rooster robbed of its June bug at Cody. He was, though, getting a little satisfaction in how he'd reacted to what Cody did to him. Maybe, on the other hand, the satisfaction came in how he hadn't reacted and that was driving Cody crazy.

He didn't know why, but he had taken the punishment for the carving on the desk, and he hadn't told a soul he wasn't the one to blame. When Mr. Schauffler kept him in at recess and asked him why he'd done it, he had looked down at the board floor and shrugged. For some reason, he felt that if he ratted on Cody, he would be no better than Cody. A tattle was a tattle, and he wasn't going to be known as a tattletale, whatever the punishment. He had hated the disappointment he'd seen in Mr. Schauffler's eyes when he confronted him. Mr. Schauffler had shaken his head and said he was surprised at Bobbie's behavior. Bobbie knew he would be punished, but he hadn't expected it to be so severe. Mr. Schauffler hadn't told him his punishment right off; he said he wanted to think about it first.

Early the following morning, he had met Bobbie at the school building at 5:00 just as Bobbie was about to light the fires. He asked Bobbie to sit down, and his teacher sat in a desk beside him. He ran his hand through his hair and said, "Bobbie, I've given this a lot of thought. It's unlike you to do something you know is wrong. I don't want to just punish you. I want you to learn from your mistake and make things right." Bobbie looked down at his hands. Mr. Schauffler continued, "For the next two weeks, you are to stay after school and clean the building—every day. You will sweep the floor, wash the blackboard, and dust the erasers." Bobbie nodded. "And this Saturday, I want you to take this sandpaper and sand out the words on that desk. I don't want you to stop until the desk is as smooth and clear as it ever was. The words aren't carved deep, so it shouldn't take you too long." He handed Bobbie a sheet of sandpaper. "Can I count on you to follow through with this punishment?"

Somehow, Bobbie had kept the moan from escaping. He nodded his head and replied, "Yes, sir."

"Good," Mr. Schauffler said. "Let's clear this problem up and get it behind us and move on." He was quiet for several minutes. Bobbie knew he was giving him a chance to explain. Bobbie ran the toe of his shoe up and down the leg of the desk in front of him. Mr. Schauffler cleared his throat and continued, "I'll leave you with something our great sixteenth president once said: I do not think much of a man who is not wiser today than he was yesterday. I have faith in you, Bobbie. You've proven yourself to be a responsible and mature young man over and over again. You've never missed a day in building the fires in the classrooms since you began. You do what you say you'll do. I believe you have learned from this experience and will be wiser for it." Mr. Schauffler slowly got to his feet and looked down at Bobbie. He put out a hand and squeezed his shoulder and walked out of the cold classroom.

Bobbie groaned, audible now. Beginning his day at school at 5:00 in the morning and not ending it until after 4:00 in the afternoon was going to make for a very long day. It was a serious matter though, and Bobbie knew Mr. Schauffler believed it to be a just punishment. He did not resent the punishment. For minor infractions, teachers sometimes stood students in a corner or, worse yet, made them put their noses in circles drawn on the board. Somehow, the circles were always just a little higher than the students' noses, so the students had to tiptoe. At other times, the teachers paddled the students. Bobbie wished Mr. Schauffler had just done that. He never liked a punishment that was drawn out. He'd much rather just get it over with. But for whatever reason, Mr. Schauffler had chosen chores.

Bobbie knew he had disappointed his momma too. Naturally, Willie nearly knocked everyone down getting out of school that afternoon making a beeline home to report Bobbie's trouble to Momma. She was waiting for him when he came dragging home, Willie peeping curiously, possibly hopeful, around the corner. She had that serious look on her face, but Bobbie sensed her hesitation to punish. Bobbie hated that look of disappointment. It was even worse than disappointing Mr. Schauffler. Her words still stung, "Bobbie, you orten of done that! I'm ashamed of you. What got into you anyway? I reckon I'm gonna have to tell Daddy." It wasn't her words that were so painful; it was the hurt in her eyes. When Daddy got home, he took Bobbie outside and warmed the seat of his pants. The belt stung like the dickens, but he could take that. It was Momma he hated to let down. He thought of telling her the truth, but he knew she'd make him tell Mr. Schauffler then, and he'd gone too far with this to go back now. He promised himself that he'd make it up to her and Mr. Schauffler one of these days.

Bobbie shifted his position under the oak. It was about time for books. He looked across the road at their ball field. It was a flat area that had a nice covering of grass in the spring and summer. Large rocks stood at the back of the field where the girls often climbed to eat their lunches in warm weather. The "rich girls" always sat up high on the big rocks so they could show off their bologna sandwiches while the poorer kids sat lower and ate their fatback sandwiches or maybe just leftover breakfast gravy on a cold, hard biscuit. Parents just sent whatever they had with their children for their lunches, and many times it wasn't very much for some of them. Often as Bobbie walked past, going home for lunch, he would hear the girls laughing and talking, trading with one another for this or that out of their lunches.

It wouldn't be long now before things started greening up and they could start up the ball teams again. They called it board ball because of the board they used as a bat. It was a flat board that was usually dried and gray. Sometimes, they'd get one of the men to whittle the handle down some, making it narrower on one end than the other and easier to grasp. For the ball, they used pieces of twine and string from feed sacks and sugar sacks and rolled it round and round until they had a ball about the size of a regular baseball. Every now and then, one of the girls would offer up the small rubber ball from her jacks set. Then they would wrap the string around that making an even better ball. Oooh-wee, he loved that game! Just thinking about it put him in a better mood.

B<small>ONG</small>! B<small>ONG</small>! B<small>ONG</small>! The bell tolled, signaling the end of recess. Three more hours of school and then another hour of cleaning the building. It made him tired just thinking about it. The students filed into the schoolroom and down the aisle to their seats. Bobbie took his seat beside Cody. Cody stiffened. He was understandably uncomfortable around Bobbie after the incident. Mr. Schauffler hurried everyone to their seats. He was anxious to get started.

"Let's have the fourth graders to the recitation seat, please. The rest of you should get started on your penmanship. I have the sentences written on the board." Papers rattled as the students scurried around getting situated. Bobbie slid out of his seat and made his way to the dreaded bench at the front of the room along with his classmates. He shuffled down to the end of the bench trying to make himself as small as possible. Maybe Mr. Schauffler wouldn't notice him. They had been reading the poem, "Mockery." Each student was given a part to memorize as homework last night. He had studied his part and even recited part of a stanza to Momma, but he couldn't remember a word of it now. He hoped the other boys knew their parts better than he.

"Okay, ladies and gentlemen, let's continue our work on our poem. Did everyone practice?" There were a few nods while others dropped their eyes, suddenly very interested in the floorboards. Their teacher continued, "Let's have the girls recite the first stanza." Bobbie looked around at the girls. They sat straight and tall, hands in laps. Montene sat on the bench beside Bobbie. Her long black hair fell in dark curls down her back. She looked over at him and smiled. Mr. Schauffler continued, "Then we'll have the boys do the second stanza. Ready?" Bobbie noticed Montene's curls bob as she nodded her head excitedly. "Okay." Mr. Schauffler raised his hand as if fixing to lead the congregation in a song at church. "The name of the poem is "Mockery," and it was written by Katherine Dixon Riggs. Girls, please begin."

The girls' voices sprang forth like a rock out of a bean flip.

Happened that the moon was up before I went to bed,
Poking through the bramble-trees her round, gold head.
I didn't stop for stocking,
I didn't stop for shoe,
But went running out to meet her—oh,
the night was blue!

"Boys," Mr. Schauffler said quietly. The boys' voices, slower and quieter than the girls', began their chant.

Barefoot down the hill road, dust beneath my toes;
Barefoot in the pasture smelling sweet of fern and rose!
Oh, night was running with me,

Tame folk were all in bed—
And the moon was just showing her wild gold head.

It was obvious that the boys lacked the enthusiasm and the commitment of the poem to memory. Their slow halted chant was somewhat monotonous. Thankfully though, they pulled it together and were able to complete the stanza.

"Good, good," Mr. Schauffler beamed. "Now let's hear the last two stanzas. Girls, you first, and then the boys will finish it up for us."

The girls were raring to go. Mr. Schauffler had scarcely finished his sentence before they bounded forward.

But before I reached the hilltop where
the bramble-trees are tall,
I looked to see my lady moon—she wasn't there at all!—
Not sitting on the hilltop,
Nor slipping through the air,
Nor hanging in the brambles by her bright gold hair!

Bobbie could hear Montene's voice above the other girls. She seemed to be leading them. Bobbie glanced back at the younger kids at their seats. They had all stopped their penmanship assignment and were listening to the poem. Bobbie felt like shouting, "For crying out loud, we don't need an audience!" His stomach did a somersault.

"Boys!" Mr. Schauffler prompted as the girls completed their section. "Boys . . ." The boys seemed to be stuck. Montene whispered beside Bobbie, "I walked slowly . . ." Some of the boys hearing her, began.

I walked slowly down the pasture and slowly up the hill,
Wondering and wondering, and very, very still.
I wouldn't look behind me,
I went at once to bed—
And poking through the window was her bold gold head!

"Bravo, bravo!" Mr. Schauffler praised. Bobbie let out the breath he'd been holding. Maybe he was going to get through this after all. "Now let's see if we understand it. What time of day is it?" Mr. Schauffler wanted to know.

Wendell raised his hand. "I think it might be late in the day," he said, "since it said the moon was just coming up. Anyway, that would be my guess."

"Yes! You're right, Wendell. Now who can tell me the time of the year or the season?" Mr. Schauffler wondered. "Allie, can you tell us?"

"Ummm, well, it says that the person was barefooted, so maybe . . . I'd guess maybe . . . it was summer?" she answered with a question in her voice.

Bobbie looked questioningly at Mr. Schauffler. Maybe some people just went without shoes in the summer, but he, for one, only wore them in the coldest weather.

"That's right," Mr. Schauffler smiled. "Also it mentioned the scent of rose and fern, and we'd expect those scents in the spring or summer, wouldn't we? Now what is the pattern of the stanzas? Bobbie, can you tell me?"

Bobbie had barely heard the question. He was still considering Allie's comment. He squirmed on the bench. "Uh, four?" he asked.

"Four?" Mr. Schauffler repeated. "No, no, I didn't ask how many stanzas, I want to know the rhythm or pattern the stanzas take."

Bobbie was silent. He had no idea what Mr. Schauffler was even asking. "That's a difficult question. Montene, can you tell us?" Mr. Schauffler continued.

"I believe it would be A A B C C, sir, since the first two lines rhyme and then the last two lines rhyme," she answered.

"You're right," Mr. Schauffler beamed. "Now let's talk about including senses into poetry. What senses did the author include in this poem? Cody?"

"Well, hummm, how about the moon?" Cody offered. "He could see the moon, couldn't he?"

"Yes," Mr. Schauffler said. "So that would be the sense of sight. Anymore?"

Bobbie, not to be outdone, raised his hand.

"Yes, Bobbie," Mr. Schauffler smiled and nodded in his direction.

"He could smell the roses, so wouldn't that be one of them?" he replied. Bobbie silently prayed he was right.

"That's correct!" Mr. Schauffler's smile spread across his face. "The author used the sense of smell." Bobbie sat up taller and slowly breathed. "I want to work with this poem some more next week," their teacher continued. "For now, I want you all to go back to your seats and try your hand at writing poetry. Try to write a three-stanza poem about someone or something in nature. I want to see an example of sensory details in your poem. We'll share them next week sometime. We have forty-five minutes to work on this before recess. Go ahead and scoot back to your seats and get started."

Bobbie

The students stood slowly and walked back to their seats. The faces of the boys looked as if they had eaten a green persimmon. It was obvious they didn't share Mr. Schauffler's passion for poetry.

Bobbie slid into his seat and took out a pencil and his Big Chief pad of paper. He didn't have a clue how to even get started. Several minutes later, he was bent over his paper, fully absorbed. He was trying to think of a word that rhymed with tree: me, see, pee, when Cody slid out of his seat and walked toward the front of the room. Bobbie looked up. He followed Cody with his eyes wondering what he was up to now. The events of the past few days had caused Bobbie to question everything Cody did. As Cody walked by Allie's desk, Bobbie noticed him quietly drop a note onto her desk. Bobbie watched her carefully to see what she would do. He thought, maybe it was wishful thinking, that she might get up and throw it away and give Cody a dirty look. However, she unfolded it ever so slowly on her lap, unnoticed by anyone else, and read it. She then folded it back up neatly and slipped it in the side pocket of her dress. Cody, after asking permission, left the room for the outhouse. Before going out the door though, he turned and flashed Allie a smile. Bobbie couldn't see Allie's face, but he hoped she didn't return his smile.

Bobbie's face burned. That scoundrel. Why did he ever think Cody was a friend? He should never have confided any of his secrets to him. He was just flirting with Allie to get to him. He wondered what else he had shared with Cody that was going to come back and bite him. As he sat stewing, a poem began to form in the corners of his mind. A sly smile inched its way across his face. He slowly picked up his pencil and bent over his tablet absorbed in his purpose. Maybe writing a poem wasn't going to be as dull as he had imagined.

The hands on the clock crawled their way toward three o'clock. Finally, Mr. Schauffler asked the students to put their things away and dismissed them. Bobbie watched as the children rushed to get out of the classroom. There was a lot of clattering and clanging as they gathered up their lunch pails and put on their coats. Finally, the last student went out the door, and it was quiet in the empty room. Bobbie sat at his desk waiting for Mr. Schauffler to give him his directions. His teacher slowly closed the leather-bound book on his desk and got to his feet. Bobbie watched him stand. Mr. Schauffler was a tall man and had a distinguished air about him. His clothes were always neatly pressed, and Bobbie had never seen him without his shirttail tucked into his trousers. He walked back to Bobbie and let out a sigh. "Are you ready to begin those chores, son?" he asked as he looked down into Bobbie's eyes.

Bobbie sat up straight in his seat and answered, "Yes, sir."

"Okay, then. You can start with cleaning the chalkboard. It needs to be erased and washed to have it clean for this Sunday's service. After that, you need to take out the ashes, sweep up the floor, and straighten the desks. Since tomorrow is Saturday, you can come by then and begin sanding on that desk. Like I said, it shouldn't take you too long."

"Okay, Mr. Schauffler." Bobbie jumped to his feet and began his chores. The old man wearily sat back down at his desk and began looking over some papers. Bobbie watched him curiously. It never occurred to Bobbie that teachers would have work to do after school. Mr. Schauffler looked so tired as he began shuffling through the papers, Bobbie almost felt sorry for him. Bobbie continued without stopping through his chores. It took him around forty-five minutes to complete them. As he went about his tasks, he continued to work on his poem in his mind. He wanted to write something that would let Cody know how mad he was at him, but he had to be careful to not be too conspicuous because Mr. Schauffler would be reading the poem too. He was in enough trouble without having an extra punishment added on for being rude to a fellow classmate. Mr. Schauffler didn't tolerate his students insulting one another. Just as Bobbie finished up with his chores, Mr. Schauffler got up from his desk. He must have been watching him to know that he was finished. He reached up and took his hat from the peg behind his desk and set it squarely on his head. As he walked out of the school building with Bobbie, he put his arm around his shoulders. "Bobbie, you did a fine job today. A person should always give his best in whatever he does, and you certainly did that today. I want to thank you for doing the work, and, more importantly, for doing it without resentment. That says a lot about a person."

"Thank you, Mr. Schauffler," Bobbie smiled up at him. "I didn't mind it at all, really. I was thinking about my poem as I worked."

That made the old man smile. "Oh, you were, were you? Now you've got me all interested. I'll be anxious to hear that poem of yours. Yes, sir, I'm anxious to hear that poem of yours!" He took his wallet from his back pocket and leafed through the contents. He took out a dollar bill and handed it to Bobbie. "I appreciate your help with the fires this week, young man," he said with a smile. "It lets me get just a few more minutes of sleep each day." He patted Bobbie on the back and smiled as they parted company. Bobbie waved bye and took out for home at a gallop.

The next day dawned sunny and bright. It was just the middle of January, but there was a break in the cold weather. It would have been the perfect day for squirrel hunting. Those bushy-tailed critters would be scampering everywhere today with the sunshine. Bobbie didn't actually have a gun, but that didn't take the fun away from his hunting. His daddy had made him a slingshot last summer. When Bobbie asked him for one, Daddy had sent him off in search of a Y-shaped piece of wood. He said persimmon or hickory worked the best. Next, he sent Bobbie over to the post office to ask Mr. Huett if he had any extra-wide rubber bands that he could have. Letters often arrived at the post office bound with the rubber bands, and Mr. Huett kept them in a big box behind the counter. When Bobbie had returned with those items, Daddy had taken an old pair of boots that he sometimes used to mend his better boots. He cut a small square from the boot leather for the rock to sit. With these items, Daddy fashioned a slingshot. Bobbie was thrilled with his new toy or should it be referred to as a weapon? It had taken him a while, but he had gotten pretty good at putting rocks where he wanted them to go. He had even made his momma's chickens dance around the yard a few times. His favorite things to shoot at, though, were squirrels. It wasn't that hard to hit a squirrel since they sat fairly still while they were eating. It had become a favorite pastime, and he hated that he wasn't going to get an early start at it this morning. That seemed like when the squirrels were the most active. Bobbie decided to hurry on up to the school and get the job completed so he could get on with his weekend.

The morning passed slowly as Bobbie sanded on the wooden desk. Wood dust collected on the desk and floor as his hand flew back and forth across the desktop. The desk grew warm underneath his hand. Bobbie breathed the dust and sneezed. As he worked, he wondered why carving on a desk was such a big deal in the little room when there were names carved all over the desks in the big room. He resented having to do Cody's cleanup too. Thinking of Cody made his hand move faster and faster across the wood. Cody should be the one in here doing this. He was probably outside in this sunshine shooting all the squirrels. Bobbie heard the door open and looked up to see Mr. Stephens walk in. Mr. Stephens was a fairly tall man with dark-brown hair and a wide grin. He was wearing a denim jumper and a brown hat. Bobbie's face reddened. Mr. Stephens was Allie's dad. Was he here to scold him? He looked up at him and nodded shyly, "Mornin', Mr. Stephens."

"Well, hello there, Bobbie," Mr. Stephens said with a smile. "I thought I'd try to get that roof fixed today while it's so nice. Getting a sunny day like this in the middle of winter is a bonus!"

"Yes, sir," Bobbie replied. "Would you like me to show you where it's leaking?"

"I was hoping you would," Mr. Stephen answered. "I stopped by Mr. Schauffler's before coming up here, and he said I would probably find you here this morning. He said you could show me just where the rain was coming in since you were the one who pointed it out to him a few days ago."

"Sure thing," Bobbie said as he jumped to his feet.

"I bet it's hard for a young boy like you to have to be at school on a Saturday," Mr. Stephens said as he glanced down at the desk where Bobbie was working.

Bobbie squirmed uncomfortably. He tried to position the sandpaper over the heart. "Yes, sir." His shoulders dropped and he considered what he wanted to say. Raising his eyes and looking at Allie's daddy squarely in the eyes, he said, "Mr. Stephens, can I tell you something in confidence?"

"A man is only as good as his word," Mr. Stephens replied. "I give you my word I'll respect your wishes."

"Well," Bobbie began as he slowly moved the sandpaper to one side revealing the heart with the names inside. "You see these names on this here desk?" Mr. Stephen looked down at the desk and then at Bobbie. He nodded.

"Well, you probably think I carved them here. Mr. Schauffler and everyone else think I did, but I didn't do it."

"Is that right?" Mr. Stephens asked with a questioning look on his face. "Did Mr. Schauffler not believe you when you told him you were innocent?"

"That's just it," Bobbie answered. "I didn't tell Mr. Schauffler I was innocent. I took the punishment because I didn't want to tattle on the boy who did it. I just let on like it was me who carved the names."

"Well, son, that is something that must have been hard to do. I respect you wanting to protect your friend, but he's not much of a friend if he let you take the blame for something he did."

Bobbie shook his head. "That's not why I did it. I wasn't trying to keep him out of trouble. Shoot! I really don't know why I took the blame; it just seemed like the right thing to do at the time. It seems a little crazy now, but since I've gone this far with it, I don't think anyone would believe me now if I said I didn't do it. I just wanted to tell you the truth though, you being Allie's dad and all. Do you believe me?"

Mr. Stephens put his hand on Bobbie's shoulder. "I believe you, son. I respect a person who does what he thinks is right. You're making decisions now that are molding you into the man you'll be one day. I think you did an admirable thing, and I give you my word that I'll keep what you told me today to myself. Now let's take a look at that roof." He squeezed Bobbie's shoulder.

Bobbie led the way to the place beside the stove and pointed out where he had seen rain coming in around the stovepipe. Then he walked outside with Mr. Stephens to see if he needed any help getting up on the roof. As they walked down the steps of the schoolhouse, Sam Shoemate, Allie's grandpa, came riding by on his mule. This was turning into a regular family reunion! Bobbie groaned.

"Howdy," the old man called as he threw up a hand and reined his mule over toward them. "Just been out to check the mail. Mother is looking for something from Sears and Roebuck."

"Your mother?" Bobbie asked in confusion.

Mr. Shoemate laughed. His belly shook as he bounced in the saddle. "Oh, not my own mother. That's just what I call my wife, Texanner. I guess you could say it's my pet name for her."

"Oh," Bobbie said to the old man.

"I do have something from my own mother I want to show you all though," he said. Bobbie watched as the heavy man slid off the mule's back. Mr. Shoemate patted his mule and turned to Allie's dad. "I was thinking that since Wednesday is Peeny's birthday, I might give her this here locket that used to be my mother's." He reached into his overall's pocket and brought out a heart locket dangling on a golden chain. "I took it with me out to the store to see if they had anything that might put a shine on it," he explained.

Mr. Stephens reached out and took the locket that Mr. Shoemate held out. He whistled. "Sam, that's a generous thing to do. Do you think she is old enough to take care of something like this? She's only turning eleven, you know. Maybe you should wait a few more years before you give it to her."

Mr. Shoemate shook his head. "Nope, I gave Winna something special on her eleventh birthday, and I want Peeny to have this. I thought I would give it to her on Wednesday when she has her cake."

Bobbie broke in. "Who's Peeny?" he asked in confusion. Looking at Mr. Stephens, he said, "I didn't know you had a daughter named Peeny."

Mr. Shoemate's booming laughter shook his belly again. "Naw, that's just my pet name for Allie. Poor girl probably doesn't think I even know her real name. If I'm not calling her Peeny, I'm calling her Polly. Don't ask me why. I've just always liked calling my granddaughters special names other than their own. Open it up, Robert," he said to Mr. Stephens.

Mr. Stephens put his thumbnail inside the clasp and opened it. "Well, look at that," he said in astonishment. "How did you get that done?"

"I rode the mail truck up to Salem last week," Grandpa said. "I had ole man Withers engrave that in there."

"What is it?" Bobbie wanted to know.

"Lookie here, son," Mr. Stephens said. "It has 'Peeny' engraved inside the heart." He showed Bobbie the lettering and then handed the locket back to Mr. Shoemate. "She'll love it, Sam," he said.

"I think she will," he said as he took the locket and put it carefully into his pocket. "Well, I'd better be getting on home. Mother is anxious for this package. I don't know what these womenfolk need so from the catalog company, but she's been waiting for it for almost a week now, so I'd better get on home with it. Bobbie, what are you doing at school on a Saturday? Don't they give kids the weekends off anymore?"

Bobbie looked down at the ground. "I got in a little trouble, sir," he said looking over at Mr. Stephens. "I'm having to do some work around here today as part of my punishment."

"I see," Mr. Shoemate answered and then cleared his throat. "Now I wouldn't be too down in the mouth about it. I have to admit I got in a mite bit of trouble myself now and then when I was a lad. Just own up to your punishment and move on. Now will I see you at services here on Sunday?"

"Ummm. I guess so," Bobbie said quietly.

"That's good," Mr. Shoemate exclaimed. "We all need to assemble on the Lord's day."

"Yes, sir," Bobbie answered. He waved to Mr. Shoemate as he climbed up on his mule and started on down the road.

Bobbie followed Mr. Stephens around the corner of the schoolhouse. He wanted to get this job finished. Time was getting by, and he still had some hunting to do.

Chapter 4

Grandpa and Grandma Shoemate lived a few yards from us during this time of my memory. I truly wish my children and grandchildren could have known my grandparents. I believe my Grandpa Sam Shoemate was the best man that I have ever known. He was not a tall man in stature, but he had the biggest and kindest heart one could ever have. He had a fat stomach and a ruddy complexion. He walked with his feet turned sort of outward. I have walked a lot of miles in his tracks behind his mule and plow. He was mostly a farmer, but he also worked at the sawmill, and he skidded logs with his mule. I have seen his chambray shirt and blue denim overalls white with salt from his sweat many, many times. I have heard people say Sam Shoemate would work just as hard when the boss wasn't around as when he was. He always gave a day's work for a day's pay, and a lot of those *workdays only paid $1. He adored my Grandma Texanner. He treated her like a queen. Grandma was a wonderful lady, and I loved her dearly. All the time I knew her, she was not strong. Her walking gait was slow and from side to side. I remember that Grandpa saddled up a horse for Grandma to ride to church because none of us had a car at that time. It was quite a chore for her to get up on the horse, but Grandpa worked to get her astride and then led the horse to and from church.*

—Allie (2010)

Allie

January 1941

Allie knelt beside her window and looked out at the darkness. She searched the blackness until she found one tiny star still twinkling in the early morning sky. Closing her eyes, she made her wish. She had willed herself to wake early on this morning, her eleventh birthday; she didn't want to miss a minute. There seemed something special about turning eleven. Somehow, it meant the little girl days were behind her. Moving nearer the teen years, she didn't know whether to be excited or scared. Her feelings were all mixed up this morning.

So much had happened to her family in the past several years. It was true they had so much to be thankful, but they had also suffered such losses. Allie couldn't help thinking about her little sisters on her birthday each year, the two little ones who had died at such young ages. How old would they have been now? Little Annetta would have been seven. How wonderful it would have been to have a seven-year-old sister to play with. Shirley would have been five, probably in her first year at the school.

Allie had only been four when Annetta Joyce died. The baby lived only six weeks. There had only been the three sisters then: Winna, Allie, and little Annetta. Allie had been so young; she couldn't remember a great deal about her. She did remember she had dark hair and eyes like Mama, and she made the cutest little faces.

On Allie's fourth birthday, Mama put little Annetta in a crib in the living room while she baked Allie's birthday cake. The wood cookstove heated up the kitchen as well as the rest of the house as the cake baked. Mama was busy and didn't notice little Annetta getting too hot, but when she went to pick her up, the baby was sweating from the heat. Whether or not it was from getting too hot, she caught a cold that quickly turned into pneumonia. The little thing died four days later. Allie shuttered. It wasn't anyone's fault that she died. She knew that. God just took her. For some reason though, Allie couldn't help but feel guilty about it since Mama was baking *her* birthday cake when she took sick. It about killed Mama losing little Annetta. She would hold her little blanket and say her arms felt so empty while tears ran down her face. Even at the young age of four, Allie could still remember the sadness in all of them.

Then three years later, God blessed the family with another baby, Shirley Racine. As fate would have it though, little Shirley lived only six months. She was a beautiful little blond toddler. She was born on September 22, 1936. The family was so thankful for her. She came down with a sickness known as membrance croup and died at only six months. The little thing coughed and coughed before she finally passed away. As sad as Mama was, she was praying for God to go ahead and take her at the end because of the way little Shirley was suffering. She died on a Tuesday. Daddy got Cap Robbins to make her little pine coffin.

That was when Mr. Roby Blue had just started teaching at the school. He and his wife lived several miles away, and he wasn't able to make the trip back and forth to school every day; it was just too far. Daddy had agreed to let Mr. Blue stay with them during the weekdays. Then he went home on the weekends to be with his wife. He was a preacher, and he was the one who preached at little Shirley's funeral. The funeral hadn't been in a church; everyone just sat on benches on the town side of the cemetery. All the community came. Mr. Blue had such a hard time preaching at her funeral. He just cried and cried. He said Shirley was the most beautiful baby he had ever seen. Since Mr. Blue was living with them at the time, he had gotten especially close to her. Shirley loved him too and would sit on his lap and make funny faces at him. Mama hugged Mr. Blue and tried to comfort him as much as he tried to be a comfort to all the family.

Why Allie always thought of her little sisters on her birthday, she didn't know. Maybe it was because she saw herself growing up and felt fortunate to be given the chance of getting older with every birthday. Her little sisters didn't get this chance. Allie looked again at the twinkling star. "Star light, star bright, the first star I see tonight, I wish I may, I wish I might, to have this wish I wish tonight." Allie closed her eyes and said a prayer that Mama would have a healthy baby and that it would have many, many birthdays.

Along about sunup, Allie heard Mama and Daddy get up. She ran into the living room, all smiles. Daddy said, "Well, look who's having a birthday!"

"Are you going to give me a whoppin'?" Allie teased.

Daddy threw back his head and laughed. "Maybe this is one day you won't have to get a whopping from me!" It was true. Allie had a stubborn streak, and many were the times Daddy would have to paddle her backside.

Allie's Daddy, Robert Stephens

Allie gave them both a hug, stretching her arms wide to go around Mama's swollen stomach. "Mama, how are you feeling this morning?"

"Well, I'm feeling like I could use a little help in the kitchen from a big eleven-year-old girl," she smiled.

Allie went with her into the kitchen. "Your grandma and grandpa will be eating supper with us tonight to help celebrate your birthday," Mama said. "Would you like a chocolate cake or a buttermilk one?"

"Well, let me think," Allie pondered. "I'm almost tempted to ask for a blackberry cobbler. You know how I love your cobblers."

Mama laughed. "That would make a pretty funny birthday cake."

"Hummm," Allie wondered aloud. "I think a buttermilk one would be perfect!"

"Then a buttermilk cake is what it will be," Mama confirmed with a nod.

After breakfast, Allie dressed for school. Mama said it would be okay to wear her new sweater set today since it was her birthday. She had gotten it for Christmas and had worn it to church but not to school. Allie loved it. It was a pale pink and the softest thing she'd ever owned. She slipped the short-sleeved sweater over her head, the static crackling and making her hair stand up. The silky softness felt as soft as lamb's ear, a plant that has velvety leaves. Then she slipped on the long-sleeved cardigan. It was the exact same color as the sweater and just as soft. She felt like a pampered princess. Allie couldn't wait for Montene and Annabelle to see it. She wished that it had been a pretty day, so she didn't have to wear a coat over her pretty sweater, but it was cold and muddy too. She drew on her long woolen stockings up under her brown skirt and then slipped her feet into her saddle oxford shoes. Daddy had worked on her shoes last night. The sole of her left shoe had gotten loose to where it flopped when she walked. Daddy could fix their shoes using a stand and last. He put Allie's shoe on the iron foot of the last and took out some little tacks. He positioned the sole back into place and nailed it back down. Allie got one pair of shoes to start school every year, and along about the first of the year, they needed some attention. She was also bad to turn her shoes over to the inside, but there wasn't much Daddy could do about that. Mama scolded some when she noticed Allie turning her shoes over, but, whether it was habit or a foot problem, Allie couldn't seem to help it. After Daddy mended the shoes, he put a fresh coat of polish on them and made them shine like a new penny. "There you go, little one," he said as he handed them back to her with a smile. "You'll be the prettiest one at school tomorrow."

When Allie arrived at school that day, she slipped off her overboots and placed them on the floor beneath the coat hooks. Her shoes were still shiny clean. That was one good thing about wearing overboots: it sure kept your shoes clean. Then she took off her coat and hung it on the hook. She smoothed down her sweater and ran a hand through her hair. Mama had put a pink ribbon in it today. She picked up her books and walked into the classroom. Montene hurried over to Allie. "Allie, you look so pretty today! Is that your new sweater set you were telling us about?"

"Yes. I got it for Christmas, and Mama let me wear it today since it's my birthday. Feel it. Isn't it soft? It feels like I'm wearing a cloud."

"Ooohhh," Montene exclaimed. "It is soft. Annabelle, come and feel Allie's sweater."

Annabelle continued to read her book. She pretended not to hear. Allie walked over to her. "Morning, Annabelle," she said as she reached out and put her hand on her friend's shoulder.

"Good morning," she answered tersely without looking up.

The second bell sounded signaling the beginning of school. Allie didn't know why her friend was so moody. Some days, she was the nicest person in the world, then another day she was distant—bordering on rude. "See you at recess, Annabelle," Allie said softly and walked to her seat.

The morning passed rather slowly. It was a rainy day, dreary really. Thunder could be heard in the distance, and rivulets of water meandered down the window glass. Of course, the children couldn't go outside for recess. Mr. Schauffler did give them a break in their studies though. Most of the boys scooted some of the desks up closer to the wall and formed a circle on the floor to play marbles. It was apparent by the whoops from Cody that he was having a good day winning marbles. His pockets bulged. When Allie glanced over at him after one of his victory cheers, he noticed her looking at him and smiled. She looked away quickly. She was shy around Cody because of the extra attention he had been giving her lately. He had even slipped her a note the other day. Allie blushed as she remembered reading it. It said she was the prettiest girl in the school, and he wanted to know if she would be his girlfriend. She hadn't written him back, of course. But she was a little pleased. She had always secretly liked Cody.

Allie joined some of the girls for a game of jacks. She was pretty good at jacks. Most of the girls could do the onesies, twosies, threesies, and even foursies, meaning they could pick up one jack at a time up through four jacks at a time. Allie had no trouble until it was time to pick up seven or eight jacks all at once. Her hands were small, and when she got up to that many, she'd end up dropping one every time.

After recess, Mr. Schauffler called the fourth-grade class up to the recitation bench. They had continued to study poetry for the past few days, and today, the students were supposed to share a poem they had written. Allie was excited. She had written a poem about Grandpa. One by one, the students settled on the bench, papers rattling in their hands. The girls' papers were folded neatly in their laps while the boys pulled crumpled wads from their pockets.

"Well now, students, I'm anxious to hear your writing. We've looked at some good examples of poetry from others and considered what they did well in their poems. I've asked you to apply some of those same techniques in your writing. Now we all are at different stages in our writing. Some of you may have been successful in these attempts of poetry writing, others may not have mastered this as yet. Remember to be considerate to one another and offer encouragement and not ridicule. As long as you're making progress, I will be pleased. Now who would like to be the first to share?"

Several hands shot up. Mr. Schauffler looked around. "Allie, since it's your birthday, why don't you go first?"

Allie smiled nervously and stood. Her paper shook a little in her hand. She reached up and tucked her hair behind her ear and cleared her throat. Then she began:

My Grandpa
On top of the garden gate I sit
Watching him walk between each row
A gentle farmer, meek and mild
Tending the plants to make them grow

I walk with him, my hand in his
Searching for berries along the path
He speaks of truths and stories told
Sometimes I cry, and then I laugh

Sitting beside him on the swing
Under the branches of whispering pine
Wrapped in the everlasting love
In the arms of this gentle Grandpa of mine

Allie's voice caught in the last words of the poem. She cleared her throat and sat down once again on the bench.

The class was silent. It was clear to all of them that Allie had written about someone dear to her heart.

Mr. Schauffler broke the silence. "Allie, that was excellent. You helped us know more about your grandpa through the few lines of your poem. You also made us feel something and that is the purpose of writing. You want others to be moved by what you write or to feel something because of your words. You made us feel your love for your grandpa. I want you to continue writing and hang on to this poem. Put it somewhere special and keep it. I'm proud of you. Okay, now, who would like to go next?"

One by one other students read their poems. Some were serious, as Allie's had been, while others were downright silly. The students listened as their classmates read their poems. They enjoyed listening to what their friends had come up with and made comments about each.

Bobbie sat listening to the others read their poems. He laughed out loud at some of them. He considered his own poem. It was about Cody's yellow-eyed marble he had won in a marble match with him. Should he read it or tell Mr. Schauffler that he didn't write one. He thought back on all the mean things Cody had done to him lately. It began when he won that stupid cat's-eye marble from him and Cody had accused him of cheating, but it hadn't stopped there. He had carved those names on the desk and blamed Bobbie, and he had told everyone Bobbie's secret that he wanted Allie to be his girlfriend. The more he thought about Cody, the madder he got. No, Cody wouldn't ever get that marble back. He'd hang on to it till kingdom come. By golly, he'd read his poem. It would serve Cody right. He didn't know if Cody would even be smart enough to figure out that it was about him. Montene was just finishing her poem about her mother's flower garden.

Mr. Schauffler had praise and encouragement for Montene and every one of the students. Finally, only one student remained. "Bobbie, I guess we're ready for you. I've been waiting anxiously to hear what you came up with."

Bobbie smoothed out the wrinkled wad of paper he had pulled from his overall's pocket and looked up at Mr. Schauffler hesitantly. He stood slowly and looked sheepishly around summoning up the courage to share his poem. His eyes fixed on Cody for a few seconds. Then he began:

The One-Eyed Cat
A cat sat looking at the moon
Could barely see it in the sky
Everything was dim and dull
Looking through a single eye

The one-eyed cat was cold and sad
Sitting alone in a garden patch
Where did his eye go you may ask
Lost to a better one in a match

This story is really very sad
I think I'll bow my head and cry
That poor old mangy yeller cat
Never to see his other eye

Bobbie sat down quickly when his poem was finished. Everybody was looking at him with puzzled expressions on their faces. Finally, Mr. Schauffler began to applaud. "Bobbie, you surprise me. That's a very original poem you have written. Is it about one of your own cats?"

"Uh, no, sir. I just thought it up, that's all," Bobbie explained.

"Well, I'm proud of you—of all my students. You were assigned a difficult task, and each of you stepped up to the plate. Good for you. Now I'd like you to go back to your desks and practice your penmanship while I listen to the third graders read from their books," Mr. Schauffler instructed.

The students made their way back to their desks. Bobbie felt a shove behind him. "Just made it up, did you? That marble will be mine again, just you wait and see!" Cody hissed in Bobbie's ear.

The school day came to an end. Mr. Schauffler dismissed the students with an admonition to read the next story in their readers. Allie was anxious to get home to her birthday supper. She stepped into her boots, but her left foot only went in about halfway. She took it off and looked inside.

It was filled about halfway with marbles. On the top was a note. Allie picked it up and read: "Roses are red, violets are blue, no one is as pretty as you, happy birthday!" Allie glanced around. Roscoe was laughing and pushing Cody out the door. It was clear who the note and marbles were from.

Allie tipped the marbles and note into her lunch bucket. The marbles rolled and rattled against the bottom and sides. She slipped on her boots and coat and hurried out the door after Winna. She smiled to herself as she skipped along. "What are you so happy about?" Winna asked.

"Mr. Schauffler liked my poem about Grandpa. I didn't get my sweater dirty like Mama was afraid I would, and I can't wait to taste my birthday cake." *And Cody gave me a love note*, she thought to herself. She would never tell Winna that, of course. "Did you know Grandma and Grandpa are eating with us?"

"Yea, Mama told me this morning. I wonder what we're having. I hope it's chicken and dumplings. I can't wait for you to see what I got for you. You're going to love it," Winna said with a smile.

Allie couldn't contain her happiness. What a wonderful day. She skipped alongside Winna reciting a favorite poem she had learned:

> Once I saw a little bird
> Come hop, hop, hop.

Allie hopped like a bird.

So I cried, "Little bird,

Will you stop, stop, stop?"

She stopped in the middle of the road, still as a pine tree.

I went to the window

To say, "How do you do?"

Allie pretended to peer through a window and wave.

But he shook his little tail,

And far away he flew.

Allie shook her bottom and pretended to fly away.

Winna laughed. "Allie, you're acting like a goofy little bird. Actually more like a birdbrain!" The sisters laughed. "And what in the world do you have in that lunch bucket? It sounds like hailstones pounding down on a tin roof!"

"Oh, just some marbles someone gave me," Allie answered. "They do make a racket, don't they?"

"You could say that. Hey, wanta sing?" Winna asked.

"Let's do! I'm so happy I feel like singing at the top of my lungs," was Allie's reply.

The sisters began singing and continued to sing all the way home. Winna began, and Allie joined in:

From the great Atlantic Ocean
to the wide Pacific shore . . .

The girls sang as they walked home, their boots making sloshing noises in the muddy road.

As soon as Allie and Winna stepped into the house, the wonderful smells from the kitchen greeted them. They could smell a chicken boiling. Mama was going to make chicken and dumplings after all. The girls hurried into the kitchen where Mama was peeling some potatoes.

"Hello, girls," Mama greeted them. "How was your day?"

"It was wonderful," Allie exclaimed.

Allie looked around the kitchen. Green beans were simmering on the stovetop. Yeast rolls were sitting inside the warming oven rising under the red-checked kitchen towel. When she peeped under the towel and took a whiff, her mouth watered. Mmmmmmmm. Then her gaze went to the table. Her eyes popped open. There sat a beautiful three-layer buttermilk cake frosted with icing that ran down the sides. Allie ran over to get a closer look. It all looked so pretty and Mama had gone to so much trouble, she puckered up and had to cry. "Mama, you're the best!" Running over to her, she stretched her arms around her big stomach. She looked up into her smiling face and asked excitedly, "What time will Grandma and Grandpa get here? Where's Daddy? Do we have any candles for the cake? What—"

"Whoa!" Mama laughed. "Grandma and Grandpa and Daddy should all be here in about an hour or so, and supper should be ready around 5:00." She reached up and smoothed Allie's hair. "Daddy was going to see if he could get some candles in town this afternoon."

Allie's dimpled smile lit up her face. "Really? Did you hear that Winna? I get to have eleven candles on my cake! That will cover the whole top!"

Winna came over to where Mama and Allie stood. "I wish every day could be a birthday day!" she said. "I can't wait until supper! Mama, that sure is a pretty cake!"

"Now if we celebrated like this every day, it wouldn't seem that special now, would it?"

Allie looked over at Mama. Mama was a little lady except that now she was round from the baby she was carrying. Her dark hair was combed back from her face and her forehead was shiny with sweat from the cookstove. She looked so tired. Her baby could come almost any day, and here she had spent her whole day making things nice for Allie. It made her feel happy and sad at the same time.

"Mama, can Winna and I do anything to help you?" Allie asked.

Mama smiled. "I think I've about got everything done for supper. Why don't you girls go ahead and get your night water before everyone gets here, so you'll be ready to relax and enjoy the birthday dinner and the company. Allie, change out of that sweater first."

"Okay, Mama," the girls answered.

Allie hurried to the backroom to change into her everyday clothes. She took off her sweater set and smoothed it out on her bed. She wanted to wear it tonight for her birthday supper.

Allie's birthday dinner was perfect. Grandpa asked the blessing on the food before they ate. He always prayed the same prayer at mealtime:

Accept our thanks, Dear Heavenly Father, for these refreshments.
Bless the hands that prepared this food.
Forgive us our sins and in heaven save us.
In Jesus' name, Amen

When they had company, Grandpa would add, "Bless those identified with us today."

Mama was such a good cook. When everyone sang happy birthday to Allie, she choked back tears. She didn't know how she was so lucky to have such a loving family. Mama and Daddy loved her so much. Winna was the best big sister anyone could ask for, and little Betty, with her chubby dimpled cheeks, was like the icing on her birthday cake. Then on top of that, she had her grandparents, aunts and uncles, and all her cousins. Allie's life couldn't have been any better.

Allie's Grandma Shoemate and Mama

After supper, Winna gave Allie a package wrapped up in brown paper and tied with a string. "Here, sister. I didn't have any money to buy you a gift, but I think you'll like what I made for you."

Allie took the package and untied the string. Inside was a cigar box that Winna had covered for her. It was covered with a red-patterned piece of cloth. Winna had covered the whole box, even the inside. It was so perfectly done, it looked store-bought. "I thought you could use it to store special things you want to keep forever," Winnie said.

"Oh, Winna, I love it!" Allie said excitedly. She opened and closed the lid several times thinking of what thing she would put in it first. She knew it had taken Winna a long time to make it, and she had done such a good job. There wasn't a wrinkle or puckered place anywhere in the material. "Thank you, sister," Allie said as she took hold of Winna's hand.

Next, Daddy took something out of his pocket. "Well, sis, I guess I was thinking like Winna. I've got a little box for you too and, like Winna's, it's homemade." Daddy handed Allie a little cedar box with a hinged lid. Allie opened it and took a whiff. The cedar scent was wonderful and the metal hinges and fastener were so bright and shiny.

"Ohhhh," Allie exclaimed. "Oh, I love it, Daddy, and I love you too! Thank you so much." She ran over and threw her arms around him.

Daddy laughed his big hearty laugh. "Well, you're mighty welcome, sis," he answered.

Grandpa cleared his throat. "I guess it's my turn." Allie turned toward Grandpa with a question on her face. Grandma and Grandpa had never given her anything for her birthday unless you counted the hugs and birthday spankings she always received from them. Grandpa reached down into his shirt pocket and took out a little sack. It was a white sack that was folded over several times into a small package. There was a red ribbon around it. "Allie, this is something that once belonged to my own mother. It's a little hard for me to part with it, but I want you to have it. I want you to know that it's very special and something you'll want to always hang on to. I had intended to wait and give it to you when you were older, but I think you're old enough to understand the significance of it and that you'll take good care of it."

Allie didn't know what to say. She had never had such a birthday in all her life. She would have been completely happy with just Mama's special birthday supper, and now she was getting three presents too. She slowly put her hand out to Grandpa's, not knowing what to say. The package was small and lightweight. "What could be inside?" she wondered. Opening the sack, she put her hand inside and took out a delicate heart necklace on a gold chain. Allie caught her breath. It was the most beautiful thing she had ever seen. Tears jumped to her eyes without her even noticing. She turned the necklace over in her hand. The front of the heart had a white mother-of-pearl overlay coating on it with three little pink flowers painted on it. There was a tiny clasp on the side. Allie put her thumbnail under the latch and opened the locket. She gasped. There inside, Grandpa's pet name for her, Peeny, was engraved in the gold. It was all just too much. Allie put her hands over her face. "I can't believe this!" she cried.

Grandpa stood and gathered Allie in his arms. "Now don't go and do that!" he chided. "This is supposed to be a happy time. Your Grandma and I just wanted to do something special for your eleventh birthday. We won't get to give you something like that for every birthday, but we thought this was the right time for it. You just take care of it, and maybe you can pass it on to a daughter of your own sometime."

Allie threw her arms around Grandpa. "I'll keep it forever," she blubbered. "I'll keep it for ever and ever and ever and never let anything happen to it."

Grandpa laughed. "I know you will," he said.

Betty had been sitting in Mama's lap up until this time. Slowly she slid off her lap and walked over to Allie. "Sissy, you can have my dolly," she said as she placed her beloved rag doll in Allie's hands.

Allie bent down and picked her up. "You can keep your dolly, Betty. I'll just keep you for my dolly!" Everyone laughed.

"Okay, now, let's cut that cake," Mama said starting to get up from her seat.

"No, Gracie, you stay put," Grandma Shoemate said. "You've been on your feet too much already today fixing this good meal and all. It's been a big enough day already without you having that young-un today too. You keep your seat. I'll serve the cake."

That night, as Allie lay in bed thinking about everything that had happened on this day, she still couldn't believe it. Her special box Winna had given her was on the dresser filled with all the marbles Cody had put in her boot today at school and the poem she had written about Grandpa. Daddy's little cedar box was beside it. Inside was the beautiful heart necklace. She had never felt so rich. Allie knew she was the happiest girl on earth that night, and her heart nearly burst with the love she had for her family. She closed her eyes and folded her hands under the covers. Silently she prayed:

Now I lay me down to sleep.
I pray the Lord my soul to keep.
If I should die before I wake,
I pray the Lord my soul to take.
God bless Mama, Daddy, Winna, Betty, and
Grandma, and Grandpa.
Please take care of Mama and the new baby she'll have
soon.
Thank you for my wonderful day.
In Jesus' name, Amen.

Chapter 5

Momma was always patching our britches. She would put patches on top of patches. I tell people that I was going with the girls before I got my first pair of shoes. Everybody went barefooted. That was just part of it. I don't remember ever having any overshoes.

—Jake (2010)

My grandpa, Ruffin Crotts, was the most gentle and kindest man in the world. I would follow him around like a little puppy dog. One of my favorite memories was when I was real small and one of my uncles or Mom got angry at me. I would go running to Grandpa. He would open his arms, and I would jump in. Then he always said, "Leave my girl alone!" And they always did!

—Oletta Ross (2010)

Bobbie

February 1941

Bobbie loved watching Momma make quilts. She would start with a box of old scraps, a kaleidoscope of colors, which would be transformed into intricate designs by her skillful fingers. Most of the pieces were just small odd-shaped scraps of old feed sacks that had been left over after someone made a dress or shirt. She never got a very big piece of cloth given to her. Women usually took even very small pieces and made them into something: a slip for a baby, a handkerchief, or maybe a patch for a pair of overalls before thinking about getting rid of them. When nothing more could be made from the material, many people gave Momma the leftover scraps. They knew she would put them to good use. You should have seen the way Momma's eyes would light up when she received a box of these "treasures." Bobbie could always tell when Momma had gotten some new scraps. She would fly through her work just itching to get at them. Bobbie would ask her, "Momma, you wouldn't have a new box of scraps, would you?"

"Law, how did you know, son?" she would answer with a giggle.

"Well, it's like a copperhead has been after you all morning the way you've been getting after your chores," he would say with a smile.

"They're calling my name, for sure," Momma would answer with a laugh. "I just can't wait to get that quilt started to see how it's gonna look."

It was amazing what Momma could do with those tiny pieces of material. She would look at the colorful tidbits and all at once announce, "I think I'm going to make a Log Cabin Quilt out of this box of scraps." Or maybe she'd say, "These are just right for finishing up that Jacob's Ladder I've been working on." It was like she could already see it in her mind, and she would grab her sewing supplies and get to town on it.

Momma didn't just make quilts; she made just about everything the family needed. Clothing was usually handmade, not store-bought. Now and then, clothes would be handed down from cousins or others in the community. Overall though, most everything worn by the family was made by Momma. Therefore, material was precious to her, and she never let any of it go to waste. When one of the children outgrew something, it was passed down to a younger sibling. When a pair of Daddy's overalls got so worn out it was downright embarrassing for him to wear them, Momma would cut out the good part and use it to make a short pair of pants for Jake or little Rex and use the leftovers as patches for a better pair of Daddy's overalls. Finally, the scraps were used for her quilts. Their clothes would have patches on top of patches. Hardly a thread would be left when she was through with a piece of material.

This afternoon, Momma was making what was called a Lazy Woman's Quilt. This quilt probably got its name because it was smaller than a regular-sized quilt, thus being a quilt that even a lazy woman could make. This certainly wasn't the case with Momma though. There wasn't a lazy bone in her body. There was usually a Lazy Woman's Quilt folded up on the end of the bed in the front room. It was just right for throwing over your legs when the house got a little chilly or for covering Jake or Rex when they curled up on the end of the bed for a little nap during the day. Momma said a person could never have too many quilts, and her family was never cold during the winter because of this.

Some of the other women in the community owned sewing machines, but not Momma. She did her sewing all by hand. She had to. Her needle would just fly up and down, up and down through those pieces of material nearly as fast as some women could sew on their machines. Momma would hum or sing while she worked. She liked gospel songs, and the rhythm of her needle going up and down and the beautiful melodic sound of her voice cast a sort of hypnotic spell on Bobbie if he were around when she was doing her sewing or mending. He'd find himself drifting off into a peaceful slumber as she sang:

Oh, Beu-lah Land, sweet Beu-Lah land,
As on thy high-est mount I stand

Momma had been sewing most of her life. Her own mother took to her bed before she was very old, so Momma had to grow up early. Bobbie didn't really know what Grandma Crotts's illness was, but she was not able to be up and around for most of her adult life. He had heard that Grandma had heart dropsy, but Bobbie wasn't sure what that was. She was a little woman, never weighing over a hundred pounds except when she was going to have a baby. For some reason though, she was sick all the time. Doc Sutton came to the house once to doctor Thurman. He had pneumonia, and Grandpa told the doctor, "When you finish with Thurman, I want you to check Berthie." When the doctor went in to check on her though, Grandma had the covers pulled up under her chin and wouldn't let him near her. She died about three weeks later.

Momma, being the oldest, had to become more or less the mother of the house when she was just a young girl. After her mother died, even though she was a married woman by then, she continued to care for her younger siblings. She had two younger sisters and three younger brothers: Alma,

Ed, Thelma, Ivel, Alfred, and Thurman. Bobbie supposed the reason Momma was so good at organizing and running their own home now was that she had been doing it for most of her life. It had been four years now since Grandma died.

Momma actually made her first dress when she was only ten years old. It was a striped dress. She cut out a round collar from the striped material too. Then she bound it around with a piece of yellow. It was getting about time to start school that year, and she didn't have anything to wear. Her daddy had gotten several pieces of material to be made into dresses for the girls, but her mother was sick and there wasn't anyone else to make one for her. So taking the matter into her own hands, Momma slipped out one of the pieces of material and whacked out a dress. She says it's a wonder she didn't ruin it. Well, it so happened that the dress turned out okay. In fact, it was so well made that she wore it to school. From that day on, she made all her clothes and clothes for everybody else in the family too. Bobbie wished Momma had kept that dress. It would have been something to see a dress his momma made when she had been his age. He was certain though that the dress had gotten passed down to Alma and then probably to Thelma. Maybe the remains of that dress were somewhere in one of Momma's quilts right now. He wished Momma had her own sewing machine. She often looked longingly at a stack of material and say that if she had a machine, she could get her sewing done in a fraction of the time. There just never seemed to be enough money for a sewing machine though. Bobbie smiled at his secret. If he had anything to do with it, she'd have one before too long.

Bobbie had a question he wanted to ask Momma, but he was afraid he already knew the answer. "Momma, do you think I could use some of your leftover material to cover a box for my valentines?" he asked.

"Well law, it is about Valentine's Day, isn't it? Time shore passes quickly. Seems like just yesterday that we were putting up a Christmas tree," Momma replied without looking up from her sewing. "I'd just love to say yes, Bobbie, but I really need most every bit of material I have for this here quilt I'm working on. I've got some catalogs you can cut pictures out of. I bet you could get Audie to look through them and find some right pretty pictures in it. You could even use your crayons and add a little color to the pictures."

"You know, Momma, that's a great idea," Bobbie replied, grateful for such good advice. "I'll go ask her and then run over to the store and see if they have any boxes we can use. I know Willie and Audie will need one too. I'm gonna see if Willie will go with me."

Bobbie found Willie out back tossing sticks for Fancy and Buck. "Want to go see if we can find some boxes up at the store for our valentines?" Bobbie asked.

"Sure," Willie said as he flung the stick one last time for the dogs.

Bobbie loved going to Jim Andy's store. It was a long building with a wide front porch that went across the front. In warm weather, old men would sit in a line across the porch chewing tobacco and shooting the bull with one another and spitting tobacco juice in a stream into the road. It was too cold this February day though for them to be outside. A bell over the door jingled as Bobbie and Willie went inside the store. Every place has its unique smells, and Jim Andy's store was no exception. As they entered, the assortment of spices: basil, cumin, cinnamon, coriander, fennel, and more seemed to fill the air. You could also detect medicinal scents like camphor, medicated ointments, salves, and balms. Wood was a dominate smell too, the store having a board floor and wooden display shelves scattered here and there. There was a little bit of everything in that store: bolts of material, all kinds of tools, flour, coffee, lard, even a doll or two scattered here and there. A person's eyes could hardly take in the assortment of items.

On the right stood a glass candy counter around seven feet long. Baskets or boxes of candy were neatly arranged on the three shelves. Horehound drops, soft peppermints, black licorice, and a chocolaty nutty bar called Kandy Kake enticed the customers with promises of a delight to the sweet tooth. Bobbie couldn't help but put his nose up against the glass counter and fix his eyes on the delectable delicacies inside. He figured he would have no trouble eating every piece of candy inside that counter. His mouth began to water just thinking about the sweet caramel and chocolate mixing together in his mouth. He would have to wait for a special occasion though. There wasn't money for such extravagance for everyday enjoyment.

A radio was playing in the back of the store. Several men sat on upturned pop crates in a semicircle around the potbellied stove listening to it. There was really more static than words coming out of the old radio, but Bobbie did hear a reporter breaking through the static every now and then talking about the war. Sid Winters was saying, "Fellers, I just think we can count on Roosevelt to stand by what he said of keeping us out of this blame war."

"I hate to disagree with you, Sid, but that Hitler feller has got to be stopped, I don't care what it takes," Tom Lancy broke in. "I say if we all pull together with the other Allies, we could take care of the whole kit and kaboodle of them. If I were a younger man, I'd be enlisting myself. I just don't feel good about them other countries fighting for what's right and us sitting over here on our backsides letting them do the fighting for us."

"I'm not saying I wouldn't be willing to do my part, you know me better than that, Lancy," Sid broke in. "I'd stand up with the best of them, but you know good as me that it's easier to get into a war than to get out of it. It'll just go from one thing to another. How long did the Great War last? Wasn't it four or five years? A lot of boys can die in that length of time, Tom, a dang lot of them. Back in September when this thang started, Roosevelt said he believed he could keep us out of it, and I, for one, want to see him stick with those words." Sid spit a stream of tobacco juice into the ash bucket by the front of the stove as if that settled the matter. The spit made a loud sizzling sound as some of it landed on the hot metal.

Bobbie leaned against the pickle jar as he listened to the old gentlemen share their opinions of the war. It was a scary time in the country. Mr. Schauffler had discussed the war some during their lessons at school. He had shown them a map of the world and pointed out the places Germany now occupied. Bobbie had learned where many of those countries were located. He thought of the people living there and wondered how it felt to have a group of people come in and take it over. He didn't say anything, but he agreed with Mr. Lancy that the United States had an obligation to help defend what was right, and if that meant going to war, so be it. If he were a little older, he might just enlist too.

One of the men sitting around the stove was Uncle Bud Hudson. Willie had gone over and sat down beside him as soon as they'd gotten there. Bobbie knew Willie loved hearing Uncle Bud's stories.

"Were you in World War I, Uncle Bud?" Willie asked.

"No sir. I was a little too old for that war. Now Claude Blair was in that war and Raydo Stroud. And I believe Will

Snider was in that war too. But let me tell you something I bet you don't know. I was around during the Civil War."

"Really?" Willie said with awe.

"I can't say that I remember much about it, being only a lad at the time," Uncle Bud continued. "I do remember though that all the men left to fight leaving the women folk and children by themselves. Yes sir, we was left to fend for ourselves. There wasn't no men left here then. And do you know what was the scariest thing about the war to us?"

"The Union soldiers?" Willie guessed.

"No, I don't remember ever seeing any soldiers, but what we did see were carpetbaggers. They just came and took what they wanted."

"There was a lot of men from Arkansas who fought in that war," Sid added. "I believe I heard something like sixty thousand."

"It was a sad time for our country," Bud said with a shake of his head, "A sad time, indeed."

The men settled into some deep thinking at that time, and Bobbie approached Mr. Andy about the boxes.

After securing three boxes from him and trading ten more of his dollar bills in for a $10 bill, Bobbie and Willie started out the door of the store. Cody was just coming in as they were going out.

"Whatcha got in them boxes?" Cody wanted to know.

"Just getting 'em ready for valentines," Bobbie answered as he headed on down the steps.

"How about a game of marbles?" Cody called after him.

"No thanks," Bobbie said over his shoulder. "I've got all the marbles I need."

"I wasn't planning on you winning," Cody said with a sneer.

"You weren't planning on me winning last time," Bobbie shot back as he headed off down the road. Willie followed with a questioning look on his face. Bobbie continued talking to Cody, "Somehow though, marbles just seem to find their way out of your pockets and into mine." Bobbie heard the door slam loudly behind him as Cody must have entered the store.

"What was that all about?" Willie wanted to know. "Are you guys still sore at each other?"

"Yep," Bobbie answered.

Once home, the boys put the boxes in the house, and Bobbie went out to the smokehouse to put his ten-dollar bill in his can. Fancy and Buck had come out from under the house and were looking out to the woods barking.

"What do you two hear?" Bobbie asked as he took time to rub their backs. He looked out into the dark woods but didn't see anything. "Is Daddy taking you two hunting tonight?" he asked. "Is that what you're all worked up about?"

Bobbie climbed into the old smokehouse and scooted the corn barrel to the side. Pulling up the loose board in the floor, he took out the old red Prince Albert can resting on the soft earth underneath. Taking out the other two tens, he closed his fingers around them. $30! That was more money than he had ever held in his hands before. Heck, it was more money than he'd ever seen before! He just needed a little more until he could buy that sewing machine for Momma. Mr. Andy said he could get a nice treadle machine for around $40. He had wanted to have that much saved by last Christmas, but there just hadn't been enough time. "What were those durn dogs barking at?"

"Fancy! Buck! Hush up!" Bobbie hollered from inside the smokehouse. Bobbie replaced the can under the board, moved the corn barrel back over the spot, and went back outside. It was about time to do his evening chores.

After supper, Bobbie, Willie, and Audie worked on their valentine boxes. Audie had cut out a variety of pictures from the Sears and Roebuck catalog. Momma had mixed up some flour and water for them to use as a paste, and they arranged the pictures over the tops and sides of the boxes. Bobbie felt a little silly making a valentine box. He thought of himself as too old for such things, but Mr. Schauffler had said it would be a good activity. He said they could practice their poetry writing when making out valentines for their friends. Bobbie didn't know about that. He'd about had his fill of poetry to do him a lifetime.

"Bobbie, I heard Mrs. Stephens had her baby. A little girl, I believe it was," Momma said as she was washing up the supper dishes. Daddy wasn't home yet, so they had gone ahead and eaten without him. Momma made Daddy a plate and set it up in the warming tray of the stove for him to have when he got home.

Bobbie, Audie, and Willie

"Yea, I heard Allie tell some of the girls that they named her Patsy, Patsy Ann, I believe."

"That's a pretty name. Four daughters," Momma laughed. "Poor Robert is going to be living in a whole house full of women before too long!"

"No, Jakey!" Audie screeched. "Momma, Jakey is wadding up my pictures."

"Ah, he's just wanting to help," Momma smiled. "Jake, do you want to come over and help me wash up these here dishes?"

Jake hopped up from the floor. Momma dried her hands and pulled a chair over to the cabinet. She helped Jake up on the chair where he immediately began splashing in the dishwater.

"Yes, sir, the Stephens' house is full to the brim with pretty little girls," Momma continued.

"Jake, did you know I used to stand up on a nail crate to cook. Yes sir, my daddy needed help with the cookin', so he got a nail crate for me to use to reach the cabinet and stove."

"Momma, where were you born?" Willie asked taking them back to the topic of babies. Willie had stayed and had supper with them. Grandma was coming over later, and he would go back home with her when she left.

"Well, kids, I was born right here in Elizabeth on February 7, 1911. Now which of you can figure out how old that makes me?" Momma turned to them with a twinkle in her eyes.

"Hummm," Bobbie figured. "1911 from 1941 is . . . thirty. You're thirty years old."

"Yep, that's right," Momma said with a nod. Sometimes I feel more like sixty though. I was just a little thing when I was born too. I weighed just over three pounds."

"Really?" answered Audie. "How little is that?"

"Well, it's not much bigger than one of Fancy's pups," answered her brother.

Momma dried her hands and went over to light the lamp. The sun had gone down, and it was beginning to get dark in the room.

Audie noticed Momma's hands as she turned the knob on the lamp making the flame rise higher. "Momma, your hands are so red and chapped they look like they're about to bleed," she said.

"I done some washing today, honey. That old scrub board takes the skin right off your hands right along with the dirt from the clothes, not to mention what the lye soap does. That stuff will eat the hide right off a body's hands, for sure!" Momma replied.

Bobbie knew life was hard for Momma and all young mothers. There was little time for anything but hard work. Momma's day started before daylight, fixing the large breakfast by lamplight. Her day didn't end even after all the children were tucked away in their beds. She still had to do the mending, churn the butter, iron clothes, stoke the fire, and the list went on and on. By the time she finally crawled into bed herself, every ounce of energy was drained out of her.

"Kids, let's get this mess picked up," Momma said. "Grandma and your uncles will be here soon. Daddy should be getting home purty soon too." Every Saturday night the radio's dial was turned to 650 to WSM radio station out of Nashville to listen to the Grand Ole Opry. It was said that this radio station could be heard from New York to California and from Canada all the way down to Mexico. Relatives without a radio would come to their house every Saturday night and gather around to listen to the likes of Pee Wee King, Eddy Arnold, and Minnie Pearl. The show was broadcast from the War Memorial Auditorium in downtown Nashville. Bobbie had heard that there was seating in that auditorium for over two thousand people. It was hard to imagine that many people in one place at one time. He had also heard that it cost twenty-five cents to get into the Grand Ole Opry. Twenty-five cents times two thousand people! Even he wasn't smart enough to figure out how much money that would be; it would be a whole lot, enough for his family to live on for a long time! What he wouldn't give to be able to see those stars in person. Maybe one of these days he'd get to go there. Roy Acuff, known as the King of Country Music, was one of his favorites. Last week, Bill Monroe and the Bluegrass Boys performed. Man, they were great!

The kids began picking up the paper scattered on the floor. Little Rex was already curled up under the covers sucking his thumb and nodding off to sleep. The grown-ups would listen to the radio station until it went off the air before calling it a day. Bobbie loved these times when the family gathered around. It would be wall-to-wall people. The house was small, and since the bed took up most of the space in the front room, everybody just had to sit where they could find a spot. Some would be piled up on the bed being careful not to waken little Rex. Others would drag a kitchen chair into the front room or stretch out on the floor using the wall for a back rest.

It wasn't long before people began gathering. Uncle Art and Aunt Alta got there first with Racine and little June. Uncle Jim and Aunt Alpha arrived next with Danny, Patsy, Jimmy, and Sue. Grandpa Crotts came in next with Thurman and Thelma and Oletta. Finally, Aunt Alma and Uncle Raymond showed up with their daughter Lanetta. How their tiny house held everyone was a mystery indeed. The kids all took off, the little girls to the bedroom with their baby dolls. They hadn't been in there five minutes until there was a squabble. Momma ran back to see what was the trouble. Audie, Racine, and Patsy were playing dolls, and all three insisted on her baby being named Judy. None could be persuaded to name her baby anything else. Momma suggested other names. "Ah, now, Linda is a pretty name or Betty. I've always liked the name Erma Lou."

"No!" they all three shouted together, hands on hips, "Judy!" The argument was finally settled when Momma suggested each "Judy" be given a middle name. That seemed to satisfy them, and the three dolls were given the names: Judy Ann, Judy Diane, and Judy Carol. After that, the three cousins played peacefully once again.

Meanwhile, the boy cousins went outside to play. Bobbie loved spending time with his older cousin, Danny. "Let's go run our wheels," Danny called to the other boys. Running their wheels was an activity they played with a metal wheel and a stick. The stick had a metal troughlike attachment that fit around the edge of the wheel. A person would get the wheel to running and then keep it going and guide it by placing the trough over the top of the wheel and pushing it along. It was such fun to race the wheels along. Sometimes that's exactly what they did with the wheels, race! Other times they would set up a kind of obstacle course using barrels, stumps, sticks of wood, buckets, or anything else they could find. Then they would see which one of them could run their wheels through the obstacle course without knocking anything over or crashing. Of course, Danny, being the oldest, was the best. Bobbie, Willie, and the other cousins looked up to him and watched his every move when he was running his wheel. They tried to imitate him not only in running their wheels, but in talk and mannerism too.

Bobbie's cousin, Danny, holding another
cousin, Jimmy, Bobbie, and Willie

It was late that evening before Bobbie finally crawled in
under the covers in the back bedroom, the kitchen being
crowded with adults. He thought about the events of the
day. He had worked on his valentine box and was able to
finish it before everyone arrived. He would take it to school
with him on Monday. The boxes would set out all week
until they got to open them on Friday. Tomorrow he'd start
making his valentines. He had gotten more excited about

making valentines as the day went on. Maybe this would be fun after all.

One by one, starting with the babies and then on up the line to Danny, sleep overtook most of the children, and they curled up and slept wherever they found an empty space. For some reason, Bobbie was wired and couldn't seem to settle down to sleep. He lay in the back bedroom and listened to the adults talk. They were talking about President Roosevelt and the changes that were taking place in the country. All the adults remembered well the hard times during the '30s. It was a time known as the Great Depression. Times were hard, and the phrase "Brother, can you spare a dime?" was something that was heard several times a day in most communities. The thing was, no one had even a single dime to spare. Bobbie heard Daddy say, "We right near starved to death."

Momma added, "There weren't narry a thing we could do. We just had to hang on and pray for better times."

Many of the people blamed President Hoover for the hard times since he was president when the Depression started. When people lost their jobs and homes, they built makeshift shacks out of anything they could find. They called these groups of shacks Hoovervilles after Herbert Hoover as an insult to him. It was no surprise to anyone when Hoover lost the election in 1932. Franklin Roosevelt won in a landslide. He had gotten most everyone's attention during his campaign when he said he wanted to help the forgotten man. The way he said it sounded like he was talking individually to each man in the country. He had promised the American people what he called a New Deal. That was something Daddy and the others in the next room understood. They were all cardplayers, and they knew what it meant to get to throw down a losing hand and be dealt a new deal. It was a way to get rid of a bad hand and get a new set of cards to play with, a way of starting over. And that's what this country had needed, a new start!

President Roosevelt hadn't wasted any time making some changes when he was sworn in. One of the first things he did was try and get the banks stable again. A big part of them had closed after the stock market crashed in 1929. People had lost money, some a lot of money. They had started keeping what little money they had at home stuffed under mattresses or some other rat hole. It made Bobbie think of his own money out in the smokehouse. But when the banks went under, the people no longer trusted them. Roosevelt had helped restore some trust in the banking business by creating an insurance that guaranteed that everyone's money was safe. It was called the FDIC for Federal Deposit Insurance Corporation. Because of this assurance that people would not lose their hard-earned money, they once again began putting their money, as little as it was, back into banks. It seemed like that was the first step in getting the country going again.

Another thing that Roosevelt had done was to start the WPA. This stood for Works Progress Administration or called by others Work Pays America. This program created paying jobs for unemployed individuals. It put a little money in their pockets and helped them buy the things they needed for their families. The effects of this program had even made a difference in their own little community. For one thing, the sawmills had gotten increased orders from the new construction going up in the area. It felt good to have big orders to fill and a little money in their pockets. Slowly but surely, the country was healing from those hard times.

Bobbie's dad: Delford James

Bobbie felt his eyes growing heavy. The grown-ups had started talking about the war overseas and whether or not they thought Roosevelt would get the Americans involved in it. It was a scary time in the country all right, but here in his bed, Bobbie had never felt safer. Momma and Daddy and most of his relatives were right in the next room. Jake was snuggled up warm against him, and he had $30 cash money. He felt rich and at peace. He was thankful for his home and the things they had.

Bobbie smiled as he heard Grandpa Crotts start humming. He knew it wouldn't be long before everyone else would grow silent and listen to him. Bobbie leaned up on his elbow and looked into the kitchen. Grandpa had turned one of the kitchen chairs over to lean back against it. Bobbie could see him sitting there on the floor leaned back up against that chair with his eyes closed. Finally, he heard Grandpa begin:

> Oh, will you not bow an' pray with me now?
> Sadly regrets that we never learned how,
> To come before Him, who only can save,
> Reaching in triumph o'er death an' the grave.
>
> Only a prayer, only a tear
> Only if sister and mother were here,

Only a song, "twill comfort and cheer,
Only a word from that book so dear.

Bobbie smiled and felt the peace of Grandpa's voice finally lull him into a peaceful sleep.

Chapter 6

Some of my fondest memories of my childhood include my many cousins. All of Dad's brothers lived in walking distance of us: Uncle Horace just down the road a piece, Uncle Elbert about two miles further on. Uncle Henry lived between Uncle Elbert and Uncle Horace. Uncle George lived across the woods at a place known then as the old home place. It is now in my field. The old home place is where the Griffith family lived. My grandma Stephens was a Griffith before she married Grandpa. Winna and I spent a lot of our playtime with all our cousins, but especially Uncle Horace and Aunt Lottie's girls, Erma Faye and Joanna, because they were closest. We seldom went to one another's houses to play, but would play between our houses. There was a certain tree that we would go to and call to them to ask Aunt Lottie if they could come up the road and play. They also had a tree or post they could come to and holler to see if Mama would let us go down and play a while. There was a huge sand bed where we built big sand castles, made roads for our cars that were made from blocks of wood, or just maybe a rock that was used as a car. We climbed trees and rode them over, and, at times, we took our catalog paper dolls. We liked to find places that had mossy spots that looked like lush carpets. We made lots of rooms and made paths between each other's houses and visited one another often. We also had playhouses where we used broken dishes our parents let us have, coffee and baking powder cans, and other things we happened to find that had been thrown away.

I want to mention my great-grandmother, Elizabeth Tinkle Rand. She was Grandma Shoemate's mother. Grandma Rand's husband was Tom Rand, but I don't remember him. Grandma Rand is buried at Elizabeth near Grandma and Grandpa Shoemate's graves. She was known as Lizzy. She was a tiny, sweet, little lady that had no real home when I knew her. There wasn't any money provided to old people back then, I reckon. She just stayed among her children. She stayed a lot with Grandma and Grandpa Shoemate. She had no teeth and liked her snuff. I remember she had all her earthly goods in what she called her red box. I've seen her open her red box and take the things out and look at them one by one and then put them back in and close the lid. It seemed sad. She died in

1947, but I really don't know from what cause. I loved this sweet lady.

—Allie (2010)

Allie

March 1941

Allie loved Aunt Ollie's donuts better than almost anything in the world. They were light, fluffy, and just melted in your mouth. The mere thought of them made Allie's mouth drool like a dog gone mad.

Aunt Ollie was actually Mama's aunt and Allie's great-aunt. However, she was just five years older than Mama. In a lot of ways, she seemed a lot closer to Winna and Allie's age than Mama's. She was the youngest sister of Grandma Shoemate, but the differences between those two sisters were like night and day. Where Grandma was tall and thin, Aunt Ollie was short and plump. Grandma was serious and levelheaded; Aunt Ollie was funny and outrageous. Grandma cooked beans and taters; Aunt Ollie made elaborate pies and mouth-watering cakes. Grandma was a whistle from a teakettle; Aunt Ollie was fireworks exploding in the sky on the Fourth of July. Everything about Aunt Ollie was big, exciting, loud, and a little bit reckless. Maybe that's why the girls loved her so much. However, Winna and Allie weren't the only ones who loved Aunt Ollie; she was a favorite of everyone. She could make people laugh their heads off one minute and have them crying a bucketful of tears the next. She was just one of those individuals who won the hearts of everyone she was around. Aunt Ollie was a wonderful cook too, and her specialty was donuts!

Aunt Ollie, Allie's Dad, Allie's Mama

This morning Mama had reluctantly agreed to let the girls make some of Aunt Ollie's donuts for breakfast even though it was Sunday—an especially busy morning for Mama. She had four girls to get ready for church now instead of three. Of course, Winna and Allie could get themselves ready for church, but Mama had to iron their dresses and help with their hair. All of this preparation made Sundays one of the busiest mornings of the week.

Winna had gotten up hungry for donuts this morning. Normally, they didn't get to have donuts unless it was a special occasion, and the only special thing about this morning was that it was warmer and sunnier than it had been in weeks. There was the hint of spring in the air, and Allie supposed that was as good a reason as any to celebrate with donuts. Allie expected Mama to tell Winna no, but, for whatever reason, Mama had agreed. Winna promised Mama that she and Allie could make them all by themselves, and she wouldn't have to help them one bit. Allie knew better. Even though they had helped Mama make donuts a time or two before, she knew they'd have a lot of questions for her once they got started. Of course, she didn't mention this to Mama. She just nodded her head vigorously along with Winna, affirming they would be responsible.

Allie clapped her hands when she heard Mama's answer and pulled the recipe box from behind the curtain of the cabinet. She looked through the few sheets of paper inside: Aunt Doll's pickled beets and eggs, Aunt Lottie's sourdough bread starter, Aunt Nellie's gingerbread, Aunt Roxie's sausage, Aunt Ollie's donuts. There it was! Allie read the recipe aloud to Winna.

Aunt Ollie's Donuts

Heat the following ingredients together in a pan until the
lard is melted:
1 ½ cups of sweet milk
2 tablespoons of white sugar
1 teaspoon salt
6 tablespoons lard

Pour melted mixture into a bowl and let it cool to
lukewarm. Add 2 packages of yeast and one egg. Add 4
cups sifted flour (2 cups at a time). Place in greased bowl.
Cover with damp towel and let rise until double in size
(about 30 minutes). Roll out. Cut into donuts. Let rise and
deep fry. Roll warm donuts in sugar icing.

This morning Mama had just a small fire in the cookstove.
That's all they really needed—just a little heat to knock the
chill out of the house for the baby. Allie leaned on the counter
and watched as Winna mixed the ingredients together in
a saucepan: 1 and 1/2 cup milk, 2 tablespoons sugar, 1
teaspoon salt, and 6 tablespoons of lard. After mixing it
together, she handed the enameled pan to Allie. Mama had
just gotten this new cookware, and she was so proud of it.
Allie was glad Mama was letting them use it to make the
donuts. "Put this on the stove, Allie, and stir it until the lard
melts," she ordered.

"You don't have to be so bossy!" Allie snapped. Sometimes Winna tried to act like a mama to Allie. She was usually so much fun, but at other times, she was a know-it-all and thought she could order Allie around like a sergeant in the army.

Allie stood in front of the stove and stirred the mixture. She watched the liquid go round and round, but the lump of lard didn't seem to be getting any smaller. The stove wasn't hot enough this morning. Her arm ached from the continued round and round motion. Her feet ached from standing in the same spot for so long. She shifted from one foot to the other. Was that lard ever going to melt?

"Allie, you've got to keep stirring, so the milk won't scorch," Mama cautioned as she noticed Allie letting the spoon rest on the side of the pan. "As soon as the lard melts, you can take it off the heat."

"I think there's a witch in it!" Allie complained to Mama. That was just an old saying Allie had heard Mama say from time to time. When Mama was anxious for some water to boil and it took a long time doing it, she'd say there was a witch in the water.

Mama looked over at her and smiled. "Sometimes it feels like it, doesn't it? Winna, why don't you get the other things ready while Allie does that? I'm afraid you girls are going to run out of time."

Little Patsy was bawling in the next room, and Betty had gotten up grumpy. She was pulling on Mama's skirt wanting to be held. Mama was pressing a pair of Daddy's britches. She was beginning to look flustered. The stove wasn't hot enough for the iron either, and Mama was having a hard time getting the wrinkles out of Daddy's pants.

Mama had two irons. She left one on the top of the cookstove warming while she used the other one to press the clothes. When the iron she was using began to cool down, she switched it for the hot one. Usually by the time one of the irons cooled, the other one was hot enough to use. It wasn't working that way this morning.

"I should have pressed these pants last night after supper," Mama complained as she set the iron down, hard, on the stovetop.

"Why does Winna get to do the easy part?" Allie whined. "Just because she's older, she always gets the easy work, and I have the hardest work! My face is hot standing by this stove, and my arm is about to fall off. It's not fair!" Allie knew she was exaggerating about the heat from the stove. Her face was not really hot; she was just bored with her task.

Allie turned and watched Winna dip the flour scoop from the flour bin. She dumped the flour into the sifter. Winna held the sifter high in the air and turned the handle. The flour fell like snow onto the counter. "How many cups of flour, Mama?" Winna asked sweetly as she turned and stuck her tongue out at Allie.

"I told you FOUR!" Allie yelled. "Winna, you never listen to a word I say. You think I'm a baby and don't know anything. I have the recipe right here in front of me, and it says four cups! Why are you ignoring me and asking Mama?"

"Alright, alright!" Winna snapped back. "You don't have to jump down my throat!" She began measuring the flour into the bowl. It looked like play to Allie. Winna held the sifter up higher and slowly turned the handle on the sifter some more. She watched the flour drift down. Allie wished she could play in the flour.

"I don't like doing this," Allie whined. "Let's just eat something else for breakfast."

"No!" Winna shot back. "We can't stop now. You said you'd help, and you're supposed to stir. That's your job. Quit whining and acting like a baby, and I'll quit treating you like one!"

"Girls!" Mama said sternly. That was all it took. Both Allie and Winna grew silent, but it didn't stop the glares going back and forth between them. The stove might not have been hot this morning, but there was definitely something steaming in the kitchen.

When the lard had finally melted completely, Allie set the pan off the stove to cool. "Allie, could you go and see if you can get Patsy to stop fretting?" Mama asked. "I need to finish these pants for Daddy. Part of the fence was down this morning, and Old Brendie got out last night. They're trying to get it fixed before church."

"Okay, Mama," Allie said. She went into Mama and Daddy's room where little Patsy lay on the bed kicking her feet and fretting. She was just a tiny thing, light blond hair and blue eyes. Allie picked her up. She had been born on the last day of January. It had been a snowy Friday evening, and Mama had suggested all three sisters go and spend the night with Aunt Ollie. The girls had been surprised. Usually they had to beg and beg to get to spend the night with their favorite aunt. Allie and Winna had been excited, but were a little disappointed that Betty had to come along too. They wanted all of Aunt Ollie's attention. It had turned out to be a fun night though. They had played hully gully until way in the night, laughing their heads off at the silly stories their aunt told them. Betty had gone to sleep early, so Allie and Winna had Aunt Ollie to themselves most of the time anyway. The next morning when they got back home, Mama was lying in the bed with little Patsy Ann beside her. The girls were so surprised.

Allie changed Patsy's diaper and patted her tummy. The wet diaper must have been what was making her cry. She began looking at her own little fingers and making baby sounds. She seemed as happy as a kitten with a string.

Going back into the kitchen, Allie saw that Winna was fixing to stir the flour into the cooled mixture. "Let me do that part!" Allie demanded. "You got to sift it, I should at least get to stir it in."

"No, I have to do this part! You won't mix it right. Move!" Winna shouted back.

Allie came up close to Winna and slapped at the air near her face. Winna slapped at Allie, her hand just missing her face. The girls often fought this way when they were angry. They knew better than to actually hit one another, but they did the next best thing. They slapped at one another's faces just managing not to touch. Allie felt the wind of Winna's hand as it went by her cheek. As she jerked back, she bumped the metal bowl on the edge of the counter. The bowl flew off the counter and crashed to the floor. CLINGGG! A cloud of white dust exploded as the flour flew up into the air and scattered over the floor. The loud noise must have startled the two younger sisters because all of a sudden there were two loud sets of bawls coming from the other room.

Mama's eyes flashed. Winna and Allie looked at one another. They knew they had gone too far. "We'll clean it up, Mama," Winna said quickly. Allie nodded, wide-eyed.

"No, I want both you girls to just get on out of the kitchen," Mama said sternly. "Allie, you get Betty ready for church, and, Winna, you get Patsy Ann cleaned up and ready. I'll finish up in here. It doesn't look like we'll have donuts for breakfast this morning after all. We'll just have to make do with biscuits and butter."

"Mama!" Allie began.

"I don't want to hear any more about it," Mama said as she bent down and began to collect the things off the floor, and Allie knew better than to argue.

The girls dropped their shoulders and went into the other room. This bright, beautiful morning had turned dark. Allie looked at Winna with a frown. It was all her fault. They could have been eating those yummy donuts in a little while if Winna hadn't been so mean. She glared at her as she went one way and Winna the other.

After washing and dressing Betty, Allie began getting herself ready for church. Sunlight came in through the window filling the room with sparkling light. It really was a pretty day. Allie could even see some crocuses starting to bloom out by the fence. Maybe Mama would finish up the donuts and let them have them for breakfast after all. Suddenly, Allie began to feel better. She remembered Mr. Schauffler's favorite saying: A smile is a curve that sets everything straight. She put on a smile as she pulled her favorite pink sweater set from the hanger. It felt so good. She took the pink hair ribbon that Mama had wound around the jelly jar to dry last night after she washed it. It had dried smooth and crisp. She pulled her hair up from the sides to the top of her head. After securing it with a rubber band, she tied the pink ribbon into a neat bow. It wasn't as neat as Mama would have made it, but it would have to do this morning. She doubted if Mama would want to mess with her hair after the incident in the kitchen. Looking down from the mirror to the dresser, Allie saw the little cedar box Daddy had given her for her birthday. Opening the lid, she reached in and took out the heart locket. She dangled it up in front of her sweater. The pink roses painted on the white overlay were the exact same color as her sweater. She put the chain around her neck and fastened it. It was so beautiful. She wished she could wear it to church and show her friends. They would be green with envy. What was the good of having something if she couldn't wear it and show it off? Hearing Winna coming, Allie quickly hid the necklace underneath her sweater. It hung unseen from her neck. Allie liked the feel of it against her chest. She also liked having a secret from Winna.

"Here!" Winna said as she handed Allie a dime. Daddy always gave the girls some money each Sunday to leave as an offering at church. The girls always tied their money up in the corner of a handkerchief. That way, the coin couldn't drop out of their pockets unnoticed. It just made it much easier to keep up with.

Church was held at the schoolhouse. The service took place in the big room with the desks in their regular school spots facing the blackboard. During gospel meetings when larger crowds were expected, the partition between the two rooms was raised, but it wasn't necessary for most Sunday services. As the desks filled with people and the hands of the clock moved to ten o'clock, Mr. Huett picked up the brown hymnals from the black metal bookcase in the corner and passed them out. He welcomed the worshippers and began the service by asking the congregation to open to page 104: "The Old Rugged Cross." The church grew quiet except for the crackle of pages being turned. Allie loved to sing along with Mr. Huett. He had a good voice and pitched the songs in a key that was easy to sing along with. Mr. Huett had five children, and they sat toward the front of the room in desks close to their mother. As the members sang the first song, Allie could hear Grandpa's gravely nasal voice above the others. Allie smiled. She glanced at Grandpa. He had his eyes closed and put all his feelings into the words:

On a hill far away
Stood an old rugged cross . . .

Allie sat beside Winna. The two sisters could harmonize beautifully together. They had remained mad at one another on the walk to church, not talking or even looking at one another, but as they sang the hymn, they looked over at the other one and smiled, their voices blending with the others in the small room. They couldn't remain mad at one another for very long while lifting their voices in praise. They both loved to sing, but, even though each was a good singer, it was when they sang together that they really sounded pretty. Mama and Daddy sat behind them; Mama looked pretty in her brown print dress, Daddy in his crisp gray trousers. Mama somehow had gotten all the wrinkles out after all. Baby Patsy was wrapped in a pink blanket, sleeping in Mama's arms. She looked like a little angel with her round face and soft blond hair. Her mouth was drawn up like a rosebud. Allie had offered up many prayers of thanksgiving for this new addition to their family. Betty sat on Daddy's knee smiling broadly, bouncing as Daddy's foot tapped to the rhythm of the song. What a sight she made with her golden curls and wide dimpled grin. She gave Allie a little wave and a giggle when she saw her looking back at her. Allie gave her a wink.

1941: Winna holding baby Patsy, Betty, and Allie

Looking down at her shoes, Allie winced. They had gotten dusty on the walk to church, coating the brown leather in a layer of dust so thick she could write her name in it. Usually, Mama brought a wet rag from home for them to wipe off their shoes when they got to the church building, but this morning had been so rushed, she must have forgotten. In the summertime, some of their cousins actually carried their shoes with them to church. Their moms would bring along a wet rag, and they'd wash their feet when they got to the church building before stepping into their clean shoes. Allie was glad Mama didn't make them do that.

Many of her cousins were at church this morning. She looked over at Aunt Lottie and Uncle Horace and sighed. She couldn't believe her cousins were fixing to have to move away. Uncle Horace had found work in Melbourne and was taking the family with him. It broke Allie's heart. She and Erma Faye were exactly the same age and had been best friends for as long as she could remember. Joanna was Winna's age, and little Carol Sue was Betty's age. It was like every time Mama had a baby, Aunt Lottie had one too. Allie and Winna loved playing with Joanna and Erma Faye. They lived just down the road from them, but the girls usually played in a place halfway between their houses. There was a certain tree that Allie and Winna were allowed to go to and holler to them and see if they could come up the road and play. Erma Faye and Joanne also had a certain post they could come to and call to Allie and Winna. Seldom were the girls allowed to go to one another's houses to play, but it suited them fine because there were so many fun things to do outside. Sometimes, they took their catalog paper dolls down the road and made rooms in the dirt and in the mossy places under the cedars for them along with their flat oat box cars. They would play for hours. They also loved playing in the huge sand beds around there. They would make sand castles and frog houses. The best sand was usually in the middle of the road where the wagon wheels kept the sand ground up fine and smooth. Many were the times when a wagon would come along and the driver would find an elaborate sand castle in the middle of his path. Reining the team to the far side of the road, the wagon would pass leaving the castle unharmed. Sometimes the girls would climb chinquapin trees and gather nuts and play hully gully. Allie's eyes filled with tears. How could she go on without her best friends? Uncle Horace had promised it wouldn't be for too long; Allie sure hoped it wasn't.

Daddy must have sensed her sadness because as they stood to sing another song, he reached out a hand and put it on Allie's shoulder and gave it a squeeze. That did make the tears come. She loved Daddy so much. He always seemed to be able to read her mind and know when she needed a loving hand. Daddy had gotten home so late this morning after helping Grandpa with the cow that they had just enough time to gobble down some biscuits and sorghum before heading out to services. Mama wouldn't think of eating without him. Thankfully, there hadn't been time for Mama to relate the events of the morning to Daddy. It had been a quiet walk to town though, and Daddy must have wondered why Allie and Winna weren't gabbing back and forth as usual. The plate of donuts that Mama had somehow managed to finish sat on the cabinet under a white cloth covering. Allie hoped they could have them for dinner when they got home.

Following the final song, Mr. Blue stood to deliver the sermon. Today, he spoke about the trials one might have to endure in life but how each difficult thing one goes through just makes him stronger. It reminded Allie of the story Mama told when times were hard for her and Daddy a few years ago. They never liked to buy things on credit. Daddy liked to pay cash for the things he bought and so did Mama. One time though, during the Depression, times were really bad. In fact, it had gotten so bad Mama needed some groceries, and she was going to have to ask Mr. Huett for some credit. Mama had prayed about it because she really just didn't feel like buying on credit was the thing to do. At last though, she didn't see any other way. So she sadly started out for the store. On her way there, she found a dollar bill lying in the road. That dollar bill bought the food they really had to have. It was like God had answered her prayer. Yes, Mama and Daddy had gone through some hard times, and Allie supposed it did make them stronger. She looked around the room at all the individuals and wondered what hard times each of them had been through. She thought of sickness, poverty, and even death. One never knew what life would bring. She shuddered. Allie wondered what hard times lay in store for each of them in this room, even herself.

After the sermon, the members partook of the Lord's Supper. Mrs. Huett prepared the bread each week by baking pie crust. She made cuts in the wafers, making sections to where it easily broke off into little squares. The congregation stood to take of the bread and fruit juice. As they finished each emblem, they sat down. Once that was done, everyone stood as the last song was sung. During the singing, members would go up to the front and place their offering on the table. Allie and Winna took their turn going forward, placing their dimes on the white linen cloth. Finally, Grandpa Shoemate was asked to say the closing prayer. He got down on one knee as was his custom and began. He finished with "Lord, be with us as we go to our places of abode and abide with us where we stay. In Jesus' name, amen."

Allie walked out with Uncle Henry and Aunt Violet and some of their children: Conrad, Willa Mae, Anna Faye, Bernard, Melvin, and Travis. Lillian and Raymond were their children too, but they were already grown and married. Aunt Violet held Uncle Henry's arm as he was blind.

It turned out to be a lazy afternoon for the most part. The fire in the cookstove had gone out when they'd gotten home from church, so they just ate a cold dinner. To Allie and Winna's dismay, Mama told them they'd save the donuts for later. Soon after, little Patsy and Betty drifted off to sleep and Daddy left for Raymond and Alma's. Raymond was Uncle Henry's son. He and Alma had the cutest little daughter Lanetta, or Nettie for short, who was about Betty's age. After Daddy left, Winna and Allie curled up on the bed to read. The house was a little chilly without a fire, so they cuddled up under the covers and read for most of the afternoon. Later, they became bored and decided to walk down and check on Daddy.

Mama was glad to see them when they got back home. "Girls, take care of the little ones while I start a fire. It's not that cold, but I think I'll build up a little chip fire to knock the chill out of the house for the babies."

"Sure, Mom," they answered. Winna got Patsy, and Allie went to play with Betty.

Allie walked over to the bed beside Betty. "Wanta string some buttons, Betty?" Allie asked.

"Buttons!" Betty parroted. Allie grabbed the button box and a needle and thread. It was a special treat to Betty to get to play with buttons. Mama wouldn't let her play with them by herself, afraid she'd put one in her mouth and get choked. Betty always jumped at the chance to string buttons. Allie climbed up on the bed and poured out some buttons. She knotted one on the end of the string and held the needle while Betty put one after another button onto the string. They clattered and clanked as they dropped down the string. "Pretty!" Betty clapped.

Mama gathered some chips from the back porch. She placed some of the dry chips in the stove and soon had a flame going. "Okay, girls," Mama said, "You all can go ahead and start after the water if you'd like."

Allie and Winna got the water buckets off the counter. They stepped out the door and started down the steps. The wind whipped their hair around like laundry on the line and caught their open sweaters blowing them out like capes behind them. They were taking a chance going after the water while still wearing their church sweaters, but they had promised Mama they would be extra careful not to snag them on the branches or get them dirty. The whole family was going down to Uncle Horace and Aunt Lottie's tonight after supper for a little going-away party. Winna and Allie wanted to keep their good clothes on to look nice for that. They were hoping maybe Joanna and Erma Faye could spend the night with them tonight since it was going to be their last night here.

"Let's stop and see if Grandma needs some water," Winna said.

Grandma was already getting supper ready. She and Grandpa went to bed with the chickens, so they had an early supper. Grandma was making biscuits. She made her biscuits in a dishpan. First, she put in a bunch of flour and a little salt and baking powder. Next, she added the shortening and worked it together using her fingers. Finally, she added the milk a little at a time and worked it until it was of the right consistency. Grandma didn't roll out her biscuit dough like Mama. She pinched off the dough and placed them in her pan. Allie loved Grandma's biscuits, and she could always find some leftover biscuits in her cupboard when she got a little hungry anytime during the day.

"Grandma, do you need any water?" Winna asked coming into the kitchen.

"Well, that is right kindly of you girls to stop and check," Grandma said, "but Papa went down and brought us two fresh buckets just a little bit ago."

"Oh, okay," Winna said.

"Grandma, are you and Grandpa going down to Uncle Horace's tonight?" Allie asked.

"I don't guess so," Grandma said. "Papa and I go to bed so early, we'd probably nod off to sleep if we did. We'll see them off in the morning though."

Allie picked up her buckets and started out the door as Grandma showed Winna the dresser scarf she had been embroidering. Grandma had been teaching Winna how to do some new stitches. Allie walked out onto the screened-in porch and happened to glance over at her own house. She screamed! Smoke was twisting up into the air and a fire about the size of chair was blazing on their shingled roof. "Our house is afire!" Allie screamed. Winna ran out of the house with Grandma and Grandpa right behind her. The fire was spreading fast and now was the size of a table. The wind whipped the fire around, and the pine shingles burned like paper.

Grandma, Grandpa, Winna, and Allie ran screaming at the top of their lungs for Mama. Mama must have heard because she ran out of the house with a baby in both arms. Her face was ghostly white, and she wore a look of horror. Grandpa and Winna ran into the house and began pulling things out. The fire was spreading fast, and, not having any water nearby, there was nothing to use to try and put it out. Mama ran over and handed little Pat to Allie. "Watch Betty!" she shouted. Mama ran into the burning house to help save what she could. Smoke was billowing now. It burned Allie's eyes, and Betty was coughing. The pine shingles popped and burning cinders flew in every direction in the wind.

"Betty, come here," Allie screamed as she pulled Betty farther from the heat. Betty was crying and Patsy was squirming and bawling too. Allie sat on the ground and tried to hold both babies. Betty clung to her, burying her face in Allie's neck.

Allie watched as Grandpa, Winna, and Mama carried things from the house. Grandma was trying to help too, but Grandpa kept telling her to get back. Suddenly, Allie heard Mama scream. She had rolled up a feather mattress and was trying to get it out the door. The mattress was too big, and Mama was stuck. Allie screamed and jumped to her feet causing both sisters to tumble onto the ground. Just then she saw Grandpa grab the mattress from the outside and pull hard. The mattress ripped from the doorway, Mama falling with it and feathers flying wildly up into the air. Just then shouts were heard coming up the lane. Daddy and the others had seen the smoke and knew it must be their house. Grandpa ran from the house for the last time carrying Mama's clock.

"Is everyone out? Is everyone out?" Daddy was screaming. Tears were streaming down his face as he looked nervously around wanting to account for each of his precious loved ones. "Is everyone out?" he said over and over. By this time, Mama, Grandpa, Grandma, and Winna were out of the house. It had started falling in and the smoke was too thick and the heat too intense for them to be very near. Raymond, Alma, Uncle Horace, and Uncle George came running behind Daddy. Mama went over to Daddy. She put her arms around him and assured him everyone was out of the house. Mama buried her head in Daddy's chest as he stood and watched all that they had go up in smoke. There was really nothing anyone could do now. Winna went over and got little Patsy from Allie. They couldn't believe this all had happened so fast. Finally, the roof fell in with a loud crash and billows of black smoke reared high into the sky. By this time, neighbors and friends were gathering on horseback, buggy, and on foot. The smoke could be seen for miles around.

That night, Allie lay in one of Grandma's beds and thought about everything that had happened. It had been a terrible day. After the fire, they had gone through the few things that had been pulled from the house. It was very little really. Mama kept saying if she had only pulled the box of baby things from under the bed. Winna kept saying how foolish she had been to not have thrown things out the windows. She said she hadn't wanted to break the windows, but looking back on it later, she realized she could have saved so much more if she had done just that. Mama felt like it was her fault in building the chip fire. The small chips must have flown up the chimney and landed on the dry pine shingles. The wind had provided the air that made the cinders burst into flame. Daddy tried to assure everyone that it was no one's fault and that he was just so very thankful that Allie saw the fire when she did and that no one was hurt.

Allie closed her eyes and let the tears roll down the side of her face into her pillow. For some reason, she thought of Great-grandma Rand.

Sara Elizabeth (Tinkle) Rand 1865–1947, William
Thomas Harrison Rand 1866–1931 Married 1881, Allie's
great-grandparents, Grandma Shoemate's parents

After Grandpa Rand died, Grandma didn't really have
a home of her own. She stayed with first one of her kids
and then another. She really didn't have much of her own;
the few things she did have she kept in a little red box.
Allie had watched her great-grandma take all the things out

of her box and lovingly handle each item. She had some dresser scarves, pillowcases, and some old doilies. After handling each item, she'd carefully place each item back in the box. It always seemed so sad to Allie watching her great-grandma do this. How sad to be without a home and things of your own. She felt a little like Great-grandma tonight. What would they do without a home? And what about all their stuff? What about her own stuff? Suddenly Allie sat bolt upright in bed. Her hand flew to her neck! Her necklace! It wasn't there! She had had her necklace on this morning. Had she taken it off? She remembered having it on when Winna came in to give her the dime from Daddy. She couldn't remember taking it back off, but she must have. It wasn't on her neck now. If only she had kept it on. Tears rolled and a sob escaped as she thought of the treasures she received for her birthday now gone. Everything gone. What must Mama and Daddy be feeling right now? What was to happen to all of them?

Chapter 7

I'll tell you a story Grandpa Crotts told me. And, and, and . . . it's a pretty good one, I think. He told me that he worked for a dollar a day for Pete Baker. They say he had an ole possum dog and in the wintertime that he'd get up early of a morning and he'd possum hunt to the sawmill. He'd catch three or four possums and get a dollar apiece for 'em. And work all day (at the sawmill) for a dollar. I told him, I said, I'd quit the durn sawmill and hunt possum straight time. And he (Grandpa) said, said, I needed that job next summer, you know. So he couldn't quit the . . . couldn't quit the job until possum season was over because if he did somebody else would get his job.

—Bobbie (1990)

Bobbie

March 1941

What a morning! It all started around 6:30 when Grandpa Crotts came by with his dog Drum. He wanted to know if Bobbie and Willie wanted to go possum hunting with him and Thurman. Thurman was Grandpa's youngest son. He was exactly in between Bobbie and Willie in age being two years younger than Bobbie and two years older than Willie. The price of possum hide had gone up, way up. A good-size pelt these days was going for $1 apiece. That was good money, and it had anyone who could halfway shoot a gun out looking for the critters. Bobbie and Willie couldn't get dressed fast enough. They loved spending time with Grandpa, and they loved most kinds of hunting.

Now possums are nocturnal animals. That means they are active during the nighttime and spend most of the day curled up in a nest somewhere hardly moving at all. So most people who hunt them have to do it at night. It's rare to see a possum in the daylight. Grandpa had an advantage over most people though when it came to possum hunting. His old dog Drum was pretty much the best possum dog in the country. He could smell out one of those rascals from close to a half mile away. This morning, Drum must have known he was going hunting because he was excited and jumping around like a skillet full of popcorn. "Come on, boys," Grandpa hollered as he waited out at the gate for them. "Drum's raring to go!"

Grandpa Crotts

The boys hurried out the door and headed off down the hill south of town following Grandpa. "Where're we going, Grandpa?" Willie asked reaching behind his shoulder and fastening his overall's suspenders. He had dressed so quickly that his shoes were on the wrong feet and the straps of his overalls were twisted and turned every which way. He was falling all over himself trying to catch up with the others.

"I thought we'd start off down by the branch," Grandpa answered looking over at him. "They like to build their dens in around water, ya know. I reckon we ought to find us a good one down in there sommers."

"Grandpa, where's your gun?" Bobbie asked as he noticed the only thing Grandpa was carrying was a stick around a foot and a half long.

"Gun?" Grandpa roared. "We're not going to mess up a durn good hide with a gunshot hole through it. No sir! I've got my trick of getting those rascals. You boys just stick around and learn somepin from yor ole grandpappie." Grandpa let out a bellowed laugh. "Yes, sir, we'll git us some hides 'fore this mornin's over, boys."

The boys hurried along after Grandpa stretching their legs to try and match the strides of his. Grandpa whistled a tune as he walked along, a mixture of "Ole Dan Tucker" and "Yankee Doodle." Grandpa was a jolly man who loved to whistle and sing. They made a funny sight this morning, Grandpa stepping it off through the field with his iron-gray hair sticking up every which way and his clothes wrinkled and patched, three tagalong Ruffins doing their best to keep up with their Grandpa Ruffin. It was a fine morning. The sun had started its slow climb up over the hills and it looked like the start to a pretty day. The birds were chirping from just about every tree limb, and the sounds of cicadas and crickets made a glorious morning song.

A half a mile or so from the house, they came upon a drove of pigs rooting around in the dirt underneath a stand of red oaks. The ground was muddy where they had trampled and dug looking for acorns to eat. Bobbie could hear the squishing and sucking sounds as the pigs' feet sunk and lifted from the manure-smeared mud. The pigs were a noisy lot. The combination of their eating, smacking, oinking, and rooting was so noisy that Thurman had to shout for the others to hear him.

"Are them some of our pigs?" he wanted to know.

Grandpa and the boys stopped for a minute to look them over. There was a mixture of black-and-white ones, solid blacks, and a few whites. Everyone in the community had hogs. The pigs just ran wild feeding on acorns and whatever else they could find. They usually traveled in small herds, and they didn't care where they went to find food, whether it was in the fields, woods, or in someone's garden. They were a downright aggravation to everyone in the area, but since everyone had hogs, it was a nuisance everyone had to endure. Momma would get so mad when they'd get in her precious garden. During the day, it was the kids' job to keep them run out, but many were the mornings Momma would wake up to find her cabbages and carrots dug up and ruined and her beans and corn trampled by them during the night.

Folks would butcher their hogs when the weather was cold enough to keep the meat from spoiling. They wanted to get the hogs just as fat as they could before butchering them so they could have plenty of fat on them to render into lard. They'd watch the hogs when they'd eat, and when a hog was so heavy, he'd not even stand up to eat, well then, he was fat enough to butcher. They hated to kill a hog that weighed less than four or five hundred pounds. They were big!

"Now you fellers know our mark, don't you?" Grandpa asked looking over at the boys with a questioning look on his face. "How can we tell our hogs from everybody else's?"

"I do," Willie boasted. "A crop and a split in the left, an under bit in the right."

"Yessir," Grandpa said with a toothless grin. "That's our mark. You boys always remember that, and always respect another feller's mark. It's a dang shame when—"

Grandpa stopped in the middle of his sentence and let out a whoop as old Drum took off running, barking loud enough to set the ground to shaking. The three hunters took out after him as the pigs squealed and took off running in the other direction.

The boys hollered words of encouragement to old Drum as they tried to catch up.

"Get him, Drum! Get us a possum hide, boy!" Willie yelled.

"Wahoo!" Bobbie joined in delight as he dodged limbs racing downhill.

Briars caught at their britches and coat sleeves as the boys zigzagged this way and that through the tangle of brush, breathless by now. They were leaving Grandpa behind. After several yards of running, he'd had to slow his pace to a walk, so the boys caught up to the dog first. Ole Drum was hunkered down on his belly clawing at the end of an old rotting tree. The tree had once stood tall and proud beside the stream, but years of flowing water around its base had washed most of the earth away, exposing its massive roots. It had finally lost its grip, whether from fierce winds or a strong current, and fallen, landing across the stream. It was lodged up against the bank on the other side making a makeshift bridge from one side of the stream to the other. Some of the branches stuck down into the muddy water, and leaves and other debris were caught up in its grasp. The water was low now, but the streambed was wide, a sure sign that it carried a lot of water during the earlier days of spring.

Drum was grunting and digging, throwing up pieces of wood and mud in his attempt to get to whatever was hiding in the trunk of that tree. Thurman ran over and grabbed hold of him just as Grandpa came stumbling out of the underbrush looking like the scarecrow in Momma's vegetable garden.

"Hold on, boys," Grandpa huffed out as he hurried over to them. "He ain't goin' nowhere."

The boys stepped back, making room for Grandpa as he hurried up to them. He was breathing heavily and put his hands on his knees as he took several deep breaths. He had a big smile on his red face, but the veins in his neck were pumping hard out and in as he finally bent down to assess the situation.

"Yessir. I think we've got us a possum pinned up in this here hole," he said with a smile. "Now watcha here while I show you how to get him outta there."

Grandpa picked up the stick he'd been carrying. The boys noticed that at one end of the stick Grandpa had cut out a fork about two inches long. It made a sort of prong on the end of it. It looked something like the pole they used for gigging fish, only smaller and shorter. Grandpa raised the stick and stuck the forked end of it into the hole. He stopped when the stick would go no farther. He nodded at the boys and then frowned in deep concentration as he started twisting the stick. He kept pressure on the stick while he gave it a couple more twists. Finally, he began slowly to ease the stick out of the hole. The boys stood on either side of Grandpa wide-eyed, watching his every move. As Grandpa pulled the stick farther and farther out of the hole, a grayish-white ball of fur appeared.

"One of you boys run over there and fetch me a club," Grandpa ordered. The boys pulled themselves away from the action at the tree and began searching for something that might serve as a club.

"How about this?" Thurman yelled holding up a good-sized limb about four inches thick.

"That orta do," Grandpa hollered, glancing over his shoulder. Not knowing quite what to expect, Bobbie and Willie gathered up clubs of their own. If Grandpa needed a club, they didn't want to be left unprotected. The boys raised their clubs higher as Grandpa pulled the possum all the way out of the hole. They could see now how he had gotten the possum out. When Grandpa had worked the stick into the hole, the forked end of the stick had stuck down into the possum's fur. The loose hide had been twisted around the stick, and Grandpa had pulled on the stick bringing the possum out of the hole.

The possum started hissing and showing its teeth. "Give me that stick, Thurman, and then you boys get on back," Grandpa said.

The boys didn't argue with Grandpa's command. That possum had a whole mouth full of teeth, and each one looked about as sharp as Momma's sewing needle. All of a sudden, the possum fell over like it was dead.

"What happened?" Willie wanted to know.

Grandpa laughed. "The old feller is playing possum. They do that when they feel threatened."

"Is he dead?" Bobbie asked.

"Not yet," Grandpa said, "but he's about to be." He raised the club Thurman had handed him and whacked the possum right smart up against his head. "He's dead now," Grandpa said with a wink.

The boys went up close to inspect the animal. It was a big possum with a long, slender body. It had a pointed snout, and its fur was a grayish white. Grandpa ran his hand over its fur, revealing the softer, lighter hair underneath. Its face was pinkish white with a pink nose and black eyes. It had large furless ears.

"Looky here at his tail," Grandpa said, holding on to its tail and lifting it up in the air. "This tail is important to a possum. It uses it to hold on with and to help it climb."

The boys noticed that most of the tail was hairless like its ears.

"How much do you think this will bring us?" Thurman wanted to know.

"Beings it is good-sized—with no bullet hole," Grandpa said as he drew his bushy eyebrows down and smiled, "I'd say we'll get us a whopping dollar bill!"

The boys smiled, dollar signs glowing in their eyes. "That sure seems like easy money," Bobbie said. "I have to work a whole week building fires at the school for a dollar."

"Yep, and I have to work a full day at the sawmill fer a dollar. I guess we can call this here our bonus money," Grandpa said with a toothless grin.

Bobbie wondered if they would eat the possum after they skinned it. He hoped not. He had eaten possum before. It was a dark meat and very greasy. He knew when times were hard a person would eat whatever they could, but he'd have to be pretty hungry to eat another possum. He decided not to ask Grandpa about that. It might give him the idea. The only useful thing Bobbie could think of for possums, besides the money they could get for their hides, was to grease your shoes with them.

After the first kill, the boys were certain they were on their way to riches. They couldn't wait to catch their next possum. "Where're we going next?" they wanted to know.

"Let's just walk this here branch and see if ole Drum can sniff us out another one," Grandpa said as he picked up his stick and handed the possum to Bobbie to carry. They started up the branch.

"I've got a riddle for you, boys," said Grandpa. The boys grinned at one another and shook their heads. Grandpa always had a riddle or joke of some kind or another. Grandpa cleared his throat and began to rapidly chant the riddle: "As I was walking through the Whirley Wheel Whackum, I met Bum Backum. I called Tum Tackum, and he run Bum Backum out of the Whirley Wheel Whackum."

The boys howled. "Grandpa, that don't mean nothing," Willie said.

"It shore does. You just gotta use that old noggin of yours," Grandpa said as he reached out and gave Bobbie's head a hard thump with his knuckles.

"I give up," Willie said.

"Well," Grandpa smiled. "The riddle is this. A guy was walking through the wheat field. He met his ole cow. He called his dog, Tum Tackum, and he run Bum Backum, his cow, out of the field, the Whirley Wheel Whackum."

All four of them had a good laugh, and Grandpa had to tell it again and again until each boy could say the riddle himself. They couldn't wait to tell it to their friends.

About that time, ole Drum's barking told them he had sniffed out another possum. "Let's go collect that dollar bill," Grandpa laughed and clicked his tongue.

This time, Drum was standing reared up on a rocky bluff. He was jumping up onto the bluff and scratching at some rocks lodged together. Gravel and sand were falling down on him as he continued his barking and clawing.

"Can I do it this time, Daddy? Can I? Can I?" Thurman begged.

Willie and Bobbie looked at one another and frowned. They each thought they should get to be the one to get him out. They were hoping Grandpa told him no.

"Let's see here, boys," Grandpa said, coming up to the bluff and looking things over. He grabbed hold of Drum and pulled him away. "It looks like he might be in there amongst those rocks. I don't think you can reach up that high, and if you go to climbing, it'll start those rocks sliding down on us."

The boys could see that Grandpa was right. There was a pile of rocks at the bottom of the bluff where some had already fallen. Grandpa made his way carefully over the shifting rocks trying to find a good steady place to stand. He pulled Drum away again and told Willie to hold on to him.

"Now let's see if we can't get us another buck," Grandpa said, slapping Thurman on the back. The boys watched as Grandpa climbed up on one of the larger rocks and began easing his stick into the crevice in the rocks. They could tell when the stick hit something because Grandpa looked down at them and gave them a big wink. He began twisting the stick. "Run, grab me a club," he hollered down. Bobbie was the one to find the first club this time. He climbed up to where Grandpa was standing ready to hand it over for the fatal blow.

The boys watched in wonder as Grandpa once again eased the stick out of the hole. Then everything happened so fast the boys really didn't know what was happening until it was over. Old Drum had not sniffed out a possum this time. What Grandpa pulled out of that hole was a big fat copperhead, and it wasn't any too happy about being dragged out of its hole. It sank its sharp fangs into Grandpa's finger that was holding on to the stick. Grandpa swore and slung the stick and the snake. The snake landed behind the boys who threw down their clubs and took off running and screaming at the top of their lungs. It was a good three or four minutes before they finally stopped running and calmed down enough to think about going back to check on Grandpa.

When they got back to the bluff, they saw that the snake was gone. They looked around nervously then up at Grandpa. He was sitting on one of the big rocks. His face was pasty white and big drops of sweat were dripping off his nose. He was digging around in the pockets of his pants.

"What are you doing, Daddy?" Thurman asked in a trembling voice.

"I gotta get that poison out," Grandpa mumbled. He took his big hanky out of his pocket and tied it around his forearm. Putting one end of it in his mouth and holding on to the other end, he pulled tighter and tighter. "Do one of you boys have a knife on you?"

"I got mine," Bobbie said as he reached down into his overalls' pocket and brought out his Christmas knife with trembling hand.

"Bring it on up here, son," Grandpa instructed.

Bobbie climbed up on the rock where Grandpa sat. He opened the knife and handed it out to Grandpa. The other boys climbed up as well. They watched as Grandpa took the knife and made a cut between the two holes in his finger. He winced and blood squirted out and ran down his hand onto the rocks. He handed the knife back to Bobbie. Then Grandpa took his finger to his mouth and sucked at the cut. He spit the bloody liquid from his mouth and repeated it two or three times. The boys couldn't move. Their legs were weak, and their chests felt like they had Cap Robbins blacksmith's hammer in there pounding; their hearts were beating so hard. Willie had started to cry, and Thurman looked as if he were about to go limp like the possum had a little while ago.

"Help me down, boys, so I can rinse my mouth out in the water," Grandpa said weakly.

The boys gathered around Grandpa and helped him off the rocks. They led him over to the edge of the branch where he stooped and took up some water. He rinsed his mouth and spit, rinsed and spit over and over. Next, he put his hand in the water and splashed it around and around over and over. Finally, he took the handkerchief from around his arm and wrapped it around his finger.

"Let's get on home, boys. I better let the doc look at this." Grandpa was as white as the belly of a frog. He splashed a little water on his face before standing. Thurman reached up and draped Grandpa's arm over his shoulder, and Willie got hold of his other arm. Bobbie called to Drum and picked up the dead possum. They began the slow trek up the hill. The fun day had turned into a terrifying day, one they would never forget.

Grandpa's snakebite caused quite a stir in the small community. Grandpa's hand had swollen double in size by the time they made it back to town. Doc. Sutton treated Grandpa's bite and sent him home to go to bed. Momma insisted Grandpa stay with her so she could keep an eye on him.

Bobbie, Willie, and Thurman stuck close to Grandpa most of the day. He slept most of the time, and Momma was in and out of the room every little bit checking on him. The boys had never seen Grandpa sick or hurt, and it hurt them about as much to see Grandpa in bed as the snakebite hurt Grandpa.

As Bobbie sat beside Grandpa's bed, he thought how much he loved this man. Grandpa was always jolly and singing. Bobbie loved to hear him sing; they all did. A person could give Grandpa just about any song, and, as long as there were musical notes with it, Grandpa could figure out the tune and how to sing it. Bobbie didn't really know where Grandpa had learned to read music like he did. He could read all those funny signs in the songbooks that told how the tune was supposed to go. He could sing the do, re, mi notes up and down the scale. Grandpa wasn't just smart with music either. He had gotten an eighth-grade education at the Old Hickory School and could do a lot of things others in the community weren't able to do.

THE SALEM HEADLIGHT

Hickory Grove School West Of
Viola, Arkansas, 1899...

Back Row, L to R: Lena Crotts, Bertha Ivester, Dr. Smith, Vinnie Jinkins, Kert Jinkins, and Steve Jinkins.
Third Row, L to R: Claud Crotts, Jesse Marotte, Ruffen Crotts, Henry Marotte, Oscar Foster, Willie Ivester, and Ethel Ivester.
L to R, Second Row: Cecil Harber, Guy Divenbless, Eliza Mroatte, Chloe Stone, Grace Divenbless, and Elizabeth Harber.
Front Row: L to R: First to are unknown, Porter Harber, Audie Ivester.

Grandpa Crotts as a boy at Old Hickory
School, third row, third from left

Bobbie supposed it was Grandpa's own pa that had given him this advantage. John Crotts, Grandpa's pa, was an educated man. He and his wife came from North Carolina from a place called Cow Pen. They moved here around 1890 and settled alongside the river at Henderson. They had a large family, ten or eleven children. Grandpa Crotts was the oldest child. Bobbie had learned their names. Ruffin (Grandpa), Claude, Leener, Dessie, Johnny, Lester, Otto, Tommie, Bertha, and Gertrude. Bertha had died when she was just seventeen. The first three kids had been born in North Carolina. Great-grandpa had owned a black slave while living in North Carolina. Really, she was more like part of the family, and she loved the three little ones so much. Bobbie knew at this time she really couldn't have been a slave because they had all been freed by then. He supposed she might have been his slave once and had chosen to stay on with the family after receiving her freedom. She had wanted to come with them when they decided to move to Arkansas, but, for whatever reason, she wasn't able to. It had broken her heart when they left her behind, Grandpa had been told. Great-grandma's name was Belinda Alice (Newton). Bobbie supposed that was where his momma got her name, Eva Alice, being named after her grandmother. He'd have to remember to ask Momma about it.

Great-grandpa had been a farmer. He'd also had a blacksmith's shop part of the time, Bobbie had learned. But what fascinated Bobbie the most was that his great-grandpa had also been a teacher. Imagine that, a teacher like Mr. Schauffler. He taught school for quite a while. In fact, on his way to Arkansas from North Carolina, he had stopped two or three different places and taught. He would teach a summer term or a winter term and earn a little extra money before moving on. He even taught at Old Hickory Road School, where Grandpa went to school when he was a boy, for quite a while once they settled in this area. Bobbie didn't know whether or not Grandpa Crotts ever had his own daddy as a teacher, but he felt proud that his great-granddad had been a teacher and that his grandpa Crotts was so smart and had gotten such a good education in a time when it was difficult to get an education in this part of the country.

Bobbie had sat too long. Thurman and Willie had wandered out of the room some time ago, but Bobbie had stayed. He was getting sleepy—best get up and stir. Grandpa was sleeping anyway, so Bobbie decided to get back outside for a while before the sun went down. He grabbed his jacket off the end of the bed and told Momma he'd be back before supper.

He walked out to the smokehouse to put his dollar that Mr. Schauffler had given him yesterday into his Prince Albert can. This was probably one of the last dollars he'd make until cold weather hit again next fall. He was sure going to miss the money. He wished he could find some way of making some money in the summer. He liked having his own money, not that he spent much of it. It was just nice knowing he had some stashed back, and he liked having it come in every week. Bobbie opened the door of the smokehouse and scooted the barrel across the floor. Lifting up the loose board, he reached his hand beneath the floorboard for the can. He moved his hand across the hard ground not feeling a thing, panic rising in his chest with each swipe of his hand. The can wasn't there! He dropped down on his stomach and stuck his hand further into the hole. The can had always been right there within easy reach. Full panic now did seize him. It had to be there. No one knew where he kept his money. He hadn't even told his parents. Bobbie jumped up and ran out of the smokehouse and into the house. Running to the cupboard, he grabbed up some matches and ran back to the smokehouse. Bending back down to the hole, he struck one match after the other and searched every inch of space underneath the smokehouse. It was no use. The Prince Albert tobacco can was nowhere. This couldn't be.

Bobbie sat down on the floor of the smokehouse and buried his head in his hands. Tears welled up in his eyes. It didn't make sense. There was no way it could have been washed away. An animal couldn't have dug it out. There was only one explanation: someone had taken it. Bobbie thought back to when he'd last seen it. It was the day he'd gone to the store and traded in ten one-dollar bills for a ten-dollar bill. He'd come back from the store and put it in the can. Willie had gone with him, but Willie wouldn't have taken it. Willie didn't even know about his money or even care. *Wait a minute. Wait just a doggone minute*, Bobbie thought. He remembered the dogs and how they were barking that night. Maybe there was someone out there. Maybe someone had followed him home. Bobbie moved the barrel back over the loose floorboard and sat for a few more minutes. Could someone have watched him? He looked at the side of the smokehouse at the wide cracks between the boards. If someone had wanted to, he could certainly have watched him move the corn barrel aside.

Slowly he opened the door. Slamming the door hard, he latched the door. He walked behind the shed to see if he could see any evidence of footprints. All he could detect were chicken tracks. Bobbie kicked at the dirt and stalked off down the road. He didn't know where he was going, but he had to walk and try to cool off. If he didn't, he was liable to punch the first person he met.

Bobbie found himself walking over toward the Stephens' place. It was shore nuff a shame about their house burning a couple of days ago. He wasn't the only one with problems, he supposed. He felt sorry for Allie and her family. He couldn't imagine losing most everything like they had. All of a sudden, his loss didn't seem quite so bad. Bobbie had actually been down at Uncle Raymond and Aunt Alma's with several others when they had seen the smoke from the Stephens' house. He'd run up to help with everybody else, but, by the time they had gotten there, the roof was starting to cave in. He'd seen they'd gotten a few things out: an ole ripped mattress, a clock, and a couple of chairs. He had especially hurt for Allie. She looked so pitiful standing over by the side of the road holding the little ones like she was—tear streaks running through the soot on her face.

Bobbie walked on. As he came up the hill, he looked over at the black heap and ashes. The empty space looked odd where the house used to stand. He looked around and began poking around in the ashes for anything that might have been overlooked. He knew Mr. Stephens must have already combed through the rubble for anything that might have come through the fire, but there wasn't any harm in a second pair of eyes looking for what another's eyes might have missed. He didn't see a thing that was still of any use. His shoes crunched on the charred and burned wood: the remains of ruined dishes, bed frames, old picture frames. Hmmm, these looked like charred donuts! Suddenly he saw a head to a hammer. That could be of use! He picked it up and tossed it out onto the grass where they were sure to find it. Mr. Stephens could add a new handle, and it would serve him well. He walked over to where Allie had been standing with the babies. She'd stood here under this tree and had to watch her home fall down timber by timber. Suddenly, something on the ground caught his eye, a flash of something bright in the late rays of the sun. He bent and picked it up. Why, it was the necklace her grandpa had given her for her birthday. He recognized the little pink roses on the front. Slipping his thumbnail in the side, he opened the heart. Inside was the name Peeny carved in the shiny metal confirming it to be the special necklace. How had the necklace ended up here? Allie must have had it on when she was standing out here with her sisters. It must have fallen off. Bobbie looked at the end of the necklace. The chain was broken. He put the necklace down inside his jacket pocket. He'd take it to school on Monday and give it back to her. Wouldn't she be surprised! Maybe that would make her take notice of him. That would serve Cody right.

Bobbie scratched his head. He didn't know whether to be mad or glad: mad about the money, glad about the necklace. One never knew what the day would bring. This day had certainly been eventful. In just a few hours he'd been rich, poor, robbed, and seen his grandpa snakebitten. Bobbie turned and started down the hill in a lope. Times like this there was only one thing to do, hightail it for home. And that's just what he did.

Chapter 8

I remember Mom telling me about a time during the Depression when they had to do without almost everything. She was walking to the store to ask George Huett for credit, which hurt and embarrassed her and Dad, when she found a dollar bill in the road. A dollar could buy a lot then, probably everything on her small list, but she struggled to know if it was right to keep it or if she should ask at the store if anyone had lost it. She knew though that everyone else was just as desperate for money as she and would state that they had lost it if asked. She thanked God for the money and bought what she needed. That almost brings tears to my eyes.

—Carol (Allie's youngest sister) (2010)

Allie

April 1941

Allie's back ached from carrying the sheet of dirty clothes she had flung over her back. The stiff cotton material cut into her shoulder as she struggled to get it down the steep hill to the spring. Her green lard bucket containing her lunch dangled from her elbow leaving a deep red groove in the bend of her arm. She wasn't going to complain though. Winna was carrying the sheet with Daddy's overalls in it, making it the heavier of the two loads. Winna also had the bucket with the starch and P&G soap. At last, they reached the bottom of the hill. The girls dropped their loads beside the bench, stretched, and groaned. Rolling their shoulders up and down, they swung their arms around in circles to work out the aches.

"I feel like a packhorse," Allie complained with a sigh. She plopped down on the mound of clothes she'd been carrying. Falling back in a heap with her arms outstretched, she resembled a rag doll carelessly tossed aside. "My bundle must have weighed at least fifty pounds," she groaned.

"I know," Winna said as she settled herself down onto her own pile. "I guess we should just be thankful we have clothes to wash though."

Allie immediately felt ashamed. Of course, they should be thankful. She didn't know what they would even be

MAKING A BEELINE HOME

wearing at this very minute or what they would have done if it hadn't been for the generosity of their kind neighbors. A few days following their house fire, they had been surprised to see a flatbed log truck pull up in front of Grandma and Grandpa's. As everyone came out of the house, they saw that the truck was piled high of all kinds of items: bedsteads, pots and pans, quilts, clothing, dishes, dishpans, buckets, and a miscellaneous assortment of other items. There were also some wooden crates that held jars of canned food, flour, sugar, and coffee. It seemed that upon hearing of their tragic fire, one of their neighbors, Pete Tyree, had gotten into his truck and driven from house to house in the community and even beyond their own community spreading the news about what had happened. Everyone was moved by their plight, and the people went through their own belongings and gave. Allie thought back on what had happened.

Pete had opened the door of the truck and climbed out. "Robert, Gracie, how are you doing?"

"We're doing okay," Daddy had answered. "We've been staying here with Sam and Texanner, and we'll be moving into Horace's house tomorrow. You heard they moved to Melbourne, didn't you?"

"Yea, we were sorry to see them go, but we're glad that it worked out for you." Pete looked to the truck and gestured to the back. "Your friends and neighbors, well, we gathered together a few items we thought you might need. We're all just so sorry about what happened. We all wanted to do something, and we hope this will help you while you all get back on your feet again."

Mama and Daddy looked at Pete, speechless. Daddy put his arm around Mama as she let out a sob and wiped her eyes.

"We don't know what to say, Pete," Daddy said. "We were wondering how we were going to manage and all. We just thank you, all of you . . ." Daddy's voice caught in his throat, and he squeezed Mama's shoulder tighter as he tried to get his emotions under control.

"It's just so thoughty of all of you," Mama managed to get out. "We thank you all so much."

"The Lord will always provide," Grandpa said with a smile as he walked up and put a hand on Daddy's shoulder. "If we put our trust in Him, we never have to worry."

It still amazed Allie. She couldn't get over the generosity of everyone. Even some of her and Winna's friends at school had given some things especially for them. She recognized Montene's yellow print dress and Annabelle's worn shoes. She thought she even recognized some of the boys' clothing.

"Can you believe we were given so much?" Allie said looking over at Winna. "I mean just think about it. They gave us things they probably really needed themselves."

"I know. I keep thinking about Thurman Crotts," Winna said with a catch in her own voice. "Allie, do you remember that fall when Mr. Kerley came up to school and told Thurman his dad wanted him down at the store?"

"Uh-huh, I remember there was a light snow on the ground, and Thurman was still coming to school barefooted," Allie said, softly picking at a loose thread in the sheet.

"Remember how tickled he was when he came back into the classroom wearing a new pair of shoes?" Winna asked. "And Thurman wasn't the only one who had to go barefooted until their folks could scrape up enough money to get them some winter shoes. We all know how that feels."

"I know it, and still they gave us all a whole truckload of things," Allie continued. "Things they needed themselves. At first, I thought I would be embarrassed wearing other kids' clothes to school, but now I'm just proud to have them, thankful too."

"Well, I guess we'd better get started with the wash. Do you want to sort while I get the water?" Winna asked.

"Okay," Allie replied.

It was a beautiful spring day, and Allie actually enjoyed wash day when the weather was nice. She was thankful for the warmth. Many were the times they would have to wash when the weather was cold and the clothes would actually freeze before they could get them hung out on the clothesline. The girls would have to work a while and then warm their own frozen hands from the steam coming up from the warm water in the kettles before continuing their work. The sun was bright today, and there was a gentle breeze this morning; that made for the perfect wash day.

Allie got up and untied the sheets. Dumping the clothes on the ground, she began to sort them. First, she made a pile for the whites: Patsy's diapers and little baby clothes, Betty's little nightgowns and underthings, Mama's apron, Daddy's long underwear. Next, she began a pile of colored clothes: their print school dresses, Daddy's shirt, Mama's blouse and skirt, and the tablecloth. Sheets, towels, and undergarments went in the third pile. Finally, Allie tossed Daddy's overalls, denim shirt, and pair of britches in the next pile. Thankfully, it really wasn't a very big wash this morning. Mama had done some small washings during this week, lessening their work considerably. All the baby clothes had burned, so Mama had to wash Patsy's few little things almost daily by hand for her to have something to wear.

Living in Uncle Horace and Aunt Lottie's house certainly had its advantages.

Photo taken at Uncle Horace and Aunt Lottie's house. Back row, far left, Winna holding Betty. Allie, middle girl, of three front girls, standing behind table behind boys

Allie still marveled at being able to go out on the back porch and draw up a bucket of fresh water any time of the day or night. She had long envied her cousins the luxury of having their own well, and it was just as nice as she always imagined it to be. She didn't miss walking to the spring every night for water one little bit. Now when Mama said it was time for the night water, she and Winna just got up and walked to the back porch to fill the buckets. Amazing! Sometimes they even fussed about who was going to get to draw it up.

Another advantage was Mama doing small washings there at the house. She didn't have her kettles or washtubs there. Aunt Lottie and Uncle Horace had taken theirs with them when they had moved, but Mama would heat up some water on the cookstove and fill some buckets and do up a little washing. When Mama had asked about hauling their own kettles and tubs up from the spring and doing laundry at the house, Daddy had told her they wouldn't be there long enough to go to that trouble. He had already started clearing some land, up on the little knoll across the road from their old house, to build their new house. With luck, they would be in it before winter.

Allie finished sorting the clothes and began to help Winna fill the rest of the tubs. It sure took a lot of water to wash; she wondered how the little spring kept from going dry on wash day! When all the tubs and the two kettles had been filled, the girls gathered some dried branches and twigs and put them underneath the kettles. Winna fetched some larger sticks of wood from a little woodpile Grandpa and Daddy always kept stocked beside the spring for this purpose.

Allie watched as Winna took the match from her pocket and struck it on the side of the kettle. She stiffened and her heart began to race as she saw the twigs ignite and the smoke rise into the air. Using her shoe, Allie dragged her foot back and forth and quickly raked at the dried grass and leaves around the kettles until the ground was scraped clean and bare of anything that might catch afire. Standing back a good ten feet, she watched the fire spread from twig to twig gobbling up the wood like a hungry monster. Visions of her own home being engulfed in flames flashed in her mind. She wondered if she would always have this fear of smoke and fire. There hadn't been a night since their house fire that she hadn't had bad dreams. She would awaken in the middle of the night certain she smelled smoke in the house and scream for Mama and Daddy. She begged Mama not to put wood in the stove during the day when Daddy was at the sawmill. Mama and Daddy both reassured the girls over and over that they were safe and to try not to think about the fire, but it was hard not to think about it.

So much had changed since the terrible fire. They were comfortable in Uncle Horace and Aunt Lottie's home and so very thankful for a place to stay. It seemed almost a miracle that her aunt and uncle were planning on moving the very next day when their house burned. Uncle Horace had insisted that they stay there. Allie was thankful to be in their house, she really was. She had always loved Aunt Lottie's house, but it just wasn't home. She felt like company in someone else's house. She missed her old familiar things: her bed, the quilt that she snuggled up in at night, Mama's shawl she sometimes wore on cold mornings, her clothes, and her precious birthday presents—all gone now. Allie felt guilty when she had thoughts like this. She knew they all had things they missed. As hard as it was on her, she knew it had to be even harder on Mama and Daddy. They didn't complain though. Daddy said everything they lost could be replaced, and Mama said they should just count their blessings. Allie couldn't understand such acceptance. She would carry on, whining to them about things she missed, but Mama would say, "Now, Allie, we've got one another and everything we really need. That's a whole lot more than what some folks have." Allie knew this was true, but still.

"Allie, come on and help!" Winna was cutting lye soap into the kettle while Allie stood daydreaming as she gazed into the fire. She went over to where Winna stood whittling the flakes of soap. The soap was an ugly gray color.

Mama made her own lye soap. The first step to making soap was to make lye water. Using ashes from the stove or gathering ashes from underneath the kettle, Mama would pour water over the ashes. That always seemed so strange to Allie, the thought of using dirty ashes to make a soap for cleaning. After the water and ashes set for a while, it becomes acidy thus being lye water. Then the lye water is added to fat. The fat came from their hogs. Each fall when Daddy would butcher a hog, Mama always saved the fat from the butchering and made it into lard. The more fat that was on a hog, the better. Much of the lard from the butchering went into cooking and frying, but some was always saved to be used in soap making. Mama made her lye soap here at the spring in the big kettle. She would heat it and stir it round and round while it boiled, adding the lye water. It took quite a while, but after a couple of hours, it would begin to thicken. Then Mama would dip it out and pour it into a flat pan. When the soap cooled, she cut it haphazardly into thick chunks. It was then wrapped in paper or cloth, ready to be stored until it was needed. Mama's soap sure supported the old saying: That's as ugly as homemade soap. Mama's soap was that ugly! Some people liked to put perfumed oils and dyes into their soap and make it into pretty shapes, but Mama considered this a waste of time and expense. She said soap was for getting things clean, not to smell like perfume or look pretty. Allie didn't argue with Mama, but she secretly thought to herself how much she loved using Aunt Ollie's soap. It had a rose scent to it and was even a pretty pink color. Allie had no doubt she'd make her soap fancy like Aunt Ollie when she grew up.

Allie walked over and picked up an armload of whites and dropped them into one of the tubs. Setting the rub board into the tub, Allie picked up one of Betty's nightgowns and began to rub it up and down on the metal humps and groves of the board. She had to be extra careful when rubbing thin material like this because it was so easy to rub your knuckles. Every wash day, Allie vowed to keep all the hide attached to her knuckles, but few were the times she finished a washing without her knuckles bleeding. Winna continued to coax the fire under the kettle. After the whites were scrubbed, they would be transferred to the kettle to boil. As Allie finished with each item, she dropped it into the kettle. Winna used the punch stick to punch them down in the sudsy water to boil them clean and to make room for more. When the kettle was full, Winna continued to punch the clothes up and down, up and down. The smoke made their eyes sting, and the soap gave off a pungent clean smell. When Winna's arms grew tired and she needed a break, Allie switched with Winna scrubbing on the scrub board and Allie using the punch stick.

"Winna, I think these whites are ready for the rinse," Allie finally called out. She dropped the punch stick and moved back from the kettle. She brushed her damp hair away from her face and wiped at her stinging eyes. Winna laughed when she looked over at her.

"You look like a little raccoon," she laughed. The smoke had darkened Allie's face, and when she wiped her eyes, two white circles were formed in the otherwise gray face. Winna came over and lifted some of the clothes from the kettle with the stick and inspected them.

"Yep, they're ready," she agreed. One by one, she transferred the white laundry to the next kettle. After the whites went through the one rinsing, they were moved to a tub for a second rinse that had bluing added to it. Allie tied three little balls of bluing up in a rag and added it to the water. The water took on a bluish tint. This was to whiten the clothes. Mama liked her white clothes white, and she could tell if the girls skipped this step. Finally, the whites were ready to be hung out. The girls twisted the clothes trying to wring out as much water as possible. Some clothes, like

Daddy's church shirt, needed to be starched. Winna took the powdered starch and measured some out into a bucket. Next, she added some water. She placed it over by the fire to heat. Using a big wooden spoon, she stirred the mixture round and round until it lost its cloudy color and became clear. She added some items to the bucket.

Daddy had made a clothesline at the spring for them to hang the clothes on.

Uncle Ed, Allie's Dad, and Betty

Sometimes when they had a big wash, they would have more clothes than the lines could hold. Then they had to drape some things on bushes or the limbs of trees. They should have plenty of line space today though. Once the whites were taken from the first washtub, Allie added the sheets, towels, and washcloths and began scrubbing them up and down. When the water quit foaming, more soap was shaved into the kettle.

"Winna, how about stopping for lunch?" Allie groaned. They had been at this for a couple of hours, and she was tired and hungry. Mama had made them a lunch this morning for them to take with them. Winna agreed and the two girls walked over and plopped down in a shady spot beside the spring and opened their pails. Mama had put some fried ham between biscuits and had cut up some slices of a yellow onion. It smelled so good! She had also put jelly between two other biscuits for their dessert. As they ate, Winna looked around.

"Hey, sis, here's some love vine," she said with a smile. "Wanta see who loves you?"

Allie laughed. "No one loves me. Let's see who loves you?"

"Let's both do it," Winna said as she looked over at Allie with a twinkle in her eyes. She pulled at the orange vine growing on a clump of bushes.

Allie didn't know the real name of the plant. It must have been some kind of parasite because it grew and twisted through weeds and bushes. It really just looked like an orange string. It didn't have roots or grow from the ground; it just grew in among other plants.

Allie and Winna each broke off three or four pieces of it. "What are you going to name yours?" Winna asked.

"Hummmm, I think I'll name this piece Cody," Allie said as she carefully wrapped a healthy piece of the plant several times around the stem of a milkweed plant. "And . . . I'll name this piece J. J." She took another long piece of the orange vine and wrapped it several times around a Princess Ann's lace plant.

"How about naming one of them Bobbie?" Winna teased.

"Don't mention that boy's name to me," Allie said crossly as she cut her eyes over to her sister. She had not forgiven him for embarrassing her.

"Oh, come on," Winna begged. "Let's just check to see if he really does love you. He did put your names together in a heart, you know," she said in a playful way.

"Fine," Allie snapped. She picked up a tiny piece of the plant and tossed it haphazardly onto a bitterweed plant. "That piece isn't going to grow, I can guarantee you that!"

Winna laughed. "We'll know the answer before too long. You may be surprised." The girls had come up with this way of telling which boys liked them. They would name each vine as they wrapped it around another plant. Then after a few days they would check on the transplanted vines. The love vine that took off and grew meant that that boy loved them. The love vine that withered and died meant that boy didn't love them. It was always exciting to return to the vines in a few days to learn which boy loved them. Winna did the same with her love vines giving each a name. Allie noticed she gave extra care to the one she named Willard.

"We'd better get back to work," Winna said as she stood up and dusted off her skirt.

Washing took all day. It was late in the afternoon when they hung the last of Daddy's overalls in the sun. By then, their knuckles were red and raw from scrubbing, and their hands were chapped from the harsh lye soap. They always saved Daddy's work clothes for last. He got them so dirty at the sawmill. It was about impossible to get the pine rosin out of them. This is a sap that oozes from pine trees. It's sticky and gooey. It was hard not to get it on your clothes working at the sawmill. The girls hated when they got even a little on their hands. They would rub sand on their hands and wash them until they were about to bleed, but usually it just had to wear off. Mama always put some kerosene on those spots on Daddy's overalls before the girls washed them hoping it would take out the rosin. Even so, some of his work clothes didn't look much cleaner when they were finished with them than when they started. They knew they were clean anyway, and Daddy never complained. He always said everybody could tell from his clothes that he was a worker. Shame wasn't in having pine rosin on your clothes, he'd say. Shame was when your clothes stayed clean because of laziness.

"I feel as wrung out as those clothes," Winna groaned as she began pouring out the water in the tubs and cleaning up.

Allie began to take down the clothes they'd done earlier in the day. Daddy's heavy overalls wouldn't be dry until tomorrow morning. "I know what you mean." They tied the ends of the sheets together and picked up their bundles. Suddenly, Allie said, "Shhhh! Did you hear that?"

"That sounded like a buzzie!" Winna said, looking nervously around. The girls weren't allowed to say the word *bull*, so they referred to a bull as a buzzie. They were terrified of them.

Winna ran over and picked up the puncher they used in washing. She looked back at Allie and saw that she had already scampered up a tree. Winna threw down the punch stick and joined Allie in the tree. They looked all around expecting any time to see an angry buzzie come into sight.

When no buzzie appeared after several minutes, the girls settled down comfortably on their perch in the tree and relaxed a little. "Remember how we used to climb trees when we lived at the Wilson place?" Winna asked.

Winna and Allie's dad had always worked at a sawmill. When Allie was seven, Dad bought a tract of timber at a place referred to as the Wilson place. The girls remembered that time as one of the most adventurous times of their childhood. It seemed to them that they had gone to a place that was just unheard of. There were no close neighbors out there in the house in the woods. There were lots of persimmon trees that had grown in a huge cluster, and there was no underbrush under them. That was the most fun place to play. They loved climbing the trees and riding them over like they were horses. Uncle Elbert and one of Uncle George's boys went with them to assist Daddy with the sawmill work. The cousin's name was Conrad. He was around fourteen years old at the time.

"I loved that place!" Allie said with excitement. "Remember how we'd play hully gully with the chinquapins?"

The chinquapins were the nuts that grew on chinquapin trees. The Ozark hills were abundant with this type of tree. These trees grew large, and farmers used them for fence posts and other wooden structures for outside as they were very resistant to rotting. They were even used sometimes as railroad ties. In addition, the wood made beautiful furniture and even musical instruments. However, as beneficial as the wood of the chinquapin proved to be, probably the best thing about the trees were the nuts that grew on them. The single nuts were encased in burrs. In the fall, these burrs fell in clusters around the tree. The forest animals such as squirrels, deer, turkeys, and even bears loved to feast on the nuts. The children though were probably the trees' greatest fans. The nuts had a sweet taste to them. Children waited for the chinquapin harvest almost as impatiently as they awaited the county fair.

It took skill, patience, and a fair amount of pain to be able to enjoy the sweetness of the nuts. This was definitely a time to bring out the shoes even though it was in the early fall that the nuts fell. First, one gathered the burr clusters from the ground. Next, using a rock, the hull was beaten until they opened revealing a shiny black nut in each pod of the cluster. These nuts had a soft shell that could be broken easily to reveal a yellowish round nut. It had a sweet, crunchy flavor. One chinquapin always made you hungry for the next.

"I've never seen so many chinquapins!" Winna answered. "I'm glad we were there during the fall when the chinquapins were falling. I think those poor squirrels around there must have been glad when we finally left. They probably went hungry that winter."

Allie laughed. "Remember how Mama ran out of salt while we were there? I guess it was too far to go into town to get any, so we just had to do without! Yuk!"

"Yea, and remember what Conrad said he was going to say when anyone ever asked him his favorite flavor. He said he was going to say his favorite flavor was salt!" Winna giggled.

"I guess that's when I smoked my first cigarette!" Allie said.

Winna laughed. "Me too," she said.

It really wasn't cigarettes that they smoked. Most men did smoke cigarettes, and Allie and Winna were curious about them. They would watch Daddy take some OBC papers and pour Prince Albert or Velvet tobacco into the papers and smoke them. So when they were out of sight of Mama or Daddy, they would pretend to smoke cigarettes. First, they would gather some of the sawdust from the sawmill and put it into one of Daddy's empty tobacco cans. Then they'd cut some little squares of paper from a catalog. Next, they'd pour out some of the sawdust into the paper and roll it up. Finally, using a little stick, they would pretend to light the "cigarette" and smoke it. What fun they had! They felt so naughty!

Allie and Winna grew tired of sitting in the tree. After hearing the bellows a few more times, they could tell from the sound that the buzzie was moving away from them. When they no longer could hear the angry bellows, they climbed down from their perch on the branch. Picking up their packs once again, they slung them over their shoulders and began their climb up the hill.

"Allie, did you know that the government used to send people around to kill people's cows when they were too poor to feed them?" Winna asked.

"Oh no! Really?" Allie looked shocked.

"Yep, during the Depression, the people were so poor they couldn't feed themselves, let along their livestock. The cows got weaker and weaker until they were starving. The drought was so bad too that there wasn't even any grass for them to find to eat. The government didn't want the poor things to suffer, so they'd send men out to kill them. Daddy said they'd bury them in some of the gullies around and cover them over with dirt."

"That's awful," Allie said. "Poor things."

Mr. Blue, Winna's teacher, explained that another reason the government did this was to try and get the economy moving again. They thought that farmers were producing too much product thereby driving the cattle prices down. By killing the sick cattle, they were getting the poor livestock out of their misery as well as decreasing the number. President Roosevelt, under the New Deal, arranged for the government to purchase livestock from these desperate farmers. Some of the animals were, indeed, destroyed and buried. Others though were slaughtered and the food given to people who were going hungry.

"You know the government does some pretty good things," Allie added. "I love it when we get those cans of pork and beans from the truck. They come from the government, don't they?"

Several times during the year, large cans of pork and beans and grapefruit juice were delivered to the school. The teachers would put the beans in a big dishpan on the top of the stove and heat them up. Then they'd serve them to the students. Those were the best days! The students would go back for seconds and thirds until the pan was scraped clean. They loved the grapefruit juice too. That was something most had never had until it was brought in to them.

"Yea, I think so," Winna answered. "Ummm, we must be getting hungry."

"If you could have any food right now that you could, what would it be?" Allie asked.

"Well, that's a hard question, but I think I'd like to have a piece of chocolate drop candy from the Huett's store," Winna answered. "Don't you just love Mrs. Huett? Do you think she gives everyone six pieces of candy for a nickel instead of five? I just love that lady!"

"I dunno," Allie replied. "She sure is nice to us though. I think if I could have anything I wanted right now, I'd choose a big juicy orange. Do you remember how Mrs. Baylor used to eat one almost every day at school?"

"I do! I can just see her now peeling those oranges with her long pretty fingers and all of us standing there watching her with our mouths drooling. I wonder where she got them. We don't have oranges around here."

The girls had reached the top of the hill by then. They saw Grandpa in the barn lot shelling out some ears of corn for the chickens. "Hey, Grandpa!" Winna called out.

"Well, howdy Molly and Polly!" Grandpa called out using his pet names for them. He took off his hat and waved it to them. "Come on over here and give me a hug."

Winna set down her bundle of clothes and hurried over. Allie continued past the barn. "I've got to get these clothes home to Mama," she called to him as she hurried by. She adjusted the bundle higher on her shoulder and made her way through the gate and across the yard. She quickly looked away when she saw the sad look on Grandpa's face.

Allie had avoided Grandpa ever since the house fire. She knew he was bothered by her distance from him, and Allie couldn't even really understand the feelings she was having herself. She just felt guilty around him like she'd done something to disappoint him. It really had to do with the heart necklace he had given her, she supposed. Allie remembered Grandpa's words, "You just take care of it, and maybe you can pass it on to a daughter of your own sometime." Allie also remembered her own words back to him, "I'll keep it forever, Grandpa!" Now the necklace was gone. The necklace that had once belonged to Grandpa's mother and that was so precious to him was now gone forever. He had trusted it to her, and she had let him down. He'd never see it again. If only Grandpa had never given it to her, he'd still have it. He'd never see it again, and it was all her fault.

Chapter 9

Grandpa had some honeybees and got the honey for us to eat. He also found trees with beehives. I would go bee hunting with him. Down to the creek we would go. Today when I take a bite of honey, I think of Grandpa. He taught me to respect bees, and the only way I ever kill one is by stepping on it before I see it.

—Oletta Ross (2010)

Uncle Bud Hudson and some of them would come down to the store, and they'd give me a quarter to shave them on Saturday. That was pretty good pay. I was just a kid. Another thing that was funny was that Jim Smith had an old telephone. You could crank it, and it would shock you. He'd put one part of the phone under one foot and hold it and hold the other part of the phone up in his hand and have me crank it. You could see his hand quivering as I'd crank. And he'd say, "You ain't a cranking it hard enough. Crank it harder!" He thought it helped his arthritis. It was shocking him, ya see. That's what it was doing.

—Wilb (Willie) (2010)

Bobbie

May 1941

Bobbie woke to a beautiful day. With only two weeks left of this school term, he was in good spirits. There's nothing quite as enticing to a young boy as the beginning of summer vacation and the endless possibilities it holds. Bobbie jumped quickly out of bed and climbed into his trousers. He wasn't going to miss a minute of this day. He found Momma in the kitchen frying up some fatback for breakfast. "Morning, son," Momma greeted him, her beautiful smile lighting her face. "You were out mighty late last night."

Bobbie walked over and gave Momma a hug. "Uh-huh."

It was late when they'd gotten home. Daddy liked to foxhunt. He took old Fancy and Buck out hunting every few nights. He probably would have gone every night, in good weather anyway, except he had to give the hounds a few days to rest up. Their feet would get sore from running on the sharp rocks and their muscles would get stiff. It would take them a day or two to get rested up before they would be ready to go again. For some reason, Daddy wanted his sons to be fox hunters too. Of course, Jake and little Rex were too small to go yet, but he insisted Bobbie and Willie go with him at least once a week. Now Bobbie liked most kinds of hunting. He loved squirrel hunting, and the few times he had been deer or turkey hunting, he'd liked that too. Foxhunting was different though. It was one kind of hunting that you didn't come back with anything to show for your work. Foxhunting was enjoyed just for the thrill of the race, and, so far, Bobbie didn't get the thrill that Daddy did. Daddy liked to listen to the barks of the dogs, and he could tell just by listening which hound was out front. He would laugh and say, "Ole Buck's hot on his heels," or "Durn it, they've lost the scent." It was the same with coon hunting. Some men around enjoyed coon hunting, but Daddy didn't do much of that.

"That smells good!" Bobbie said taking a big whiff of the pork Momma was frying up. "Where is everybody anyway?"

"Daddy has already left for the sawmill. They didn't get everything finished they wanted to yesterday, ya know. Jake and Rex are still snoozing, and Audie's gone down to the spring for the butter and milk. Grandpa's out on the front porch though with Thurman and Oletta. He's fixin' to go bee hunting and thought you might want to go."

"I shore do," Bobbie said excitedly as he scrambled out the kitchen and through the front room. He rushed outside determined not to be left behind.

"Morning, Grandpa," he said breathlessly as the screen door slammed behind him. Grandpa was sitting in the ladder-backed rocker, the porch boards groaning with the back-and-forth motion of the chair. He was wearing his overalls and his big straw hat. The stem of his pipe was held between his lips, and he wore a peaceful, relaxed look as he gazed out across the green fields. Grandpa was never far from his pipe. A few years ago, he had to have a little surgery of some kind or another at the hospital. The doctors gave him something to put him to sleep while they worked on him. He was out several hours. Momma sat with him until he woke up. She said when he finally came to, the first words out of his mouth were, "Where's my pipe?" Bobbie watched him now as he took a couple of puffs and blew the smoke slowly into the air. The sweet clouds of smoke drifted lazily up and out across the yard fading gently into the morning like the pleasant thoughts Grandpa seemed to be having. Grandpa blew out another puff of smoke and smiled his toothless grin at his grandson.

"Well, I shore nuff thought you were gonna sleep till noon!" he said. His smile disappeared all of a sudden and he made a click of his tongue, a sign that he was downright disappointed in Bobbie. "A feller can't get ahead in this ole world laying up in the bed till all hours of the day. No sir!"

Grandpa Crotts

"Shucks, Grandpa, it's not that late." Bobbie explained. "Besides, I didn't get in bed very early last night. You know I went foxhunting with Daddy, don't you?"

"Yep, yer Momma told me you all didn't get home till sommers after midnight. That's a shame. I guess you're plum too tuckered out to help me hunt bees this morning, and I was shore needing your help." Grandpa shook his head as he took another pull on his pipe and looked over at Bobbie out of the corner of his eyes.

Bobbie smiled. He knew Grandpa was kidding him. "Grandpa, you know I'd never be too tuckered out for that," he said. "Why I'd go bee hunting with you if I was so tired I had to crawl around on my hands and knees. I'm raring to go. Do we have time to eat a little breakfast first, or was you aiming to head out right now?"

"Now a feller cain't hunt bees on an empty stomach, can he?" Grandpa laughed his hearty laugh. "There ain't no telling how far we're gonna have to walk to find us them bees. Newwwwwwww, I wouldn't want to start out with an empty belly, no siree." Grandpa took his pipe from his mouth. Leaning down, he gently tapped the cup of the pipe on the edge of the porch. The loose tobacco fell from the pipe and dropped into the dirt. Grandpa wiped the pipe on his pants' leg and dropped it down into his shirt pocket. Resting his hands on the arms of the rocker, he pushed himself up with a grunt. "Let's go and see if your momma has them eggs fried yet," he said with a wink. "First, go around back there and fetch Thurman and Oletta and tell 'em to come on in to breakfast."

"Okay," Bobbie answered as he swung his legs over the banister of the porch.

Suddenly Grandpa stopped, his hand still on the door handle. "Hold on there a minute," he said as he turned back around to look at Bobbie. That word *fetched* just put me in mind me of a riddle I've been itching to ask ya."

Bobbie looked up at Grandpa with an expectant grin. Where in the world did his grandpa come up with all his riddles? "Okay," he said. "I'm ready."

"Okay, now here it goes. At night, they come without being *fetched*," Grandpa put emphasis on the word he'd just used. "And by day, they are lost without being stolen. What are they?" Grandpa eyed Bobbie as he waited for his answer.

Bobbie thought. The word *stolen* hit a sore note with him, but he wasn't going to get into that with Grandpa. He shook his head. It was no use. He never could figure out one of Grandpa's riddles. "I dunno, Grandpa," he finally had to admit.

Grandpa grinned and pointed up, "Stars," he said. "Stars. They come at night without being fetched, and they are lost in the day without being stolen." He gave Bobbie an openmouthed wink and said, "Think about it! Boy, you're gonna have to learn to use that noggin of yours."

Bobbie laughed and jumped down to the ground to go fetch his uncle and cousin. "Grandpa, you're smarter than Mr. Schauffler, I do believe!"

Bobbie walked out behind the house. The spring rains and sun had caused the grass to grow thick and long the past few weeks. It felt soft under his bare feet. He had near bout grown out of his shoes this year, and with the warm weather, his shoes had been oiled down and put away for Willie to wear come cold weather again. None of the children even considered wearing shoes in warm weather. Bobbie, being the oldest boy in the family, usually got the new pair of shoes when it was time for school to start in the fall. He liked going barefoot though and shed his shoes after the last frost. His feet were still a little tender right now, but it wouldn't be long before they'd be toughened up so he could run over the sharp rocks without flinching at all. The sounds of the morning were all around him. Henny Penny was still crowing her fool head off as if everybody in their right minds weren't already out of bed. The hens were scratching around in the loose dirt, clucking and squawking as they argued with one another over the last few kernels of corn Audie had thrown out earlier. Those lazy hens should be able to find their own food this time of year. Bobbie didn't see Thurman or Oletta, but he could hear them on the other side of the barn talking and laughing. "What are ya'all doing?" he asked coming upon them. Thurman had a rusty chain looped through the collar on old Buck's neck and was leading him around. One would have thought the dog was a trained monkey the way he was following along obediently behind Thurman never missing a step. Not far behind Thurman was Oletta. She had tied a raveled old rope around Fancy's neck and had led her over to an old rusty pan where she was lapping greedily at the cool water. Her rope was as thin as a spider's web and one tug from Fancy would have broken it for sure, but good old Fancy was on her best behavior. When she raised up from her drink, she followed along after Oletta like she was a prisoner in chains. *Those poor dogs*, thought Bobbie as he shook his head. They had run all over tarnation last night chasing those red-tailed foxes. He figured they were still worn to a frazzle and could use some rest, but here they were catering to the wishes of these two young-ens.

Grandpa Crotts and some of his children and one grandchild:
Ival, Grandpa, Thurman, Alma, Thelma, Oletta

"Hey, ya'll ready to come on in and eat some breakfast? I think Momma has it ready. Then after breakfast, Grandpa is gonna go bee hunting, and he said we could go." Bobbie bent down to stroke the heads of both dogs. Fancy leaned her head into Bobbie's gentle hands enjoying the caress. Buck, on the other hand, stood still as a fence post acting like he didn't care a thing for the petting he was getting. He didn't fool Bobbie though. Buck's eyes shone brightly and there was a hint of a smile on the old dog's face.

"Yea!" Oletta said, jumping up and down and clapping her hands. Her blond curls bounced up and down to match her jumping. "Bee hunting, bee hunting, I getta go bee hunting!" Bobbie smiled even though he felt like groaning. He was hoping she'd rather stay here and play dolls with Audie. He really wished Grandpa didn't think he had to take her along everywhere he went. She wasn't even quite three years old and would have to be carried the whole way. She'd probably end up making so much noise she'd scare off any bees they might be lucky enough to find. Bobbie knew better than to suggest leaving her behind to Grandpa though. Oletta was Grandpa's pet. Just like she could lead Fancy all around the yard on a rope that was as weak as a thread, she more or less could lead Grandpa around in the same way. All she had to do was stretch those little arms of hers up to him and say, "Prease, Gampa!" and he couldn't resist. He'd smile and his old gray head would start bobbing like a puppet on a string. He just couldn't say no to her! She got to go just about anywhere or do just about anything she wanted when Grandpa was around.

Bobbie could sort of understand Grandpa's soft spot for her though. After all, Oletta lived in the same house with four older uncles. Most of them were so much older that they paid little attention to her. All except Thurman, that is. He and Oletta were like a licorice stick all twisted together. You hardly saw one without the other. Those other three uncles though could be downright ornery when they wanted to be. Oletta's mother lived with them as well. Any time one of the uncles or even Oletta's mother, Thelma, got on to

Oletta for something or another, all she had to do was to go running to Grandpa. He'd open up his arms, and she would jump into them. Then Grandpa would say real sternly, "You leave my girl alone!" Yep, she could lead Grandpa around as easily as she was leading ole Fancy, and Bobbie had no doubt that Oletta would be going bee hunting with them today.

Grandpa, Ruffin Crotts, with a granddaughter

After breakfast was over, Grandpa, Bobbie, Thurman, and yes, little Oletta headed out in search of bees. Grandpa had some of his own honeybees. He had built some beehives out in the woods behind the house. He kept the family supplied with sweet honey the year around. Momma used honey for most of her sweets instead of using the expensive white sugar you could buy at the store. Even though Grandpa had his own bees, every now and then he'd get it in his head to go out and hunt some wild bees. It was more of a sport to him than anything else. Just like Daddy enjoyed his foxhunting, Grandpa liked to bee hunt. Bobbie had been with him one or two times when he coursed bees as it was called, and it always amazed him at the old man's ability to be able to watch bees and follow them with his eyes as they flew through the air. He could usually wind up following them all the way to their hive. Bobbie couldn't wait to see if they'd be able to find some honey today.

It was such a pretty morning. The redbuds were fully bloomed, purple splashes in the dark-green foliage. The green of the trees against the brilliant-blue of the morning sky made a contrast so intense it almost hurt your eyes to look at it. The dogwood trees were budding getting ready to burst open. Bobbie always thought of the story his momma had told him when he looked at dogwood trees. She said the dogwood trees used to be large and strong. Now they were scrawny, twisted, and small. She said it was because the Roman soldiers used the dogwood tree to make the cross where they crucified Jesus. Because of that, God cursed the tree and it never again grew to be large and strong. Also if you look closely at the dogwood blossom, you can see some other things about the crucifixion. In the center of each flower is a round section that resembles the crown of thorns placed on Jesus' head. The flower has four petals representing the four parts of the cross, and at the end of each petal is a reddish-brown indented part that represents the nail scars. It was a sobering thought. Bobbie didn't know if the dogwood tree really had been used for the cross, but the petals sure seemed to support Momma's story.

Bobbie and Thurman followed along behind Grandpa, Oletta riding high on his back. She was singing a silly song, and Grandpa was whistling along with her in tune:

> Mary had a wittle wamb
> Wittle wamb
> Wittle wamb
> Mary had a wittle wamb
> Its freece was white as snow.

Bobbie and Thurman rolled their eyes at one another behind Grandpa's back. Something happened to Grandpa when he got around Oletta, Audie, or his other little granddaughter, Nettie. He got all soft and silly. And girls! Bobbie could tell Oletta was going to be like all those other girls at school liking those silly stories and songs. He enjoyed Grandpa a whole lot more when *girls* weren't around.

"Grandpa, where you figuring on going to look for the bees?" Bobbie asked, more of a way to draw Grandpa out of his foolishness with Oletta than as something he wanted to know.

"Now, boys," Grandpa began. "Bees have got to have water, don't ya know. That's how they keep the temperature in their hives from getting too hot or dried out. If the temperature gets too hot, the wax could start melting, and that would cause all kinds of trouble for them. Those bees are smart critters. They each have a job, and they work together for the good of all of them. I've heard tell that a single bee may make around fifty trips a day to a watering hole to collect water. So when you're wanting to find a bee tree, the first place to start looking is around some moving water. Once a bee starts getting water from a certain spot, they're likely to keep using that spot."

The boys were silent as Grandpa explained about the bees. Bobbie knew without a doubt now that Grandpa had to be smarter than his teacher. He had never heard Mr. Schauffler go into such detail about a particular topic.

Grandpa adjusted Oletta a little higher on his back and continued. "We're going to start down at the creek," he said looking back over his shoulder at his son and grandson. "I wish we'd have asked your momma to fix us up a little picnic lunch, Bobbie. We may have to sit for a spell before we find us a bee to follow. A person has to have perseverance when he goes to hunting bees."

Bobbie didn't have a clue what perser—whatever it was that Grandpa just said, but he wasn't about to ask what it meant. His head was already spinning.

"Daddy, I don't see how you can follow a little bee," Thurman said. "I just don't get it. They're so little, how can you keep up with em when they're flying through the air?"

Grandpa laughed. "Well, sonny, it's just like anything else. It just takes practice, and when you've lived as many years as I have, you've had plenty of time for practice!" He chuckled again. "I'm not saying I find a bee tree every time I course bees. Newwwwwwwwwww! Sometimes I course a bee and have to give it up and go home without ery a bit of honey."

"What do you do when you lose a bee, Grandpa?" Bobbie asked.

"Well now, if I can get the general direction it is traveling before I lose it, then I can sometimes still find the tree. You know? Bees like trees that are old and rotten. So if you're to go and lose your bee, but you know the direction he was headed, you can sometimes scout around and find it. It's not gonna be too far off. A beehive will generally not be more than a mile away from some water. A bee always flies in a straight line back to the tree. That's where we get the old saying: making a beeline to get sommers. Anyway, soes if you head off in that straight line, keeping your eyes up at the tops of the trees, you're likely to find the tree," Grandpa explained. "You can also keep your eyes open for bear claw marks on a tree or coon droppings around the base of a tree. We're not the only ones looking for honey, you know. That's one reason the bees usually have their hives up high in a tree so other critters can't get to it as easy."

Bobbie scratched his head. Who knew you had to know so much about bees to be able to find their hives? "I heard some of the men at the store talking about baiting for the bees and finding their hives that way," he said.

"Yep, some folks like to do that. The only way some people will course bees is soaking corncobs in sugar water and putting that out to attract them. I've tried it a few times myself," Grandpa admitted. "Some folks even like to use a little anise mixed in with some honey or sugar water. That's supposed to really attract the bees."

"Anise?" Bobbie and Thurman asked together.

This was turning into a regular schoolroom lesson. Bobbie had expected Grandpa to just tell them a little secret to finding beehives. He hadn't expected a whole durned lecture about them.

"Yep," Grandpa said. "It does seem to work. I used to get some anise off of your grandpa, Bobbie."

"You mean Grandpa James?" Bobbie asked. He knew Grandpa James used to sell spices. He carried a satchel around with him that had all kinds of spices and flavorings in it. In fact, it had earned him his nickname. Grandpa's real name was George Lafayette James, but everybody round these parts always just called him George Riley. That was on account of him selling Riley products. He carried his Riley products with him when he carried the mail or near bouts everywhere he went, and he would sell them to people. Bobbie had always just thought Grandpa's name *was* George Riley until when he died just a couple of years ago. He'd asked Daddy why the preacher kept calling him George Lafayette at the funeral when his name was George Riley. That's when he'd learned that Riley wasn't his real name.

"Yep," Grandpa answered. "Many a times I would get some anise off of him and mix some in with a little honey. I'd put it down in a bucket or jar and put a few sticks in with it. Bees can get all stuck up in honey if you're not careful, so you have to put some sticks or leaves or something in on top of the honey for them to sit on while they collect the sweet stuff," Grandpa went on. "Yessir, I used to go about attracting bees thata way, but wonced I got better able to foller them with my eyes, I took to just watching for them at the water holes."

By this time, they were going down the hill to the creek. Grandpa put Oletta down to walk in the smooth sand. Bobbie enjoyed walking in the sand too. It felt cool on his hot feet. The temperature seemed to drop a good five or ten degrees as they neared the water and chill bumps popped out on his arms. The water was crystal clear as it bubbled and ran over the smooth stones. It was shady around the creek with trees leaning out over the water, some of the limbs reaching their leafy fingers down into the cool water as if to tickle the creatures living beneath the surface.

"Let's find us sommers to sit," Grandpa suggested looking around.

"Wanta make some frog hills?" Thurman asked Oletta.

"Yea!" she squealed.

Thurman commenced to helping Oletta make the structures. To make a frog hill, first, you dig with your toes down into sand. Then you cover your whole foot with the damp sand and pack it down hard. Finally, you slowly draw your foot out of the sand leaving a little tunnel-like house. For some reason, these were called frog hills or frog houses. Maybe it was because frogs were attracted to the cool, damp holes; at least the children thought so. Oletta wasn't able to maneuver the steps involved in making these all by herself. Thurman though was tireless in helping her make one after another. Before long, there was a string of them lining the creek.

Grandpa and Bobbie had settled onto a log lodged up against a willow. They sat watching Thurman and Oletta play in the sand. "We're never gonna find a bee with them making so much noise," Bobbie complained.

"Oh, I wouldn't say that," Grandpa reassured him. "Besides, being out enjoying this purty scenery and watching the young-uns play is one of the reasons I like bee hunting. It gives me an excuse to just sit and watch all of God's creation around me for a while. Watching Oletta and Thurman have fun playing in the sand is as much fun to me as coursing a bee. Why don't ya move on over there?" Grandpa pointed to a shady spot downstream. "It'll be quieter there, and I bet it won't be long till you spot one."

Bobbie wasn't as convinced as Grandpa sounded. He still didn't like the noise. If Thurman and Oletta just wanted to build frog houses, they could have done that at home. He shot a disgusted look in their direction where they were obviously having a grand ole time and waded out to sit on a rock that was sticking up a good three feet out of the water.

The water was freezing. The rock, Bobbie discovered, was smooth and made a perfect seat. He settled himself on the top and found a comfortable position. Looking down into the water, he discovered all kinds of activity. Minnows and crawdads were scurrying everywhere. To his surprise, there were some pretty big fish swimming around too. He began to watch the fish darting this way and that, aggravated at himself that he hadn't thought to bring a fishing pole. He loved to fish and what was better to eat than crispy deep-fried fish? He decided that he'd spend a good part of his summer sitting right here on this very rock fishing for perch or crappie. Momma loved for him to bring home fish all during the summer months. She'd actually can them. Now canned fish were nowhere near as good as fresh fish, but when they got to the bottom of the barrel, so to speak, in the wintertime, it was always good to have something canned to fall back on. Momma made sure there was always something to eat at their house.

Tiring of watching the critters under the water, Bobbie lay down on his side and watched a dragonfly as it dipped and soared over the water's surface. He had never noticed how truly large their wings were. Their eyes seemed enormous too. That insect must be able to see for miles. He wished he could see that well. Maybe then, he'd be able to spot a bee. As Bobbie watched, the dragonfly seemed to go in circles. Round and round it went. It was never going to get anywhere that way. Suddenly, it swooped down toward the water apparently after some prey. As Bobbie watched, a little black-and-yellow bee darted out of its way. Bobbie sat up quickly. He watched the bee as it darted out of the dragonfly's way and once again landed on the water's surface. Bobbie glanced over at Grandpa. He was busy watching Oletta chase Thurman around the dozens of frog houses scattered in the sand. Bobbie whistled softly.

Grandpa, hearing the whistle, looked over at him. Pointing to the bee, he gave Grandpa the thumbs up sign. Grandpa's smile spread across his face. Hopping up, he ran over to the children. He said something softly to them and lifted Oletta up onto his shoulders. Wading the water, they eased up close to Bobbie. The bee flew along the water's edge and then began to rise up higher into the air. Grandpa set Oletta down on the rock next to Bobbie and followed the bee with his eyes. His head moved ever so slowly as the bee moved away from the water and over the treetops. Suddenly, Grandpa grabbed up Oletta, threw her onto his back, and took off. "Come on!" he yelled. "He's going home!" Thurman and Bobbie jumped to their feet and took off after Grandpa. Water splashed in every direction as they stumbled across the slippery stones. Grandpa took off through the trees. He was ripping through the woods, one hand behind him holding Oletta, the other hand out front pushing limbs and brush out of his way.

Bobbie was so excited he was darting around about like that crazy dragonfly had been doing a minute ago. He strained his eyes for a glimpse of the bee. How could Grandpa see something so tiny? Grandpa was way ahead his eyes focused on that tiny bee. Bobbie was several yards behind Grandpa, and he could hear Thurman stumbling along behind him. Suddenly, Bobbie saw Grandpa stop. Still looking up, he turned his head this way and that. The boys stopped too, not moving a muscle. Suddenly, Grandpa let out a whoop and threw his hat into the air. "We've got us a bee tree, boys!" he shouted. The boys ran up breathless behind Grandpa. Poor Oletta was considerably shaken after her wild ride on Grandpa's back. Her knuckles were white where they grasped his overall straps.

"Are you sure, Grandpa?" Bobbie asked.

"Sure as shootin'!" he said as he pulled Oletta from his back and set her down on the ground. She grabbed onto his trousers' leg not sure what all this commotion was about.

Grandpa pointed to a scraggly limb toward the top of the tree. "Looky up there, boys," he said. "See that hole up near that dangling limb?"

The boys strained their eyes. Sure enough, there right near the limb was a dark hole. They could see a few bees circling here and there around the hole.

"Are you going to chop down the tree?" Thurman asked. "Where's your ax, Daddy?"

"Newwwwwwwwwww, we're not gonna chop down the tree today, boys. We'll let those bees alone until sometime in the fall—let 'em make us a little more honey. But I am gonna put my mark on this tree. That will tell anyone else who might come upon this hive that it's already been spoken for."

"Ain't you afraid you won't be able to find the tree again?" asked Bobbie.

"Naw, we'll be able to find it. Look around and find some landmarks that will help us. You boys need to start learning to do things like that."

Bobbie and Thurman looked around and tried to memorize the spot while Grandpa made his mark on the tree. "There we go," Grandpa said coming back to them. "We've got us a honey tree just waiting for us to collect the honey. Speaking of honey, I'm getting hungry. What about ya'all? Let's start back home and get us something to eat." He picked up Oletta and swung her onto his back.

Bobbie and Thurman were speechless. They fell into step alongside Grandpa. They looked up at him and then back to the bee tree still amazed at the events of this day. How Grandpa was able to do all the things he did was a mystery to them. They looked at each other and smiled. They knew they were looking at the wisest man in the world.

Chapter 10

I guess that when I was a child the month of May was the most eventful and exciting time for me. School was out, and the weather was warm enough that Mama let Winna and me take off our undershirts and long stockings. I can still remember the brushing of the hem of my dress on my naked legs. We could also start going barefoot, and I loved the feel of the sand on my feet when I dug my toes in the huge sand bed that was just down the road. It did take a while to toughen our feet up when we walked on the sharp rocks.

It was a very busy time for Mama though because Decoration Day was coming up the fourth Sunday in May, and she had to make dresses for us girls. In those days, one could order material from the catalog. Mama and Dad ordered most of the things they needed from Sears and Roebuck or Montgomery

Ward. Getting ready for Decoration Day also meant that we got new patent leather dress shoes, either black or white, and new white anklets. I think they were ordered from the catalogs too. Winna and I would choose a dress that we saw in the catalog and tell Mama that we wanted our dresses made like it. I do not know how she made them without a pattern, but she did, and we were always so proud of our dresses.

Besides the sewing and gardening that Mama had to do, she had to start making the crepe paper flowers to decorate the graves. She did not like making the flowers because, being the perfectionist that she was, they never turned out to suit her. Grandma Shoemate and Aunt Ollie had to make theirs also. Aunt Ollie was a master at turning out beautiful roses. Grandma always did her work very slowly, but her rose petals drooped and the leaves sometimes came off. Bless her heart. With all the work they did, the first spring shower ruined them completely.

I remember one decoration I had made a ribbon out of crepe paper and tied it across my head with the bow at my center part. My ribbon was red, and I believe Winna's was blue. It came up a rain while we were there, and the crepe paper faded all over our hair! Some of the women started wiping our hair with their handkerchiefs, but it didn't help much. I loved Decoration Day and looked forward to it all year.

—Allie (2010)

Allie

May 1941

Allie and Winna walked into the cemetery arms loaded with colorful crepe paper flowers. Paper streamers were tied around their heads with big bows at the center parts of their hair. Feeling as pretty as the lovely flowers they carried, they strolled slowly around the cemetery. They were feeling very grown-up. "Just wait until Cody sees you today," Winna said. "He will sure enough think you're the prettiest girl in school."

"I think all the boys here will be looking at the both of us, and why wouldn't they?" Allie said with a smile. "We are just about as pretty as these flowers we're carrying around."

Winna laughed. "Now aren't you a little overconfident today?"

Allie and Winna loved Decoration and had looked forward to this day for weeks. They were going to savor every minute of it and stretch it out as long as they could. They not only looked pretty, they felt special and important too. This year Mama had entrusted them with the job of putting the flowers on the graves of their loved ones. This was the first year that they could ever remember Mama not coming to the Decoration. Patsy had gotten up fussy and was running a temperature this morning, so Mama had decided to keep her and Betty at home. How sad that must be for Mama to miss this special day.

Bobbie's Aunt Alta James, with daughters,
Racine and June, in Elizabeth Cemetery

Allie looked down at the handmade flowers they carried. It had actually been Mama, Grandma, and Aunt Ollie who had made most of the flowers. Each of these ladies had their specialties. Aunt Ollie could make beautiful roses.

Mama's specialty was mums, and Grandma turned out lovely peonies. They had been working for weeks on these delicate flowers. Bits of colored crepe paper littered every room and even trailed out of the house into the yard, a rainbow broken into bits and pieces. Mama's poor fingers were raw and blistered from twisting the paper and wires. Winna and Allie had tried to help and had been successful in making a few of the simple flowers, but they hadn't quite mastered the art of flower making and had to leave most of the work to their elders.

The flowers were made from crepe paper: blue, yellow, pink, red, and lavender. Petals were cut from the paper and then attached to wire stems one petal at a time, wrapping a piece of wire securely around each petal as it was fitted into place. More and more petals were added until there was a cluster of them on the end of the wire. Then using a knife, each petal's edge was gently pulled and stretched making it curl on the ends. This was what made the flowers appear so real. Finally, the stem was wrapped in green crepe paper and a few leaves added about halfway down the stem. Usually the petals were formed around a yellow or black center that was folded over the end of the wire. The flowers seemed so natural and real that Allie halfway expected to catch a whiff of their wonderful scent as she lifted them to her nose. Yes, they all had certainly spent a lot of time making flowers for this special day, and a lot of love was put into each and every one.

May was probably Mama's busiest month of the year. There were so many things that had to be done. Besides making flowers, all four of Mama's daughters got new dresses for Decoration.

Sometime about the first of April, Winna and Allie began going out to the post office every afternoon after school in hopes of getting their new Sears and Roebuck catalog. They loved going to the post office. Mr. Huett, the postmaster, worked behind the oak partition that separated the post office from the general store. Allie would watch him through the glass, very serious and official, as he took the big canvas mailbag, delivered by mail buggy, and emptied the contents onto a sorting table. Then piece by piece, he would carefully go through the mail and begin putting the letters into the little cubicles. The letters made thumping noises as he popped them expertly into each recipient's slot.

The post office front was beautiful. Allie would rub her hands gently over the rich dark grain of the wood and admire the delicate scroll-like carving etched into the wood. It was a dark wood resembling rich glistening molasses. Several little boxes covered the front. Forty-eight little boxes sat up against the glass-paneled front. People with these boxes could look through the glass into their boxes to see if they had mail, but they couldn't get to their mail. If one of these customers saw that he had something in his box, he would have to ask Mr. Huett for it. Then Mr. Huett would have to stop what he was doing and take it out of the box and pass it out to him through the bars of the little window in the front of the panel. This little window even had two small doors on the inside that could be shut. When it was time for the post office to close, Mr. Huett would close the little doors and that meant post office business hours were over for the day. Some of the boxes though had little knobs on the outside of the boxes. If you had one of those boxes, you could get your mail anytime the store was open without bothering Mr. Huett. You had to know your box's combination though. Each of these special mailboxes had two little knobs on the door with numbers on it. Turning the knobs just right popped the doors open. It was so much fun getting the mail, and Allie always felt so important twisting the knobs. She tried to appear confident while secretly holding her breath each time she was entrusted to get the mail, praying the door would open. Their post office box was number 84, and their secret combination was to turn the left knob to the right until the little arrow lined up at L1A, and the right knob had to be turned to the left until the number 1 was between X and N. It really took a lot of concentration, and if the numbers weren't lined up exactly, the door wouldn't open. Then you'd have to start all over again. When Allie was younger, it often took several attempts to get the door open, but now she could usually do it on the first try.

However, as exciting as it was to turn the little knobs and open the post office box, it was even more exciting to hear Mr. Huett say, "Just a minute, girls. You have something that wouldn't fit in your box." Then he would have to raise the little glass window on the left side of the post office front and hand out a package or catalog. There was a little shelf underneath the window, and he would set the package on the shelf. Oh, how Allie loved to hear him say that. It was almost like getting a Christmas present. That was why, beginning around the first of April, Winna and Allie checked their mail daily in hopes of receiving a catalog through the post office window.

It was fun getting catalogs for several reasons. First, Allie and Winna loved to play with paper dolls, and Mama allowed them to use scissors to cut paper dolls from the catalogs. They would use oat boxes for cars or wagons and play for hours in the sand beds and under the cedar trees with their paper doll families. Nothing was quite as much fun as playing with paper dolls.

Another reason they loved getting the catalogs, though, was Mama always let them pick out one dress from the girls' section of the catalog for her to use as a pattern for their Decoration dresses. It was such a difficult decision! There were so many dresses, and all of them were pretty. What made it even more difficult was that Winna and Allie insisted their dresses be made exactly alike, so finding a dress they both liked sometimes took quite a long time and, sadly, often a fair amount of arguing. They would change their minds at least a dozen times before finally announcing to Mama their choice. Mama would consider their decision carefully before finally exclaiming, "Yes, I think I should be able to make you both a dress like that." Mama was amazing. How she was able to just look at a picture and cut out the pattern herself was a mystery to the girls.

When she was finished, the girls each had a dress that was made just like the picture in the catalog. Mama was somewhat of a perfectionist. She wasn't satisfied unless every seam was smooth and every line matched up perfectly with the next. Winna and Allie were always in such a hurry for Mama to finish them; they pleaded for her to work more quickly. However, no amount of coaxing and pleading seemed to convince Mama to take any shortcuts. The wait was always worth the extra time when Mama finally slipped those special dresses over their heads. They squealed with delight as they went twirling and sashaying around the room, their wide skirts brushing their bare legs making them giggle.

Some of the time Mama bought material from the catalog, but usually she had to use flour sacks. Flour came in printed cotton sacks. Once the flour had been emptied into the flour bin, Mama took out the stitches in the sack so the material would lie in one big flat piece. Next, she would wash the material and iron it. Finally, it was ready to be cut out and sewn into a dress. Picking out a sack of flour was an exciting time for a person because that flour sack just might become your next dress.

This year Allie's dress was red. Tiny white flowers dotted the material like cherry blossoms caught in a spring breeze. Mama made the dress with pearl-like buttons going down the back and a white sash was tied in a bow at her back. Winna's dress was just like Allie's, only her dress was purple with pink berries scattered across it. Purple was Winna's favorite color, so whenever they got a piece of purple material, it went without saying that it would be Winna's. Her sash was pink to match the pink berries on the purple material. The best thing about their dresses this year though was the hem. It didn't go straight across the bottom the way dresses usually did; the bottom was scalloped, a wavy hemline that was sure to be the envy of all their friends. Mama had hesitated when they had shown her the picture of the fancy dress, but, just like they'd expected, Mama finally agreed.

It felt so good to not be wearing their long stockings that Allie could hardly keep from dancing through the cemetery. She detested wearing stockings. They were heavy, scratchy, and they never stayed put. She was always having to pull them up and twist them into place. Her favorite part of summer was going barefoot and barelegged. Oh, how she loved the feeling of running and playing without worrying about her stockings falling down.

Allie remembered a funny story Audie had told them about her mom. It seems that one day when Mrs. James was just a little girl she was playing pop the whip with her classmates. She was running and jumping when all of a sudden—down came her drawers, stockings, and all. How embarrassed she had been. The girls had laughed until tears rolled down their cheeks when Audie had told them that story. Allie could only imagine how embarrassing that would be. That would even be worse than having a boy write your name on his desk. Poor Mrs. James! It went without saying that Allie was always careful when she was playing any rowdy games after hearing that story, making sure her stockings were pulled up under her armpits.

The girls made their way through the cemetery to the graves of their little sisters, such tiny graves in among the larger ones. The stones, embedded with shiny specks of quartz, stood side by side marking the two spots. A miniature pink rosebush shaded the little mounds, the tiny blossoms giving off a sweet aroma so appropriate for their sweet dispositions. The sisters took pink carnations from their bouquets and placed one on each of their baby sister's graves. Allie placed hers on Shirley's grave, and Winna put her delicate flower on Annetta Joyce's grave, standing in silence for several minutes showing their respect and love. Their little sisters' graves were always the first place they placed flowers each Decoration Day. It seemed only fitting. Slowly they began walking on, making their way in and out among the graves of other family members placing flowers on the earthen mounds they had become so familiar with over the years. Some of the graves had monuments with engraved names, but many, like their sisters', had only flat rocks with the names and dates scratched into the stone with crude tools. Daddy and Mama planned to get monuments someday for their young daughters. Even without fancy headstones, no graves were given any greater care than theirs. The girls always felt bad that some of the graves didn't even get flowers put on them at Decoration or any time. Many graves seemed to have been forgotten as the years passed. Winna and Allie took it as a personal responsibility to decorate as many of those graves as possible. As soon as all of their own flowers had been placed on graves, they ran around picking fresh flowers from the peonies, roses, and jonquils growing in and around the cemetery putting them on the graves that were still bare.

The sound of gospel singing caught the girls' attention. Looking to the west side of the cemetery, they saw that everyone was walking that way, gathering under the trees. Many people were already sitting on the rough plank boards that were set across stumps which served as pews; pastel dresses, dark trousers, wide-brimmed hats, and bonnets clustered together under the shade of the white oak trees. This was another reason why Decoration Day was so special. Instead of having church services in the school building, they got to have their service outside under the trees. Winna put the last of her jonquils on the unmarked grave she was working on and ran with Allie over to join the others. They scooted in beside their cousins as the crowd sang on:

Shall we gather at the river,
Where bright angel feet have trod . . .

Decoration Day was a time of the year when they got to see some of their cousins on their Daddy's side. Uncle Henry and Aunt Violet sat on the pew in front of them. Their children, Conrad, Willa Mae, Anna Faye, Bernard, Melvin, and Travis, were scattered here and there along the wooden planks. Their older son Raymond with his lovely wife Alma and little daughter Nettie were sitting with them as well. Allie didn't see their other daughter Lillian, but knew she would be joining the rest before too long. She was older and married. Allie looked forward to getting to see her and her small children.

A light wind began to blow making the crepe paper ribbon brush across Allie's face. The leaves danced in the breeze and the birds blended their sweet sounds to the voices of the worshippers. Allie reached over and squeezed Winna's hand. She was so happy she could scarcely sit still. Why couldn't every day be this wonderful? It was a beautiful day. She was surrounded by her loving family, and she felt so pretty in her new dress, shoes, and socks. She swung her legs back and forth admiring her new white shoes and lacy socks. She was going to be so careful with these shoes and not turn them over like she did so many of her shoes. After all, she was growing up. She should start wearing shoes some during the summer months and not run around barefooted all summer long. She was fixing to be a young lady after all.

Allie looked around for Cody. She didn't care what those love vines said, she knew he liked her. A few days after Allie and Winna had scattered the love vines on the plants to see which boys liked them, she had secretly gone to the spring to see which love vines had grown. Allie blushed when she remembered how Bobbie's love vine had grown up and down and all over the bitterweed she had thrown it on. The ones she had put on the other two plants had barely grown at all. Oh well, it was just a silly old game anyway. It didn't mean anything. Allie had pulled the love vine, bitterweed, and all up by the roots before Winna could see it. Winna would have loved to have seen that to tease Allie. Allie smoothed her dress and tried to pay attention to the service. She caught a whiff of fried chicken.

She couldn't wait for lunch. She knew a wonderful lunch, spread on blankets beneath the white oaks across the road from the cemetery, awaited her. She couldn't wait to dig into Aunt Nora's pies. Aunt Nora always stacked her pies. Allie used to not understand why she did that. Mama finally explained to her that Aunt Nora just had one pie pan. She would make an apple pie and turn it out on a plate. Then she'd make another apple pie and stack it on the first one. She'd do that five or six times. She'd end up with a stack of pies as high as a three-layer cake. She stacked them as a way of transporting them as easily as possibly. Stacking them made them set in the tubs more easily and didn't take up as much room. They were delicious, and it was always a treat to everyone to get a big slice of Aunt Nora's apple pies. Aunt Nora had a big family, so she always brought a lot of food to the Decoration. Even though Mama didn't come today, she had sent a basketful of food with them. Allie loved Mama's cooking the best. Mama made wonderful dressing, yeast rolls, raisin pie, and chicken and dumplings. Allie felt her mouth drooling. She sucked it back in before it rolled out the corner of her mouth.

The song came to an end, and Mr. Robbins rose to deliver the lesson.

"We are here today with our family and friends . . ." Allie's mind wandered as the preacher continued on. She looked at the sky and noticed some dark clouds gathering in the west. The wind seemed to have grown a little stronger, whipping her dress against her legs making the scalloped edge ripple. She had been right. Her dress had been the envy of some of the girls. Montene had asked if her mom could borrow Mama's pattern. Allie smoothed down her dress and looked around. Some of the women tied their bonnets a little more securely under their chins. Allie caught sight of one of the paper flowers from a nearby grave come loose and go flying up into the air, spinning round and round when it came down like a maple seed before settling onto a different grave. She sure hoped it didn't rain and ruin this beautiful day. Allie was brought back to the sermon. Something Mr. Robbins was saying caught her attention. He was saying something about things we have learned from our ancestors, many of whose graves were around us today. "They not only knew what the good book said about honesty and trust, they lived it."

Allie's face grew hot. Why was he preaching about honesty? She didn't feel honest. She hadn't felt honest for several weeks now. She turned and glanced over her right shoulder to where Grandpa Shoemate was sitting. He was looking straight at her. He knew! He knew she wasn't honest. Allie whipped back around and faced the preacher. Grandpa knew she had disobeyed him and had worn the locket when he had asked her not to. It had been his own mother's locket, and he'd never see it again. How could he know though? Allie wasn't even sure herself if she had kept the necklace on or had taken it off the day of the fire. Either way though, the necklace was gone. It would have burned up if it had been in the house anyway. Why did it keep haunting her? Why did she feel so guilty about it? She wished Grandpa had never given it to her in the first place. He would still have it if he hadn't! Tears stung her eyes. She missed Grandpa. She missed his hugs and his laughter. She missed spending time with him. It had been so long since she sat on his lap or taken his hand for a walk. Allie had continued to avoid him for weeks now, ever since the day of the awful fire. It was like the necklace had come between them.

When the sermon ended, Mr. Huett led them in one last song. A final prayer was said asking a blessing on the food they were about to eat. Allie and Winna stood and wandered with the rest of the family to the spot where they always spread their lunch at Decoration. The sun had gone behind the clouds, and the sound of thunder was growing a little louder. The women began scurrying around getting baskets and tubs of food from the wagon beds. Allie walked over and patted Grandpa Stephens' mule. All of a sudden, she wasn't very hungry.

Grandpa's mule, Sure Foot, stood behind Grandpa's wagon munching on grain from the gray canvas feed sack tied around his neck. Sure Foot was Grandpa's pride and joy. Grandpa claimed his mule could climb the steepest cliff of any mountain and not miss a step. In fact, that's how Sure Foot had gotten his name. Grandpa had bought him off a man in Eureka a couple of years ago. Grandpa said he'd never been over such a steep rocky trail as he had that day when he'd gone after him. He said that on the way home that mule never missed a step. After that, Grandpa said he'd put Sure Foot up against anyone's mule. Allie rubbed his dusty charcoal hair. His hair felt stiff and coarse underneath her hands, like the straw in one of Mama's brooms. His ears twitched as a horsefly buzzed in and out around them. "Want to know a secret?" Allie whispered softly in his ear, brushing away the fly. She continued to stroke his neck. Sure Foot's left eye rolled sideways to look at her. "I let down someone I love, and now I feel just awful about it." Sure Foot's head bobbed. Allie's hand stopped suddenly, and she looked quizzically at Sure Foot. She smiled wondering if Sure Foot had really nodded that he understood and then went on. "You see, I really didn't mean to let him down. I only wanted to try on this necklace he gave me, but then Winna had to come in and I hid the necklace and I forgot that I had it on. Then we went to church and then the house caught on fire, and it would have burned anyway." Tears welled up in Allie's eyes. Sure Foot's jaw went side to side as his teeth ground the grain. Allie laid her head against his neck feeling the rhythm of the chewing. Her head swayed back and forth with the motion. "I'm afraid Grandpa will never trust me again," she said. "It was his mother's, and he trusted it with me, and I let him down."

"Allie, are you talking to a mule?" Winna laughed. "Come on and fix you a plate before these hungry cousins of ours eat every scrap."

Allie gave Sure Foot one final pat. "I wish I was as steady and dependable as you are!" she said as she walked away.

The meal was delicious as usual, but, soon after, it began to rain, lightly at first and then a steady downpour. Everyone ran for whatever cover they could find. Allie and Winna grabbed a blanket and headed for cover under Grandpa Stephens' wagon box. They lay on their stomachs and looked out at the falling rain. The petals of the beautiful paper flowers first drooped and then dropped, leaving sharp metal stems poking sharply out of the ground. The hours and hours of work were ruined in only a few minutes. The graves, beautiful only moments before, now ugly once again. "It's just not fair," Allie complained looking out at the ruined flowers. "Just think of all the hours Mama, Grandma, and Aunt Ollie spent on those flowers."

"Not only them," Winna sniffed. "All the ladies in the whole community. It's all they've been doing for weeks. All that time wasted!" The girls were sobbing openly now. Allie looked over at Winna about to say something else. All at once, Allie burst out laughing. Winna, startled, looked at Allie, thinking she had surely lost her mind. As soon as she did, she too burst out laughing. The rain had soaked their hair and the paper ribbons tied around their heads causing the crepe paper to fade and run. The color had streaked down their faces and hair. Allie's face and hair were streaked with red and Winna's was streaked with blue. They laughed so hard. Their tears of disappointment mixed with their tears of joy had joined the rain already on their faces. What a hideous sight they made. This day that had started with them feeling so beautiful loaded with gorgeous flowers and feeling so elegant had ended with them sitting underneath a wagon box in the mud with colored faces and hair! "I don't know about you, sister," Winna said as she leaned into Allie, "but I kinda doubt if the boys would be too impressed with us right now!" Allie doubled into squeals of laughter thinking what Cody would think of her if he could see her now.

"Boys!" she said in between laughter and hiccups. "Who needs them anyway?"

Chapter 11

We had the first TV in Elizabeth. In about the mid-fifties, we were picking cotton in the bottoms. The people we were picking for asked Dad and Mom over to watch TV on a Friday night. They watched boxing. Dad loved it, so he bought us a TV. Down there where we were, you could put the antenna on the ground and lean it up against the side of the house and get all the channels in Memphis. When we got home that winter, Dad, Jake, and Rex hooked up the TV. They put the antenna on the ground and leaned it up against the side of the house. Nothing! Next, they put the antenna on a pole. Nothing! Finally, they put the pole on top of the house. We barely got channels 3 and 10 from Springfield. Dad was mad as heck. If he had known that, he never would have gotten the TV. Grandpa Crotts lived with us then. When his brothers and their wives would come and visit us, Mom would cover *the TV with a tablecloth. Grandpa's family called the TV A Devil's Box!*

—Betty (Bobbie's younger sister) (2010)

June 1941

Bobbie

Grandpa bounced little Rex up and down on his foot. His foot pumped in time to his musical chant:

> Ride a little horsey, go to town,
> You'd better be careful and don't fall down!

Grandpa quickly dropped his worn boot to the porch floor, making Rex take a plunge. Rex squealed with laughter and climbed hurriedly back onto Grandpa's foot. He wrapped his chubby little arms around Grandpa's leg and jumped up and down, obviously ready for another ride.

"More!" he begged. Grandpa groaned, lifted his leg with Rex still hanging on, and crossed his right leg over his left. Taking a deep breath, he started pumping his boot up and down, slowly at first and then faster and faster. He began the second verse of the song:

Ride a little horsey, pacey nanny
Here he goes to see his granny!

Once again, Grandpa dropped his foot at the end of the verse when he said "granny," causing Rex to plunge quickly to the floor. Rex's fine baby hair stuck straight up as his bottom sailed straight down to the rough boards of the porch. Rex laughed in delight. He had barely reached the floor before he begged, "More!" Poor Grandpa! He'd been at this for close to an hour, alternating between riding Rex and then Jake on one foot and then another. His legs must be about to fall off.

Grandpa lifted Rex off his foot and patted his behind. "You two little cowpokes run along now and see if your momma can't wrestle you up something to eat. Cowboys gotta get nourishment, ya know. Riding broncos is hard work."

The two toddlers galloped off whooping and making pretend they were still riding Grandpa's foot. Grandpa watched them go and chuckled. He turned to his older grandsons, Bobbie and Willie, and his son, Thurman, and asked, "Did I ever tell you boys about how I used to ride broncos?"

The boys looked up in surprise. Grandpa never ceased to amaze them. Bobbie's hand froze in midair around his knife. He was whittling a hickory stick. His shavings had continued to get thinner and thinner. Thin white slivers of the stick lay all around his legs. With each stroke, he tried to slide the knife's edge all the way down the side of the slender stick to the bottom without breaking his stroke. He just about had it mastered. "You rode broncos, Grandpa?" he asked.

"Yes sir, I shore nuff did," Grandpa said with enthusiasm. He slapped his leg and grabbed his gray felt hat off his head. He twirled it in the air and rocked in his chair imitating the motion of sitting atop the back of a bucking horse.

The boys looked at one another in stunned surprise and laughed.

"Did you ever get busted?" Willie asked with a snaggletoothed grin. Willie had recently lost most of his front teeth, and he looked about as toothless as Grandpa.

"Newwwwwwwwww! Busted?" Grandpa looked at them in shocked disbelief. "Whacha talking about? Me, busted?"

"When did you do that, Pa?" Thurman wanted to know. "I never knowed of you riding broncos."

"Well, sir, it was way back before any of you boys were born when I was just a young man." Grandpa settled back in his chair and commenced to rocking. He took out his own pocketknife and began cleaning out his fingernails. Bobbie had noticed the nail of the finger where Grandpa had gotten snakebit had grown out curved like a bird's talon. Bobbie supposed the snake's venom had done something to do with it. Grandpa continued, "Bobbie, it was when your and Willie's Momma was just a little bitty thing. Grandma and

I moved out to Kansas for three or four years. We weren't making a good enough living here, and I heard tell of work out thata way. We loaded up our two young-ens in the back of our covered wagon and moved west. I got a job out there working for a man named Johnson on a big cattle ranch."

Bobbie thought of his Grandma as a young mother loading up her precious young children and moving to an unknown place. He couldn't remember his Grandma Crotts that well. Bobbie had only been seven years old when she died. He did know Grandma was just a little thing all her life. He wished he could have known her when she had been young and energetic, not old and bedridden. She had to have been very brave to climb into a covered wagon with her babies, agreeing to move to an unknown place away from her own family, not knowing what might lay in store for them.

"What else did you do besides ride broncos out there?" he asked Grandpa.

"Well, now, fellers, I worked hard. I did things out there I wouldn't ask you all to do."

"Like what, Pa?" Thurman wanted to know.

"Well, I slopped the hogs, milked the cows, hoed the garden, broke horses, and just about anything else the farmhands asked me to do," Grandpa answered.

"We do most of them things, besides breaking horses," Thurman said. He and Willie had scooted over close to Grandpa and were hanging on to his every word.

"Yessir," Grandpa replied, "but you don't do 'em from sunup to sundown, do ya, now?"

"No, sir," Willie admitted.

"That's what I'm talking about," Grandpa responded. "Back then, I only got sommers between five or six hours of sleep a night. The workday started 'fore daylight and ended way after dark. If I hadn't been a young man, I wouldn't of been able to hold up to it."

"Why did ya have to work so hard, Pa?" Thurman wanted to know.

"Well, son, I had to make a living for my family, don't ya know. There I was just a young man still wet behind the ears with a family depending on me."

Bobbie, Willie, and Thurman looked at one another, dumbfounded.

"Why were your ears wet, Grandpa?" Willie asked the question they all wanted to know. Bobbie's eyes trailed to Grandpa's ears to see if he detected any wetness still there.

Grandpa threw back his head and laughed. "Now that's a cowboy phrase, boys. I can see how you'd be a little confused by that expression. Well, let me explain it to you. You know when a little calf is born it's all wet, covered with the mucus from its mother's womb."

Bobbie thought back to the newborn calf he'd seen just a few days ago down at Raydo Strouds'. It was so cute as it struggled to stand, and it had been, as Grandpa said, wet all over. Grandpa continued, "Well, in a little bit, that calf starts drying off, don't ya know. First the thin hair on its legs starts drying and then the hair on its face and back. The last place, though, that gets dry is behind its ears. A little wet behind the ears is just an expression that means someone is a little inexperienced or doesn't know too much about something—they're still a little 'new' at something just like a newborn calf. That's what I meant when I said I was wet behind the ears. I just meant that I was just a young man and didn't know too much about taking care of a family or making a living."

"Hummm," Bobbie mused, nodding his head. "I guess that makes sense. Holding up his knife, he said with a lopsided smile, "Kinda like I'm still learning to whittle. I guess my ears are still a little wet when it comes to whittling."

Grandpa laughed and hit his knee with his hand. "Shore nuff, son, something like that anyway," he said. He chuckled again and went to rocking in his chair once again.

Bobbie settled back against the post of the porch and resumed his whittling. Why did every conversation with Grandpa turn into a lesson of some kind or another? He thought Grandpa should have been a teacher like his own pa had been. He did like that expression "wet behind the ears" though. He'd store it back in "his gray matter" as Mr. Schauffler called your brain and pull it out and use it every now and again. His attention focused back to Grandpa who had started talking again. He sure was in a talking mood this morning. Whew! It was hard to keep up with the old man!

"Bertha and I were married back in 1910, it was. The very next year we had our first child, Eva, Eva Alice, named after my own mother, Belinda Alice. Then a couple of years later we had Ed. It wasn't long after that that we decided to try a go of it in Kansas. Like I said, we were just having too hard of a time of it here. Gonna get a fresh start, that's what we wanted to do. Jobs round here were few and far between, scarce as hen's teeth, they were." Grandpa carefully folded his pocketknife and put it down into his overall's pocket. He reached down into his shirt pocket and took out his pipe.

Bobbie, Willie, and Thurman looked at one another. What in the world did Grandpa mean by "as scarce as hen's teeth?" Ever so slightly they shook their heads at one another. Each one of them knew what those shakes of their heads meant: keep your mouths shut. No use getting Grandpa going on that one. One lesson a day from Grandpa was more than enough.

Grandpa took out his packet of tobacco and pulled some of the moist, loose leaves from the pouch. He stuffed it down into his smoke-stained pipe. Striking a match on the bottom of his boot, he held the flame up to his pipe. The flickering flame ducked its head down into the pipe as Grandpa took a long draw. He blew out a stream of gray smoke. Grandpa closed his eyes in apparent relaxation and leaned his head against the back of the chair. The smoke drifted past Bobbie. It had a sweet, musty smell to it. Bobbie liked the smell. The smoke continued on its way circling up off the porch drifting lazily out into the trees. Grandpa sat enjoying his pipe a few minutes, seemingly lost in thought before continuing.

Opening his eyes, he took the pipe from his mouth. "While we were in Kansas," he said suddenly, startling the boys, "we had Alma, purtest little thing you ever saw. So there I was with a young wife and three young children. I guess that gets me back to your question, Thurman. When a man's got a wife and three little ones depending on him, he's gotta work hard. There's no way around it. The way I look at it, if a man won't provide for his family, now that's a pretty sorry man. No, sir, I'm not talking about a man who can't provide for his family. There's a difference, don't ya know. I've seen that happen now and again. There's been times when I haven't been able to care for my own family the way I would have liked, but I've always done the best I could, let me tell ya. I'm just saying it's a shame when a man doesn't make the effort." Grandpa leaned back and puffed on his pipe. He had a faraway look in his eyes. Did Bobbie see tears in Grandpa's eyes? Bobbie quickly looked away. If Grandpa did have tears in his eyes, Bobbie didn't want to stare.

Bobbie looked down at his whittling. He knew what Grandpa was talking about when he said he wasn't always able to take care of his own family the way he would have liked. Even though Grandpa's family had seen some very hard times, it was never on account of Grandpa not working. Grandpa was a hard worker, always had been. Bobbie remembered an especially hard winter a couple of years ago. Grandpa had gotten a job that year clearing some land for Mr. Dodge, a man who lived south of town. He had several acres of land that he wanted the timber cleared and the land smoothed for pasture. Grandpa was thankful for the job and started work on that land midsummer. He worked hard every day, seven days a week. Well, fall came and he still wasn't quite finished. He went to Mr. Dodge and asked if he might get part of the money he'd already earned so he could go ahead and buy his kids some shoes before cold weather hit. Mr. Dodge told him no, that he wasn't going to pay a thing until the job was completely finished. Well, Grandpa worked even longer hours. He kept his older boys out of school to help him. They would hitch their mules up before daylight, and it would be way after dark when they'd come dragging back in. Finally, they finished the job somewhere around the middle of November. By then, the weather was downright cold of a morning, but there hadn't been a heavy frost yet.

Well, when Grandpa went to Mr. Dodge to collect his earnings, Mr. Dodge told him he didn't have the money and that Grandpa would just have to wait until he sold some of his hogs before he could get paid. Grandpa didn't like it, understandably so, but what could he do about it? That was the year Thurman and some of his brothers went without shoes until after the first snow. Bobbie would never forget the pained look on Grandpa's face when he'd told his kids they would have to make do without shoes for a few more weeks. Yes, Grandpa had seen hard times, but it wasn't because he didn't try. Bobbie thought back on what Grandpa had said about being wet behind the ears when he'd been a young family man. Bobbie figured Grandpa's ears hadn't stayed wet for very long.

Grandpa Crotts with granddaughter Lanetta

The sound of squealing and laughter interrupted Bobbie's thoughts. Grandpa stirred in his chair. "What are those young-uns up to now?" he chuckled as he got up from his chair. Bobbie, Willie, and Thurman stood as well. Grandpa went through the house to go outside as the three boys climbed over the banisters of the porch and went around the corner of the house. Rex and Jake were playing at the side of the house with Grandma James' dog, Jiggs. Jiggs was a little brown house dog. He wasn't much bigger than a red squirrel and about as quick as one too. Jiggs was running around the yard with Jake and Rex hot on his heels.

When Grandpa James died a couple of years ago, some of Grandma's relatives came to see her from California. They brought her a little dog all the way from the west coast. They thought she needed a pet to keep her company with the loss of Grandpa. Grandma had objected at first, thinking a house dog was silly. Folks in these parts of the country didn't know anything about cute little house dogs. Her relatives insisted though, and it wasn't too long before Grandma became attached to him. In a few weeks, Jiggs was sleeping right up in the bed with her. Jiggs stayed in the house with Grandma most of the time now, so when he got out of the house, he went a little crazy.

Right now, he was running lickety-split all over the yard, like Jake or Rex did when Momma had her switch after them. Jiggs would run in a circle and all of a sudden stop and lie down. He'd act like he wasn't paying any attention to the little boys and let Rex and Jake get right up to him. Then the minute one of them would reach out to touch him, he'd jump up and take off running again. The little boys would scream at the top of their lungs with delight and take to chasing him again. Grandpa and the older boys watched them and laughed at the show about as much as the little ones laughed in their fun. Grandpa and the older grandsons walked over and sat down underneath the shade of the walnut tree at the side of the yard.

"Grandma James sure loves that little dog, doesn't she?" Bobbie said as he commenced to whittling again.

"He's about like her baby now," Grandpa answered. Grandpa sat enjoying his pipe for a few more minutes, watching his younger grandsons chasing Jiggs. "Now talking about someone who had a hard time," Grandpa began again, "Your Grandma Adeline James had about as hard a time as any a person I've ever known. You know that she's three-quarter Indian, don't you?"

The boys nodded. Bobbie and Willie knew they had Indian blood running in their veins. Grandma had the characteristics of an Indian, light-brown skin and brown eyes. Her hair was gray now, but it had once been dark, and it was coarse and straight like an Indian's. Bobbie supposed he had inherited some of Grandma's characteristics with his dark hair. Grandma was tall too. She had been taller than Grandpa. She had also been known to go on the warpath every now and then too. Bobbie grinned at this. She did have a stern disposition and wasn't bashful about telling you her opinion. He did love his Grandma though. Willie was especially close to her, staying at her house more so than their own. Grandma more or less claimed Willie as her own, and as much as this may have irritated Momma privately, she never confronted Grandma about it. Grandma had come from Randolph County over close to Mammoth Springs. Bobbie knew she had grown up poor living in a dirt-floor cabin with her own parents, older sister, and younger siblings. Bobbie guessed growing up so hard may have been one reason for Grandma's stern way.

Bobbie looked up as Grandpa continued, "Margaret was your grandma's older sister. She carried a pistol in her dress pocket every day. Know why she carried that pistol?"

"To shoot the white men?" Willie guessed. He had heard about cowboys and Indians, and he supposed that since she was an Indian, she needed the gun to protect herself from the cowboys who must have been white. Why else would she need a pistol?

"Nope," Grandpa said shaking his head. He looked over at the boys. "That's how they got supper on the table. As Margaret and your grandma went about doing the chores for the day, Margaret kept that pistol handy and shot whatever animal she got the chance to shoot. That's what they had for supper that night. Your grandma and her sister, Margaret, were the two oldest kids in the family, and it was up to them to help get food for the family."

"What about their dad and mom?" Bobbie wanted to know.

"Well, son, times were hard, like we were talking about earlier, even a lot more so for this family though. Their dad was probably out trying to scratch out a living working sommers, and their momma was probably tied down with young-uns at home. I know we've seen some hard times in our own family here, but there are folks who have it a lot harder than we ever have. A feller needs to remember that any time he's down on his luck. All he has to do is look around. It won't be long before he sees somebody else a lot worse off than he is himself."

Bobbie thought about a person wondering about where his next meal was coming from. He couldn't imagine times being harder than that. Using one of Grandpa's favorite expressions, a feller like that had to be at the "bottom of the barrel," so to speak. Bobbie didn't care how hard a person looked around; he didn't think you could ever find a person worse off than that.

Bobbie with younger cousins and siblings

"Was it that way with you and Momma when you moved out to Kansas?" Thurman wanted to know.

"Well, Thurman, it was about that bad. We didn't know where our next meal was coming from, I can tell you that," Grandpa said. He shook his head and clicked his tongue. "Times were hard, real hard."

Bobbie looked up as he heard the back door slam. Momma came out and tossed some scraps over the fence. She stopped a few minutes to watch the boys still chasing Jiggs around the yard. She laughed and threw up her hand at Grandpa and the boys. Dusting off her apron, Momma went back inside.

"That little dog must be getting tired," Bobbie said. "Those boys though," Bobbie laughed, "They NEVER run out of energy!"

"Grandpa, why did you and Grandma come back from Kansas?" Willie asked Grandpa. "If times were so hard here, why didn't you all just stay in Kansas?"

"Well, sir, the job at the ranch ran out after a few years. We could have stayed on out there though 'cause by that time, they had started drilling for oil out there. Most all the men in the area were going to work in the oil fields. I gave Berthie a choice. I told her I could go to work climbing the derricks of the oil rigs or we could just come on back home. She told me she thought we should come back. So that's what we did. We made a beeline for home. I figure she was afraid I'd get hurt out there in the oil fields. Anyway, that's how we ended up back here."

A loud growl and a piercing scream made all four of them jump. "What in tarnation?" Grandpa shouted as he sprung off the ground. He took off running up the hill as fast as he could with Bobbie, Willie, and Thurman right behind him. Momma ran out the house, the door slamming behind her, at about the same time, a look of terror on her face. Little Rex was sitting on the ground screaming at the top of his lungs.

As Bobbie came upon them, Grandpa had already scooped Rex up into his arms. Momma was beside them. Blood was running down Rex's face and Grandpa's shirtsleeve was already soaked with blood. Bobbie looked closer and could see a gaping hole in Rex's cheek. Everything was happening so quickly, he had a hard time taking it all in. Rex was reaching for Momma, screaming and crying. Momma was crying and reaching for him. Grandpa was kicking and screaming at Jiggs. Jake was crying about as loudly as Rex and was pulling at Momma's skirt. Everybody was making so much racket, it seemed as if all nature had stopped its normal activities and sounds to watch and listen to them. Thurman seemed to be the only one who had kept a calm head through all of this. Slipping up close beside Bobbie and Willie, he whispered, "Come on! Let's go get the doc."

Bobbie nodded, and all three boys took off running as fast as their legs would carry them up the road to the community doctor's house. Doc Sutton lived just north of town, about a half-mile away. The doctor was outside getting some things out of his buggy when the boys arrived, breathless. The doctor could tell by their appearance and actions that something was wrong, but couldn't understand their garbled words. Finally, giving up, he just motioned them up into the buggy. Going around to the back of the house, he quickly caught his horse and hitched him up to the buggy. He ran into the house, grabbed his black medical bag, climbed up onto the narrow seat of the buggy, and took off down the road.

By the time the boys had calmed down enough to explain to the doctor what they thought had happened, the buggy was halfway down the road to their house. Apparently, when Momma had thrown the scraps over the fence, there had been some tasty tidbits in there that Jiggs had wanted to eat. When Rex and Jake had continued to play and had run upon him, he had snapped at them and had caught Rex on the cheek. They told the doctor there was an awfully lot of blood, and Bobbie said he had seen a bad gash on Rex's cheek. The doctor began at once bombarding them with questions: "Whose dog was it? How long has your Grandma had him? Is it an inside or an outside dog?" Bobbie grew a little more tense with every question. Then the doctor asked a question that made Bobbie's blood run cold. "Has Jiggs been acting strange lately?" The questions began to click in Bobbie's mind. He knew why the doctor was so concerned. Bobbie looked at Willie and Thurman. He saw the scared looks on their faces as well.

The yard was quiet when they pulled up; apparently, everyone was in the house by now. Thankfully, the awful screaming and crying had stopped. The doctor handed Bobbie the horse's reins, grabbed his bag, and hopped down from the carriage. The boys watched as he ran inside. Bobbie, Willie, and Thurman slowly climbed down from the buggy and tied the horse to the post. They wandered into the yard. They didn't really want to go into the house for fear of what they might see or hear, but they didn't feel like doing anything else until they found out if their youngest brother was going to be okay. They sat down on the floor of the porch to wait for the news. The boys were unnaturally quiet. None of them mentioned what they most feared. Bobbie took out his knife and picked up a stick. Willie lay down with his hands under his head and looked off into space. Thurman sat down beside ole Buck, gently rubbing his head and ears.

The same thoughts were going through all of their minds: rabies or hydrophobia. This was a sickness that sometimes spread through animals in an area. It had gone through their own community before. Bobbie didn't remember it, but he had heard the older men talk about it. It wasn't known exactly how the sickness started, but it was known how the disease was spread. An animal that contracted the disease went mad. When it did so, it would bite other animals causing those animals to go mad as well. The disease would make an animal behave in ways that it normally wouldn't.

For example, a nocturnal animal such as a raccoon might come wandering out during the daylight. They would often become aggressive, biting for no reason. Often an animal with the disease could be recognized by foaming or slobbering at the mouth. For some reason, not all animals were susceptible to the disease. Daddy said skunks, foxes, raccoons, and coyotes were some of the worst to get it. What had Bobbie so scared though was that Daddy said cats and dogs could get it too.

Daddy always made sure his fox dogs were vaccinated for rabies. Since he took them foxhunting, he said there was a good chance they could pick up the disease from the foxes since foxes can carry the disease. Once a year, someone came to town offering free rabies shots to all the dogs. Bobbie remembered Daddy taking Buck and Fancy up there the last time the shots were offered. For the life of him though, he couldn't remember Grandma taking Jiggs up there.

Rex's screaming had started up again. It sent chills down Bobbie's spine. He got up and wandered out into the yard. Bobbie hated to think what they might be doing to him. That gash had been deep, and just touching it was sure to be painful. What did they do to bad cuts? Rex was still just a baby, and what about poor Momma? He knew how things like this upset her. It was going to be a long day.

The day passed slowly. News of the dog bite traveled throughout the community, and wherever Bobbie went, everyone was upset about it and wanted to know how it happened. Doc Sutton spent most of the afternoon at the house. Bobbie learned that the first thing he did was to wash the wound thoroughly with soap and water. He told them that it had been a good thing that the gash had bled so much. He explained to them how blood cleanses a wound. It took thirteen stitches to close the cut in Rex's cheek, and Bobbie supposed it would take that many more to close the wound in Momma's heart. Rex was Momma's baby, and she hadn't had dry eyes since it happened. The doctor must have given Rex something to relax him or to make him sleep because he slept the rest of the afternoon and all that night. Bobbie had overheard the doctor talking to Daddy about rabies. The doctor explained that since Jiggs was a house dog and hadn't been acting strangely, he was certain he did not have the disease. He did suggest that Grandma get Jiggs vaccinated the next time the shots were offered in the area, just to be on the safe side.

Grandma James felt just awful about what happened and said that for the life of her she couldn't understand what had made Jiggs act that way. Bobbie knew it would be a long time before she would let any of them play with Jiggs again. There were two reasons for this. For one thing, she certainly didn't want anything like this to ever happen to any of her grandchildren or anyone again. She loved them all, and it broke her heart to see little Rex hurt like he was. She would keep Jiggs in the house and watch him and make sure he could be trusted before allowing him to be around any of them again. She said herself that she might never let him be around any of the babies ever again. There was another reason though that she was going to be cautious with Jiggs, a reason that probably had to do more with Jiggs' safety than with the grandchildren's. Bobbie winced when he thought of Daddy's words. He didn't even like to think about what Daddy said he'd do to Jiggs if anything like this ever happened again. He hoped for all of their sakes it never did.

Chapter 12

I loved going to my grandpa and grandma Stephens' house. I almost felt like "Alice in Wonderland" when I wandered around in the orchard and through the grape arbor. Their chicken houses were among a grove of plum trees that had branches low enough to catch in our hair if we didn't stoop down. Grandma had a variety of chickens. There were some hens that had no feathers on their necks. They were very ugly, and whenever I ate an egg for breakfast, I always wondered if one of those hens laid that egg!

My Grandpa was a fox hunter, and he always kept at least two hounds. He kept them tied out at the back fence, and he had big barrels filled with straw for their shelter. I loved hearing him blow his fox horn that he used to call his dogs when they were gone after a foxhunt. His dogs knew the sound of his horn from all the other fox hunters' horns.

I can remember every facet of their house, inside and out. The house was made of rough planks painted white with a long porch across the front. There were banisters with cedar posts painted red. The house looked large from the outside, but there were only four rooms. There was a screened-in back porch that you had to go through to go into the dining room and kitchen. The living room was small, but it held the double bed that they slept in, a chair for each of them, the heating stove, a settee, which some would call a cot, and a dresser that held the radio and kerosene lamp. The dresser had a mirror that was one of those that you could look into and it either made you look very long faced, or if you changed positions, you looked broad and fat. We had so much fun looking in that mirror. Grandma's rocking chair was low, but had a very high back. Both the seat and back had a cushion. I always thought Grandma looked so small in that big chair. I can't remember Grandpa's chair. Grandma slept in a long flannel gown with long sleeves. She wore a nightcap that was white and had strings that tied under her chin. I guess Grandpa slept in his long handles.

Just off the living room was a bedroom that had two double beds, a stand table between the beds for the lamp, an organ, Grandma's treadle sewing machine, and a big camelback *trunk. At the door leading out on the screened-in porch, there was a door that opened to go upstairs. There they kept apples stored for the winter. I remember them wrapping the apples in paper and putting them in baskets. One type of apple interested me so much. It was dark red, almost black on the outside but the inside was as white as snow. It was my favorite because of its uniqueness. There were other things in the upstairs besides apples. There were some high-top button up shoes. They didn't have strings, but tiny buttons with elastic cords to fasten them with. There were numerous buttons, and it took a long time to get them all buttoned up. I loved putting them on and strutting around, but only upstairs! I am sure there were other things up there, but the apples and shoes were my favorite. It was neat and tidy as I remember. Going to Grandma and Grandpa's was always an adventure!*

—Allie (2010)

I remember something my sisters and I did after we were grown-up. Dad bought a car. Before this, we had only Dad's truck he used to haul off lumber from the mill. We would sometimes go to West Plains or Mountain Home with him. Apparently, we didn't have a radio in the car. We would sing on the way. We girls would sing soprano, Mom alto, and Dad bass. It was always church songs that we all knew by heart. One day, Dad wasn't in a very good mood. Carol, Betty, and

I started singing as soon as we were all in the car. Dad asked couldn't we wait until we at least got started! (Carol was a younger sister born in 1943.)

—Pat (Patsy) (2010)

Allie

July 1941

Allie tilted her head into the breeze, enjoying the wind hitting her full in the face making her hair whip back and forth against her cheeks. Even though the day was hot, she was not a bit uncomfortable riding along in the comforts of this glorious automobile. She bounced up and down on the wooden plank that stretched across the bed of the '38 black Ford pickup truck. She laughed gaily and grabbed at the side of the truck as they went over an especially big bump coming down hard on the seat. Even that was fun. So what if her bottom acquired a few bruises! She found it amazing to be traveling this fast. Her eyes could scarcely take in all the sights at this speed. Something would come into view for just the briefest second before it was left behind in the dust and there would be something new to see. Allie's head was already dizzy from twisting her neck from one side to the other trying to look at everything. She rarely got to travel out of their small community, and she didn't want to miss a thing! There was so much to see!

Allie had ridden in a vehicle before, but only a time or two. Very few individuals in their small town were fortunate enough to own one of the new contraptions. Most still depended on the horse and wagon, and some did not even have that luxury. Many families still had to walk wherever they needed to go. Allie's own parents did not even have a wagon, but Grandma and Grandpa Shoemate did. Many of the kids at school came from families whose only transportation was their own two feet, and a lot of these families lived a long, long way from town. Allie was thankful her own family only lived about a mile from town. She thought of the Stroud, Baker, and Kerley families who lived a good four miles away. No wonder their children were sick with colds so often in the winter months.

Allie was so happy and excited she felt like singing. She was just too happy to keep quiet. With the smile that was spread across her face, she would be lucky if she didn't catch a fat green June bug between her front teeth before they got there. It was just that she couldn't believe her good fortune in getting to ride in a vehicle. For a while, it had been a big enough thrill just to see an automobile. She would never forget the first automobile she ever saw. She had gone with Daddy to deliver a load of lumber to a place over on the Baker place. Sitting up in the wagon box, she had been chattering away, excited to be spending the day with Daddy.

It had been just Daddy and her. That was another great thing! Winna hadn't been there. She had Daddy all to herself, and as luck would have it, that was the exciting day they had seen their first automobile. She had gotten to brag about that for a very long time to Winna! It had been the dust that day that had gotten her attention first. Not knowing what it was in the distance, she pointed it out to Daddy. Watching it closely for a few minutes, he said it was probably a dust storm. Then Daddy shook his head and clicked his tongue. "That sure brings back bad memories," he said. "There were sure some terrible dust storms a few years back." Allie nodded. She had heard Daddy tell of those dust storms that could blacken out the whole sky for people living in Kansas, Texas, and Oklahoma. She had listened to Daddy and some of her uncles talk about those terrible storms. The drought had been bad in Arkansas too, but they hadn't experienced the blinding dust storms that the states to their west had. She shivered. If something like that could cause Daddy to worry, it was something to be feared for sure. She hoped that wasn't happening again.

Allie watched Daddy eyeing the dust with curiosity as it drew closer and closer. Next, they heard the noise. Daddy sat up straighter in his seat. It was a sound unlike one she had ever heard before, a sort of rumbling and chugging. It had a sort of rhythm to it. Allie remembered moving over closer to Daddy on the wagon seat and taking his hand. Then here it came, a big black box-looking thing clawing its way up over the hill, churning up the dust as it came, making it swirl in every direction. Daddy pulled the wagon over to the edge of the road as far as he could to let it pass. The people inside the black box honked the horn as they passed and threw up their hands in a friendly wave as she and Daddy sat there openmouthed. Allie, at last losing her fear, stood up on the wagon box to get a better look, and Daddy said, "Well, look at that!" Allie had heard of automobiles. They all had, but she had never dreamed they would be such noisy things. No, she would never forget that day. Allie didn't remember exactly how old she had been when she'd seen that first vehicle, maybe three or four. Now here she was actually riding in the back of one! They were probably traveling at least twenty miles an hour. Just think of it! She wished Mr. McGuffey would toot his horn. She wanted the whole world to see her riding in the back of this grand automobile and stand up on something to watch her as she passed just like she had climbed up on the wagon seat years ago.

Allie looked over at Winna and smiled. Winna looked so grown-up this morning. Her light-brown hair was pulled back in a short ponytail with a black scarf tied around it. A few tendrils had worked loose and were blowing in the wind. It looked like she had even put on some light-pink lipstick this morning. Winna was pretty. Her complexion was clear and smooth, and she had a beautiful smile with dimples. Her long lavender dress was tucked neatly under her legs to keep it from blowing up in the wind, and she had on short anklets and white leather shoes, shoes in the middle of summer! Allie could hardly believe it! Winna must surely be growing up. She looked down at her own feet, dusty and brown. Her legs looked like a mad cat had gotten hold of her, so many red scratches zigzagged from her ankles up her legs to under the hem of her skirt. The scratches hadn't actually come from a cat though. She had gotten them from climbing trees and riding the young saplings up and down like horses. She learned to do that from her cousins, Joanna and Erma Faye. That had been one of their favorite things to do before the girls had moved away. Allie and her cousins would climb the young trees and ride them over like horses. The trees, being thin and limber, would bend and spring back easily. The weight of the girls' bodies would bend them double, but the minute the girls' feet would touch the ground, they would kick off and spring back into the air. Once again, their weight would bend the trees back down where they would kick back up. Now talk about fun! It had to be almost as much fun as riding a real horse! They would see who could ride their "horses" the highest without getting thrown. Allie had ridden all alone this week, her legs often brushing up against limbs and briars or getting bucked off, resulting in the many scratches to her legs. Winna had grown too old for this sort of fun. Even though it had been fun for Allie this week, it just wasn't the same without her cousins. She missed them so much. She hoped they would get to come to the family reunion this weekend.

Allie's skirt blew up in the wind exposing a good-sized scab on her left knee. She had gotten it from the tumble she'd taken from her Tommy Walkers. Some people called them stilts. Allie didn't know where the name came from, but that's what they were known as. Daddy had made hers from some chinquapin limbs. He would have to search long and hard to find just the perfect ones with the limbs sticking out in the right places for her feet to go. Allie knew her daddy was busy, but he always had time to help her find sticks for Tommy Walkers or whatever else she needed. When it came to her Tommy Walkers, Allie knew no fear. She didn't walk on them, she ran. She would hop on, grab the top of the poles, and take off. Tommy Walkers were not only fun, they were very useful. Often in the summertime, the ground would be too downright hot to walk on. That's when you could just hop on your Tommy Walkers and give your poor feet a break. They were also handy for getting to the high apples on trees or walking over briar patches or through chinquapins groves over the stickery burrs. Allie didn't know how she could handle summertime without them. It never failed though that she ended up with a skinned knee or a bruise before she put them away. She loved them, and the pain was always worth the fun and benefits.

Looking at her scab, her cousin Joanna came to mind. She smiled as she thought of her chubby cousin. Joanna liked to play hard just like Allie. When she would fall, she was usually just fine; that is, unless she saw blood. If Joanna happened to look down and see blood, she puckered and bawled like a panther. Allie felt like puckering up and bawling right now, thinking about how she missed her cousins. They had been gone four months! It felt like a lifetime. She crossed her fingers that she'd get to see them at the family reunion. However, she knew that seeing them would just make her miss them that much more. Those cousins sure knew how to have fun. Allie looked again at her older sister. Winna might be growing up, but not Allie. She wasn't ready to grow up just yet. There was too much fun to be had! There would be time for that grown-up stuff later on.

Allie's foot bumped up against her small travel satchel that sat at her feet. Winna had one just like it sitting beside her. The last two summers the girls had packed their satchels and caught the mail car up to Pickren Hall to spend a few days with Grandma and Grandpa Stephens. The summers before that, Daddy had taken them up in the wagon. That was where they were heading today. One of the highlights of their summers was getting to spend some time with their other grandparents, Daddy's parents. Winna and Allie had looked forward to this trip for weeks. It seemed like they were taking such a long journey by themselves so far from home. The trip there on the mail car was almost as much fun as the time spent with their grandparents. What an adventure!

Allie started humming, softly at first and then more loudly. Winna looked over and grinned and joined in, and, pretty soon, their voices were harmonizing some of their favorite songs.

Way too soon, the mail truck was pulling to the stop where Pickren Hall gravel road intersected with the main 62 road that ran east and west. Winna and Allie gathered up their satchels. They handed their bags down to Mr. McGuffey as he hopped out of the cab of the truck, Winna took Mr. McGuffey's hand and was careful to descend in a ladylike manner. Allie hopped over the side, her skirt catching briefly on the running board of the truck. Taking their nickels out of the corners of their handkerchiefs, they each handed him their coins.

"It seems a downright shame to charge five cents apiece to haul pretty girls in my mail truck. You know that's two cents more than it costs to mail a drab ole letter," Mr. McGuffey said with a smile.

The girls smiled and thanked him for the ride. "Believe me, it was well worth the money," Allie said, and she meant it. "I loved every minute of the ride."

Mr. McGuffey laughed. "Anytime. Now what day will you need a ride back?" he asked.

"Oh, we won't need to be catching a ride back," Winna explained. "Our whole family will be having a reunion on

Saturday at Uncle Earl and Aunt Bertha's. Daddy and Mama will be bringing Grandpa's wagon up for that, so we'll ride home with them."

"Oh, is that right?" Mr. McGuffey answered. "A family reunion? That's a little disappointing. Since my truck doesn't have a radio, I wouldn't mind hauling you girls around with me every day so you could entertain me with your pretty singing." Winna and Allie looked at each other and smiled. Nothing pleased them much more than a compliment on their singing. "Tell your grandma and grandpa howdy for me, ya hear? You all have a good time at your grandparents'," Mr. McGuffey said as he crawled back into the truck and pulled the door closed. Looking out the window one last time, he tipped his hat to the girls.

"Okay. Good-bye!" the girls called out to him. "Thanks again for the ride." They watched as he drove down the dusty road. *What fun*, Allie thought, *it must be to drive around in a truck all day*. The girls picked up their satchels. Winna began walking up the gravel road.

"Wait!" Allie commanded.

"What's wrong?" Winna asked, stopping suddenly in her tracks and looking around in alarm.

"We've got to wait for the mockingbird call," Allie explained.

Winna set down her satchel and rolled her eyes. "Allie, not that again," she said with a sigh. "I thought you'd seen a snake or something."

"You know it won't be long," Allie insisted. As if to prove her point, no sooner had the words left her mouth when the shrill call of a mockingbird echoed from a nearby tree. Allie looked at Winna and smiled. It never failed. For some reason, the path that led from the road to their grandparents' home always had an abundance of mockingbirds. Allie had named the road Mockingbird Meadow. Even though it wasn't really a meadow, she liked the sound of it. She worried last spring when the field that joined the path burned. She had been afraid the mockingbirds would move away and find somewhere more lush and green to live. However, it didn't seem to lessen the number of birds at all. If anything, their numbers seemed to increase.

Allie looked around and caught sight of one of the birds sitting on a low limb of a nearby tree. The bird's gray slim body blended in with the gray burned bark of the tree. The tail of a mockingbird is long. The bird is mostly gray. However, there are patches of white and black on its wings and tail. Even though it is a pretty bird, it's the bird's remarkable ability to mimic the calls of other birds that gives it its name and makes it so unique. Its ability to sound so amazingly like other birds can not be explained. Allie wondered if the birds' mocking irritated the birds it mimicked the way her own mocking irritated her sister. Often, just for fun, she would repeat everything Winna would say. She would call it the mockingbird game. Winna would grow tired of it right away, and it would soon escalate into a fight. Allie couldn't blame her. It wasn't much fun to have everything you said repeated.

Allie picked up her satchel and fell into step behind Winna down the road, wondering, as she always did, why the mockingbirds favored this particular area.

The road, really more of a path, to Grandma and Grandpa Stephens' was narrow and winding. It wound around and Allie and Winna took their time walking the familiar path enjoying the walk, anticipating the week ahead. They loved spending time with their daddy's parents and their many cousins they didn't get to see as often as their cousins on their mama's side. Daddy had four brothers: Uncle Elbert, Uncle George, Uncle Henry, and Uncle Horace. One of his brothers, Elmer, died of a snakebite when he was only twelve years old. Daddy also had five sisters: Aunt Roxie, Aunt Nora, Aunt Myrtle, Aunt Bertha, and Aunt Gladys. Aunt Rose died when she was just twenty-three. The family reunion was to take place at Uncle Earl and Aunt Bertha's and most of the family was planning on being there. Allie couldn't wait!

Around a particularly sharp curve in the road, the sight of their grandparents' house came into view. Grandma and Grandpa's house was what was known as a clapboard house. It was a rough board house painted white. A wide porch ran across the front with concrete banisters. Posts of knotty pine went up from the banisters to the roof of the porch, and they were painted red. It was a pretty house and looked big on the outside. However, once inside, there didn't seem to be that much room. Allie and Winna stopped as they always did and took in the peaceful, serene setting.

The house set nestled under tall poplars along the side, and a tall crab apple tree grew in the front. The limbs of the trees seemed to wrap their protecting arms over the abode, sheltering it from harm. Across the road from the house were the barn and the pond. Ducks could almost always be found floating on the pond's smooth surface. Today though, most of the ducks waddled along the steep bank, searching in the tall weeds for grasshoppers or maybe June bugs. However, two small yellow ducks paddled here and there on the surface in the water. As Allie watched, one little duck turned his little tail up as his head went under, no doubt in search of a tasty tidbit. Allie loved to watch the ducks. It always made her a little nervous to see the little ones out on the pond like that. She knew there were snapping turtles in the pond. Sometimes, the turtles would lie in wait for the young ducks and grab them and eat them. Allie had seen Grandpa take a shovel out to the pond. He would stand at the side with his shovel raised. If he saw one of the snapping turtles stick its ugly head above the water, he would give its head a whack with the shovel. That turtle wouldn't be getting any of the little ducks again.

Out behind the house was the orchard. Grandpa kept a variety of fruit trees: all kinds of apple trees and a variety of peaches. There were also several plum trees with low hanging limbs. Allie loved going out into the orchard to pick the fruit. Grandma canned a lot of fruit, and rarely was the table set without some kind of fruit being part of the meal.

Grandpa and Grandma Stephens

In the yard, Grandpa had a grape arbor. That was Allie's favorite place on the whole farm. The frame, or arbor, was made of wood, and the grape vines grew on each side and up over the top. This made a shady tunnel-like structure that was always so cool and nice. Allie loved to sit beneath the arbor with the clusters of grapes hanging above her head. They were beautiful as well as very tasty. Allie looked at the arbor today and noticed the young grapes were already beginning to change from a light-green to a purplish-pink color. She hoped she would be able to make another visit to the farm when the grapes were fully ripe.

Winna spotted Grandma first and called out a hello. Grandma stopped in the middle of hanging out clothes and a warm smile spread across her sweet face. Although Grandma was too far away for Allie to be able to see her eyes, she knew Grandma's smile began first in her eyes before it spread to her mouth. It always did. Grandma was a small woman. Her hair was long, parted in the middle and pulled back in a low bun at the back of her neck. She, like most women, wore a long dress, almost to the ground. Grandma always wore a long apron over her dress. Her apron had a bodice that buttoned at the back of her neck. The skirt of the apron was gathered at the waist and was almost as long as her dress. It protected her dress, keeping it clean as she went about the chores of the day. Grandma didn't always put on a clean dress every morning, but she always did put on a clean fresh apron, always looking tidy. Grandma put down the shirt she was fixing to hang on the clothesline and hurried to the front gate to greet her granddaughters. Allie ran and threw her arms around her grandmother who was not much bigger than herself, and so began her wonderful week at her grandparents'.

After a supper of sweet peas, summer squash, fresh lettuce, roasting ears of corn, and sliced peaches, Allie and Winna went out on the porch to watch Grandpa as he checked his bee gums. Grandpa kept bees for a couple of reasons. First, honey was used as a sweetener, so having their own honeybees made it very convenient as well as being very economical for Grandma and Grandpa. Sugar was expensive and used mainly for special occasions. Honey was used for everyday sweetener. However, bees were also important to Grandpa because of his many fruit trees. Without bees, the blossoms wouldn't be pollinated adequately resulting in less fruit. Grandpa's fruit trees were very important to him, so the bees were more important to him as pollinators than they were as honey makers. Grandpa kept a close eye on his bees, and Allie and Winna had been thrilled when Grandpa announced at supper that he needed to check on them.

Allie, being more adventurous than her sister, would have climbed right into the beehive with the bees if Grandpa would have allowed it. He insisted though that they not get off the porch. They could see the hives clearly from there, he said, and would have plenty of time to skedaddle into the house should the bees become upset and decide to swarm. Allie was disappointed that she would be so far from the action, but she would never dream of arguing with Grandpa. She sat on the banister of the porch and dangled her red scratched legs over the edge. Winna sat properly in one of the chairs, content to watch from afar. Allie watched Grandpa walk across the yard where the hives sat in a row beside the road.

Grandpa was dressed in his bee costume. He didn't own fancy attire like some of the pictures Allie had seen in books. He did have on a long-sleeved shirt buttoned to the neck and at the sleeves. He had a bee bonnet that Grandma had made by attaching a section of an old slip made of netting to a wide-brimmed hat. This netting came down over his face and neck. Grandpa told the girls that for some reason bees were attracted to a person's breath so that was where they tended to go when disturbed. Therefore, it was important for a person to keep his face protected. Grandpa swung an old smoking hickory stick with him. "Smoke calms bees," Grandpa explained when Allie had asked about the smoking stick. Allie was so excited about the whole ordeal, she could hardly sit still. She wriggled on the rough concrete ledge squirming like a worm on a hook.

"What is he checking them for?" she called over her shoulder to Winna.

"Well, the way I understand it," Winna explained, "there are three kinds of bees in a hive: the workers, the drones, and the most important one, the queen bee. Grandpa has to keep an eye on the hive to make sure that the hive isn't getting too crowded. If it gets too crowded, sometimes the bees will swarm to start a new colony, and Grandpa would lose a lot of his bees if that happened. He has to check on the queen too and make sure she's doing okay. After all, she's the most important bee of all."

Allie turned around to stare at Winna. Her mouth dropped open. She turned back around to look at Grandpa. She hadn't expected so much from Winna. How in the world did her sister know so much about bees? Come to think about it, she was pretty much an expert on most things. Winna was a reader though, so Allie guessed that's what made her so smart. Winna could lie in bed all day with her nose in a book and be completely contented. How she could stay cooped up in the house all day was a mystery to Allie. Allie wanted to be outside and be a part of whatever was going on. Right now, she had tucked her legs up under her and was sitting on them in fear that they would take off and go running across the yard to be with Grandpa to check those bees before she could stop them. Winna sat quietly rocking back and forth in her chair as calmly as could be.

Grandma and Grandpa Stephens

Allie turned out to be a little disappointed in the whole bee checking adventure. Grandpa didn't get stung once. He didn't yell, jump, run, or even flinch. Allie kept waiting for some action, but none ever came. She and Winna didn't have to run for cover into the house or anything. Grandpa reported that everything looked fine with the bees and that it wouldn't be long before he would need to rob their hives. Allie begged him to wait until her next visit before he gathered the honey and could she please, please help him if

Mama would make her a bee hunting outfit. Grandpa just laughed and ruffled her hair. "I'm not sure Robert didn't get himself half a boy with you," he said as he continued with his hearty hahaha laughter as he walked into the house. Allie frowned. Why couldn't anyone take her seriously?

Grandma and Grandpa went to bed early, not too long after sundown. Winna and Allie pulled on their nightgowns and prepared for bed, much too soon for their liking. After donning their nightgowns, Allie brushed Winna's hair for her and Winna brushed Allie's. Their hair was sure a mess of tangles after the ride in the mail truck!

The girls would be sleeping in the bedroom in one of Grandma's feather beds. Allie had to admit she was a bit tired, and the bed did look inviting. She loved feather beds. She had one foot in the bed and was anticipating jumping into the bed's cloudlike softness when she heard Grandma's light footsteps.

"Do you girls need to go to the door before you go to bed?" Grandma asked softly, almost in a whisper. Allie's foot froze in midair. Grandma stood in the doorway in her long faded-blue nightgown. Her white nightcap was tied snugly under her chin. She reminded Allie of what Mrs. Santa Claus might look like bundled up like she was. Allie wondered why Grandma needed a nightcap in the summer. She blushed at Grandma's question. She looked over at Winna to see her reaction because she herself was at a loss at what to say to Grandma's question. Did Grandma actually think they might get her feather bed wet during the night?

"Sure, Grandma," Winna said without hesitation. "Come on, Allie," she said. "Good night, Grandma."

"Goodnight, girls," Grandma said with a sweet smile. "I hope you girls sleep well."

Winna and Allie "went to the door" more to please Grandma than of any necessity. After coming back into the house, they dusted any grass and leaves from their feet and finally crawled into the feathery softness of the feather bed. Ummmmm! It felt so heavenly; Allie groaned in delight. She didn't know a bed could be this comfortable. She couldn't help but feel a bit sorry though for all those chickens who gave up the millions and millions of feathers in this mattress for her comfort.

Allie lay in bed and listened to the different noises around her. It was strange how each different house had its own unique sounds. She could hear Grandpa's dogs bark and then the sound of the metal chain as it bumped against the metal water bucket as one of the dogs lapped from it. A whippoorwill from not too far away called its song, "Whippoor-will, whippoor-will." Far off another answered, "Chip butter in a white oak, Chip butter in a white oak!" Grandpa, it must have been Grandpa who turned over in the bed, making a loud squeak of the bedsprings. Then Allie noticed the frogs and crickets. They were deafening. When one really listened to all the night sounds, it was a wonder anyone could even sleep at all. Winna's soft breathing beside her let Allie know that she had fallen asleep. Then came a snore. Allie wished Grandpa Stephens would turn over. He snored almost as loudly as Grandpa Shoemate. Grandpa Shoemate had the loudest snore of anyone she knew! Suddenly, Allie missed home. She missed Grandpa Shoemate. She missed him so much. Tears welled in her eyes and ran from her eyes down her face into her pillow. Why had she let her secret about the locket come between them? Grandpa had always been her guiding light, the person she went to for advice. He had always loved her no matter what. Why did she think he would stop loving her or be mad because of the locket? She had to make things right between them again. She couldn't go on without having him right there for her. The tears kept coming. The more she tried to keep them in, the more they came. Did Grandpa think she didn't love him anymore? She did love him so, so much! Why shouldn't he think that though, the way she had ignored him these past several weeks? Allie hiccupped loudly. Her shoulders shook the more she tried to hold back the tears.

"Allie, are you crying? What in the world is wrong?" Winna asked, coming up on her elbow.

Allie sniffed and wiped her eyes with the edge of her nightgown. "I'm missing home, I guess," she told the half lie.

"You're what?" Winna asked in disbelief. "You've never been homesick before."

"I can't help it," Allie continued to sniffle.

Winna was baffled. She had never seen Allie so beside herself.

Winna cuddled up beside Allie and put her arm around her. "Well, you'd better stop that crying. You're going to get the bed wet, and you know how Grandma feels about her feather bed getting wet," she said with a giggle.

Allie stopped crying. She remembered Grandma's words asking if they needed to go to the door. She had to giggle at that. Soon the giggle turned into a laugh. It wasn't long before the laugh turned hysterical.

"Shhhhhh!" Winna said. "Oh, Allie, if it's not one thing with you, it's another! You're going to wake Grandpa if you don't quiet down!"

"I can't help it!" Allie said in between hiccups. The thought of waking Grandpa did have a calming effect on her though. Grandpa and his stern disposition always intimidated Allie somewhat. After a few minutes, she was able to calm down a bit.

"Finally!" Winna said. "Now try and get to sleep!"

The girls were silent for a few minutes. Winna's breathing had slowed into a sleep pattern again. Allie lay listening to the night sounds around her once again. After several minutes, she stirred and rose up on her elbow. "Winna?" she whispered. Winna had evidently drifted back asleep.

PAM ESTES

"Winna!" she whispered more loudly, nudging her in the arm.

"Hummm?"

"I think I need to go to the door," Allie whispered.

"Oh, Allie!" Winna groaned.

Grandma and Grandpa may have gone to bed early, but they slept late too. It just seemed to take a lot of sleep for them for some reason. Allie felt like she must have lain awake in bed a full hour before she finally heard the bed squeak and Grandpa's feet hit the floor. She figured it must be around 7:45. Grandpa always got up in time to listen to the 8:00 news on his battery radio. In a few minutes, she heard the radio come on and Grandma getting around. Allie continued to lie in bed for several more minutes until she felt it was okay to get up. She knew though that she had to be quiet until Grandpa had his first cup of coffee and had finished listening to the news. She decided to tiptoe out to the kitchen to help Grandma with breakfast. She slipped quietly out of bed, careful not to wake Winna.

Allie walked into her grandmother's kitchen. "Well, good morning, sweetheart," Grandma said with a warm smile. "How did you sleep?"

"Just fine," Allie said with a smile. "I wish I had my own feather bed. I felt like I was sleeping on air!"

"They are comfy, aren't they?" Grandma said.

Allie looked around Grandmother's kitchen. She admired the china cabinet. Grandma kept her pretty dishes in there.

It had a curved glass front. Close to the china cabinet was the cabinet where Grandma prepared her food. It had a flour bin in the front that pulled out from the cabinet. Shelving went across the top of the cabinet for her baking supplies: salt, baking powder, soda, white sugar, and brown sugar. Away from the cabinet, on the same side, was a table where Grandma kept some of her supplies: canned fruit, jellies and preserves, and other food items. Across from that table was her wood cookstove with its warming closets on top and water reservoir on the side. A teakettle sat on top of the stove. There was a fire going in the wood cookstove already, so the room was already growing warm this morning. How did Grandma get a fire going so quickly? There must have been some coals left from cooking the supper last night. The kitchen and dining room were separated from the rest of the house, and you couldn't get to them without going through a narrow screened-in porch. Because of this, Allie felt like she had Grandma all to herself this morning.

Allie pulled a wooden stool to the cabinet where Grandma was already gathering the ingredients to make her biscuits: flour, baking powder, lard, salt, and milk. Grandma shuffled around in her little high-top button shoes and long stockings. The shoes made pitter-patter sounds on the wooden floor as she scurried around. Grandma made sure she had everything she needed before beginning her task: measuring spoons, measuring cup, and her wooden paddle. Grandma measured everything. Allie watched in wonder wondering how many times Grandma had gone through these same steps before. She probably could have completed this task blindfolded.

Grandmother had a sort of ritual when it came to making her biscuits. Allie was trying to memorize these steps so one day when she was a young woman on her own, she could make them just like Grandma. She tried to predict what Grandma would do next before she actually did it. First, she mixed her flour, baking powder, and salt in a large stoneware bowl. Next, she used her fingers to mix in the lard. Finally, she added the milk. Then came Allie's favorite part. She watched as Grandma picked up the smooth, long-handled, wooden paddle and mixed the dough all together. Allie watched the paddle move round and round the bowl scraping every bit of flour down into the mixture. When Grandma got it all mixed up, she took a spoon and scraped the dough from the wooden paddle onto the flour board. Then she rolled the dough with her rolling pin, smoothing the dough carefully getting ready to cut out the biscuits. Grandma seemed very careful and exact in her cooking.

"Grandma, tell me the story again about how my daddy made that wooden paddle when he was just a boy."

Grandma put down her rolling pin and grinned over at her granddaughter, giving Allie her full attention. Allie saw Grandma's eyes twinkle and then the hint of a tear along with her sweet smile. Grandma loved this story as much as she, and Grandma always loved to talk about her son, Allie's daddy. Allie loved the way she spoke Daddy's name with such affection and softness pronouncing Robert into two soft quiet syllables, Ro-bert.

"Well, one day I was watching Ro-bert whittle. He was just a little boy about your own age. I asked him, 'Ro-bert, what are you making?' He said, 'Oh, Mother, I'm just whittling.' I told him, 'Well, son, I think I can have a use for that when you're finished with it, if you don't mind. It's so nice and smooth.'"

Grandma smiled. "I think it pleased your Daddy that I wanted it. Well, I did have a use for it. I began using it that very day for making my biscuits, and I've been using it ever since. It's very special to me, and I always think of him when I use it to make my biscuits." Grandma picked up her rolling pin and began rolling the dough once again.

"Allie, would you like to cut out the biscuits?" she asked.

Allie smiled and nodded. Picking up the biscuit cutter, she began pushing the small cutter down into the dough. Grandma made little delicate biscuits. Allie thought about the wooden paddle. She secretly hoped Grandma would give the wooden paddle to her one day. She would love to have something that her daddy made when he was just a boy about her own age. Grandma took the pan from the oven where she had placed it to heat while she mixed up the biscuit dough. She picked up the biscuits as Allie cut them out and placed them into the hot grease. When they were all in the pan, she slipped the pan into the hot oven. Allie cleaned up the counter while Grandma cut off slices of pork and placed them in the skillet to fry as the biscuits were baking.

When the meat was done, Grandma made the gravy and fried the eggs. After placing it all on the table, Grandma got out the churned butter, jelly, and a bowl of canned fruit. Grandma always had sorghum. That was one of Allie's favorite things to eat with Grandma's hot delicious biscuits. Finally, she called Grandpa and Winna to join them, and all four of them sat down to their meal. It was a wonderful breakfast, and when Allie was finished, she thought she would not be hungry again for at least a week. After everybody had had their fill and Grandpa had slurped down several cups of steaming hot coffee, everyone went out except Grandma and Allie. Allie helped Grandma tidy up the kitchen.

When the kitchen was clean, Allie left the kitchen and went to the back porch. The narrow porch was screened-in. This was where they kept their water bucket with the dipper, wash pan, and soap. The towel hung on a nail above the wash pan. Allie noticed dark clouds had gathered, and it had started to rain. Her shoulders drooped. She was disappointed that it looked like it was going to be a rainy day. She had wanted to play in the orchard today and run around the farm. She didn't want to waste a minute of this week. Not really knowing what to do, Allie wandered up into the attic. The attic smelled of a mixture of apples and spices.

It wasn't long until the rain began to come down harder. It drummed down on the housetop, the raindrops bouncing loudly on the metal roof. Droplets of water chased one another down the pane of glass in the window in the front of the little room. Allie stood at the window and looked out at the beehives, the road, the barn, and the pond. The ducks seemed to be enjoying the rain, lifting their wings and stretching them, seeming to want to collect as many raindrops as possible. Allie looked down on the pink blossoms of the crab apple tree, such a beautiful pale-pink color among the green of the leaves. Next, she spied Grandpa going out toward the barn carrying his milk bucket, rain dripping off the brim of his hat. Grandpa was tall. His hair was gray as well as his moustache. His moustache was long, hanging down on either side of his mouth. Allie loved everything about Grandpa, especially his deep hahaha laugh. She watched as he whistled to his mules, Kit and Beck. They pricked up their ears at the sound of Grandpa's familiar whistle. Allie looked out to see if she could see Sure Foot anywhere. She would have to remember to ask Grandpa about him.

Allie watched Grandpa until he was out of sight and then wandered over to the apple baskets. Looking down, she saw two lonely apples still lying in the bottom of the basket wrapped in newspapers. Unwrapping one, she was delighted to see that it was one of her favorites, an apple so very dark it was almost black. Even though Allie had just had breakfast, she bit into the apple. It had softened with age, but the meat of the apple was still snow-white. It amazed Allie how this type of apple could be so dark on the outside and snow-white on the inside. She wondered if she saved one of the seeds of this apple if she could grow her own apple tree that would grow those dark apples. She finished the apple and tucked the seeds into her dress pocket.

Allie's face lit up as she spied a pair of Grandma's high-top button shoes lined up neatly by the stairwell next to the wall. Sitting on the floor, she pulled them on. She took time to fasten each elastic loop over each leather-covered button. Allie couldn't believe how long it took! It was worth the wait though when she finally stood up and looked down at her feet. She had never felt so tall and elegant. She walked clumsily over to the phonograph player. Turning the crank then lifting the needle, she played the song, "The Old Black Crow in the Hickory Nut Tree." Allie danced or attempted to dance around to the music. Those darn shoes kept twisting and her ankles kept turning over as she danced from one end of the attic to the other. Once the song went off, she decided she might need a little practice walking before moving on to dancing. Allie stood and strutted the length of the attic several times. She tried walking with her head held high and proud. Just when she knew she looked as glamorous as any movie star, over went her ankle and she'd almost fall. Allie supposed it took practice to learn to walk in heels. She would ask Aunt Ollie to give her some tips; Aunt Ollie knew all the beauty and fashion tips.

What she needed was some makeup. Allie wished, wished, wished she had some makeup she could put on. She knew without a doubt that Grandma didn't have any. Maybe Winna brought some lipstick with her. She might snoop around in her satchel later to see if maybe she could find some. Sitting down on a rug, Allie thumbed through an old catalog from a stack Grandma had stored in the corner of the attic. She flipped first to the makeup. She and Winna had looked at makeup before, so she recognized the Tangee brand. She searched until she found the natural color of lipstick, knowing it didn't look natural at all when it was on your lips rather a pink color. If only she had her own money, she would buy a tube of Tangee natural color lipstick to carry with her. Wouldn't her friends be surprised to see her slip out a tube of it and run it over her lips? Allie wanted to paint her lips so badly at that moment, she was tempted to see if she could find some pokeberries somewhere on the farm and smear the purple stain of the berries on her lips. She had been told though that pokeberries were poisonous. She wasn't quite that desperate for colored lips. Allie decided she'd have to wait until a later time to primp. She closed the catalogs and placed them back in the corner.

Walking back to the stairwell, she took off the shoes. In her bare feet, Allie walked over to the far end of the room seeing what else she might discover. She spotted a trunk she had never noticed before. She ran her hand over its dusty smooth lid and slowly opened it. The hinges groaned as the trunk yawned open its mouth it had no doubt kept shut for a long time. The trunk was filled with many official-looking papers. What could they be? They must be Grandpa's papers. They were all so official looking. She felt proud that Grandpa seemed so important. She knew when he was younger he had been the justice of the peace and had owned a grocery store. She looked at the official documents and looked lovingly at his signature among the other signatures on the page. W. C. Stephens was written on the documents over and over again. Allie knew this stood for William Cranford Stephens. He was known by everyone though as Cran. This particular document was dated September 30, 1889, Cushman Arkansas. Grandpa's signature was so well written. It was written with lots of loops and curls. Mr. Schauffler would certainly think Grandpa's penmanship was excellent. Allie ran her finger over the loops and curls of his handwritten signature. Allie picked up another sheet of paper. It was yellowed and looked very old. It had Grandma's name on it, but it was from Grandpa. It seemed to be a poem, a love poem?

To Lucy Aldora Stephens

Remember me when this you see
though many a mile apart we may be
for I'll always think of you.
I remain your love forever
W. C. Stephens

Allie blinked. It was difficult to think of Grandpa writing something like this to her grandma. She quickly folded the paper and placed it back in the trunk. This was a love letter to Grandma from Grandpa, somewhat like the letter Cody had written to her. Her face grew hot. When did Grandpa write this? Did Mama and Daddy write love letters to one another? Allie shook her head. She couldn't imagine them doing that. She looked through some more of the papers. Allie found paper after paper where Grandpa had written Grandma's name over and over again, Lucy Aldora Stephens. Each time he had written it, it had been written so elegantly and seemed to be written with so much love. Allie placed the letters back where they had been. She closed the lid, trying not to make a sound. What would Grandpa think if he knew she was going through these papers?

Allie walked back over to the window. She wanted to see if she saw Grandpa anywhere. Yea, the rain had stopped. She turned on her heels and ran down the stairs ready for another adventure.

The week passed quickly at Grandma and Grandpa's, and before Allie knew it, she was in the wagon box with Mama and Daddy headed for home. She was so exhausted she could hardly wiggle. As exhausted as she was though, she was also very contented. It had been a wonderful week. She had so enjoyed her time with Grandma and Grandpa and then the family reunion had been wonderful. She couldn't believe the crowd that showed up at Uncle Earl and Aunt Bertha's. Once a year, the family had a family reunion somewhere. The reunion was always planned for when Aunt Roxy and Uncle George Wilson and their family came in for their yearly visit from Oklahoma City. Sometimes, it was at Uncle Horace and Aunt Lottie's house. Other times, like this year, it was at Uncle Earl and Aunt Bertha's. They lived in an old store building, so there was lots of room.

Allie thought back on the day. Almost everybody had been there: Uncle Elbert and Aunt Cora, Uncle George and Aunt Esta, Uncle Henry and Aunt Violet, Uncle Horace and Aunt Lottie, Mama and Daddy, Aunt Nora, Aunt Myrtle, Aunt Bertha and Uncle Earl, and Aunt Gladys. Then the cousins: Carol Sue, Rosemary, Jacquita, David, Russell, Betty Jean, Ruthie, Qualline, Curtis, Catherine, Virginia, Joyce, Lucy, Willa Mae, Anna Faye, Marjorie, Adalee, and other boy cousins galore.

And yes, Erma Faye and Joanna had been there. It had been glorious seeing her favorite cousins again. Allie's thoughts raced about the time she had spent with her cousins. They had changed somehow though. They talked about school in Melbourne and their new friends. Erma Faye even had a boyfriend and kept bringing him into the conversation! They both seemed so much more grown-up. When Allie suggested seeing if they could find some trees to ride, neither of the girls seemed very interested. They said they had on their best dresses and didn't want to get them dirty.

Her cousins hadn't been very interested in a lot of things Allie had suggested doing, like playing in the barn loft or having races around the pond and back. They had been interested when Allie told them about looking through the catalog at the lipstick and dancing in the high-top shoes in the attic. They wanted to know about all the kids at school, especially about some of the boys. Allie wondered if she had seemed as different and changed to them as they had to her. Funny how a few months had a way of making people change their minds about what was fun or important. Allie found herself changing too. She had to admit that. At times she felt like running and playing while at other times she wanted to be more grown-up. Allie didn't know if she liked the changes or not.

Family reunion

Aunt Bertha Harber pulling the wagon with her children, Russell, Jacquita, David, and Rose Mary. Allie is standing on the porch, and her parents are sitting on the steps. Allie's

Grandma Stephens and sister Betty are
beside her on the porch.

Right before everybody began leaving the reunion, they all gathered on the porch of the house for a family picture. Allie wondered how a camera could fit them all into a single picture, there were so many of them. She did love them all so much though, and she was thankful for her good fortune at being a part of this wonderful family. She closed her eyes and let the rocking motion lull her to sleep as she rested on the pallet Mama had spread for them on the bed of the wagon. It would be good to get back home.

Chapter 13

Paths were everywhere when I was a little boy, shortcuts to everyone's houses and to town. Only a few people had a truck or car, so the paths were shortcuts to save a lot of steps and time. Mom would go down to Grandpa Crotts' house real often to help him out and visit, and we kids would be along. The path went off down behind our house and up the hill to Grandpa's house. There was a good spring down by Raydo's, and we would stop there and rest and get a drink of water. Back then, Mom would buy some flavored drinks in little plastic bottles to mix with water. She would take a pitcher and cups and mix up some in that good cold spring water. We would sit in the shade on some big rocks there by the spring and drink our flavored drinks, and boy, did it taste good!

—Jake (2010)

I remember once Mom was going to go into the smokehouse to get some jars. As soon as she opened the door, she heard a noise and looked up. Jake, Rex, and Wilb had a great big grab hook on the end of a pole for gigging frogs. They had hung it up on some nails over the door inside the smokehouse. When Mom opened the door and looked up, the pole fell. The hook caught in her eyelid. Audene (Audie) was with her, and she went ballistic, screaming and bawling. Mom couldn't get out of the smokehouse because of the long pole. George Huett heard Audene screaming and came running and so did Tilford Hammond. They had a hard time getting her out of the building because of the pole. Then finally, Tilford held the pole while Mr. Huett sawed the handle off short enough to get Mom in Tilford's car. When I got home from school, Mom was in the bed. That was something she never did. I was in the first grade.

—Betty (Bobbie's younger sister) (2010)

Bobbie

August 1941

Bobbie rolled over onto his side on the quilt pallet that was spread on the porch and stretched his arms up over his head. Barely opening his eyes, he squinted as the sun's first rays, coming through the porch slats, made diagonal stripes across his face and body. He turned his face to the house, leaving the sun's glare to his back. Bobbie wasn't quite ready to rise and shine this morning as much as Henny Penny, Momma's rooster, was coaxing him to do so. Sleep wanted to hang around even with the sunrise. Bobbie hadn't slept well last night. It wasn't that he'd been uncomfortable. The pallet Momma spread for him on the porch was almost as soft as his own bed. It wasn't even the temperature. It was definitely cooler on the porch than inside the house. It was so hot inside the house during the summer months, even with the doors and windows left wide open, it was hard at times to catch a breath. That was why he preferred to sleep outside on the porch or even out in the yard during the summer. It wasn't even the cicadas, owls, frogs, and whippoorwills that had kept him awake with their songs all night. Cripes, they could be so loud at times! No, it was something else, something that kept nagging at the corners of his mind.

Bobbie tossed again on his pallet. He hated it when a certain thought skirted around here and there just outside the boundaries of his consciousness, close enough to make itself known, but not close enough for Bobbie to grab its meaning. That's the way it had been last night. Something had gnawed at him all night. He hadn't been able to put his finger on it, but it had been there, and, doggone it, that had kept him tossing from one side of his pallet to the other half the night. Bobbie turned on this back and threw his arm over his eyes to shade them from the sun. He gazed through the crack in his arms up at the roof of the porch. The roof sheltered the porch that came off the front room of the house. The porch was high up off the ground and had no stairs leading down to the ground; more of a balcony, he supposed, than a porch. You could only get to the porch from inside the house unless you shinnied up the support poles the way he sometimes did to take a shortcut. A railing went around the porch. There were several trees in the backyard, and, most of the time, their branches kept the porch in the shade, a cool place to sit, especially in the afternoon when the sun was to the back of the house. Momma liked to sit out there and sew in the afternoon. It made a nice place for her to sit because she had a view of the road leading to town. Sitting up high on the porch, she had a bird's-eye view of people walking to town or riding back and forth in their wagons or on horseback. They would often stop and chat a while with Momma as she sat there with her sewing in her lap.

Momma's sewing! Bobbie sat up suddenly. There it was. That was what was bothering him. He looked off across the yard through the slats in the porch as he thought back over the last few weeks. He thought of the money he had saved for Momma's sewing machine and how it had disappeared. It angered him, actually made his face turn red, to think that just when he'd finally saved enough money to buy her a sewing machine, he'd had it stolen right from under his nose. Who would have done such a thing? He had a pretty good idea of who did it, but there was no way he could prove it. It wasn't just the fact either of not being able to buy Momma that sewing machine. He'd gotten used to having money in his pocket, well, not exactly in his pocket. He had gotten used to having money, his own money. He'd tried not to spend his money, tried to save most all of it for the sewing machine, but he did have money. That had felt good. He didn't like not having any spending money, no money at all of his own. He wouldn't have any either not until school took back up in the fall, and then it would be late fall before he'd start building fires again and start earning his dollar a week. Then it would be starting all over again, one dollar at a time.

Bobbie and Audie: later years

Bobbie supposed he'd messed up by keeping his money hidden in the smokehouse and not in his pocket. No, he would probably have lost it if he'd kept it in his pocket too. He thought back to Allie's locket, how he'd put the locket down in his pocket, meaning to give it to her. That sure hadn't gone the way he'd wanted it to, losing it before he'd even gotten home with it. That kept eating at him too. How in the world could he have lost it? Bobbie brought his fist down hard on the pallet. He knew what Mr. Schauffler would call his behavior, irresponsible. Well, that did it. He had chased sleep away for this morning, that was for sure and for certain. He was too blooming mad to get any sleep now. Talk about getting up on the wrong side of the bed; he wasn't even up yet, and he was already in such a bad mood he was ready to bite the head off the first person who said the first word to him.

Bobbie stood slowly and stretched. He could smell something cooking in the kitchen. Momma was humming a song as she clattered pots and pans around. Bobbie figured she was canning. The garden was putting off really well right now, and Momma liked to get her canning done early in the day before it got too hot. Bobbie smiled in spite of his bad mood. Did Momma ever get in a bad mood? She had to work so hard, and if she was worried about not having a sewing machine or anything else for that matter, you would never know it. Momma seemed to just make do with however much or however little she had. Bobbie slipped on his trousers and pulled his suspenders up over his bare shoulders and walked into the kitchen.

"Good morning, son," Momma greeted Bobbie with a smile. "You're sleeping later and later. You know school will be taking up before too long, don't you? You're gonna have to get used to getting up earlier." Yep, Momma was canning this morning. The kitchen was hot with the fire in the cookstove. Her face was red, and strands of her hair were wet and sticking to her face. Several jars of green beans were already lined up on the table standing straight in a line like fence posts where Momma had placed them to cool. It looked like she had already canned several cookers full this morning by the looks of the jars. He wondered what time she rolled out of bed. Canning was a hot job and a hard one too. The pressure cooker was heavy, especially when it had all those jars of food and water inside. Bobbie didn't know how Momma was able to get that cooker on and off the stove like she did. She wasn't a big woman, but she was strong in every sense of the word. He admired his momma so much and knew he should be around to help her out more than he did. He went over now to lend her a hand.

"Let me help you, Momma." He helped her set the pressure cooker back on to the hot stovetop. Momma scooted the cooker to the middle of the stove and wiped her hair away from her face.

"Thanks, son," she said as she put down her pot holder. "These beans will shore taste good this winter. Now getting back to school, I believe it takes up in a couple of weeks, doesn't it?"

"Yea, I think it does," Bobbie said gloomily. "Where did you go to school when you were a little girl, Momma?"

"Law, I went to Dewey Town School most of the time anyway. Now that's been a while ago," she said with a laugh.

"Did they not have this school here at Elizabeth then?" Bobbie asked.

"Well, I think it was here, but we didn't live here then. We lived farther south of here," Momma continued. "Not that we lived close to Dewey Town School either. I walked two and a half miles to school every day and didn't think a thing in the world about it. Everybody walked, just like a lot of the kids still have to walk today. We're just fortunate that you children don't have to walk any farther than you do to school."

"Did you get summers off like we do?" Bobbie wanted to know.

"Our school terms were a little different than yours," Momma explained. "We went to school two months in the summer and three months in the winter. We would go to school in July and August and then we'd be off until cold weather. It all centered around fieldwork. They needed the kids to help with harvesting the crops, so school never started until the cotton and other crops had been picked."

"Sounds like you all had to do more work on the farm than we even do," Bobbie said with a groan.

"Oh, Bobbie, I don't know how families would have gotten along without their children when I was a little girl. That's one reason people wanted big families to have help with the fields and help raising the younger kids. Why, I didn't know nothing but work by the time I was just a little thing," Momma said with a sigh. "I did as much work as my momma by the time I was your age. I was nine years old when I commenced to doing the washing. Yes, sir, kids worked hard."

"It was probably a break for you to go to school, wasn't it?" Bobbie asked.

"Ah, law, I did love to go to school," Momma said with a laugh. "I went to school through eighth grade at Dewey Town. I always went there unless there wasn't any school going on down there. Sometimes Dewey Town School would run out of money and not have as long a term as Glade School did, so we'd have to go over there for a while. Then there were times when the Glade School ran out of money and those children had to come over to Dewey Town and go with us. Children just had to go where they could. Schools sometimes would run out of money, and they would have to shut down until they could afford to pay the teacher again."

"I kinda know how they feel about running out of money. In a way, I'll be glad when school starts up again so I can begin earning some money," Bobbie said as he reached for another biscuit.

"Ah, what are you worried about money for?" Momma wanted to know. "Just enjoy being a kid while you can. Don't you have everything you need right here? I bet you have quite a lot of money saved up already. Haven't you been saving all that money you've been making these last couple of years?"

Bobbie cringed. Should he confide in Momma that the money had been taken? Would it make her think he had been irresponsible to tell her he didn't have it anymore? He was silent a few minutes, and then he asked hesitantly, "Momma, have you ever had something stolen from you?"

Momma paused for just the briefest minute as she wiped up a spill on the table. Then she continued on. "Yes, sir, I have. Your daddy has to. I recollect once not too long after we were married, we went with Waymon and Bertie Owens to a dialogue up at the school. I think now you children may call them plays, but in my day, we called them dialogues. Oh, we just thought those were something to go to! All the parents and everybody went in wagons, don't ya know. Well, I rode in the back of the wagon with Bertie 'cause you were just a baby. Your daddy rode on horseback, rode ole Blaze." Momma stopped in the story and laughed. She always knew how to tell a story, but often had a hard time because of her giggling. She tried to continue the story but had to stop several time to laugh. "Well, somebody stole ole

Blaze's bridle reins that night while we were inside watching the dialogue, just left the horse standing there. Ole Blaze just stood there. We got ready to go, and I seen your daddy coming along behind the wagon, and the horse didn't have no bridle reins. When I asked about the reins, your daddy just said, 'Well, somebody needed them worse than I did, I guess'," Momma laughed again.

"Didn't Daddy get mad and try to find out who took them?" Bobbie asked.

"Naw," Momma said, "Wouldn't of done no good. Anyways, like Daddy said, somebody probably needed them worse than we did. You know, Bobbie, it's like that a lot of the time. Now I know sometimes people take things just to be mean, but sometimes people take things 'cause they just don't see no other way. They're desperate, you see. I'm not saying it makes it right. It's never right to take what doesn't belong to you. I'm just saying we don't need to be too quick to judge what others do when we don't know all the circumstances. We never know when we might be in that same kind of circumstance ourselves."

Bobbie walked over to the warming oven on the stove and grabbed another biscuit and some meat from breakfast. He guessed he understood what Momma was saying. It was a lot like what Grandpa was saying the other day about people going through hard times. Seems like the harder times people lived through, the more understanding they were of what other people did.

Bobbie

Bobbie kissed Momma on the cheek and wandered on out in the yard. Billy and Jack were running their wheels, and Bobbie walked over to join them.

"Hey, Bobbie," Jack said as Bobbie came up to them just finishing the remains of his breakfast. "Billy and I were thinking of taking our fishing poles down to the creek to see if maybe we could catch a mess of fish. We were waiting around to see if you wanted to come along. Whatta you say?"

"Count me in!" Bobbie said with a wide grin. "Let me grab my pole, and I'll be ready to go."

It was around ten o'clock when the boys dropped their lines into the waters of the glistening creek. The sun was reflecting off the water making diamonds seem to sparkle and dance on the surface. Even though the sun was bright and the summer temperature was close to ninety degrees, it was cool on the creek bank. Dragonflies darted here and there over the surface, and one even glided to a stop right on the water's surface on the shallow transparent edge of the creek. A large fish briefly surfaced sending sparkling ripples that followed one another to the bank in rapid succession. Bobbie caught Billy's eye and grinned. Without a word, both boys claimed that silver fish as his own.

Further downstream, Jack was having some luck where the creek ran over some rocks making its way downstream. He whooped as he held up a good-sized perch. Before long, Jack's luck traveled upstream to Bobbie and Billy. The morning passed pleasantly for the boys. Consequently by the early afternoon, a dozen or more good-sized fish had the misfortune of finding themselves at the end of the long metal stringer.

"Did you think to bring anything to eat?" Bobbie asked his fishing partners as rumblings began to stir in his now empty stomach. The meager breakfast had long ago left him.

"Not a thing," Billy said, and they all moaned.

"Well, the way I see it, we got our dinner right here," Jack said nodding at the fish. "Boys, let's get us a fire started and cook us up a fish to eat."

"Ah, how we gonna do that? We don't have any matches for a fire," Bobbie complained.

"Nope, we don't have any matches, but I just happen to have some flint," Jack said with a smile as he began digging in his pockets. He dug down into his trousers and pulled out one item after another: a knife, three acorns, a marble, a dried-up night crawler, a fishing lure, a ball of twine, a pencil stub, a smooth rock, and finally two pieces of flint. Bobbie and Billy stood in amazement staring down at Jack's assortment of items. "Gather up some kindling, and let's get us a fire started," Jack instructed them.

The other two boys scattered with smiles on their faces, the taste of sizzling smoked fish already tickling their taste buds. They came running back with a handful of dried twigs and grass.

"It's got to be finer," Jack explained after inspecting their kindling. "Use your knife, Bobbie, and split it. It's got to be as fine as frog hairs."

Bobbie grinned at the expression and took out his knife. Shaving the dried kindling over and over, they soon had a small ball of powdery fluff. He was pleased with himself in the way he had mastered using his knife. He could indeed make the wood shavings very fine now.

Next, Jack took the flint and began striking the two gray stones together above the ball. Tiny sparks jumped here and there. "Hold the ball right under the flint," he instructed the boys. Billy picked up the ball. "Bobbie, you blow when the sparks hit the ball," he said. With the cooperation of all three boys, they had a small fire before too long. Placing larger twigs and sticks on the fire, it soon grew large enough for cooking the fish. Putting fish on the end of sharpened sticks, they cooked the fish in this manner. It wasn't long before the scent of juicy fish filled the air. Their mouths began to water, and when they finally pulled back the skin and picked the white flesh from the bones, the fish about melted in their mouths. Billy laughed and suggested Jack add a shaker of salt to the assortment of items he kept in his pocket, but, all in all, they were satisfied with the outcome of their meal. Bobbie knew he'd learned a skill from Jack that day that he'd carry from then on.

The smoke from their fire sauntered up over the creek and out over the treetops. The boys sat on the sandy shore picking the tender meat from the bones and watched the smoke make its ascent before it disappeared into the air.

Suddenly, Billy stood up. Shading his eyes in the sun's afternoon glare, he pointed to a rocky ledge. "Hey, you see that dark hole up there in the face of that rock wall?"

"Whereabouts?" Bobbie asked looking in the general direction of where Billy was pointing, still too busy enjoying this incredible meal to be distracted very much. He felt like he was going to need a nap after this big feast.

"There! Just to the right of that sycamore tree. See?"

Bobbie and Jack, interest mounting, stood to get a better look. "Yea, I think I see it," Jack said. "What do you think it is, a hole of some kind?"

"It could be," Billy said with a sly grin. "Might even be a cave. You never know. Want to go see?"

The boys looked at one another, excitement showing on their grease-smeared faces. It was obvious they were in agreement as to what they wanted to do. They definitely had to climb the bluff and see if the hole Billy saw might actually turn out to be a cave. After all, this creek was called the Tunnel for some reason. It must have gotten its name for a cave or tunnel of some kind. They knew caves existed in these Ozark Mountains. They quickly devoured the rest of their fish, put out the fire, and stashed their fishing gear on some rocks. Then they lit out at a rapid pace down the creek bed toward the rock bluffs.

The walk down the creek and then the climb up the hill to the rock bluff was a weary journey to say the least, even for three spry, young boys. By the time they clawed their way to the rocky edifice that was their destination, their breath was coming from way down deep in their chests. Sweat rolled down their faces and necks. For several minutes, all they could do was lie on their backs to try to catch their breaths. Finally, Billy crawled to the back of the ledge and peered into the dark cavity. The hole went back about two yards and then seemed to angle down. It wasn't large, about a yard and a half wide and only about that tall. Billie leaned down and went cautiously inside. Bobbie and Jack were right behind him.

It was dark inside and cool. The walls were damp, and moss grew right inside the opening. A large brown toad jumped from its resting spot, startling the boys. Bobbie jumped. Thump! He groaned as he bumped his head on the ceiling when he jumped in his alarm from the toad. Jack laughed in spite of Bobbie's pained expression.

"How far back does it go?" Bobbie asked Billie, still rubbing his head.

"I can't really tell. It drops down, and it's too dark to see," Billy called back, peering down into the darkness.

"I wish we had thought to bring one of those burning sticks," Jack said.

"Come on up here," Billy said, "It gets wider up here."

The other two boys squeezed up to sit beside Billy. He was right. The tunnel did open up to where all three could sit side by side. The light from outside was at their backs, but, up above, there was only blackness. It was cool and damp inside the hole. One could only guess how far the tunnel traveled on ahead.

"Man! This is really something!" Bobbie said excitedly. "I've never heard anyone mention anything about this before. Why haven't we thought to ask someone about how the Tunnel got its name?"

"Hello!" Jack hollered ignoring Bobbie's question.

"Hellooooo" came a faint echo.

Billy raked his hand over the ground in search of a stone. He plucked one up and threw it up ahead. It bounced and seemed to travel some distance as it plummeted down into the darkness.

"Want to go a little farther?" Billy asked unable to contain his excitement.

"How long is that string in your pocket?" Bobbie asked Jack, remembering the string he'd seen earlier.

"I don't know. Why?"

"I thought we could tie it onto something out here. That way, we could follow it back and not get lost," Bobbie suggested.

Jack rummaged around in his pocket and brought out the string. He began unwinding it. It was indeed fairly long, somewhere around fifteen or twenty feet.

"What can we tie it on to?" Jack wanted to know.

Bobbie took the end of it and went back a few steps. He found a small plant, more of a weed really, and tied one end of the string to it. "We can't pull hard," he explained, "but it will lead us back to the opening."

"Okay, let's go!" Billy said with enthusiasm.

"Let that string out as you go," Bobbie instructed Jack.

The three adventurers crawled on. They crawled side by side. The floor was damp and muddy. It was eerily quiet. Bobbie could feel the knees of his pants growing damp from the damp earth. He could hear the beat of his own heart. It was rattling like Momma's pots and pans. They really hadn't gone far when suddenly the ground dropped unexpectedly. It quite literally dropped out from under all three of them. They found themselves falling.

"Aahhhhhhhhhh!" they screamed. All three boys clawed at whatever they could as they fell, fingernails digging at the soft clay. All traces of sunlight vanished as the three boys plummeted straight down. Ommph! They landed at the bottom of a deep pit. "Ouch!" Bobbie felt a sharp stab of pain in his side where he landed on something sharp. One of the boys landed on top of him, and it took a few minutes for him to catch his breath. It was pitch-black. "Watch it!" one of them managed to get out.

"What happened?" someone asked weakly.

"Is everyone okay?" Bobbie asked. No one answered. Everyone was too startled trying to assess the situation to even know.

With the silence, reality seemed to settle in. The boys were sitting in a thin puddle of water at the bottom of some kind of hole it seemed. It was pitch-black. They had no idea of how deep the hole was or whether or not they would be able to get out. No one knew where they were.

"You guys okay?" Bobbie asked again.

"I'm okay, I think," Jack said weakly.

"I don't know about my left arm," Billy said. "It really hurts."

"What about you?" Jack asked Bobbie.

"Yeah, I think so," Bobbie answered. "We've just got to figure out how to get out of here.

The boys rose and began to feel around. Their breaths were coming quick now. Bobbie could feel his own heart beating hard in his chest. Would they be stuck in here? Tears sprang to his eyes. He didn't like the dark. He didn't like this closed-in feeling. Everything was confusing. It was difficult trying to determine which direction was toward the front of the cave and which direction was further on toward the back.

"We've got to stay together," Jack warned. "Don't wander off from one another."

"Hey! Do you still have that string?" Bobbie wanted to know.

"No, I must have lost it in the fall. Let's see if we can find it dangling anywhere," Jack suggested. "If we can find that string, at least we will know that's the direction out."

"Good idea," Billy answered.

The boys' words seemed overly loud in the confines of the dark hole. Water squished with each footstep, and the boys bumped into one another as they wandered around in the inky black. "It's no use," Jack finally admitted after they had searched for a long while. "I feel like I'm going in circles."

"Wait!" Billy yelled. "Here is a wall that goes straight up. We had to have come in this way. We've got to climb up this wall to get out."

Bobbie and Jack moved toward Billy's voice. The boys stood side by side and ran their hands along the wall. It was cold and wet. The wall did go straight up with virtually no hand or footholds. The wall seemed to be made of clay, slick smooth clay. Bobbie and Jack agreed this must be the way they had come into the hole. "How far did we fall?" Jack wanted to know.

"It couldn't have been that far, or we would have been hurt more," Bobbie reasoned.

"So . . . the wall can't be that tall," Jack deduced.

Jack and Bobbie began trying to climb the wall, but not being able to see where to place a hand or foot, they didn't make much progress. "I can't climb, guys, with this arm," Billy complained.

After an hour or so, Bobbie and Jack had to admit that they weren't doing any good either. All three sat down together to try and develop a plan.

"I'm getting worried, guys," Jack voiced what they were all feeling. "I don't know if we're going to be able to climb out of this hole. No one knows where we are. I know people will start looking for us when we don't show up back home, and they're bound to find our fishing gear at the creek, but there's nothing to make them look here. How will they ever find us?"

"If we hear them hollering for us," Bobbie said, "we can holler back. Maybe they'll be able to hear us."

"They might be able to," Jack said. "What do we do until then?"

"There's not much we can do," Billy said. "We just have to stick together, keep trying at that wall every now and then. At least we've got water. That's a good thing, and it's not that cold or uncomfortable in here. Plus our bellies are full," he said with a laugh.

The other two laughed too, or at least they attempted to.

Time passed slowly. Every now and then, one of the boys would get up and work at climbing the wall. Once, Bobbie even climbed on Jack's shoulders to reach higher up on the wall. It was pretty scary though, doing it in pitch-blackness. Jack almost lost his balance and fell. It was hard for Billy to do much climbing at all with his hurt arm. They were convinced now that it was surely broken.

When the sound came out of nowhere, all three boys jumped to their feet like they had been shot. A voice! "Hello?" the voice asked.

"We're here!" all three boys shrieked jumping to their feet, falling over one another in their excitement.

"What are you all doing?" the voice asked. It was Cody's voice.

"Cody?" Bobbie asked, unbelieving.

"Yea, what are you guys doing in there?"

"We're trapped. We fell in a hole. Don't come any closer, or you might fall in too. Can you get help or get us out?" Bobbie asked desperately.

"Yea. You guys hang on. I'll be right back with help," Cody called.

The boys whooped and jumped up and down in the blackness as they heard Cody leaving the cave. They were saved! They were saved! How in the world, they wondered, had Cody discovered them?

It so happened that Cody had been doing a little fishing himself that day a little farther down the creek. Seeing the boys leave the fishing area, he had become curious and followed them—at a distance of course. Cody had missed his best friend Bobbie during the past several months. He had secretly spied on his friend on more than one occasion, and this was one time it had definitely paid off.

After seeing them go into the cave, he had waited and waited for them to come out. When they remained in there for what seemed like hours, he finally came to the conclusion that something must have gone wrong. That's when he discovered their plight. Cody hightailed it home, enlisting the help of several men in town to help get the boys out of the cave.

It had been a frightening experience that would haunt Bobbie, Jack, and Billy for many years. Rocks were piled at the entrance to the cave to prevent this occurrence from happening again. As Bobbie came out of the cave into the bright light, he squinted. He secretly said a prayer of thanks and then took off running through the woods down the path that would take him home. There would be plenty of time to collect his fishing gear later. Right now, there was only one place he wanted to be, home!

They say every dark cloud has a silver lining, and that saying was definitely true with this frightening day. Cody and Bobbie's friendship was mended that very day and grew stronger than it had ever been before. Things soon got back to normal with these two boys. Bobbie challenged Cody to a marble game the very next day and as fate or friendship would have it, Cody won back his beloved yellow-eyed marble in that very game. Amazingly too, Bobbie discovered his Prince Albert tobacco can, still stuffed with all its money, on his pillow beside him when he awoke a couple of days later on his pallet on the porch. Best of all though, the boys put aside all hard feelings and never brought up what had happened in the past. They left hard feelings behind and looked forward to good times in the future. After all, isn't that what true friendship is all about?

Chapter 14

When August rolled around, everyone started getting excited about going to the reunion at Mammoth Springs. It was always the third week in August and lasted the full week. It wasn't only the young that went to the reunion, the older men and women went also. Jim James or one of the men that had a log truck with a flatbed set a time that we would gather at the store to load up for the long trip. The men and older boys and the braver women would sit on the edge of the truck and hang their feet off. The other women and children sat in the middle on quilts. It was quite a load when we all got loaded up. The roads were rough and dusty, but we bounced along happy and excited about what we would do and see when we got to the big event.

The first thing we saw when it came into view was the huge Ferris wheel, and we heard the sound of the music from the rides. When we got there all dusty and windblown, we all unloaded. The driver that took us always set a time for us to gather back to the truck for the trip back home. The crowds were enormous and milling around everywhere. The smells that came from the hamburger stands made our mouths water. We didn't have hamburgers and hotdogs except at the reunion. There were all sorts of rides to choose from, but the Ferris wheel was where I headed. Dad gave Winna and me fifty cents or maybe a dollar to spend. Anyone could buy tickets for whatever rides they chose. There was Tilt-A-Whirl that two to four people could ride in each seat, and there were several seats on that ride. It would go up and down, spin and whirl, and sling you around every which way. It was really just too wild for me. There were stands where you could throw darts at balloons and see how many you could burst, and if you burst them all, you could win a teddy bear or some other prize. Other stands had pin balls to knock down and many other stands that you could play games for them to get your money. The Ferris wheel was my favorite ride though. I surely stayed away from the swings that were close to the big spring that the town was named after. I had heard that the spring had no bottom, and I always wondered where you would go if you ever fell in. The swings were chairs attached to long chains fastened to a long pole at the center. The chairs hung at the end of the chains. When the swings started going around, they would go faster and faster. The chairs swung on the chains very far out from the pole when they were going their fastest. I just knew I probably would fall off and end up in the bottomless spring, so I stayed clear of that ride.

Winna and I would meet up with Mom and Dad at one of the hamburger stands for what we were sure were the best things we had ever eaten. Dad paid for our hamburgers and orangeades or lemonades. What a treat it was!

When it was finally time to start back for home, everyone started gathering back at the truck. After all the heads were counted, we headed home, tired but excited from all the things we saw and did. By the time we pulled in at the Elizabeth store, there were many sleeping babies and tired mothers.

—Allie (2010)

Allie

August 1941

Allie really didn't know when she'd been more excited. They were going to the reunion in Mammoth Springs! She and Winna couldn't believe it! Each year they crossed their fingers and hoped and hoped they would get to go, but something always seemed to keep them from being a part of this experience. When Betty was little, Mama had said it would be too hard on her trying to manage a baby on such a long trip. Another year Daddy had been too busy with his work at the sawmill for them to go. This year Allie and Winna were certain they would not get to go because of baby Patsy and because of their house burning and all the extra expenses of Daddy building the new house. It had been such an unexpected surprise when they'd overheard Daddy talking to Mama this morning about the upcoming event.

The reunion was short for the Old Soldier, Sailor, Marine, and Air Force Reunion. This event was held the third week in August in Mammoth Springs and lasted the full week. It was like a carnival with rides, exhibits, food stands, game booths, and other types of entertainment. People in the area looked forward to this event all year and came from miles around.

Winna and Allie had been cutting out paper dolls from the Sears and Roebuck catalog in the bedroom when they'd overheard Daddy mention the reunion to Mama.

"Jim James said he's willing to take his flatbed truck to the reunion this year and anyone who wants is welcome to ride along."

Allie and Winna stopped what they were doing, their scissors frozen in midair.

"You're not thinking of going, are you?" Mama asked, surprise registering in her voice.

"I was thinking it would be good for us all to go," Daddy said.

"With Betty and Patsy as little as they are?" Mama said. "That doesn't seem like a very good idea."

"Gracie, it's been such a hard year for all of us, but especially for the girls. You know how they have struggled since the fire, having those nightmares over and over. I just think it would be a good thing for us all to get away and enjoy this time together as a family."

"I don't know, Robert."

In the bedroom, Allie and Winna looked worriedly at one another. Allie's eyes were opened very wide in surprise and anticipation. Winna reached out and took her hand. They both knew Mama had such influence with Daddy. If Mama was convinced they shouldn't go, the girls knew she could sway Daddy to her way of thinking.

"I was thinking we could take some quilts for the girls to sit on," Daddy continued. "You know there will be a lot of people sitting around the outside of the truck bed, if it's the trip you're worried about. The girls can sit in the middle. I'll help you with them."

"It's not just the trip, Robert," Mama went on. "The girls will get tired and will want to be carried. I just don't have enough arms for them all." Allie couldn't see Mama, but she could picture the expression on her face, the slight shake of her head, and one side of her mouth slightly pulled down.

"Once we get there, Winna and Allie are old enough to pretty much be on their own," Daddy continued. "That leaves the two of us with the two little ones. I think we can manage them between us. What do you say? I think you need this as much as the girls, Gracie. You've been working way too hard."

Allie had to give it to Daddy. He wasn't giving up easily.

The girls heard Mama sigh. That was a good sign. *Come on, Mama!* they were thinking.

"What time are they wanting to leave?" Mama asked Daddy.

"Jim said that whoever was going needed to meet at the store at 4:30 Friday afternoon. That should put us getting over there around 6:30. I figure we'd stay until 10:00 or so. I know the girls would sleep on the way back. You could too if you wanted."

"Well . . . I know the girls would love to," Mama admitted.

"Then let's do," Daddy confirmed. "I think it's just what we all need."

By this time, Winna and Allie were holding on to one another in a tight grip trying very hard not to scream out loud. Allie actually pulled her hands away from Winna's and stuffed them into her mouth to keep her joys of excitement from escaping. They knew they should not be eavesdropping, but how could they resist!

"I guess it may be what we do need," Mama admitted. "It doesn't come around often, and it does seem a shame to deprive the girls of this fun opportunity."

Tears sprang to Winna and Allie's eyes. The reunion! How could they possibly wait until Friday night?

Allie and Winna had been to the reunion only once before. It had been several years ago before Betty was even born. Winna had been about seven, and Allie around five. Allie could remember it though. She could remember the lights, the rides, and the wonderful food. They had gone in Grandpa's wagon that time, starting the trip early on a Friday morning and not getting back until late Sunday night. They had spent two nights with some relatives in Mammoth because of the long trip in the wagon. It had been a three-day event, one day for the trip there, one day at the reunion, and the third day for the trip back. Allie could hardly believe they could do it all in one day, now that they would be going in an automobile. They had had so much fun before. Allie remembered that they had even had their pictures taken. Allie had put her hands up by her face the way the cameraman had asked her to do and smiled when her picture was taken, and Winna had put her hands behind her head and smiled.

Allie

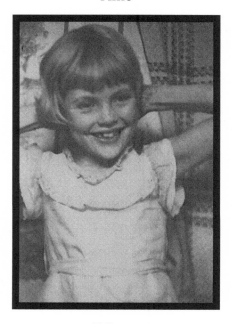

Winna

Daddy and Mama had even had their pictures taken. What fun they'd all had! Allie's heart was already racing a mile a minute and Friday was still four days away. What would she wear? What would she ride first? Would she eat a hot dog or a hamburger? Drink orangeade or a lemonade? Oh, there was so much to think about!

Allie thought Friday would never arrive. The days seem to crawl. The girls were so afraid something would happen before Friday that would prevent them from going on their trip. Winna and Allie were especially good and helpful to Mama all week, just to be on the safe side. They didn't want Mama to reconsider and think going to the reunion was indeed going to be too much trouble after all. Mama hardly had to do a thing for the next few days. When it was time to eat, Allie jumped up and set the table, once actually snatching the plates right out of Mama's hands. After the meal, the girls grabbed the dishes right off the table and began washing the dishes before Daddy had hardly finished his last bite. They even took care of their little sisters. Mama hardly saw her smallest daughters for the next few days.

Allie played outside with Betty for hours at a time. She showed her how to make hollyhock dolls. Allie would pick a fully bloomed hollyhock flower, leaving a short stem attached to the bottom of the bloom and turn it upside down. Next, she would pick a hollyhock bud. Pulling the green covering from the bud, the inside revealed a lovely cone bud with a pale bottom. This very much resembled a lady's face with a fancy hat. The bottom of the bud had a tiny hole in it. This was placed on the stem on the flower bottom. When completed, it looked like a lovely lady in a beautiful dress and hat. Betty would clap her hands and beg for more. Allie would comply and make rows of them to Betty's delight: a row of beautiful maidens all lined up at a dance waiting for their beaus. Allie would pick flowers from different hollyhock bushes for different color dresses: pink, red, orange, and purple. She had to admit to herself, they were quite beautiful.

Next, she would take Betty to the barn to visit the kittens. Taking along some doll dresses, they would play for hours dressing the kittens. Allie would slip a little pink print dress over the calico kitten's head and button it up the back. Next, she'd put the little bonnet on her head and tie the strings under the kitten's chin. Finally, she'd wrap her in the flannel blanket and hand the squirming kitten to Betty who giggled with delight. When one kitten grew too squirmy to handle, Allie would move on to the next kitten. It wasn't too long before all the kittens ran for cover to hide. All the girls could see of them were their little pink noses sticking out of the cracks under the barn and between bales of hay. Then the girls would have to move on to other sources of fun.

While Allie entertained Betty, Winna took care of Patsy. Patsy was an adorable baby. She would giggle and coo and wave bye-bye. Just about anything Winna did brought a smile to Patsy's chubby face. Winna carried Patsy around and showed her the chickens, donkeys, and kittens. She spread Mama's Sunbonnet Sue quilt under the trees and lay for hours playing with her baby sister, watching the leaves make the sunlight dance on the quilt. Mama commented that she had never gotten so much done in so little time and maybe they should plan an outing every week.

Often the girls would take the little ones up to visit Daddy. Daddy was busy, as always, rebuilding the house. He was determined to have his family in their new home by the first snowfall. Uncle Horace and Aunt Lottie would be moving back into their home soon, and Daddy wanted to be out of their house by the time they returned. He joked that his own family had to make do as best they could while their house was being built. With most of his earnings going for the lumber for the new house, there wasn't much money left for anything else. Daddy often said, "One day we eat beans and taters, and the next day we eat taters and beans." He was making progress on the house though. Daddy had seen a house in Dolph that he liked, and he was building their new house after that model. The girls walked through the skeleton of the house: the living room, kitchen, dining room, and a bedroom. The new wood of the house looked so pale and smooth and had a wonderful fresh pine scent. Daddy had cut the wood for their new house from his own sawmill. Allie marveled that Daddy had felled the trees, skidded the logs, split the logs into lumber, hauled the lumber to the house site, and now was nailing the lumber into place to build the house. He was doing it all, building their house from the tree up so to say. Allie couldn't wait until they were back in their own home again. Allie's heart nearly burst with excitement and pride in both the new house and in her Daddy's work. He had such talent as a carpenter.

Friday afternoon was a long time coming, but it finally arrived. Allie and Winna yanked the bobby pins from their hair, pulling out handfuls of hair with them too, in their excitement. They had worn the hairpins all day. They wanted their hair to look perfect for this special occasion. Their hair fell in tight Shirley Temple curls down to their shoulders. The girls had seen pictures of this young star and wanted to copy her adorable hairstyle. After fixing their hair, Allie and Winna slipped into their Sunday dresses that Mama had pressed crisp and fresh for them. Then they slipped on their anklets and shoes and were all set to go in record time. Then they had to sit quietly and try not to get dirty or wrinkled while Mama got the little ones dressed.

Mama had other preparations to do as well. She packed a basket with some items she thought they might need on their trip: sandwiches, snacks, diapers, water, washcloths, and blankets, even a pillow for the little girls. Allie felt as if they were going on such a long journey.

Finally, with Betty riding on Daddy's back, Winna carrying Patsy, and Mama and Allie carrying the basket, the family began the first part of their journey by walking from their house to the store. Allie could only imagine what adventures lay in store for them!

Upon reaching the store, however, Allie gasped in surprise and disappointment. There were so many people. People stood in the road and crowded on the store porch. Some were sitting on the benches; others were standing around here and there. There were men, women, and children running everywhere. Surely, Mr. James' truck couldn't hold everyone. Allie desperately began trying to count everyone and to calculate the space on the bed of the truck. There must be twenty or thirty people here at least. How many people could a truck hold? Daddy was always so polite; Allie knew he would surely suggest his family stay behind if there were not enough room for everyone. Her stomach began to ache, and she twisted her handkerchief in her hands. How disappointing it would be to have to walk home after all the excitement of the week. Allie imagined them walking home and having to put away the items in the basket and taking off their pretty clothes. Her worries must have shown on her face because Mama asked, "Allie, what in the world is the matter?"

"Oh, Mama! I'm afraid there won't be enough room for everyone. Just look at everyone!" Allie confessed, looking up at Mama, a look of horror on her face.

Mama laughed. "Funny girl! It won't take too much room for the ones who sit along the edge. Don't you worry. I think there will be room for everyone. We can sit close together."

Allie hoped Mama was right. Soon the women with young children began spreading their quilts and blankets in the middle of the bed. They situated the little ones there and then sat beside them. Next, the younger children climbed up beside their mothers. Finally, Daddy helped Allie up onto the bed of the truck. She walked over and sat down on the edge of Mama's quilt. Allie had butterflies in her stomach. She couldn't believe she was getting to ride in an automobile again so soon. In just one summer, she was getting to ride two times in a vehicle. She supposed times were changing. Pretty soon, it might get to be something that wasn't so amazing. Right now, the trip to and from the reunion in the back of the truck was almost, just almost as exciting as going to the reunion itself.

Finally, the men and boys began to climb on. They sat along the edge of the truck bed and dangled their feet off the side. Allie wondered what would keep them from bouncing off when the truck hit a bump. The road was rough and filled with holes. It seemed so reckless and dangerous to her. She hoped Daddy wouldn't sit on the side like that. Allie held her breath as more and more people climbed on. Everyone scooted closer and closer together. Just as she suspected, Daddy stood to the side until everyone else was seated. Finally, he climbed aboard too. Allie let out the breath she'd been holding! There was room for everyone! However, there was not an inch to be spared. Daddy squeezed in on the quilt beside Mama and held Betty on his lap. Allie looked up at Mama and smiled. They were actually getting to go! It was going to happen!

Allie looked around now and noticed some of the boys and girls from school were on the truck. Now that she saw everyone was going to fit on the truck, she relaxed a little and noticed who was actually there on the truck with her. She saw Cody and Bobbie together, sitting at the back of the truck dangling their feet. Why did that not surprise her to see them being reckless? They seemed to be friends again. She also noticed some of the older boys with them: Danny, Shine, Billy, and Jack. Billy was wearing a cast on his arm. Allie had heard the scary story of the boys falling into a deep hole of some kind or another. Winna was sitting beside Allie with her friends from school next to her. Allie was disappointed that none of her own friends were along. Finally, Mr. James stood and hollered back to them, "Is everyone all set?"

There was a loud uproar of "Yea," "Let's go," "Wahoo," and the likes. Then he started the engine, and they were off with a jerk. Everyone laughed and grabbed on to something, and the truck started down the road. A cloud of thick dust jumped up from the road and chased after the truck, seeming to want to go along and be a part of this fun journey. Allie looked around at all the excited faces. She caught Daddy's eye, and he winked at her.

The ride was bumpy, dusty, and hot. Allie was so excited, she couldn't keep the wide grin off her face. She found out soon though that the dust from the road wanted to settle on her teeth. It made them gritty. After that, she tried to smile with her mouth closed. The wind blew Allie's curls all over her head, and she had to tuck her dress underneath her legs to keep it from blowing up in the wind. Poor Mama had spent so much time pressing it only to have it wrinkled so soon by being stuffed under her legs. She looked over at Mama holding little Patsy. The jostling of the truck had already rocked her youngest sister to sleep in Mama's arms. Betty wasn't sleeping though. She wasn't going to go to sleep and miss the fun. She was old enough to know something exciting was happening. Betty clapped her hands and bounced on Daddy's lap, grinning from ear to ear and waving her hands at everyone.

Winna and her friends began to talk of all they would do when they got to the reunion. Soon some of the older boys turned around and joined in. Many of the kids attended each year, so they considered themselves experts, giving advice to all the others. Allie listened intently to learn all she could. Having only attended once and that being six years ago, she knew she had a lot to learn.

"Save you money, and don't go in to see the three-headed monster," one boy advised. "Most of those sideshows are just rip-offs anyway."

"That game where you try to knock down the bottles with the baseballs is a steal," said another. "I lost five dollars there last year and didn't win a blame thing. I think the bottles are weighted down."

"Five dollars! Who has five dollars anyway?" Shine hollered.

"I lost every bit of my money at that card game," another boy cut in. "This year those card sharks aren't getting a red cent of my moola!"

Allie held her handkerchief tightly. Her five dimes were tied securely in the corner. The way these kids were talking, there would be people there ready to yank her money right out of her hands the minute she got there. Her hands began to grow damp from her tight grip.

"I'm going to spend every single penny of my money riding the Ferris wheel," Winna said confidently. Allie looked over at her sister, surprised. That seemed very bold of Winna.

"Yep, I'm gonna ride and ride and ride until the reunion closes down," Winna said.

Allie suddenly didn't think she knew her sister. Winna, who always seemed so sensible and levelheaded, was talking like a crazy person; ride until the reunion closes down? Allie didn't know what she was going to do. Was she going to ride with Winna? She really didn't know if she wanted to ride the Ferris wheel. She remembered it was so big. Would everyone laugh at her if she were afraid to ride? Would Winna leave her behind in her excitement to ride and ride and ride? There was so much to consider.

"My first stop is going to be the Tilt-a-Whirl! That's my fav!" exclaimed an older girl. "It slings you all over the place! I rode it so many times last year I puked my brains out."

"Super-duper! Count me in!" remarked someone at the far corner of the truck bed. There were other exclamations of joy all around Allie as if throwing up were the most exciting thing in the world. Allie looked at the faces of the teenagers around her and wondered if they had all lost their minds.

"Have you ever ridden the swings? They take you out over the spring. You know that spring doesn't have a bottom, don't you?" a teenage boy said.

Allie's eyes popped open. How could a spring not have a bottom? Oh my, what if she fell in? Where would she go? If you fell in a spring with no bottom, where would you end up? She had to ponder that for a while. She knew that was one ride she definitely would not be riding on or getting anywhere around. Suddenly, she wasn't as excited about the reunion as she had been. She scooted an inch closer to Mama. She decided to face the front of the truck and concentrate on the sights they were passing. Mama looked over at Allie and gave her a reassuring smile.

Allie smiled back tentatively. She took a moment to study her mother and father as they sat there side by side on the patchwork quilt in the bed of the truck. As she compared her parents to the other fathers and mothers sitting around them, it occurred to her what a very attractive couple they truly were. She'd never really thought about it before; they were just Mama and Daddy. Tonight though, them being among all the other parents, Allie did make a comparison.

Allie's Daddy and Mama

Mama looked so pretty with her dark hair, brown eyes, and olive skin. Daddy looked more handsome than any of the other men, tall and slim with a broad smile and sparkling eyes. Daddy was talking to another man beside him. All of a sudden, he threw back his head and laughed loudly. Yes, that was Daddy. His and Mama's personalities were very different. Daddy was laughter, jokes, hugs, and kisses. Mama was more serious, calm, and not as free with her affection. Mama loved them dearly; that went without saying, but she just wasn't as affectionate as Daddy. Allie sometimes wondered if Mama might feel a little left out or neglected the way Daddy got so many hugs and kisses and just more attention from his daughters than she did. It wasn't that the girls loved Daddy more than Mama; it was just that Daddy's arms were always open. Allie looked over at Mama now. She reached out and squeezed Mama's hand. Mama smiled warmly. What a comfort it was to have Mama and Daddy to snuggle up to when she felt uneasy or insecure. She decided this was where she wanted to sit for the rest of the trip.

As they neared the town of Mammoth Springs, they began to faintly hear the carnival music. Excitement ran through the bed of the truck. Everyone began straining their necks to try and catch a glimpse of the carnival. Sure enough the tall Ferris wheel could be seen above the treetops. The lights of the carnival were reflected in the waters of Mammoth Springs. Before long, the music could be heard loudly, and with each increased volume in the music, it was matched in the level of excitement among the passengers of the truck. Allie fully expected some of the boys to hop from the truck bed and take off running as they neared the gate, thinking they could outrun the speed of the truck.

Mr. James turned the corner and pulled the truck onto the wooden bridge that took them across the spring to the reunion. Allie held her breath. She sure hoped the bridge didn't break. Thumpity, thumpity, thumpity. The truck bounced over each loose board in the bridge. Allie's mind thought of the water underneath the bridge. She couldn't comprehend a spring with no bottom. Did it go on and on like outer space was said to go on and on, never ending? It was something she couldn't understand, something that never ended. She really didn't think it was a good idea for them to cross such a dangerous spring with no bottom. What if Mr. James ran off the side? She breathed a sigh of relief when the truck finally bumped its way onto the other side.

Mr. James pulled the truck into a grassy area alongside the many other trucks and wagons parked there. They were here! They were finally at the reunion! Pulling his watch from his pocket, their driver said, "Now everyone listen up! This truck is going to pull out of here at 10:30 sharp. If you're aiming on catching this truck home, you'd better be here by then." Everyone nodded and affirmed they would be back at the appointed time and climbed down. The boys took off at a run, but the men and women spent a few minutes dusting one another off and running a comb through their hair. Mama brought out her washcloth and poured some water on it. She washed the babies and smoothed down their hair. Then she handed the cloth to Winna and Allie. As much as they were in a hurry to get to the midway, they took time to wipe the dust from their faces.

"Now, you girls, be careful," Mama said sternly. "If you want us or need us, meet at the Ferris wheel. Daddy and I will go there every so often to check for you. Just stay there if you need us, and we'll be there directly. That's a good place to meet because you can see the Ferris wheel from all over the field. Do you have your money?"

"Yes, Mama," Winna and Allie answered holding up their handkerchiefs. Mama was holding Patsy who had started to squirm and whimper, and Daddy had Betty's little hand in his.

"Okay, you girls have fun, and stay together," Daddy cautioned.

And just like that Daddy and Mama turned and walked off with the other adults leaving the girls alone. Allie was somewhat surprised that Daddy and Mama would let them loose in such a crowded place so easily. She didn't know what she thought of being left alone. She couldn't help but wonder if she'd ever see them again.

"Come on," Winna called excitedly behind her to Allie as she took off with some of the other kids. Allie started off in a run to catch up. Winna was intent on keeping up with her friends, so she was walking fast. Allie wished again that some of her own friends were here. She felt like a tagalong with Winna and her friends. She wished she had Winna all to herself. They always had so much fun together. Allie tried her best to keep up. Her little matchstick legs were taking giant steps, sidestepping popcorn boxes, soda bottles, electrical cords, and construction boxes to try and keep up with the older kids. Her bouncy curls swung as her head slung first one way and then the other trying to see everything. Her eyes were as big as Mama's dinner plates. Winna was laughing and talking with her friends. She didn't seem to be paying that much attention to her younger sister at all.

Sounds and lights came at Allie from all sides. Lively carousal music circled round and round her up and down and round and round. Colorful lights blinked on and off: blue, yellow, orange, green, purple, green, yellow, blue, round and round and up and down. The Ferris wheel with its lights rolled up and down and round and round and the chairs swayed back and forth as they went higher and higher and then crested to move down again. Allie thought Winna and her friends would stop at the Ferris wheel. After all, Winna had said that was where she was going to ride and ride, but to Allie's surprise, the group walked right past the Ferris wheel.

"Step right up, ladies and gentlemen. Never seen before . . . most amazing sight . . . one of a kind!" And the crowds. People were everywhere bumping into her, nearly knocking her down!

Allie's head was spinning like the Tilt-a-Whirl they passed. Then a woman in a turban caught Allie's eye. The woman's face was painted. The lady's eyelids were bright blue with black lines going out from the upper and lower lids toward her ears. She had on huge hoop earrings and a long flowing, glittering purple robe. Her hair was piled high on her head caught up underneath the yellow turban. Allie had never seen anyone like her before. She was beckoning to Allie, motioning to her to come. "Come on over. Learn your future. Let me read your palm. What does the future hold for you, my dear?"

She was looking right at Allie. Should she go over? It seemed so rude to just walk away and ignore the woman. Allie didn't know what to do. "Come on over, little girl," the woman said reassuringly. "I can read your palm and tell you what will be in your future."

Allie stopped and then walked over hesitantly. The lady seemed so nice. Allie seemed to be pulled to her by some invisible force. The lady smiled warmly. "There you go. You're a lovely young lady. Let me see your hand, dear."

Allie held out her hand uncertainly to the lady.

"Ah, look at this!" the lady said with surprise in her voice. "I see . . . I see . . . I see a long, long trip in store for you. You will go on a very long journey very, very soon!" She smiled at Allie, revealing long, slightly yellowed teeth behind very red lips. Up close her smile was scary. Her smile was too big. The lines outlining her eyes made the lady look fierce. Suddenly Allie was afraid. Where was Winna? Allie looked around. She tried to jerk her hand away, but the lady held onto it.

"I . . . I . . . I've got to go," Allie stammered as she pulled her hand harder. She finally jerked it away and started backing away.

"Not so fast, sweetie," the woman said sweetly. "That will be ten cents for your fortune."

Allie didn't know what to do. Should she bolt and run? Would the woman chase her? If she could read the future, she could surely find her if she ran and hid. Tears swam in her eyes. Allie slowly took her handkerchief out of her pocket. She untied the corner where her money was safely tied and took out a dime. Putting it on the table, she turned and ran.

People were everywhere. There was shouting and laughter behind her. Babies were crying, children tugging at their parents, and noise everywhere. Allie couldn't think. Where could Winna be? Allie wandered from one place to another. Where should she go?

Allie was being pushed along with the crowd. She had never been in such a place. Where had all these people come from? Where were they all going? "Step this way, ladies and gentlemen!" "One of a kind!" Voices were beckoning customers from all sides. The August air was stifling hot. Allie's hair was sticking to her neck and forehead. It was difficult to breathe in the crowd. The air was thick with dust and strange smells. Allie's throat felt dry and hot. She was thirsty. She needed some fresh air. She felt like she was smothering, being so short in this crowd of tall people. Allie saw a break in the crowd. She ducked and ran through the mass of people to the side. Breaking into an opening in the crowd, Allie opened her mouth to take in a deep breath of fresh air. Just as she took in a deep breath though, she screamed. It wasn't just a little gasp, a shriek, or a yelp. It was an out and out bloodcurdling scream. Standing right in front of Allie was a man holding the longest, fiercest-looking snake Allie had ever seen. The man not only was holding the snake, he had it draped around his neck, and it was hanging down on one side of his neck almost to the ground. The snake was brown with darker brown markings on it. The man held the snake's head in his hand, and the snake was looking straight at Allie. Allie had always been terrified of snakes, and here was the biggest, meanest snake she had ever seen, not three feet away from her with its beady eyes glued right on her. She couldn't quit screaming. She was paralyzed with fear. People around her began laughing. Some tried to comfort her and pull her away, but it was no use. Allie continued to scream. And then somehow, Allie found her feet. She took off running as fast as her spindly legs would carry her. She did just like she remembered her Mama telling her, "You can see the Ferris wheel from anywhere you go at the reunion." Allie looked up and saw the lights of the big Ferris wheel. She ran toward it without stopping. She didn't slow down. She may have knocked people down. She may have ran between mothers and children and caused people to drop things. She really didn't know. She really didn't care. Her eyes were glued on that bright big object in the night sky, and she didn't take her eyes off it once.

To Allie's great relief, Mama, Daddy, Winna, and her little sisters were all waiting for her at the Ferris wheel. Allie ran and jumped into Daddy's arms. They were all just as happy and relieved to see her as she was to see them. Winna was especially happy! She had told Mama and Daddy, "One minute she was there and the next she was gone!" They didn't have to worry about Allie getting away from them again that night. She clung to them like pine rosin.

The rest of the night was lots of fun for Allie. She and Winna must have ridden the Ferris wheel five or six times. By the end, she completely agreed with Winna and would be saying herself the next time they went to the reunion, "I'm going to ride, ride, ride that Ferris wheel until it closes down." She even rode the merry-go-round with Betty. One thing was sure. Never did she let her family out of her sight, not for one second!

Before they left, Daddy took them all to one of the hamburger stands. Oh, the food and drinks were just so good. The orangeade and lemonade were in big glass jars, and the girls had a glass of each. There were orange rings floating in the orangeade and lemon rings floating in the lemonade. Winna got a hamburger and shared it with Allie, and Allie got a hotdog and shared it with Winna. The girls knew they had never tasted anything so wonderful; that is until Daddy bought them each a caramel apple. Winna and Allie would talk about that wonderful treat for weeks and weeks!

All too soon it was time to begin their trip back home. After the noses had been counted, everyone settled down for the long trip back home. Allie curled up on Mama's quilt and settled in for the long ride. The trip home was quieter and much more subdued than the trip there had been. Most everyone had a few tales to exchange when they had first begun the trip back but soon settled down into a quiet slumber. Patsy and Betty were snoozing before they were even out of sight of the lights of the reunion. Mama lay her head in Daddy's lap and was soon sleeping as well. Allie slept most of the way home too. When they were nearing the Elizabeth store, she briefly woke and wondered if they would ever get home. It seemed like they had been riding forever. She smiled as she realized the fortune lady had been right. She guessed she had made a very long journey. But what a night it had been! This night had brought good times and scary times. Allie thought of the caramel apples, hamburgers, hot dogs, the Ferris wheel, the orangeade, the lemonade, and the merry-go-round. No, she would never forget this wonderful night. She thought again of the bottomless spring and the awful snake and she shivered. Maybe, just maybe, that's where that awful scary snake had ended up—at the bottom of the bottomless spring!

Chapter 15

While Bob was overseas, he sent Rex, Erma Lou, Linda, and me jackets with our names on the front. It also had a picture of the place he was stationed on the jacket. It was called Formosa. We sure got a lot of attention with those jackets.

—Betty (Bobbie's sister) (2010)

Bob bought her (his mom) her first sewing machine. After she got it, boy, she went to sewing right then! It was a treadle machine that Bob bought her. It was a Singer. Mom sewed all the time after that, but that's what set Mom up—when he bought her that sewing machine.

—Wilb (Willie) (2010)

Bobbie

December 1941

A brisk wind whipped snowflakes from one landing spot to another, ripping them up angrily as soon as they landed slinging them somewhere else, only to be whipped up and slung around again. The wind seemed angry and bitter this afternoon, never settling but continually gusting with unusually wild force. It matched the mood of the members in the small community. However in addition to being bitter and angry, everyone was also in a state of confusion, panic, and extreme sadness. Just this afternoon around 1:45, Bud Landrum had run out of the store shouting the news: "Japan has bombed our naval base in Pearl Harbor, Hawaii! We've been attacked by Japan! We've been attacked!"

It wasn't long until everyone in town gathered around the old radio in the store trying to catch the latest news reports coming in through the broken static over the wires. Men, women, boys, and girls huddled around the old brown box, every ear turned toward it, trying not to miss a single word. All faces wore the same look of dread and disbelief. It couldn't be! Their own country attacked! How could this have happened? Suddenly even their own small community seemed vulnerable, susceptible to the world. They were not closed off and protected any more.

Bobbie joined the others, his jaw dropped. His eyes frantically searched the faces of the older ones around the circle for clues of how really bad it was. It was like the ice on the pond had finally broken, and they had all fallen through. Bobbie had known they had been skating on thin ice for some time now really. The ice had been cracking. He had known that; they all had, but had stubbornly refused to believe it, turned their heads instead of facing the truth. Bobbie remembered Daddy and his uncles talking of the problems in Europe, whispering of the invasions. It was all so unstable there. He had listened as the old men at the store had gone on and on about the conflicts in Europe and this man called Hitler who seemed to be behind it all. They had only been fooling themselves when they said maybe Roosevelt could keep the United States out of the conflict. The old ones knew. They had seen trouble brewing before. These men had been around during the Great War and knew the signs of a coming conflict. Is that what this invasion was leading up to? Would it be a world war again? Would this country now be drawn into this war? It was almost like Japan wanted to pull us into the war by attacking our naval base, destroying ships and killing our soldiers. Could Roosevelt overlook this? The men gathered there today answered with a resounding no! This couldn't be overlooked. This meant war for the United States!

Bobbie stood and walked slowly down the aisle of the store and out the door. He had to think, needed some fresh air. The wind whipped the door shut behind him with a bang, blowing the driving snow into his face. The flakes were bigger now and coming down harder. Bobbie pulled the collar of his coat up and his cap down more snuggly over his ears. He didn't know where he wanted to go or what he wanted to do, but he was uneasy and had to stir. He could never sit still when there was trouble, always seemed to have the need to walk it off, spend time alone.

Bobbie was lost in thought and didn't even realize where he was until he found his hand pulling open the old wooden gate to the cemetery. He hesitated. What had brought him here? He supposed he was drawn to this place on account of the talk at the store. The men had been talking about all the young boys who gave up their lives during the Great War and the ones who were likely to be called up to go overseas if there were another. Bobbie shivered now as he thought of friends of his, old enough to be called to go off to fight if they were asked to do so. Which of them would end up here? Which of them would not make it back? He couldn't stand the thought of it. He couldn't think like this. This was too close to home. Even his cousin Danny was almost old enough to go. Some of the Huett boys were that age. Bobbie thought back on some of the men who were veterans of World War I: Claude Blair, Claude Case, Jasper Haynes, Will Snyder, and Raydo Stroud. Then there was Clovis Hodges and others who never came back from the war. If there were another war, how long would it last?

Bobbie knew he wasn't that far from military age himself. So many questions.

Bobbie's Dad holding baby daughter

Wandering through the cemetery from grave to grave, Bobbie noticed the names and ages on the gravestones that seemed to have been soldiers. Making somewhat of a circle, he ended up at his own family's burial plot. He walked over to his grandpa James' grave. Bobbie looked down at his grave. Grandpa had only been gone two years now. Looking at the dates on the stone, Bobbie saw that he had been born in 1871 and died in 1939. He had been a mail carrier. Grandpa would carry the mail from Elizabeth to Dolph and to Calico every day, there and back. At other times he carried the mail to Bakersfield. Either way, it was around fifteen miles one way. Bobbie closed his eyes and pictured Grandpa with his heavy mailbag on his back. Bobbie knew Grandpa had to be exhausted after doing that every day, six days a week. One day he'd do it on horseback and the next he'd do it in a buggy. The reason he took the buggy every other day was that people would send eggs and cream to the market with him, so every other day, Grandpa would take the mail in the buggy so he could haul their dairy products to the store for them. Grandpa carried a shotgun on the mail route with him too. He liked to eat squirrel, and he'd kill squirrel all year with that gun as he drove his mail route. Bobbie smiled at the thought of Grandpa walking down the road slinging a couple of squirrel. Just like Grandma used to carry a gun around with her when she was a girl to shoot whatever she could for her family's supper, Grandpa ended up carrying a gun with him and doing the same when he got older. Grandpa was a jolly man, always laughing. Bobbie loved that about him. He was a peddler too, sold Riley products, and he carried his products with him as he carried the mail. He'd sell Zemo, 3-S Tonic, Redbud Salve, and all kinds of extracts to the people along his route. Grandpa also had an old cotton gin up at the store. Bobbie loved to watch that old contraption work to remove the seeds from the cotton bolls. Grandpa always kept busy and made a little money during his lifetime, not much, but enough to get by on. Bobbie sure missed him. Grandpa's lifetime: carrying mail, shooting squirrel, selling Riley products, playing with the grandkids. It was over too fast. "A lifetime sure goes by fast," Bobbie said aloud. He lovingly touched Grandpa's headstone.

Bobbie's Grandma and Grandpa James

Grandpa had married Grandma, an Indian, and they moved to Elizabeth around 1901 or 1902. Grandma had been born the same year as him, 1871. She was raised south of Mammoth Springs in Randolph County. Grandma had told them her stories of how hard they had it when she was a little girl. Her family was very poor. She told Bobbie it was her job to work the oxen and to work the cotton as well as help her sister Margaret get supper on the table. They would pick the cotton and put it in the house, and then during the winter months when it was cold, they'd work the cotton, pulling the seeds and leaves and stuff out of it. Grandma's mother was a full-blooded Indian and her father half-Indian. His name was Andrew Jackson Tyree. He was named after our seventh president. Bobbie always thought that somewhat odd since President Jackson was the one who had signed the Indian Removal Act back in 1830 when he was president. For whatever reason though, his great-grandfather had been named after this popular president. Great-grandpa Tyree wasn't buried in this cemetery at Elizabeth though, but in a cemetery down close to Wild Cherry. Bobbie had visited that cemetery once or twice and seen where his great-grandpa was buried. Great-grandpa had actually died while visiting Grandma and Grandpa James. Since he died in this part of the country, this was where he was buried.

Bobbie rubbed his hands together to try and warm them. He needed some gloves. The wind was brutal. It continued to whip around, and the snow stung his hands chapping them as well as his face. The flakes continued to come down turning the graves into white mounds. Bobbie's hands were numb and his feet were stiff with cold. His socks were wet where the snow was coming in through the holes in his boots. Bobbie guessed he needed to buy himself a new pair of boots since these had so many holes in them. He was trying to make do with last year's boots even though they had seen their better days, and his toes were curled up at the ends. He had thought these boots would get passed down to Willie this year, but Daddy thought maybe he could get a few more months out of them. Bobbie told himself he would check on a new pair if he had any money left after he bought Momma's sewing machine.

Bobbie had asked Jim Andy to order the machine several weeks ago, and it should be in any day now. He couldn't wait to see Momma's face when she saw it. Bobbie's heart nearly burst with excitement over the surprise. He could scarcely be in the same room with Momma for fear that he would lose all control and the words would come pouring out of his mouth about his surprise for her. After the events of today, at least that was going to be one bright spot in an otherwise bleak month. Bobbie had it all planned out. He'd set the machine beside the Christmas tree after Momma went to bed Christmas Eve, and it would be there when she got up Christmas morning. What a wonderful Christmas it would be!

Bobbie blew on his hands to warm them. He knew he needed to get home and begin his night chores. Momma and Daddy would be wondering about him. He began walking toward the cemetery gate. Passing another tombstone with a military cross etched into the stone, he wondered how this young man had felt about leaving home to serve his country. Had he been anxious to serve or had he been hesitant? He had been so young when he died, only eighteen. It seemed such a shame that he had to make such a sacrifice, to give his life at such a young age. He had never had the chance to do all the things young boys dreamt of doing. He'd been cheated out of all of that. Bobbie really didn't know what to think about being called up to serve. Part of him was scared, scared to leave home, scared to fight, scared to think of dying. Part of him though was furious, and that made him want to fight, ready to fight. Was that how this young boy had felt too?

Bobbie thought back to the reports that had been shared from the *New York Times*. It had told of a massacre of Jews. Could this killing of innocent people actually be happening? Could this man named Hitler have so much power and influence over individuals that they would carry out such orders? Could there actually be places such as the concentration camps that were described in the paper? If so, was that not worth fighting for? Bobbie didn't know if what they were hearing about these places was truth or not. At times like this, he felt his community was so isolated from the rest of the country. He didn't know what to believe. He wished they had access to big city newspapers or radio stations that came in loud and clear without static cutting out half of what was being said.

Bobbie got very little sleep that night. Grandpa and his uncles were at the house until way in the night discussing the events of the day and what might happen. Momma didn't even bother cooking supper that night, something Bobbie couldn't remember ever happening before. Everyone just ate cold biscuits and leftover meat, whatever they could find for supper. It seemed the whole town, probably the whole country, was in an uproar, holding its breath for what was to come. The very thought of Japanese planes invading America's shores and killing American servicemen made them unable to rest. Bobbie tossed all night. Was Daddy too old to fight? What ages of men would be called? What would happen to his own family if Daddy were called up? Bobbie felt as if his whole world was about to be turned upside down.

The next morning Bobbie woke at his usual time and made his early morning trip to school to light the fires. He didn't know if there would be school today. He had heard that President Roosevelt was supposed to deliver a message to the nation and to Congress around noon. He figured the community would gather for that. One way or the other though, the school building would be needed, and with the cold and snow, he needed to get the building warm.

School began at the usual time, but that was about all that was normal about school that day. The students came into the building very quiet and subdued. They took their seats without even being asked to do so by Mr. Blue. It was even quiet in the little room. Bobbie noticed that Mr. Schauffler didn't sing his usual Mr. Zip song with the little kids this morning. It was like the zip had been zapped right out of all of them. The students and teachers alike moved like they had no energy at all. Mr. Blue assigned the students in the big room seat work to do. Along around noon, adults began arriving. President Roosevelt was going to give a speech at 12:30, and the community was going to congregate at the school so they could all be together when they heard what he had to say.

Mr. Schauffler and Mr. Blue dismissed the students to eat their lunches while they prepared the classrooms to accommodate more and more people as they arrived. Mr. Blue got on one side of the large partition while Mr. Schauffler got on the other end. After instructing all the small children to stand back, they began raising the heavy wall. Bobbie and some of the larger boys assisted their teachers. Once the wall was raised, posts were placed at either end to keep it in place. Next the seats were positioned to where they were all facing the same direction toward the battery-powered radio that sat at the front of the building.

Before long the seats began to fill: Ot and Elda Foster, Jim and Josie Smith, the Haughns, the Comstocks, the Strouds, the Bakers, the Kerleys, George and Edna Huett, Sam and Texanner Shoemate, Mr. and Mrs. Landrum, Momma and

Daddy with Grandpa Crotts, Otis and Sally Owens, Jim and Alph James, Art and Alta James, Mr. and Mrs. Stephens, and they kept coming. The line of people stretched back through the door down the front steps.

Mr. Blue asked the students to move from the chairs and either stand or sit on the floor as more and more people crowded into the room. Bill Tyree and Zona, Cap Robbins and Maude, Otis Harris and Vern, Troy and Ida Belle, Bud Hutson, Alma Foster, George and Ruth Foster, Lynn and Azlee Zimmer, and Lee Campbell. Now the adults had to stand too. Every space in the building was filled, but as each person came inside, he did so silently and with only a nod or brief smile at a neighbor or friend.

Bobbie noticed the way some of the parents of military-age boys were already hovering over their sons in a protective way. Mr. and Mrs. Lance had Lester sitting between them determined to keep him away from harm nestled there between the two of them. Bobbie could understand their feelings. Suddenly, he felt the need to have Willie and Audie beside him. Getting up from his spot beside some of the older boys, he moved over to where the younger kids sat. It took some wriggling, but he finally wedged his way in between the two of them. Audie looked up, somewhat surprised to see him so close beside her. Bobbie just nodded briefly and continued to look around at the crowd.

When everyone was settled, Mr. Blue stood. "Ladies and gentlemen, we're happy to have all of you here today.

I'm just filled with sorrow that it's such a troubled time that brings us all together." He paused and gestured back to the radio. "Mr. Schauffler and I have put new batteries in our radio here, so we should be able to hear President Roosevelt's speech in its entirety. I know we're somewhat cramped for space in here, but I don't think it will be a long speech. Is everyone okay where they are? Is there anyone standing who has a condition that he should sit?" Mr. Blue looked around. When no one voiced a problem or concern, he continued. "Very well then. I've asked Sam Shoemate to lead us in a prayer before the President's speech. I know we need to lean on one another at times like this. I know it's important to have faith in our President and our Congress to do the right thing for our country, but we need to look to our greatest help as well. That's why I've asked Mr. Shoemate to lead us in this prayer. Sam?"

Mr. Shoemate rose from where he was sitting and then struggled to get down on one knee. He reached out and took hold of the seat in front of him with one hand and bowed his head. There was a slight rustling in the room as men, sitting here and there, removed their hats and bowed their heads as well. The room grew silent, and Mr. Shoemate began his prayer.

Mr. Shoemate prayed from the heart, that was evident. He humbly asked that God be with the leaders of this great land as well as the leaders around the world that they would make wise decisions to lead the world out of this conflict into more peaceful times. He asked for the safety and protection of the servicemen and women, especially those of our own number who might be called to serve. Finally he asked that the Father be with the family members who had lost loved ones during the recent air raids in Pearl Harbor. It wasn't a long prayer, but it seemed to voice the feelings and concerns that everyone was having. An echoing amen followed his own when he finished.

At last, Mr. Schauffler turned on the radio. The reception from the radio was especially clear today. Each person sat stiffly, anxious for, yet dreading what he would hear.

Finally, President Roosevelt's voice came strongly over the wires:

Mr. Vice President, Mr. Speaker, Members of the Senate, and of the House of Representatives:

Yesterday, December 7, 1941—a date which will live in infamy—the United States of America was suddenly and deliberately attacked by naval and air forces of the Empire of Japan.

The United States was at peace with that nation and, at the solicitation of Japan, was still in conversation with its government and its emperor looking toward the maintenance of peace in the Pacific.

Indeed, one hour after Japanese air squadrons had commenced bombing in the American island of Oahu, the Japanese ambassador to the United States and his colleague delivered to our Secretary of State a formal reply to a recent American message. And while this reply stated that it seemed useless to continue the existing diplomatic negotiations, it contained no threat or hint of war or of armed attack.

It will be recorded that the distance of Hawaii from Japan makes it obvious that the attack was deliberately planned many days or even weeks ago. During the intervening time, the Japanese government has deliberately sought to deceive the United States by false statements and expressions of hope for continued peace.

The attack yesterday on the Hawaiian Islands has caused severe damage to American naval and military forces. I regret to tell you that very many American lives have been lost.

A gasp went up from the crowd.

Bobbie watched as some of the women dabbed at their eyes. It was what they all suspected. They had heard that there were several killed. Mr. Roosevelt went on.

> *In addition, American ships have been reported torpedoed on the high seas between San Francisco and Honolulu.*
>
> *Yesterday, the Japanese government also launched an attack against Malaya.*
>
> *Last night, Japanese forces attacked Hong Kong.*
>
> *Last night, Japanese forces attacked Guam.*
>
> *Last night, Japanese forces attacked the Philippine Islands.*
>
> *Last night, the Japanese attacked Wake Island.*
>
> *And this morning, the Japanese attacked Midway Island.*
>
> *Japan has, therefore, undertaken a surprise offensive extending throughout the Pacific area. The facts of yesterday and today speak for themselves. The*

people of the United States have already formed their opinions and well understand the implications to the very life and safety of our nation.

As commander in chief of the Army and Navy, I have directed that all measures be taken for our defense. But always will our whole nation remember the character of the onslaught against us.

At this point in the President's speech, the Congress and those present at his speech applauded. The ones sitting around Bobbie nodded too, showing they agreed with what the President just said. No doubt our nation would remember the onslaught against us on this day. The President continued once the applause died down.

No matter how long it may take us to overcome this premeditated invasion, the American people in their righteous might will win through to absolute victory.

The people applauded greatly at this point, giving the President their unwavering confidence and support. There was applause and shouts in the school building as well. It wasn't shouts of joy, but shouts of approval in what the President had to say.

I believe that I interpret the will of the Congress and of the people when I assert that we will not only defend ourselves to the uttermost, but will make it very certain that this form of treachery shall never again endanger us.

Once again, the President had to yield to the applause of the crowd. His speech was moving. The crowd was in agreement with what he was saying. They had been betrayed, and they wanted to make it known that they would not tolerate this form of treachery.

Hostilities exist. There is no blinking at the fact that our people, our territory, and our interests are in grave danger.

With confidence in our armed forces, with the unbounding determination of our people, we will gain the inevitable triumph—so help us, God.

The people were greatly moved at this point. Bobbie couldn't see the crowd around President Roosevelt, of course, but he suspected they were standing to show they greatly supported him. Bobbie too was moved by his words.

I ask that the Congress declare that since the unprovoked and dastardly attack by Japan on

Sunday, December 7, 1941, a state of war has existed between the United States and the Japanese empire.

Bobbie (left) in later years, serving his country

This completed the President's speech. Once again, the people applauded. There were mixed emotions from the ones gathered in the school building. Some of the women held their hands over their mouths in apparent shock and fear. Many of the men appeared determined and satisfied. Some were angry while a few wept. Bobbie looked back to his own parents. It was hard to read Daddy's expression, but Momma was looking right at him. It was not hard to read the worry in her sad eyes, in probably every mother's eyes there. Within the hour, Congress had officially declared war against Japan, and the United States was a part of the war. School was dismissed for the remainder of the day, and the crowd of people began to slowly leave the school building. All emotion was drained from them. It had been an exhausting two days, and no one knew what to expect in the coming days. Willie bent down and picked up Jake and put him on his back and carried him home that way, obviously feeling the need to be near his little brother. Bobbie reached down and took Audie's hand in his as they walked behind Momma and Daddy and the others through the snowy road. And even though they were in a crowd of people, Audie kept her little hand tucked snugly in his the whole way.

Lanetta Stephens, Thurman, Jake, Rex, Willie,
Erma Lou (Bobbie's younger sister, born later)

Chapter 16

I remember on Christmas morning, Daddy would get up and build a fire to let the house warm up and go back to bed until it did. Pat, Carol, and I would get out of bed and peek into the living room to see if Santa Claus had come. The glow from the stove would let us see that he had. We could see some dolls sitting under the tree and a few more packages, and our stockings would be full and bulging. We jumped back in bed, whispering and giggling so anxious to get up. "Can we get up now, Mama?"

"No, not yet, let the house warm up a little more, girls," Mom would say. Finally, it seemed like forever, Mom would say, "Okay, you can get up now." We would jump up and run to the tree to see which doll was ours and what all Santa Claus had left. There would be some doll dresses for our

dolls, made out of material just like some of our dresses. How did Santa know we had dresses like that? We were so surprised! There would be apples, oranges, nuts, and hard candy in our stockings. Usually a coconut was under the tree with more nuts and hard candy. Oh! What wonderful, magical Christmas times those were!

—Betty (2010)

Allie

December 1941

Christmas Eve dawned sunny and bright. Patches of the earlier snow lingered in the shade of the pines and on the north side of the house, but most of the snow had melted leaving in its place thick, gooey, slick mud. The road had deep ruts where the wagon wheels had cut grooves through the soft earth, and just last night, Daddy and Grandpa had to help push an automobile out of the ditch. Allie had hoped for a white Christmas, but it looked like it was going to be a brown one.

It didn't matter though. In the corner stood the cedar Christmas tree decorated with the paper chains the three sisters had made. They had taken notebook paper and colored the lines, each a different color. Next, they cut the paper apart. Then using flour and water, they mixed it together into glue and fastened the strips, looping them together forming the chain. Also adorning the tree was the popcorn chain. It was all so beautiful. Allie would hold Patsy in front of the tree, her little chubby hands patting at the chains making them bobble back and forth. Allie couldn't believe how her little sister had grown. She was eleven months now! When she smiled, two little teeth shone like white pearl buttons in her little pink mouth. She had just enough fuzzy golden hair to make a little curl on top of her head, and Winna and Allie were in a race, each wanting her to say their own name first. "Owie," Allie would say over and over forming the word slowly and deliberately. "Winnie," Winna would repeat over and over until everyone begged her to stop. Even little Betty, not to be outdone, joined in. "Bett!" she would scream right up in little Patsy's face. Patsy would look startled and then pucker up and bawl when Betty did this. The poor thing probably was afraid to even try to talk with all those faces right in her own, coaxing her to mimic them.

Yes, it was turning out to be a beautiful Christmas even though it wasn't white. The best part though was they were back in their own home. Allie couldn't believe it was less than a year since their awful fire. Daddy had started clearing the land across the road from their old home right after their fire. Then he'd lost no time falling trees for the new home. Even though living in Uncle Horace and Aunt Lottie's house had been great, it really had been great; it just never had felt like home to Allie. She had always felt like company there. Allie finally felt like she was home again and they were a family. She would go from room to room in their new home, running her hands along the rough walls. These were their walls. True, the walls were bare; Mama and Daddy hadn't had time to put building papers or even newspapers on the walls yet, but there would be time for that. The floors were still just rough wood with no rugs yet, and Daddy had already had to dig a few splinters out of little feet, but it was worth it. It was their floor! Daddy had said he would have his family in their new house before the first snow, and he'd done it, just barely, but he had done it! They had been here almost four weeks now. Allie still couldn't believe it! She was so happy too that Uncle Horace and his family were back home again! This would be such a wonderful Christmas with everyone back where they should be.

Their new house had four rooms. The front room, which also had Mama and Daddy's bed in it, the dining room, the kitchen, and the bedroom where the girls slept. It was okay that the inside of the house wasn't quite finished yet because Daddy would have time to work on it during the winter months when it was too cold or wet to work outside at the sawmill.

"I'm going down to wish Grandma and Grandpa a merry Christmas Eve," Allie called to her mama as she grabbed her coat and headed out the door. Christmas Eve was almost as much fun to Allie at Grandpa's as Christmas. She fairly ran across the road and burst into the house.

"Christmas Eve gift!" came a bellowed voice before Allie even got both feet in the door.

"Grandpa, you beat me every time!" Allie laughed. It was true. She was determined every year to wish Grandpa a Christmas Eve gift before he wished it to her, but in all her years, she had never succeeded. Then came her next favorite part. Where it came from, Allie couldn't remember, but, even though she was getting a little too old for it, Grandpa too, Allie would have been so disappointed if Grandpa didn't do it.

Grandpa jumped up from his rocker and grabbed Allie up in a Christmas hug. "It's time for your Christmas Eve gift!" he laughed. Allie screamed and laughed at the same time.

"No!" she begged and giggled as she struggled to get away from him. Grandma stood in the doorway with her wooden spoon in her hand, ready to watch the show. She was smiling. Grandma must have been right in the middle of making breakfast, but she took time out for this.

Grandpa pulled Allie along to the bed. Dropping down to the floor, which at Grandpa's size was no easy task to do, he pulled Allie down and began rolling her under the bed. Allie laughed and laughed and struggled. Grandpa was laughing as loudly as she. This was what he called her Christmas Eve gift. He rolled her under the bed. It got a little harder each year with Grandpa's age and size, not to mention Allie's longer legs each year.

"There you go, Peeny! You got your Christmas Eve gift!" Grandpa said as he put his hands on his knees and grunted as he stood. He reached down and pulled his granddaughter to her feet.

Allie stood and wrapped her little arms around her Grandpa's fat stomach. "I love you so much, Grandpa!" she said. "Merry Christmas Eve to you!"

"I love you too, my Peeny!" he said. "Come over here and sit with me for a while while Mother finishes up breakfast."

Grandma smiled and sidled off into the kitchen, ready to continue her chores. Allie saw her shaking her head and could hear her chuckling as she went.

"Peeny, I've been wanting to talk to you about something," Grandpa said as he began pulling her down beside him. Allie lay over him, feeling the rise and fall of his chest against her cheek. She knew what Grandpa was going to say, and she dreaded his words. She had finally gotten over her guilty feelings about the necklace and had resumed her affections with Grandpa, but she knew he had been hurt by the way she had treated him for all those weeks after the fire. She knew he had to be confused by it. Allie didn't know what she would say. How could she make him understand that it had nothing to do with her feelings about him? It was her own guilty feelings about herself.

"Peeny—" Grandpa began.

"Grandpa," Allie interrupted. "I love you more than I can even tell you. Don't ever doubt that." She was quiet for a minute. "I don't know why I acted that way. Well, no, I can't honestly say that. I guess I do know why I acted that way, I just don't know if I can explain it." Allie reached down and rubbed at the back of Grandpa's hand, stroking the vein-lined skin. He remained quiet allowing her time to gather her thoughts together. Grandpa wasn't one to rush. She knew he would sit with her all day if that's what she needed.

Allie could hear Grandma in the kitchen preparing her biscuit mixture. Allie had watched her Grandma make biscuits so many times, she visualized where she was in the process right now. Allie could see Grandma making a well in the flour in the big bowl, getting ready to pour in the milk.

Allie looked up at Grandpa with tears in her eyes. He squeezed her shoulder, giving her the confidence to go on. "It's because of the locket, Grandpa," she finally got out in a choke. "I tried it on the morning of the fire. I wanted to wear it to church. I know I shouldn't have. I wasn't supposed to wear it, but it was just so pretty. I can't remember if I took it off or not, but either way, it's gone." Tears were rolling down her face now. She had kept her secret in for so long that letting it out to Grandpa now somehow felt good. She hurried on. "When I couldn't find it after the fire, I just felt like I had let you down. I felt like I had disobeyed you. I felt guilty. You gave it to me to keep forever, and I promised you that I'd keep it safe and never lose it. I know it was one of the last things that belonged to your own mother, and now it's gone!"

Allie sobbed now. She buried her face in Grandpa's overalls and sobbed and sobbed. Grandma came to the corner of the front room and looked in on Allie and Grandpa.

Grandma Shoemate

Grandpa gently shook his head at Grandma, and she returned to the kitchen. "Come up here, Polly," Grandpa said lovingly after a few minutes. Even though Allie's legs dangled almost to the floor, Grandpa scooped her up on his lap and held her. He patted her back and soothed her.

"Baby girl, don't you know you're worth more to me than a thousand lockets? There's not a thing you could do that would stop me from loving you. Yes, I loved that locket because it had been my mother's, but it wasn't my mother. It was just an object. And it wasn't your fault that it was lost or burned in the fire. It just hurt me to think I had done something that had upset you."

"Oh, Grandpa," Allie sobbed, "you could never do that."

"I tell you what," Grandpa said in a matter-of-fact way. "Let's make a promise, you and me. Let's promise to always be open and honest with one another. If something is bothering us, let's just talk to one another about it. But you listen here, Miss Peeny. You never doubt my love for you, for all my grandchildren. You are God's most precious gifts to me, and there is nothing, and I mean nothing that will keep me from loving you. You never forget that!"

Allie hugged Grandpa even tighter. "It's a deal," she promised.

"Are you two almost ready for some biscuits and sorghum?" Grandma called from the kitchen.

"Ummm! That sounds wonderful!" Allie said. She wiped her face, and she and Grandpa got up and joined Grandma in the warm kitchen.

Winna was pouting when Allie got back home. "I can't believe it's Christmas and it's so warm!" she said. "You barely need a light jacket out there."

"What's so bad about that?" Allie wanted to know.

"Remember last Christmas when we skated on Mr. Landrum's pond?" Winna asked.

Allie did remember. It had been so much fun. They had taken the lids from milk cans. They would slip one foot in one lid and use the other foot to push off with and balance. Then they would skate and skate. Several more kids joined them on his pond. Mr. Landrum was such a nice man. He had come out and watched them, so afraid that someone would fall and get hurt or that the ice would crack. Allie loved that man, and it had been so much fun skating. She could understand Winna being disappointed. "It will turn cold again, sis, and we'll be able to skate," she said.

"I know, but there is just something special about going ice skating at Christmas time," Winna replied.

"Girls," Mama called from the kitchen. "Would you mind running out to the store and picking up a bottle of vanilla for me? I'm running low, and I know I'll need some tomorrow for the cake."

"Sure, Mama," Winna and Allie answered. They were feeling the need to get out anyway. Christmas Eve always seemed to drag, waiting for Christmas Day.

"I don't have anything but a big coat to wear," complained Allie, "and it's not that cold out there today."

Mama stopped what she was doing. "Just a minute, Allie," she said. Mama went to the bedroom and pulled a box from under the bed. "Seems like I remember a jacket someone gave us after the fire that might fit you." She brought out a worn denim jumper and held it up to Allie. "This might be a little big, but it should about fit."

"No!" Allie shrieked. "That used to belong to that James boy. I won't wear anything of his."

"Allie Grace!" Mama said sternly. "If someone is nice enough to give you something to wear, you will not be too nicey nicey to wear it. You put this jacket on and wear it this minute, young lady."

"Mama!" Allie whined. "It wasn't him who gave it to me in the first place, it was probably his mother. Do I have to?"

"Yes, you do. Like you said, it's not cold enough for anything too heavy today. This jacket should be just right."

Allie groaned again, but slipped her arms into the jacket. Winna kissed Betty, and Allie pouted as she and Winna headed out the door. "Check the mail too," Mama said. "We might have a Christmas card from Aunt Roxy and Uncle George."

The girls started out. Allie couldn't be down for long. It felt too glorious to be out in this wonderful weather, knowing, too, that this was Christmas Eve. How exciting! "Santa Claus comes tonight," they had been telling Betty all day. Betty had clapped her hands and stood at the window with her nose pressed up against the glass. "Where's Santa?" she asked over and over, expecting to see his sleigh pull up any minute.

"Winna, do you think there's any way Daddy would be called up to fight?" Allie asked the question that had been bothering her since war had been declared.

"I don't know, sis," Winna admitted. "I think it will depend on how long the war lasts. I think they call up boys from eighteen to twenty-one first who aren't married. They may not even have to call up anyone the way men are standing in line at the recruiting offices though."

"Oh, I have been so worried about Daddy. Surely they wouldn't call up someone with four kids!" Allied reasoned.

"I feel so sorry for mothers who have boys that age," Winna said, glancing over at Allie. "At times like this, I'm glad we don't have brothers."

"I know what you mean," Allie agreed. "Winna, let's try to sing that song about Pearl Harbor we've been hearing on the radio."

"Oh, sister, I don't think we know enough of it to be able to," Winna said.

Allie and Winna loved to listen to the radio to learn new songs. They had a system of trying to get down the words of a new song. When a new song came on the radio that they were trying to learn the words to, Winna would try and write down the words to one line, and Allie would try and write down the words to the next line. If it worked out like it was supposed to, when they put their lines together, they would have the song in its entirety when they were through. Often though, they would get confused and end up writing down the same lines. They had both fallen in love with the new song about Pearl Harbor. Somehow though, they could never manage to get down all the words.

"I know, and I can't even really remember what we wrote down, but let's try," Allie begged.

"Okay," Winna consented.

Winna began the sad song, and Allie joined in. They were silent a few minutes after they had finished. They knew they didn't get all the words right, but the message and feelings were certainly there. They knew they were living at a scary but exciting time in history. Allie couldn't help but feel chills go up her spine even with the warm sun shining down on them.

"Winna, let's sing that marching song about the war," Allie said with a smile. "We can march along as we sing it."

The girls began the lively marching song and sang and marched all the way into town. Nearing the store, Allie noticed Cody and some of the boys from school standing on the porch as they walked by. She was determined not to look over at them, but suddenly a dirty snowball hit her squarely on the back. "Ouch!" she said as she laughed and turned around. She and Winna ran to the side of the store and picked up some snow and made snowballs of their own. Soon, snowballs were flying from one side of the road to the other. Laughter and shrieks filled the road.

"We give up!" Cody finally conceded, holding up his hands. The other boys did the same.

Allie and Winna laughed. "Merry Christmas!" Winna called to them waving her hand.

"Merry Christmas to you!" they called back.

The girls hurried on. "My hands are freezing," Allie said as she stuffed them down in the jacket's pockets.

"Mine too!" Winna confessed, rubbing them together and blowing on them.

Slowly, Allie brought something out of the jacket pocket and held it out in front of her. She gasped. It was a chain with a heart locket dangling on the end of it. Allie screamed at the top of her lungs. She began crying, laughing, and screaming all at the same time.

Winna didn't know what to think, "Allie?"

"My locket! My locket! It's my locket! Oh my goodness, how in the world? Winna, it's my birthday locket! I can't believe it. It's like a miracle!" Allie was jumping up and down. She opened the locket and looked at the name inside just to be sure it was hers. "See, it is mine, it is!"

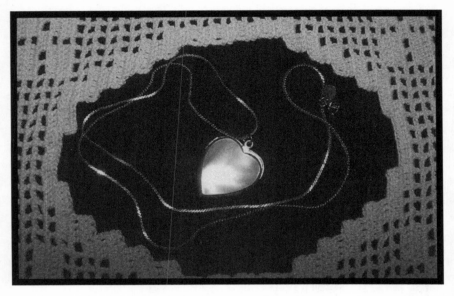

Allie's heart necklace

By this time, Cody, Jack, Billy, and others had gathered around them, thinking something surely was wrong. Allie was laughing and crying, at the same time trying to explain how she thought her birthday locket had burned in the fire, or had been lost, but here it was in the pocket of this jacket.

Suddenly, Allie stopped laughing. "How in the world did it get in Bobbie's jacket pocket?" she asked seriously. Allie got an accusing look on her face. "How did that boy get my locket? All this time I've been worried it burned in the fire, and he knew where it was. He had to have known." Winna and the others stared at Allie with confused expressions.

They certainly didn't have an answer to her question. They were more confused than she.

Hearing the door slam to Jim Andy's store, the group looked up to see Bobbie and Willie coming out of the store carrying a big box. "Hey, you all," Bobbie hollered with a big smile on his face. "I'd wave, but as you can see my hands are pretty much tied up!" His grin stayed on his face as he started down the steps backward being careful not to trip. "Careful, Willie," he cautioned.

"You!" Allie screamed! She ran over to Bobbie. "I've never trusted you, and now I understand why. I never have forgiven you for carving my name on that desk. Do you know how much that embarrassed me? How come you did that? I've never done anything to you. And how do you explain this?" Allie held up the locket in front of Bobbie's face.

"Your locket!" Bobbie exclaimed.

"Yes, it's my locket, and it was in YOUR jacket pocket. All this time I was so sick and worried about it, and it was in your pocket all along. How could you be so mean and not tell me where it was?"

Bobbie had one foot on one step and another foot on the next. His face was red, and his arms were aching from the weight of the heavy box. He had never in his life heard Allie speak so many words all at once, and every one of her words were being thrown right at him.

"I—" he began.

"I know this is your jacket," she began again. "Don't even try to say it's not yours. I didn't want to wear it, but my mama made me. I bet you didn't even know your momma gave it to us. I bet you didn't know what happened to it. I bet you were going to keep this necklace for yourself. Why were you going to keep it for yourself? You're just a mean boy, that's why!" Allie said answering her own question. She spun around and started walking away.

Bobbie tried again, "Allie, I found your necklace."

Allie whirled back around. "You found it? Where?"

"Do you mind if I set this box down?" Bobbie asked. He nodded to Willie to go back up on the porch. Setting the box down ever so carefully, he walked over to Allie. "After the fire, I walked over to your house, er . . . where your house had been. I walked around among the ashes to see if I could find anything your dad might could use that he missed." Bobbie stopped and looked around at the others. All eyes were on him. They weren't going to miss a single word. "Well, then I happened to notice this necklace lying in the grass, under the trees where you must have stood while your house burned. I picked it up and dropped it in my pocket. I was aiming on taking it to school and giving it to you. You see, I knew it was yours because I was with your dad when your grandpa showed it to him. When I saw the necklace, I knew it was yours."

Allie stood staring at Bobbie. She hadn't even blinked. Her mouth stood open, not knowing whether or not to believe this unbelievable story. Bobbie continued.

"Well, when I got home and looked for the locket, I couldn't find it." He blushed. "I guess by that time I had taken my jacket off, and I had a hole in my pocket in my britches, so I figured it fell out. I guess I forgot I dropped the necklace in my jacket pocket and not my britches. I went back out and looked and looked, but I couldn't find it. Anyhow, I just didn't mention it to you since I thought I had gone and lost it again. I didn't see how it would help you any telling you how I found it only to lose it again."

It had started to make a little sense to Allie. She could see how it could have happened the way he was explaining it. "Then your momma packed up some things for us," she said, "and one of the things she packed up happened to be this jacket?" Allie finished.

"Yes," Bobbie nodded. "I didn't even know she'd given you all this jacket until a few days later when I was looking for it, and she said it was in with the things she'd given ya'll."

Allie felt awful. "I guess I owe you an apology," she said looking down at the ground.

"No, I'm just sorry I never told you about the locket. Maybe if I had, we could have figured it out or at least you wouldn't have worried so much about it," Bobbie said softly.

"Well, I guess this is as good a time as any to explain something else to you, Allie," Cody said coming up to stand beside her.

Allie turned in surprise to look at Cody. "What do you mean?" she asked, wondering what in the world Cody could have to add to this event.

"Well, Bobbie didn't carve the name in the desk that day at school, I did," he said sheepishly as he dropped his head.

"What are you talking about?" Allie stammered. She looked from one boy to the other. "Why would you do that, and why would you," looking at Bobbie, "take the blame for it?"

Both boys shrugged. "It's just a long story, Allie, but we're both sorry," Cody said as he fingered the cat's-eye marble in his pocket. "I just don't want you to keep being sore at Bobbie for it though when I was the one who did it. I've already apologized to him, but I just realized I needed to let you know it was me who did it!"

Allie narrowed her eyes at Cody. "All this time when I was mad at Bobbie, I should have been mad at you." Turning to Bobbie, she said, "I guess I owe you another apology."

"Hey, it's Christmas!" Bobbie said. "Let's just everyone forget it and everyone be friends."

"I'll second that!" Cody said with a laugh. "Think you can do that, Allie?"

Allie held the necklace up in front of her. How could she stay angry when she had her precious necklace back in her possession again? "It's a deal!" she said for the second time that day.

"What have you got in that box?" Cody asked Bobbie. Bobbie smiled as he remembered another time Cody asked him the same question.

Bobbie's eyes lit up. "I've got my momma a new sewing machine," he said, "and I can't wait to see the way her eyes will light up tomorrow morning when she sees it! I've got to get home to wrap it up and put a big bow on it. See you all later."

Bobbie's Momma, Eva Crotts James

"And I can't wait to see how my grandpa's eyes will light up when he sees this necklace! Merry Christmas!" Allie exclaimed.

Allie turned one way, Bobbie the other, and they each took off in a run making a beeline home!

Later that night, Allie lay listening to the soft breathing of her sisters beside her. Betty had her little hand in Allie's own. She had tossed and turned for a good hour, getting up to look out the window several times for Santa before finally drifting off to sleep. Winna, on the other side of Allie, stirred gently in her sleep, throwing an arm over Allie's shoulder. Allie's eyes filled with tears as she felt the love she had for her sisters and her family, confident of the love they also had for her. How very fortunate she was to be a part of this family.

She thought back to Grandpa's surprise when he'd seen the locket this afternoon. "Now, Polly, I want you to wear this pretty locket sometimes. Your great-grandmother would have wanted you to enjoy it like she did. And if anything should ever happen to it, you and I both know she would certainly understand." Then he'd caught her up in one of his loving embraces, and Allie knew in her heart that she would never again doubt Grandpa's love for her.

Allie fingered the locket that she clutched in her hand. Had she even put the locket down once since discovering it this afternoon? All this time when she'd been sure she'd never see it again, it had been tucked away in Bobbie's jacket pocket within arm's length of her. Funny how things had turned out, her hating Bobbie, blaming him for things he wasn't even responsible for. Could it be she had Bobbie pegged wrong all this time? Daddy seemed to think so. Allie thought back to something Daddy had said once when Allie had been berating Bobbie. "Allie, I think you need to give Bobbie the benefit of the doubt and not be so quick to judge him. I think he's a fine young man." Allie had been stunned at Daddy's words at the time and had told him he was wrong. But now, she wasn't so sure. She thought she might ask Daddy what he meant by what he said. Bobbie did have his good points, Allie could see that now. It was touching the way he was so excited about the gift of the sewing machine for his mother. Cody had told them Bobbie used his own money to buy it for her. How many boys would spend their money on something like that? Allie also couldn't help but admire Bobbie in the way he had accepted the punishment for Cody for carving on the desk. She still didn't understand it, but in a strange way, she respected him for it. Yes, she would have to keep her eye on this dark-headed James boy. She still was a little leery of him, but she was beginning to look at him in a little different way. Allie smiled to herself in the darkness. She didn't think she would be quite as upset as before if the names Bobbie and Allie showed up again one of these days inside a big heart on a desk at school. Who knew . . . she just might be the one responsible next time in those names getting there!

Edwards Brothers Malloy
Oxnard, CA USA
May 30, 2013